KILL
WITH
KINDNESS

ALSO BY ED JAMES

KILL
WITH
KINDNESS

ED JAMES

THOMAS & MERCER

Published by Thomas & Mercer, Seattle

www.apub.com

Amazon, the Amazon logo, and Thomas & Mercer are trademarks of Amazon.com, Inc., or its affiliates.

ISBN-13: 9781503948013
ISBN-10: 1503948013

Cover design by @blacksheep-uk.com

Printed in the United States of America

KILL
WITH
KINDNESS

Day 1
Saturday, 9th September 2017

Chapter One

T here, there, there.' DI Simon Fenchurch picked his son up from the cot, stuffed with too many cuddly toys, and hugged him tight. 'Hey, my little man.'

Baby Al. The name hurt now his namesake was dead. Eight months old, two of them premature. Did that mean they didn't count? Was that the root of the problem?

He kissed the boy's perfect head and breathed his smell deep into his lungs.

Baby Al coughed hard, like he was tearing his lungs apart. Then again, and again. The antiseptic reek of the hospital came back.

Fenchurch felt his stomach roll and he held Baby Al out. 'Can you take him, love?'

'He might need a feed.' Abi took him, cradling him in her arms as he coughed yet again. She didn't say anything, just whispered sweet nothings to her son, still coughing. Her cheeks were still puffed up, her dark hair cut short, just the right side of severe. Made her look elfin, maybe. She started undoing the buttons on her black blouse then unhooked the left side of her bra.

Fenchurch reached out and stroked the baby's soft cheek. Even got a tiny smile for his trouble. 'I just want him to have a night at home.'

'I know.' Abi flared her nostrils as she let Baby Al latch on to her nipple, supporting his body with one arm, his head with the other. 'I want to raise him after everything that happened with Chloe. I want him home with us until he sods off to university.'

'That's a long time away.'

Abi grinned wide. 'You'll be an old man by then.'

'And you'll be—'

The door swept open and Stephenson, Baby Al's doctor, charged in, his forehead knotted like someone had tightened it too hard with a wrench. Everything about the man was grey, from his suit and shirt to the complexion of his skin, just his white coat deviating from the party line. He stopped and seemed to realise where he was. His forehead slackened off as he caught sight of Baby Al sucking away. 'Ah, that's a good sign.'

'He tires so quickly, though.' Whoever was doing the tightening now went to work on Abi's forehead, dragging her eyebrows down in the middle. She pulled Baby Al away and tucked her breast back in her bra. 'See? That's him done now and he only just started.'

'Well.' Stephenson let his shoulders go, his arms hanging lank at his sides. 'We've got the results back and . . . I'm afraid that the news isn't positive.'

Fenchurch clenched his fists. 'You told us he was getting better.'

'I told you I *thought* that there was a *chance* that he *might be* getting better. That's not the same as getting better. And him tiring while—'

'You need to find out what's—'

'*Simon.*' Abi flared her nostrils again, then gave a professional smile as she handed Baby Al to Stephenson. 'What's happened?'

'To put it bluntly, the catheter procedure didn't take.' Stephenson sat on the chair and rested Al on his chest. 'The tissue is supposed to grow over the closure device and, well, it hasn't. Baby Al still has a hole in his heart.'

Fenchurch felt his skin tingle. Wanted to grab the baby and run off, far away to somewhere this shit wasn't happening, where everything was okay and he was teaching Al to kick a football and drink his first beer, and meeting his future wife and . . .

Abi's face was curled up, tears welling in her eyes.

Fenchurch went over and held her, shielding her from Stephenson and his bad news. 'What options do we have?'

'The good news is there are still some.' Stephenson stared deep into Baby Al's eyes and grinned. 'As it stands, the hole in his heart isn't shrinking like we'd hoped.'

'It's getting bigger?'

'Potentially. The mere presence of the closure device makes it some-what challenging to identify just how large the, ah, hole is.'

'Is there any other surgery we can try?'

'The, ah, *particular* way in which his heart *hasn't* regrown makes surgery somewhat *more* challenging.'

Fenchurch's skin tingled again, like ants were crawling up his spine. 'He's going to die?'

Stephenson was jiggling Baby Al up and down, sticking out his bottom lip. Then his face set into granite as he focused on Fenchurch. 'We're not *quite* at that stage yet.'

'When people say "not quite" it usually means they're way past it.'

'In most cases, this would be a death sentence.' Stephenson hugged Baby Al close, his eyes turning to steel. 'But I'm not giving up on your son.'

'I just want to take him home.' Abi broke free of Fenchurch and started pacing the room. 'Just one night in his short life.'

'I understand.' Stephenson handed Baby Al back to Fenchurch, but couldn't take his eyes off the kid. 'There's nothing we can do at this stage other than to assess the options and say our prayers.' He rubbed the back of his neck. 'Now, you can spend as much time with your son as you need, okay?'

'We've got an appointment, unfortunately.' Fenchurch hugged Baby Al tight and kissed his forehead. 'But we'll be back later. I hope you've got some positive news by then.'

⌣

'We need to keep talking.'

Fenchurch parked in the shade of one of the giant oaks overlooking the crematorium entrance. 'You're right.' He glanced at Abi in the passenger seat. 'That's what all that counselling is for.' He got out of the car into the burning hot sun. His *London Post* from the previous day flopped out of the door pocket, TEACHER-PUPIL SEX SHAME on the cover. *Waste of bloody money.* He dumped it on the back seat and waited for his wife. 'All throughout this shit we need to—'

Abi slammed the door and leaned against the car, arms folded, head bowed. 'Nothing is making the hole in his heart regrow.'

Fenchurch hurried round to her side and tried to take her in his arms, but she wasn't making it easy. 'This is the hardest thing.'

Abi bared her teeth. 'As bad as this feels right now, losing our daughter was worse.'

'I know.' Fenchurch managed to get her away from the car and started brushing dust off her black skirt. 'But with Chloe it felt like there was always something I could do. Someone I'd not dangled out of a window or—' He sighed. 'Someone kidnapped her, scooped out bits of her brain, brought her up and . . . they robbed us of the chance. We should've been taking her swimming and dropping her at school and . . . It's still burning away at me that there *was* something, that someone knew something that could've . . . Who am I kidding?'

'Simon, I get it; believe me, I do. You should've talked to me. You should be doing it now.'

'I know.' The regret weighed Fenchurch down like someone had doubled gravity. 'I wish I had, every single day. But I'm trying now. Our boy's fighting for his life and it's just killing me that there's nothing I can *do* to save him.' He grabbed her hand. 'But I want to go through this with you, okay?'

Abi gave the faintest squeeze. 'Being born just to . . . Sometimes I . . .' She let go. 'Sometimes I wish we hadn't had him.'

'It's okay to think that . . .' Fenchurch hugged her tight again. 'But we chose to have him. For as long as he's alive and we're capable, we've got to look after him. He still needs us and I still need you.'

'Okay.' She brushed her tears away. 'Come on. We've got a funeral to get through.'

Fenchurch felt Abi's hand tighten as they approached the crematorium. A crowd of people stood outside the low building, some crying, some laughing, others either staring into their phones or sharing the displays with people around them.

Mary Docherty stood firm, her jaw tight. Dressed in black, though her coat was a few sizes too big and far too warm for September. She got a hug from an obvious ex-copper, all scar tissue and big shoulders.

Fenchurch stopped. Couldn't walk another step. 'This is too hard.'

Mary spotted Fenchurch. 'Oh, Simon.' She dashed across and embraced him, her sweet perfume cloaking him. 'I miss him.'

'Me too, Mary.' Fenchurch wrapped his arms around her frail body. 'Me too.' He blinked away tears.

'He had longer than we were first told, Simon.' Mary gripped Fenchurch with a strength he didn't think she had. 'I got to treasure that time with him. Almost ten months.'

Fenchurch briefly felt gravity switch back to normal, then Baby Al's face flashed in front of his eyes and the weight started crushing him again. He let Mary go and stepped aside to let Abi console her.

'Thank you for naming your son after Alan.'

Abi didn't say anything.

'It's the least we could do.' Fenchurch chanced a glance into the bright-blue sky. 'I'm sure the old bugger's looking down at me from wherever he is and tearing lumps out of my work.'

'Sure he is, Simon.' Mary smiled for a brief moment. 'Oh, I met your daughter. She's a lovely girl. What happened to her . . . It . . . Alan tried to . . .' She broke off, tears flooding her cheeks.

'Oh, Mary.' The ex-copper stepped back in, wrapping her in his arms. He mouthed, 'I'm her brother.'

Abi gave him a smile then led Fenchurch towards the crematorium. 'Well played, Rambo.'

'Sorry, I'm just saying how I feel.'

'When it's appropriate.' Abi led him through the thick crowd towards the loudest laughter. 'Speaking of inappropriate . . .'

Fenchurch's father stood with a gang of grizzled old men, red faces and silver hair, all laughing and joking. 'Simon, Abi.'

Behind them, Chloe was checking her phone, lips pressed together, eyes narrow. Her dark hair hung low, shrouding her face. Then she spotted Fenchurch and her face glowed. 'Dad!' She kissed him on the cheek, then did the same to her mother. 'How's Al?'

'How's Al . . .?' Abi frowned. 'We're seeing him later. You'll come with us, won't you?'

'Only if you want me to?'

'Chloe, of course we do. We've missed so much of your life . . . You and him should be inseparable.'

'Okay.' Chloe grinned, then a wave of laughter from Dad's cronies made her grimace. 'Is that normal for a cop's funeral?'

'Is what normal?' Dad squeezed Chloe's nose like she was three again, not twenty. 'We were just remembering a few of Docherty's finer moments. Not just your old man who worked with him, is it?'

Chloe rolled her eyes. 'And they say nepotism's dead . . .'

'Alive and kicking in the Met, my little princess.' Dad had to look up at Chloe, at least four inches taller than him. Didn't stop him pinching her cheek. His eyes twinkled with the usual mischief as he focused on Fenchurch. 'Don't know if I told you this, Simon, but one day we were raiding this squat in Limehouse . . .'

At least eighteen times. Fenchurch gave a tight smile. 'Yeah, I've—'

'Docherty was a DC back then. Tall as you like, and skinny as a rake. Even though he was on the old fast track, his Scotch accent made even the Krays quake in fear.'

'Dad, you're not old enough to—'

'Fastest runner outside the Olympics. Anyway, we pitched up at this flat and Doc was first up. Flipped up the letterbox to peer inside, only someone had covered it with dog mess. Docherty got it all over his nose and fingers.'

Chloe's polite laugh didn't quite stretch to her eyes. She turned away from Dad and spoke low to Fenchurch. 'This is what they've been like. Telling all these stories at the guy's funeral.'

'It's a copper thing.'

'Finding humour in a friend's death . . .?'

'Gallows humour. Otherwise we'd all be locked up in rooms with walls you can bounce off.' Fenchurch squeezed her shoulders. 'They're celebrating his life.' He pointed at the other cops in Dad's gang. 'When we're inside, just you watch. They'll be bawling like your brother. This is their way of showing how much they loved Docherty.'

Chloe looked like she was processing the gallows humour but not quite understanding.

'What do I always say, Simon?' Dad slapped Fenchurch on the back. Hard. 'You shouldn't be angry that it's over—'

'—be glad that it happened.' Fenchurch nodded, trying to bat him away.

'Doc was a great man and a great cop.' A dark look settled on Dad's face. 'Nobody wants to remember a bag of bones, do they?'

The door opened and the crowd started slipping into the chapel.

Dad wrapped his arms around his son and granddaughter as he led them inside. 'Simon, do you mind if I have the aisle seat? Had a few pints with the boys and you know what my bladder's like these days.'

⌣

Fenchurch blinked hard, his eyes struggling to adjust to the sunshine, his tears dried to crystals. He stood aside from everyone and took a moment to think about Docherty.

All the support, all the help, all the . . . everything. Gone. Ripped away by the cancer that ate him up. Stupid bastard could've got treatment if he'd been quick enough, but he hadn't. Gone far too soon.

'Simon?' Dad was standing with Chloe, who looked like she was going to throttle him. 'Your daughter won't admit that she loved seeing West Ham with us.'

'Grandpa, is this the place . . .?'

'Supporting West Ham's like attending a funeral every Saturday, love.' Dad gave his son a knowing wink. 'Anyway, I'm glad you're not going to that camp in America this year. A London summer is something to savour and enjoy.'

Fenchurch spotted Detective Superintendent Julian Loftus leaving the crematorium, the sunlight catching his bald head. Then he put his cap on. Never seemed to be out of his uniform. Probably slept in it.

'Back in a sec.' Fenchurch walked over to meet Loftus. 'Thanks for attending, sir.'

'Couldn't miss this.' Loftus grimaced, his wide jaw pulsing, like he was grinding his teeth to sharp points. 'Hell of a business. Taken from us so young.'

'I saw him a week ago, just before—' Fenchurch hadn't spotted his new boss standing behind Loftus.

'I did, too.' Acting DCI Dawn Mulholland. Black trouser suit, black scarf. Pale skin, lined around the eyes, her face an unreadable mask. 'He thought he'd get longer.'

When he looked at her, Fenchurch still got the same pang of . . . what? Anger? Hate? Fear?

It burned away at his gut.

You sat on information that could've found Chloe earlier, even interviewed one of the men who'd abducted her, but treated him like a witness instead of a suspect.

Fenchurch was kidding himself. He'd raised it but nobody cared. Just him. Hard to feel anything other than a stab in the heart when he thought about it.

'He got much longer than I expected, Dawn.' Fenchurch felt a different sting, one that scratched the back of his throat. 'In November when . . . he got diagnosed, they gave him six weeks. He ended up with almost ten *months*. Got to see the Grand Canyon and the Great Wall of China.'

Mulholland looked him up and down, slowly, a bitter smile flashing on to her lips. 'Even so, it was very sudden at the end.'

Fenchurch tried to swallow but something stuck. 'Fuck cancer.'

'Indeed.' Loftus stared off into the distance. He looked genuinely upset, like the emotion was enough to cut through his usual professional composure. 'You know, the last time I saw Alan, he said, "Don't be sad that it's over, be glad that it happened." I'll take that to the grave.'

Mulholland's phone burst out, the slick funk of 'Maneater' by Hall & Oates. 'Sorry, sir.' She walked off, ignoring the disgusted looks.

'We need to celebrate his life.' Loftus watched Mulholland walk away frowning as she talked into her mobile. 'We get so lost in the everyday, in the cases. This job insulates us from emotion until we can't feel anything. Right now, we're running twelve murder cases tracing back to this super-strong ecstasy. I'm sure you've heard of it, Simon.

Blockchain.' His jaw pulsed again. 'I suspect that's what Dawn's been called away for. Or someone else has had acid thrown over them.'

Another one. Some poor sod with a face burnt by whatever corrosive substance some vermin could get hold of. Kerosene, acid. If they were lucky: reconstructive surgery and PTSD. If they weren't . . . And all for the most stupid of reasons: looking at a drug dealer's girlfriend; scratching a drug dealer's car.

Fenchurch clenched his jaw. 'It's been a shit summer, sir.'

'Horrendous year. And I thought 2016 was bad. This one's even worse.' Loftus tapped Fenchurch's arm. 'I see your daughter is here. That's progress, yes?'

'Well, she's living with us again, so yeah.' Fenchurch felt a tickle of pride and happiness as he nodded.

'Simon.' Mulholland beckoned him over as she pocketed her phone.

'See you later, sir.' Fenchurch strode over to Mulholland. 'What's up?'

'I need you to visit a crime scene. A murder.'

Called to a murder scene on a Saturday is bad enough, but when they've just turned your mentor into ashes . . .

Fenchurch felt his back quiver. 'Dawn, I'm at a funeral.'

'I'm asking you, Simon. As a favour.' Genuine fear twisted her forehead. 'I've got half of my team out on secondment to the drug squad and we had another acid attack in Hackney just half an hour ago.'

Fenchurch caught a flash of the training course he'd been on, photos of faces twisted and scarred, swollen and distorted by some little arsehole splashing a tiny amount of acid or kerosene on to their skin. Wouldn't wish it on his worst enemy.

What would Docherty want?

That's all it comes down to.

Fenchurch sucked in a deep breath. 'Give me a minute.' He stomped off, kicking up pebbles, the veins in his head pounding, towards Abi and Chloe standing near Dad's cronies. He shot a glare over to Mulholland, though she was oblivious. 'Love, I've been called in. A murder.'

'Simon, it's fine, okay?' Abi ran a hand down his arm. 'I know she rubs you up the wrong way, but right now someone's son or daughter is dead and you need to bring their killer to justice.'

Fenchurch kept his focus on Mulholland, the throbbing in his temple getting worse. 'Today's hard, you know?'

'I know. Chloe and I are going to hospital to be with Baby Al. You come when you've caught them, okay?'

Fenchurch nodded slowly. *She's right.*

It's what Docherty would want. What he'd expect.

Chapter Two

Alone woman stood at the side of the road, thigh-high boots and a tight dress, ponytail hanging down her back.

Fenchurch let his window down as he slowed. 'Bloody hell, Kay, you look like you're on the game.'

'Thanks a lot.' DS Kay Reed clacked round the side of the car and got in. Almost took the door off. She tugged at the seatbelt and eventually got it to click into place, then started fiddling with her boot straps. 'Just on my way to my sister's baby shower and—'

'You're wearing *that* to a baby shower?'

'What's wrong with it?'

'Abi said you had a thing on. Didn't realise she was talking about your outfit.' Fenchurch looked at her short skirt again, like she was out in Newcastle or Bristol.

Reed's glare told him not to push it. 'So I'm swapping trains at bloody Bank and I get a call from that witch.'

'Mulholland?'

'I should be so lucky.' Reed kicked off her boots and got a pair of trainers from the back seat. 'The Sorcerer's Apprentice. Just you wait, guv, soon as Mulholland's made full DCI, Ashkani will get her old job.'

Fenchurch set off but tried not to give her any satisfaction.

Reed huffed as she reached down to tie her laces. 'I'm still on Crete time. Got off the plane at ten last night. Not supposed to be back on until Monday. Dave was right — we should've taken those extra two nights.' She sat back and let out a breath. 'How was the funeral?'

'Rather have been in Crete, Kay. Maybe not with you and Dave. Even a baby shower—'

'Guv, I could've flown back.'

'Kay, you're enough of a nightmare having *had* a holiday.'

'Would've given me a chance to get away from my kids, though.' Reed sat back, arms folded. 'You haven't answered my question: how was the funeral?'

'Not a dry eye in the house and all that.' Fenchurch honked at a clown sitting at the lights. 'Dad and his cronies will be giving him a good send-off, I hope.'

'Hope doesn't come into it, guv.' Reed raised her pencil-thin eyebrows. 'They'll be six pints in already. "Hey, do you remember when he got dog shit all over his fingers and nose?"'

'Already had that. Never stops making them laugh.'

'Oh, I'm being a bitch.' Reed let out a sigh. 'It's good that people remember Docherty.'

Fenchurch tightened his grip on the wheel as they set off again. 'Listen, we had some bad news about—'

'Abi called me.' Reed reached over and stroked his arm. 'I hope he's going to be okay, guv.'

'Kay . . .' Fenchurch took a back lane and pulled up just at the start of the Minories. Three storeys of generic buildings on either side of a long straight street, yellow cranes bunching up at the end. Every day was a working day in the City, even down here on the fringes. He turned off the engine and let the traffic hurtle past.

The Hotel Bennaceur was just up the road, the door for once staffed by a uniform with a clipboard rather than a bouncer with an earpiece and an anger-management problem.

'Let's get on with it, then.' Fenchurch got out and locked the car. He passed the Third Planet, a rowdy bar filled with Arsenal and Spurs fans shouting at each other like they'd bothered to attend the match. A couple of them near the window watched Reed walk past, leering at her like they were on a building site.

She snatched the clipboard from the Crime Scene Manager. 'Is DS Ashkani here yet?'

'No sign of her, Sarge.'

Fenchurch grabbed a crime scene suit from the pile. 'When she deigns to honour us with her presence, tell her we're inside.'

Always the hard part, waiting outside the crime scene. Waiting for the details to crystallise. The victim could be anyone, could've had anything happen to them.

218 was stencilled on the door's pale-white wood. Very arty, like the rest of the place. White walls and coffee-coloured floorboards lined the corridor. Classy, probably described as a boutique hotel online. Fenchurch hated to think how much they charged for it.

Fenchurch sucked in a breath and nudged the door open.

A small room, the Scenes of Crime Officers getting in each other's way. Wall-mounted TV and posh furniture. A camera flash caught Fenchurch through his mask and he had to blink it away. He navigated a path through the SOCOs over to the bed.

A woman lay on the white bed sheets, naked, her skin pale. Late twenties, maybe. Dark hair, eyes shut, but it was like she was smiling. Pink handcuffs around her wrists tied her to the bed frame. No obvious signs of attack, but her head was leaning over to the left. And the faint smell of diarrhoea.

'No clothes, no wallet, no phone.' Could tell by the depressed posture that it was Mick Clooney, the lead SOCO, pointing at the body. His mask betrayed yet another new eyebrow piercing. 'Got a wedding ring, though, Si. She's someone's wife. You need to find her husband.'

'Or her wife, Mick.' Fenchurch took in the body again. The gold wedding band was outshone by the platinum engagement ring's huge diamond. His eyes kept going back to the face, though. Seemed familiar, but he couldn't place it. 'Kay, do you recognise her?'

'No.' Reed stood next to him, her suit crinkling as she frowned. 'Know what you mean, though. Is she off the telly?'

'Nah. It's something else.'

'She's been nagging at my non-existent as well.' William Pratt was over the other side of the bed, the pathologist on his knees in front of the body, like he'd given her at least one of the rings. '*Om-pom-tiddly-om-pom.*' He stood up in instalments, the click of his back louder than either of the cameras. 'I've just settled on her having one of those faces. *Om-pom-pom.* Which is very different from one that you'd never tire of punching, eh, Michael?' His eyes wrinkled up though his mask.

Clooney took a step towards him. 'That joke smells worse than this room, William.'

'Oh, the diarrhoea? Well, it's common with corpses, you know, Michael.'

'It's a lot stronger than usual.'

'And that remains a mystery, my dearest simpleton.' Pratt reached out a finger and prodded the body, like the victim was an experiment. 'The deepest of mysteries.'

Fenchurch joined him by the body. Still couldn't place her. 'Okay, so anything on the cause of death?'

'Certainly nothing obvious.' Pratt lifted her head. 'Aha, there's a blow to her left temple. And that smell, though, and the staining under the body.' He reached over to lift the victim.

Clooney slapped his wrist. 'She's not yours yet.'

'Sorry.' Pratt settled for a prod of the victim's buttock from the side. 'I suspect the . . . *effluent* was perimortem, which is intriguing. But the clincher . . .' He gestured at the handcuffs. 'The presence of these probably means we can rule out suicide.'

Reed leaned low and stared at the cuffs. 'Maybe she took a couple of bottles of pills and tied herself up just so she couldn't run to the toilet and stick her fingers down her throat?'

Clooney folded his arms and tilted his head to the side. 'You ever tried snapping cuffs on yourself?'

'Mick, any new recruit will tell you it's easily done. Hard part is getting them off before someone finds out.' Reed smirked. 'And you're the expert at making the beast with one back, so you tell me how easy it'd be to get them off when you've tied yourself to a bed frame?'

'Calling me a wanker?'

'You are a wanker.'

'*Kay.*' Fenchurch waved her off. Then he joined Pratt around the other side of the bed. 'So we've got suspicious circumstances, yeah?'

'Well, yes. *Om-pom-pom.*' Pratt pointed at the marks on her wrists. 'It looks to me like someone forced these on. This wasn't one of Mr Clooney's danger wa—'

'*William*, I've told you—'

'Enough!' Fenchurch peered at the victim's left wrist. The cuffs had dug into the flesh, despite their fluffiness, and left a series of rings on the skin. 'Sure she wasn't just struggling when the poison or whatever it was kicked in?'

'These are incredibly tight.' Pratt's eyes wrinkled again. 'I doubt even Mr Clooney in one of his ten greatest auto-erotic sessions would be able to get them *that* tight.'

'Look, if you wanted them that tight, you'd hit the cuffs off the—' Clooney threw his arms wide. 'Piss off.'

'Snared.' Pratt winked at him. 'Regardless, though, Michael, you've raised a valid point. Could our poor victim here have got the cuffs that tight by knocking them against the bed frame?' He reached over and shook them again. 'It's doubtful. No, someone has tied her up, very deliberately, and left her to die.'

Fenchurch shut his eyes, tasting the burn in his throat. The ants were crawling up his back again. 'Poison?'

'Could be anything, really. *Om-pom-pom*. Nothing is jumping out at me. *Om-pom-tiddly-om-pom*. Though there are a few things we can discount. I'll not bore you with the detail.'

'That's what the post-mortem's for.' Reed's eyes narrowed through her mask. 'Could it be this super-strong ecstasy?'

'Ah, the infamous Blockchain.' Pratt scratched at his throat. His beard puffed his suit out like an old settee. 'Had a number of young ladies and gentlemen on my slab at Lewisham who died of overdoses from that stuff but . . . Mm. I shall investigate, but my money's on poison. Just . . . which one?'

'If it was drugs, why would you take strong E in a hotel?' Clooney was tapping a note on his tablet. 'Safer to use the club toilets, right? If it's a hotel, you'd just be chopping out lines of coke, yeah? And Tammy's done the bog here. Clean, like she'd barely had a piss.'

'Charming as ever, Mick. *Om-pom-pom*. Don't ever change.'

'See, this Blockchain, though?' Clooney stuffed his tablet under his armpit, head tilted to the side. 'Isn't that something to do with Bitcoin?'

'Full marks.' Pratt was still staring at the body. 'I would suggest some smart-arse drug dealer has paid for some product using Bitcoin as a currency in a dark web market. Then, when said dealer did some digging into Bitcoin, he discovered the wonders of the blockchain, hence christening the drug du jour Blockchain.'

'Still don't know what a Bitcoin looks like.'

'Well, Mick, as I'm sure you don't know from your pit of ignorance, it doesn't look like anything. It's a cryptocurrency, it's entirely virtual. I'll not bore you with the details, but the real innovation is the blockchain. Every transaction updates a shared and open ledger of who owns what. It's completely transparent.' Pratt looked up, his eyes full of wonder. 'Ah, do you know the applications in medicine alone will—'

'Just the time of death, William.' Fenchurch folded his arms. 'Any chance of that?'

Pratt narrowed his eyes. 'Friday night.'

'She's been lying here overnight?'

'That's for certain. But . . . Mm. My calculations give me a time of death of around eleven thirty.' Pratt fiddled with the body, prodding and poking again. 'Now, our poor victim is quite cool.' His eyes warmed up again, the wonder returning. 'I validated the room's heating schedule with the chap on the front desk and I have a jolly good idea of the room temperature in the intervening period. *Om-pom-pom.* But. *Om-pom-tiddly-om-pom.* I'm finding some intriguing anomalies on the body, which I shall have to defer until later.'

'William, this might be an intriguing thought experiment to you, but I need to find someone who was in this room at that time. Am I looking at eleven p.m. or earlier?'

'I'll need to defer that until—'

'William, I need to find someone who was in here when she was killed. When should I focus on?'

Pratt jerked down to a crouch and got eye level with the victim. 'These bonds. This blood. And this blow to her skull. Hmm. I'd suggest we're looking at an initial attack of twenty-one fifteen, give or take half an hour.'

'You said she was poisoned. Do you—'

'Yes.'

'I didn't even finish my thought, let alone my question.'

'Well, my dear Inspector, I would suggest the most likely chain of events is that this poor woman was attacked at around nine fifteen last night. Then, two hours later, she died.'

Fenchurch's skin prickled. 'She was *dying* for two hours?'

'All I know is that she was poisoned during that two-hour period using an unknown toxin.'

'William, I need the post-mortem fast-tracked.'

Pratt shot to his feet with a crack. 'It's a weekend, Simon. I've got a chess match at—'

'I don't give a shit about your chess match. I need to know how she died and when.'

'I suppose I *could* postpone, but—'

'Thanks, William. Let me know when and where.' Fenchurch switched his glare to Clooney. 'So, Mick, how—'

'Forget it, Si.' Clooney waved his hands around, taking in the number of his officers working away. 'The body's in a hotel room. Any DNA we find is very unlikely to be useful. Could be someone who stayed here three weeks ago or a cleaner or someone at the laundry or—'

'Or it could be the killer.' Fenchurch tried a slightly stronger glare. 'Let me know what budget you need me to find.'

'Yeah, good luck getting a penny out of that dragon.'

'Don't let Mulholland hear you calling her that.'

Clooney winked at him. 'I didn't call her it. You did.'

Chapter Three

'See? Even Mick Clooney hates Mulholland.' Fenchurch dumped his crime scene suit in the discard pile, ready for processing. 'And he's a wanker.'

He led back through the hotel to the reception area. White walls with tasteful artworks — a series of red-and-black variations on a theme which seemed to be the pyramids. Two desks at right angles. The empty reception desk, dark wood and marble, guarded access to the rooms. The other was the tall security desk, with two heads poking up above the partition.

'I've told you a hundred times!' DC Lisa Bridge sat next to the guard, her blonde hair tucked behind her ears. Legs crossed, arms folded. 'I need access to all of the CCTV, inside and out.'

'And I heard you the first hundred times.' The red-faced security guard looked like he was sitting in a child's seat. Must be close to seven foot. And his eyes naturally bulged like he'd seen a ghost. 'It's not simple. I need approval from the owners.'

'No, you don't.' Reed got between them and settled into a low crouch. 'Lisa, can you work with your usual guy to get the external footage?'

'Fine.' Bridge got up and trudged off.

Reed stopped the guard getting up. 'We've got a warrant and if I see you so much as looking at the equipment, you're getting locked up.'

'I know the drill. Don't have to brief me.' Then the guard gave Fenchurch a cheeky wink. 'I know you.' He joined them standing, looming tall. A chain dangled round his neck, holding a keycard and a tiny USB drive. 'Simon Fenchurch, isn't it?' He held out a hand. 'Jim Muscat. PC Muscat, as was. Based at Leman Street until March, but I got my twenty-five and got out. You must remember me?'

Fenchurch would have imagined so with those eyes, but he just couldn't recall. Then he gave Muscat a professional smile. 'How you finding this?'

'Cakewalk, mate.' Muscat's mouth hung open and he thumbed behind him. 'Until someone finds a dead body on your watch. It's common in hotels, but this is my first one.'

'Did you find her?'

'Nah, the cleaner did. Joanna. Half past one.' Muscat's voice had slid up an octave. 'Poor thing's in a bit of a state. She told me and . . . Not sure what I could do other than call it in, you know?'

'Wondering if you can help me, Jim.' Fenchurch settled a serious gaze on Muscat, treating him like he was still on the Job. 'We've got a bit of a mystery concerning the guest's identity.'

'I know what you mean.' Muscat frowned. 'Thought I recognised her from somewhere but . . .'

He knows her face as well. Bloody hell.

'One thing you might be able to help with, Jim. How did the killer get in the room?'

'Why you asking me?'

Fenchurch pointed at the security console behind the desk.

'Oh. I already looked for DC Bridge. The machine's on the blink. Got a guy coming to fix it next week.'

'Can you get them in any sooner?' Fenchurch clapped Muscat's arm. 'Anyway, how about you flex those old police officer's muscles and look up the guest on the system?'

'Would love to help.' Muscat tugged at his collar. 'Trouble is, I've not been here that long and young Katerina hasn't showed me the system yet. She's the receptionist. Well, for weekends anyway.'

'Do you know where the girl who found the body is?'

'Joanna. She's with a cop. Uzma Ashkani, used to know her from my time on the force. Lovely girl. Not many Indians on the force, though.'

And Uzma was supposed to check in when she arrived . . .

Fenchurch motioned at Reed as he set off. 'Kay, can you work with Jim here and see if he can get us a name?'

———

'Simon.' DS Uzma Ashkani stood in the doorway, hand on hip, her expression as dark as her hair. Her smile betrayed how much she liked herself. She joined him in the corridor and pulled the door behind her, marked Staff Only. 'So Dawn asked me to step in and make sure everything's above board.'

Nothing like being audited.

'Sergeant, you were asked to let me know when you'd arrived.'

'And you were busy.' Uzma put her hands on her hips again. One of her less annoying habits. 'You dislike me because I've worked for DCI Mulholland for six years, don't you?'

'It's nothing to do with that. So long as you remember who you work for, we won't have a problem.' Fenchurch held her gaze until she looked away. 'Have you spoken to the cleaner yet?'

Uzma motioned inside the room at a middle-aged woman sitting on a sofa, eyes red, a tissue bunched up in her fist. She looked up at them and Fenchurch could see in her eyes that sitting there red-faced and crying wasn't exactly a novel experience. 'Name's Joanna Page. She found the body. You're welcome to join me.'

Fenchurch entered the room and leaned against the nearest wall. Bare breeze blocks. Six comfy sofas paired off. A fridge hummed next to a water cooler.

Uzma put her notebook on the table and sat back, running a hand through her hair. Still hadn't lost that supercilious smile. She spoke in a soothing tone. 'Can you take us through what happened today?'

Joanna took a moment to compose herself, tugging at her skirt and tights. 'I'm a cleaner here at the weekend. Just doing my rounds, listening to that new St Vincent album, when I opened that door and . . . Jesus Christ. Got a bit of a fright. I mean, I often see guests in their beds, even at that time, but she wasn't answering. And she was smiling at me? I mean, it freaked me out. I went inside and—' Joanna burst into tears, her body racking with each fresh wave.

Fenchurch leaned in to Uzma. 'Stay with her and see what else you can get.'

Uzma raised her eyebrows. Then shifted over to the other seat and put an arm around Joanna. 'Hey, it's okay.'

───⏝───

Reed was in the bar. The Third Planet: all marble and glass and stripped wood. A giant wall of whisky sat by the cash register, a priceless collection of Scotch from all over the world, if that was still Scotch. The Arsenal and Spurs fans had left their drinks, half-finished pints of Peroni and Stella still covering most tables. The giant TV screen had moved on from the live match to some pundits talking shit in a studio high up in the stadium.

A couple of DCs were taking statements from hotel staff.

Reed wandered over, her trainers squeaking on the floor. 'You okay, guv?'

'Uzma. Say no more.' Fenchurch grimaced. 'What you up to?'

A beanpole trudged up to them. At least six foot six. Skin and bones. And he looked young, despite his failed attempt at a beard. He held out his hand. 'Oliver Muscat-Smith.'

Fenchurch shook it. 'Any relation to Jim Muscat?'

'My old man.' His eyes bulged, just like his father's. 'Parents never married. Not together any more. I'm the bar manager here.'

'You seem a bit young.'

'Okay. Deputy bar manager.' Oliver sighed. 'Okay, I'm a trainee barman, but . . .'

'So, Oliver.' Reed folded her arms. 'You were saying?'

'Was I?' Oliver looked her up and down, teenage lust twinkling in his eyes. 'Oh yeah. I was telling DS Reed here that I didn't see anything weird.' He gave her another appraisal. 'I've got a good eye for the unusual and special.'

Reed puckered her lips. 'Have you, now?'

'Anyone pops in here, I can tell you when they were last in, what they were drinking, how much they tipped me. Whether they tried to hit on me.'

'You sound quite experienced for your age.'

'Happy to show you what I can do.'

'I bet you are, son.' Fenchurch laughed. 'You still at school?'

'Nah, left in the summer. I'm eighteen, in case you're wondering. Started this gig full-time in July. Before that, I did back-office admin, then I worked reception. Cushy number, that, but this is me now. Training to be a proper cocktail waiter. Get a gig on a cruise ship, maybe on someone's private yacht. Big bucks out there.' Oliver's eyes scanned around the bar area. 'Not in here, mind.'

'You know the victim?'

'Not seen her, sorry. I try to keep out of that part of the hotel as much as I can in case someone asks me to do something.' Oliver grinned wide. 'You know, I'm six foot seven. Means I can reach things a lot of people can't.' He flashed his eyebrows at Reed. 'Got size sixteen shoes.'

Fenchurch glowered at him. 'We don't know the victim's identity.'

'*I* didn't kill her, mate.'

'Not saying you did. You said you worked reception. Wonder if you can maybe get us the victim's name?'

'Why can't Kat do it?'

'Who?'

'The receptionist.' Reed's face tightened and she spoke in an undertone. 'Guv, I tried speaking to her but Uzma stopped me when she gave her age. Still a minor. Waiting on her mother turning up. And besides, she's crying. She saw the body and it freaked her out.'

'Okay. So, Oliver, given that your old man says he doesn't know how to use the system . . .?'

Oliver rolled his eyes. 'Can barely use the bloody telly . . . Follow me.' He marched through to reception, strutting like he was on a dance floor, and walked over to where his father was scowling at the computer. 'All right, old timer?' He pushed his dad away and knelt in front of the desk. 'What's the room number?'

'218.' Muscat shot his son a wink. 'Sometimes you need an old-timer, eh?'

'Not very often.' Oliver typed at the machine. 'Okay. She checked in just before seven last night.' Then he frowned. 'Oh, bloody hell.'

'What's up?'

'Name is Elizabeth Windsor. Oh, someone's having a laugh, ain't they?'

'Did she book it?'

'Course she didn't. She's the Queen.'

'I mean whoever is pretending to be her.'

'Right. No. Says here that the booking was made by Maximum Exposure PR.'

A PR agency? Great . . .

27

Chapter Four

I t's still nagging at me, guv.' Reed was out of the car first, buses and lorries buzzing past behind. Her forehead twisted again. 'People keep saying they recognise the victim.' She slammed the door and charged off down the road. 'Who is she?'

Fenchurch caught up with her by the building, a brick pile in prime Hackney, a few doors down from the Empire. Buses, trucks and cars thundered past, a cacophony of engine noise and dubstep. He pressed the buzzer more in hope than expectation. MAXIMUM EXPOSURE was etched in battered brass on the door.

'Max Exposure, how can I help?' The sort of voice you'd hear on kids' TV, all lilting and jaunty.

'Police.'

And the door clicked open, just like that.

'Staffed on a Saturday. Interesting.' Fenchurch stepped through to a large reception area, bigger than the hotel's.

Reed walked up to the desk and flashed her warrant card. 'Is Mr Maxfield in?'

The receptionist peered over his thick glasses, obviously more for show than function. 'Ben's not taking visitors.'

'We're police, son. Be a good lad and get him, yeah?' Reed smiled at the lad then watched him trudging off.

Fenchurch rested against the reception desk, the white plastic dented in a few places. Too low, as well.

'It's good to get back to work, though.' Reed pressed her lips together. 'Two weeks with Dave and my kids. Driving me bloody potty.'

The receptionist reappeared. 'Guys, I'm afraid that Mr Maxfield is very definitely *not* taking any visitors today, so—'

'Just get him out here, son.' Reed waved him back. 'Now.' She watched him traipse off again, though he was slightly faster this time. 'The evidence trail stops at the hotel room door. Need Sherlock bloody Holmes to solve this.' Then she licked her lips. 'Benedict Cumberbatch can solve me any day.'

'Grow up.' Fenchurch poked his fingernails into the reception desk's cracked plastic. 'It's not a locked-room mystery. That cleaner told us the door was open. It's how she got in.'

'Suppose.'

Something clattered behind the desk and the receptionist was back, though this time he was accompanied by a middle-aged man. Spiky black hair, obviously dyed, his face lost under stubble and Botox. Wearing teenagers' clothes: skinny-fit jeans that looked like they stopped the blood flow to his feet. Ben Maxfield, his jaw clenched. 'What can I do for you?'

Reed held out her warrant card. 'Mr Maxfield, we've got a dead body at the Bennaceur in the Minories. Room was booked by your firm, in the name of Elizabeth Windsor.'

'Very, very pleased for you.' Everything he said was dry, sarcastic, like he barely meant any of it.

'We need to identify the victim.'

'I'm afraid that I've got far too much work to get involved with this.' Maxfield sat behind the desk, feet up on the cracked plastic. 'Now, you need to leave.'

'Are you refusing to speak to us?'

'I'd *love* the luxury of a couple of hours just chatting with you, Sergeant. As it is, my phone's ringing every five minutes with some tedious, tedious editor trying to get me on the bleeding record about— Well. That would be telling.' He smirked. 'Now, I really need to get back to it, okay?'

Reed bent down to him, their foreheads level. 'You caught the bit about a dead body, yeah?'

'I haven't killed anyone since 1985.' Maxfield's head jerked back as his hands shot up, palms out. 'Joke!' He settled on his elbows, tilting his head to the side. 'Sergeant, I have every sympathy for you, I really, *really* do. It's just that I've got so, so, *so* much work on.'

'So you're not going to speak to us?'

Maxfield pushed himself back up to standing. 'Not even if you took me back to the police station.' The phone on the desk started ringing and Maxfield reached for it.

Fenchurch grabbed his arm. 'Now, do you want to come to the station, or are you going to talk?'

Maxfield got up and walked over to lean against the window, silhouetted by the sun. 'When I saw it was *you*, a celebrity, I wondered if you'd like representation?'

'I'm hardly famous.'

'It's not just celebs, you know. Those news stories about you and your daughter? So, so heartwarming.'

'We just need the name of the woman in the hotel room.'

'I tell you, I could've done a much, *much* better job of finding your daughter.' Maxfield clapped his hands together. 'And without so, so many deaths. It was like an Arnold Schwarzenegger film by the end, wasn't it?'

'*Sir.*' Fenchurch crossed his arms. 'The victim's identity. *Please.*'

Maxfield ran his palms together, slowly. 'Part of my trade is keeping my lips sealed.'

'You going to open them for me?'

'What do you think?'

'Come on, then.' Fenchurch grabbed Maxfield's shirtsleeve. 'You get to choose which cells you spend the night in.' He left a pause. 'Hackney or Leman Street. Either one gets pretty rough on a Saturday. The sort of people we lock up are very good at hiding blades where we can't find them.'

'Trying to intimidate me won't work. I've dealt with much, much better than you.'

'Is the victim a client?'

'Oh, are we playing twenty questions?' Maxfield rolled his eyes. 'Of course she's a client. I don't pay for random strangers' hotel rooms.'

'Name, now.'

'Simon, Simon, Simon. I can only give yes or no answers. I mean, *come on.*'

'Is she a celebrity?'

Maxfield weighed it up, staring out of his window, then back down. 'Ish?'

'That's neither yes nor no.'

'Well spotted. You might make a detective one day.'

'Just tell me.'

'But I'm having *so* much fun here!'

Don't let him get to you. Fenchurch cleared his throat. 'I just need her name. That's it.'

'I've got a policy to only talk once I've seen a body. You could be up to anything here. So until I see her cold, dead flesh, then I'm not talking.' Maxfield rubbed his fingertips together, his forehead creasing. Then he stuffed his hands in his pockets. 'And besides, I've been on holiday. Splashed all over the *Sun* and the *Mail* and the *Star*, if you've been following it.'

'I don't read those papers.'

'You don't look like you *can* read.' Maxfield covered his mouth with his hands. 'Sorry. Look, if you must know, I was staying on a client's yacht in the Med. Glorious, glorious weather. Such, such gorgeous Pinot, too. They own a vineyard in California. Invited me out in October for Halloween in a Californian vineyard. *Divine.*'

'I assume the yacht's owner isn't the client I found murdered in a hotel room?'

'You're welcome to assume anything, but you'd be very, very *right*, my good sir. Ding ding ding!' Maxfield looked at Reed for a reaction, mouth open, eyes wide, like a gameshow host. Then he grumbled and leaned back against the window. 'Different client entirely.'

'You're not going to tell us, are you?'

'Probably not. I mean, it's like they don't train you lot to ask the right questions, isn't it? I'm world-class at avoiding them, so you'd think—'

'What do you think, Kay?' Fenchurch took his time walking to the door. 'Perverting the course of justice?'

'I'm not perverting anything!'

'Two-year sentence. Minimum.'

Maxfield caught himself. Then shut his eyes like he was meditating. 'Okay.' His brow creased. 'Look, an associate was dealing with this while I was away. I genuinely, *genuinely* don't know anything about this case.'

'So why all this evasion?'

'It's like a sport with me. I enjoy making the little people squirm.'

'Just tell me who's lying dead in that hotel room.'

'All I'll tell you, until you prove that she's dead, is that my client is a woman who needs her profile managing over a week or two.' Maxfield puckered his lips. 'I just can't tell you. Sorry.'

'You're choosing this—' Fenchurch stopped himself, otherwise he'd end up knocking his block off. 'Listen to me. The victim has a husband or maybe a wife, someone who'll mourn her death, who'll want justice. Don't you want to help them instead of playing charades?'

Maxfield winked. 'Two words. It's a saying. First word.' He started thrusting his hips. 'Second word.' He thumbed at the door.

'Very funny.' Fenchurch jabbed a finger at Maxfield. 'Someone will mourn this woman's death. I just need a name. That's it.'

'Sorry, but I can't help.' Maxfield yawned into a fist. 'Please leave.'

———

'What a prick.' Fenchurch got in the car and sent a raging glower at the Maximum Exposure office like it would do anything. 'You ever see anything like that?'

'A few times.' Reed yawned, like she'd caught it off Maxfield. 'You think he'll help?'

'Not a chance.'

Fenchurch gripped his keys tight in his pocket. 'I'm so tempted to chuck him down some steps, Kay.'

'At least wait until I've put the big spikes at the bottom.'

Fenchurch laughed. 'He knows her identity, doesn't he? Why is he mucking us about?'

'He's playing us. That or he just doesn't believe you.'

Fenchurch stabbed his key in the ignition and twisted like it was Ben Maxfield's throat. 'The victim's face, Kay. I know it from some-where. A film? A TV show? Is she a singer?'

'Maybe it's just someone from the news?' Reed smirked at him. 'Though she'd have to be one of those dolly birds on Sky Sports News, right?'

'Not one of them, Kay.' Fenchurch's throat tightened. 'Maybe she's an MP or some minor celebrity or . . . I don't know.'

'Tell you what, I'll get someone to look into it. Okay?'

Fenchurch started the car. 'You know, I'd much rather you did it than gave it to some idiot.'

Reed slumped back in her seat. 'Guv . . .'

'Come on, Kay. Look, I'll see what's happening at the hotel, you find her identity. That's a much sexier job.'

Chapter Five

Fenchurch held open the hotel's front door to let someone leave. Then grabbed their sleeve as they passed. 'Not so fast, Mick.'

'Oh, it's you.' Clooney tried to walk off but Fenchurch's grip held him in place. 'I've got to head up to sunny Hackney. Acid attack outside a bar.' His lip curled. 'It just gets worse, Si. Feels like we're living in the end times.'

'I'll look for you wearing a sandwich board at Old Street tube.' Fenchurch still didn't let go. 'Have you got any forensics for me?'

'Some.' Clooney tried another tug at his sleeve and just gave up. 'Listen, Tammy's in charge here and you've got twelve of my best. I'll give you an update by close of play, okay?'

Fenchurch let his grip go. 'By six at the latest.'

And Clooney was gone.

Fenchurch entered the building. His turn to get his arm grabbed.

A short man, boyish looks fading into middle-aged seediness. Sleeves short like the wearer, who barely came up to Fenchurch's armpits. Name badge: RODERICK. MANAGER. Spelled trouble. 'Are you Fenchurch?'

'That's me.' He pushed his hand away. 'Take it you're in charge?'

'For what that's worth.' Roderick breathed on to his badge and rubbed it against his shirt tails. 'You need to let me reopen the hotel.

The owners are jumping on my balls. With this place shut, they're not making any money. And when they're—'

'They'll have insurance for this sort of thing.'

Roderick tucked in his shirt. 'Wouldn't be so sure of it.'

'They should be more worried that there's been a murder here.'

'I—'

'Not until forensics have been completed, sir. But that floor is staying shut.'

'You really don't get it, do you?' Roderick walked off, muttering to himself as he pushed through to the staff area.

What a guy . . .

Bridge was behind the reception desk working at a laptop. She grinned at him as he approached. 'Need a room for the night, sir?'

'Prefer one without a dead body.' Fenchurch motioned at the still-swinging door. 'The manager causing you any hassle?'

'Nothing I can't handle, sir.'

'What sort of thing?'

'Oh, nothing much, just . . . He's pushy. Trying to get this place opened, that kind of thing.'

'Any more of that and you point him at me, okay?' Fenchurch took another look around. Suspicious lack of any police officers. 'Got an ID yet?'

'Not yet, sir.' Bridge closed her laptop and leaned forward. 'DS Ashkani is having a briefing. I wasn't invited.'

'I take it you're working on something too important?'

'Well.' Bridge opened the laptop again. 'Like Jim Muscat said, sir, there's barely any CCTV inside.' She pointed up at the ceiling. 'Just those two in here and a couple of corridors on the ground floor. Nothing outside the victim's room or anywhere near. That I've found, anyway. I had a look, but I couldn't spot any.'

'They can be well hidden.'

'Don't have to tell me, sir.'

'So there's no useful CCTV?'

'Well. There's this.' Bridge turned her laptop so he could see the screen. The reception area, frozen. A man was walking out, carrying a blow-up doll under his arm like he was lugging a lilo to the beach.

'What the hell is this?'

'Your guess is as good as mine.' Bridge turned the laptop back round. 'I've been going through the footage between nine and nine thirty. Ten people left, two arrived.' She stopped Fenchurch before he started. 'And the two arriving are part of the ten.'

'And what about outside our window? Someone getting here early, lying in wait, killing her, then leaving when the coast's clear?'

'That's next on my list, sir.' Bridge slouched back in the chair. 'Putting names to that initial set of faces has been tricky enough. The rest is going to take ages.'

'You're doing a great job, Lisa.'

'Always seem to get landed with this, sir.'

'We'll need to do something about that.' Fenchurch gave her a smile. 'So, this list?'

'Thanks for speaking to us, sir.' Bridge sat in the staff canteen area, her leg jogging. 'You arrived here—'

'I can explain this.' Sam Cornwall was tall, with a sharp haircut and huge bags under his red eyes. Bristol or Swindon accent. Wearing a potato sack. Had to keep tucking it down to preserve his modesty. 'My mates glued it on last night. It's my stag weekend and those bastards . . .' He laughed like he was still pissed. Probably was. 'What's this about, anyway?'

Fenchurch cut in: 'Someone was murdered in a room on your floor.'

'Shut up.' Sam's drunken laugh died on his lips. 'Really? Shit. Look. Mate, the only person I killed last night was myself. Very slowly.'

'We still need to understand your movements at the time in question.'

Another drunken laugh. He'd clearly forgotten the death. 'You'll have to help me with the time.'

'You left here just after nine. Did you see anything on your way out?'

'Mate, I'm lucky I even got out. Those bastards.'

'Can anyone verify your movements?'

'Four of us staying here. They'll be able to confirm.'

'You need a hand getting that sack off?'

Sam gave Bridge another grin. 'I've got to keep it on tonight.'

———

'Aye, I was out with Sam.' Ed was Scottish, no sign of a hangover except for a deep voice. A frown danced across his forehead, almost getting lost in his thick eyebrows. 'Did we glue Sam—?' He coughed. 'Nah, didn't see anything on our way out. Last thing I remember is Chris opening bottles of sambuca and Jägermeister in Dave's. He reckons it's—'

———

'—much cheaper if you buy bottles rather than shots.' The chubby guy next to Fenchurch pushed his glasses up his nose, eyes bulging. Northern accent, but hard to place. 'I left here with Dave but he—'

———

'—got a kebab on my way back.' Another Scot, big and burly. Looked like someone off the TV, but hard to picture who. 'Woke up this morning and I'd only eaten the meat. What was I thinking? The pitta, soaked in the fat and chilli sauce, that's the best bit!'

'Did you see anything on your way out?'

'After a bottle of sambuca, I was lucky to even get out, doll.'

'Had a day from hell.' A businessman in a shirt-and-jumper combo, though both were struggling to contain his gut. 'Up and down the Northern Line seeing clients all day long. I know what I'll be doing when I die and go to hell. Then I had a . . . meeting on Mansell Street.'

'We have you on CCTV arriving back here at nine oh five.' Bridge twirled her pen. 'Seems like a long meeting.'

'I had a few light ales with . . . an ex-colleague. We were going for a curry up on Brick Lane, but I wanted to drop off my laptop.'

'And this ex-colleague can confirm the story?'

'They could . . .'

'It's a woman, isn't it?'

He rubbed his neck. 'It might be.'

'And if we looked at CCTV from later, we wouldn't find you and her coming back here, would we?'

He cleared his throat. 'What's this about?'

'Someone was murdered in a room down the corridor from yours.'

He gulped. Then again. Then his cheeks bulged and he ran off towards the toilet.

'And Jenny didn't even get here until lunchtime today.' Hen 1 pointed at Hen 2. Black dress, stinking of sour perfume. Geordie accent. Fake tan. Sitting on a sofa next to a clone of her, opposite another two clones. 'Here, hon, you want to sit between us?'

'I'm fine.' Fenchurch was standing between the sofas. 'Just wondering if you saw anything?'

Hen 1 pointed at Hen 3. 'Ash here thought it'd be a good idea to have a quiet night in the rooms and go big tonight, like.'

'Quiet night with this lot and three bottles of vodka?' Hen 3 bellowed out laughter. 'We ran out of booze at nine! Then went to a club!'

'This slag here!' Hen 1 pointed at Hen 3. 'She got finger—'

Fenchurch reached in and clicked on the lights. They flashed on, showing a load of cleaning equipment.

Bridge followed him in. 'Getting nowhere, sir.' She looked like she was going to kick a steel bucket. 'An hour to herd those cats, then none of them saw anything. Wasting our time.'

'Not quite.' Fenchurch held up his hands, palms out. 'We started today with ten leaving, two of whom came back. We're now down to two arriving, one leaving. That's progress.'

Bridge gave a slight shrug. 'I suppose.'

'It's good.' Fenchurch leaned back against the door. 'Can I see the photos of the missing two?'

'Both women.' Bridge pulled up two shots on her laptop.

Hard to be more different. One was short and stocky, her hair shining in the grainy black-and-white. The other was tall and overly thin with dark hair.

Neither was their victim.

Fenchurch pushed it back. 'Can you find them, please?'

'I'll try.' Bridge pinched her nose and waved a hand out of the door. 'I can get that barman to get us home addresses for the others?'

'Do it.' Fenchurch opened the door and peered out. Uzma was walking towards them. 'Keep me updated.' He met Uzma halfway along the corridor. 'Sergeant, nice to—'

'Need your help, Simon.' Uzma jerked her thumb behind her. 'Jim Muscat . . . He's hiding something. Won't speak to me. Says he'll talk to you. Did he work for you?'

'No, but he thinks he did . . .'

Chapter Six

'Jim, you know how this looks, yeah?' Uzma sat on the guard's desk, swinging her legs. 'You need to keep talking to us.'

Muscat was on his own chair, staring at the floor, shoulders slouched.

Uzma raised her eyebrows at Fenchurch.

He joined her sitting on the desk and smiled at Muscat. 'You ever been to a cop's funeral, Jim?'

Muscat looked up at him, squinting.

'Course you have.' Fenchurch nodded slowly. 'Must've been to, what, ten? Twenty?'

Muscat gave a shrug. 'About that.'

'My old boss got cremated this afternoon.' Fenchurch felt the lump in his throat again. 'I worked for him for twelve years, on and off. My old man worked with him, too, back in the day. Said to me, you shouldn't be angry that it's over—'

'—but be glad that it happened.' Muscat exhaled through his nostrils, nodding. 'My old man was a copper, too. East Ham, Shoreditch, Lewisham. Twenty-five years on the beat. Can't see my son signing up.'

Or mine . . .

Pain stabbed Fenchurch's gut. He cleared his throat.

'Course, you met my boy earlier, didn't you? You'll know what I mean, mate. Ollie's walking his own path and it's not public service, that's for sure.' Muscat rocked back in his chair, getting an almighty crack from the mechanism. 'Maybe one day he'll decide to do something worthwhile. Me, I always wanted to be a copper. Broke my heart when I failed my medical and had to leave. You?'

'Keep passing my medicals. But if you're talking about wanting to be a cop, well, I was a bit of an arsehole in my teens.' Fenchurch sat back on the table. 'Some people say I've got worse.'

'Heard that.' Muscat laughed. 'Heard that, all right!'

Fenchurch joined in the laughter and let it run for a few seconds. 'Jim, I need your help finding these women.' He passed him some CCTV prints of the two missing guests. 'They arrived here last night. She left. She stayed.'

Muscat snatched the prints with gusto and stared hard at them like he was back on duty again.

Fenchurch scanned the foyer while Muscat looked at the photos. 'My DC said you don't have internal CCTV here?'

'Afraid not, mate. Keep asking for it, but it falls on deaf ears. The brothers who own this place . . . Pair of crooks.' Muscat tossed the photos on the cabinet next to him. 'They're penny-pinching bastards. Everything's so tight here. Always about the bottom line. I swear, that CCTV's just the tip of the iceberg.'

'Anything we should look into?'

'Nah, mate. Just not the best geezers to work for.'

Something's not right here.

Fenchurch picked up the photos again. 'You recognise them, don't you?'

'No.'

Fenchurch showed him the photo of the short woman. 'Is it her?'

'What? Do me a favour.'

'So it's this woman.' Fenchurch pointed at the tall woman. 'Who is she?' He waited, but Muscat just stared at the floor. 'What the hell's going on, Jim?'

'Nothing, I swear.'

Fenchurch focused on the image. A well-to-do woman, young, arriving back at the hotel. *What is he hiding?* 'Someone killed our victim and got out of here without a trace. If you're up to something, mate, you want to—'

'You take me for a common criminal? Eh?'

'Jim, I don't know you from Adam.' Fenchurch held up both photos. 'I just want to find these two.'

Muscat snatched them back, a vein throbbing in his temple. 'If it was me and I wanted to murder someone here and then get out on the QT, I'd use the back door. It's unmarked.'

———

The hotel kitchen smelled of burnt toast and rotting fish. Fenchurch tried a door. 'It's locked, Jim.'

Muscat got out a key. 'I shouldn't be showing you this.' He unlocked the door and opened it on to some cobbles. Vine Street. Back-street boozers and hipster cafés. Further down it opened out for some office buildings. Cigarette smoke billowed down from somewhere.

Uzma followed him out, Bridge just behind her. 'There's got to be a camera round here.'

'I'm looking.' Bridge spun around, cross-referencing with her laptop.

'You got that one?' Uzma pointed above the smoking area outside the next-door office block, a couple of cleaners huddling under the bike shed, sucking on roll-ups.

'What? Oh.' Bridge hit the keyboard like she was tenderising a steak. 'This is us now.' She rested the laptop on a bollard, close enough for Fenchurch to see. Onscreen, the three of them were standing around on the street, staring at Bridge's laptop. She wound the footage back to the night before.

The lane was dark and empty except for a fox sniffing about. At 20.48, a couple walked out of one of the back entrances to a bar, hand in hand, then walked over to a white van. She knelt down out of sight and the man rested back against the wall. Could see a ponytail bobbing back and forth every so often.

'Oh, Jesus Christ.' Bridge sped it up. Nine minutes later and the man was screaming with delight. 'Impressive stamina.'

'Look at the state of them, though.' Uzma watched the couple stagger off down the lane back into the bar. 'Surprised he could even get it up.'

Then nothing, just a fox rooting around near a bin.

Some headlights shone as a car pulled up. It sat there, idling, the exhaust pluming behind it.

Fenchurch leaned in close. 'Lisa, can you find the driver for me?'

'Sir.' Bridge frowned at her laptop. 'It's a partial plate. Might take me a while.' She set it playing again. 'I'll see if—'

The hotel's back door opened and a short woman left the building. She got in the car and it drove off.

Bridge tapped the screen. 'Sir, this is at ten. Around the time of the murder.'

Uzma leaned in close. 'I know who this is.'

Chapter Seven

Uzma led towards the staff room, shaking her head. 'It's the receptionist. Katerina.'

Fenchurch looked around the room as he sat next to her. 'Did you get anything out of her earlier?'

'Well. Muscat said her shift ended at ten. Trouble is, she's under eighteen so I've asked her mother to head to Leman Street. Still not shown up yet. Had her life story on the phone about how her husband left her and died in a car crash and—'

'Did you get anything out of the cleaner?'

'Don't think she knows anything. Sent her home with her husband. She was pretty shaken up.'

A thump at the door. Roderick, the manager. Wild-eyed and twitchy, like he'd drunk a jar of coffee. He clicked his fingers in Fenchurch's face. 'I really need a word with you. Now.' He set off down the corridor.

'Right.' Fenchurch made eye contact with Uzma. 'Can you chase up this girl's mother?' Then he followed Roderick out into the reception area. 'What?'

'In here.' Roderick opened the door marked Manager's Office. 'Nazar, here's the—'

'I see who it is.' A man sat behind the desk, thin and well dressed. He spoke in the plummy tones of a private education, but looked Middle Eastern. Whether he was the son of immigrants or just educated over here wasn't clear. Late forties, his dark hair tousled into an almost-perfect flow, catching the light just right. Guy was good-looking and he knew it. Behind him, a signed Shadwell United shirt hung on the wall. Number 9, WALSH, the white-and-gold hoops splattered with mud, grass and blue-ink signatures. Nazar shot a glare into the corner of the room. 'Sutekh!'

An almost-exact copy of Nazar sat slumped on a chair, just heavier and balding. Mouth hanging open, head rocking back and forth, snoring like a burst drain. He didn't have his twin brother's dress sense, instead settling for a black-and-white tracksuit.

Nazar flicked a hand at Roderick. 'Get us coffees. Now.' He waited for him to comply, then stood up, offering a hand and a smile to Fenchurch. 'Sutekh?' Sleepy just snored. 'Sutekh?' Still nothing, so Nazar just gave a polite smile. 'This is a horrific business, Inspector, and we are very glad that you're taking your time to investigate fully. I was wondering if we could work towards a—'

'Open the goddamn hotel!' Sutekh was awake now, fury burning in his eyes as he got up, jabbing a finger in the air. He'd either never got his brother's accent or had lost it, instead finding a Middlesex grunt behind some bins somewhere. 'We're losing goddamn money here! Hand over goddamn fist! Open up! Open up!'

Fenchurch just stood there. *If it's a good cop/bad cop thing, they're terrible at it.*

'Sutekh, that's not our prime concern here.' Nazar snapped a hand in the direction of his brother. Then gave a polite smile to Fenchurch. 'They told me when we bought this place that we'd get suicides — at least ten a year in a place this size. We've owned this hotel nine years and had only five deaths. All explained, all suicides.' A smile parted his lips, his pearly whites shining through. 'This, though . . . A murder? Here? It's shocking. *Shocking.*'

'Open the goddamn doors!'

'Sutekh!' Another snap of the wrist. 'My brother and I, we *really* want to help. We want to support you doing anything in your power to find the culprit and bring them to justice.'

'Sir, thanks for your support but I need to get back to the investigation.'

Snoring droned from the corner again. Sutekh's head was on his chest.

Fenchurch scowled. 'Is he okay?'

'I'm sorry.' Nazar tiptoed across the room. 'My brother suffers from narcolepsy. We're twins, identical as you can see, but I'm lucky, as I somehow didn't get the family affliction. I can only apologise for him — I know how it looks. Indifference. Apathy. Ignorance. But Sutekh has the heart of a bull.' His forehead knotted. 'The brain of one at times.' He nudged his brother on the shoulder.

'Goddamn prick!' Sutekh grabbed his brother's finger and twisted it. Then seemed to realise where he was and slackened off. He focused on Fenchurch, that fire back in his glare. 'When are you going to open our goddamn hotel? Eh?'

'Sir, your hotel will be shut for the foreseeable future. I'd advise that you cancel all bookings for the next few days at least, then claim on any insurance pol—'

'No!' Sutekh hauled himself to his feet and squared up to Fenchurch. 'You need to let us open the goddamn doors. Now! Or we will sue the police for loss of income!'

'You will, will you?' Fenchurch stood his ground, nodding slowly. 'See, if you'd had insurance, you'd not be in this mess.'

'Insurance is the work of the devil!' Sutekh thumped his chest. 'Why the hell should I pay for someone else's goddamn murdering?'

'Sutekh, let the officer get on with his job.'

Fenchurch waved Nazar off, keeping his gaze on his brother. 'You're not involved in this, are you?'

'What did you say to me?'

'Mr Bennaceur, you don't seem to care that someone's wife is lying upstairs, dead.' Fenchurch got in his face, going eyeball to eyeball. 'Most murderers are sociopaths. They kill without remorse because they can't care about other living things. I could put you in a room and ask you a lot of difficult questions about where you were last night.'

'I was in Nice.' Sutekh stepped back but snapped his own wrist in his brother's direction. 'We both were.'

Fenchurch smirked at Nazar. 'Sure your sleeping isn't just a coke comedown?' He stared at Sutekh until he looked away then made for the door. 'As part of this case, we'll look into your backgrounds. We might just have that chat, okay?' He left the room and slammed the door.

Pair of arseholes.

Are they up to something? Hiding a murder? Or just another pair of cheap bastards worried about the bottom line?

Always so hard to tell.

Fenchurch found Katerina Raptis with Uzma in Leman Street's nicest interview room, not that it was up to much. Katerina was short, her legs barely touching the ground, and had an impish look about her. Round cheeks and jet-black hair. Even though she was crying, she still looked like she was taking the piss. She rocked back and forth, avoiding looking at Uzma. Then she screwed up her face, gasping as tears flooded her cheeks.

'Katerina, it's okay.' Uzma walked over and rubbed the girl's back, standing like that for a few seconds. Then she leaned round and smiled at her. 'Your mother is just about here.'

Katerina finally looked up at her, a snarl on her lips, then burst into tears again, covering her face. Bunched-up tissues in both hands, her fists twisting and twisting. Still no sign of the girl's mother.

Fenchurch leaned back against the interview room door. 'Why is she crying?'

'No idea.' Uzma kept her gaze on the girl. 'Been like this since I got here.'

Raised voices out in the corridor, someone shouting. Fenchurch opened the door and peered out.

'Where is she?' A woman flounced along the corridor, just out of a uniform's reach. Heavy make-up plastering over lines, perfect hair and the stench of floral perfume. She caught sight of Fenchurch and raced over to him. 'Where's my baby?'

'Mrs Raptis?'

'I prefer Ms these days.' She tilted her head at Fenchurch, then raised her pristine eyebrows, thin pencil-width lines. 'Call me Jocasta. Or Jo, if you prefer?'

'I'll stick with—'

'Oh my God!' Jocasta put a hand to her mouth. 'It's you!' Then both hands out wide, like her eyes. 'Simon Fenchurch!' She bit her lip, frowning. 'We followed your story in the papers. Me and Katerina. Heartbreaking story, you poor thing.' She reached out and stroked his chin. 'You poor lamb.'

'Right.' Fenchurch brushed her hand away. 'Well.'

'Thought I recognised you, but it was maybe just that you look like that Jason Statham.' She pouted. 'Your story resonated with us. Me and Katerina. You must've gone through hell. I read someone online saying it was the same group as Maddy McCann?'

'We don't think it's in any way connected, no.'

Her eyebrows turned in on themselves. Then she tried to peer behind him. 'Where's my girl?'

'Through there.' Fenchurch made sure the door was shut. 'A colleague is working through some details in her statement.' He gave her a stern look. 'I'll warn you now: she's been through a traumatic event and I recommend counselling.'

'Katerina? Counselling?' Jocasta threw her head back. 'Do me a favour! I tried to get her to see a headshrinker when her—' She huffed out a sigh. 'She ran rings round the poor woman. Didn't make Kat any better, neither.'

'Well.' Fenchurch nudged the handle down. 'I need to just check on progress, so—'

Jocasta barged past him. 'Kat!' She raced over and smothered her daughter in a hug. 'Are you okay?'

'Mum.' Katerina flinched, jerking away from her mother. 'I want to help.'

'That can wait. Let's get you home!'

Katerina was on her feet, face twisted. 'Mum, back off!' She brushed some tears from her face and gave Fenchurch a slight nod. 'What do you want to know?'

Fenchurch sat opposite them and leaned forward. 'Let's start with you leaving the hotel.'

'I got my coat from the staff room . . .'

'What time was that?'

'Ten. Just after? It was pretty quiet for a Friday, but Siresh was late so I had to stay on and . . .' Katerina sat back and brushed her hair out of her eyes.

Fenchurch held out his hands. 'We still don't have an ID on—'

'Mrs Fisher.'

Uzma jerked round, scowling at Katerina. 'You *know* her?'

'I checked her in.' Katerina ran her teeth over her top lip, stretching it out. 'She's my English teacher.'

'What?'

'Joanna freaked out. She let me see her body.' She started crying again, her breath coming in slow bursts. 'Mrs Fisher was . . . I can't . . . She was so nice. We were really close. And I can't . . . can't . . .'

'Do you know her first name? Where she lives? Anything like that?'

Katerina shook her head, biting into her lip. 'I don't know anything other than she's called Gayle.'

'We need to tell someone their wife's dead. Anything—'

'Her husband's a teacher at the school too.' Katerina sniffed. 'Mr Fisher. Steve, I think.'

Chapter Eight

A brick terraced house in Elephant and Castle, the sort of area where a brick terraced house was now insanely expensive. Three storeys of acid-cleaned brickwork, even had a small front garden.

'Very swish.' Fenchurch peered through the window. Empty. Certainly no signs of movement. Cream walls, wooden floors. Nice telly, big wooden mirror. 'Which floor is it?'

Reed was over at the door, grinning. 'Guv, there's only one buzzer here.'

'It's the whole house?' Fenchurch let out a deep breath. 'This is much more than a teacher can afford, isn't it?'

'Her husband must do something flash.' Reed tried the buzzer again. 'Maybe he's a City boy like my Dave.'

'Katerina said he's a teacher, too.'

'Weird.' Reed hit the buzzer one last time. 'Either way, it doesn't look like there's anyone in.'

Fenchurch stepped back out on to the street, a block away from their pool car. Thumping bass came from a nearby house, football commentary and crowd noise from another. Distant traffic rumbled, probably the Old Kent Road. 'Not like we can just nip over the side wall to have a shufti.'

'Next best thing.' Reed stepped over the short brick wall into the neighbour's garden and knocked on the door.

It opened slowly and a little old lady peered out, her face like one of the many gnomes in her garden. Accompanied by a waft of cat piss and cigarette smoke. The wallpaper was chipped and torn. 'What do you want?' Old, Cockney accent, probably born in the house during the last ice age. 'Eh?'

'Police, madam.' Reed flashed her warrant card. 'Looking to speak to—'

'My husband died in 1996!' The door started to close. 'You lot can't torment him any more!'

Reed grabbed the door and stopped it shutting. 'We're not after—'

'You bloody are!' The woman shot an evil look at Reed, like she was dealing with the devil himself. 'You think he was in the Guildford Four! Trying to make out he was number five!'

'We just need to—'

'Well, he's in heaven now, no thanks to you lot!'

'Madam, can I take your name, please?'

'No, you bloody can't!'

'Madam, this is about your—'

'Lawyer! I want a lawyer!'

Fenchurch stepped over the wall and put another hand on the door. 'Madam, we're murder squad detectives looking—'

'He didn't kill that copper! You can—'

Fenchurch grabbed her by the arms. 'Madam, we don't give a shit about your husband.'

Spit lashed his cheek.

'You bloody should! Twenty-two years you lot were stalking him, making his life a pigging misery. And for what, eh? He was as Irish as you are.'

'What was your husband's name?'

'Edward Deeley, God rest his soul.'

'I'm very sorry for your loss, madam, but—'

A sharp pain hit Fenchurch in his bad knee. The other one cracked off the pavement as he went down.

Reed grabbed the gnome woman round the waist and lifted the old dear off her feet, legs kicking out. 'Madam, we're looking for your neighbours.'

'Lies!'

'What's going on?' Footsteps thumped from behind. A burly woman in her fifties was jogging from the other side of the road. 'Marjory, are you okay?'

'They're here about my Edward!'

Fenchurch showed his warrant card before he could get any hassle. 'Madam, we're investigating a murder.'

'But her Edward died of a heart attack twenty-odd years ago?'

'It's about her neighbour. Gayle Fisher.'

'Oh my God.' Her mouth hung open. 'What happened?'

'We have reason to believe we've found Mrs Fisher's body in a hotel room.'

'Lord save us.' She crossed herself.

Fenchurch led her away from the old bat's house, his knee throbbing. 'Can I take your name?'

She stopped on the opposite side of the road. 'Bethany.' Didn't look like a Bethany.

'We need Mrs Fisher's husband to identify the body. And, well, we just need to find him.'

'I'd love to help.' Bethany gave a shifty look at the house, like she couldn't stare at it without sucking in a demon's spawn. 'Thing is, they keep themselves to themselves. Didn't even know their names until the other day.' She sneered at Fenchurch. 'But I tell you, that couple. Always having blazing rows. Had one yesterday evening.'

'What?'

'Be about half five, maybe earlier. She can handle herself. They was out on the street, and she was giving that husband of hers what for. Shouting and bawling. Never heard the like.'

If she's telling the truth, there's a four-hour gap between this argument and . . . someone poisoning Gayle.

Fenchurch checked back at the house. Reed was still with old Marjory. 'Have you seen either of them since?'

'He got in his motor and hotfooted it. Not been back since.'

'This was definitely last night?'

'You saying I've lost the plot?' Her eyebrows locked together in fury. 'You calling me a liar?'

'No, I just need to know exactly what happened.'

Bethany's rage slackened. 'I could check my notebook, give you an exact time.'

'That'd be helpful, thanks.'

'Just doing my bit for the community.' Bethany walked off towards a block that hadn't been acid-cleaned.

'Bloody hell, guv.' Reed joined him, nostrils flaring. 'Can I do that old bat for anything?'

'Battering my knee.' Fenchurch reached down and rubbed the lump. 'We need to find this husband.' He waved at Bethany's house. 'Stay here and wait for her story. Get some more officers out here and start a door-to-door.'

'This isn't rocket science, Constable.' Uzma was back at the reception desk, gripping both chair backs. Bridge sat in front of her, not looking impressed. 'We need to get confirmation of all movements in and around the hotel. Don't know what you were told during training but that's how policing works. Okay?'

Bridge barely glanced at her. 'Sarge.'

'Can you at least—?' Uzma clocked Fenchurch and stood up tall. She cleared her throat. 'Simon, didn't see you there.'

'So I see.' Fenchurch beckoned her over to the hotel entrance. 'What's going on?'

'I've got them going through CCTV from outside, but they're just not up to it.'

'That right?' Fenchurch held her gaze. 'Because what I see is a DS bullying a DC.'

'People need pressure, Simon. Positive stress.'

'Back down, okay? DC Bridge is a good officer.'

'Like you're a good judge of character.' Uzma walked off, putting her phone to her ear.

What have I done to deserve her?

Fenchurch joined Bridge. 'Lisa, how you getting on?'

'I'm struggling to pin down the timeline.' Bridge swivelled her laptop round. 'But I've got Gayle Fisher's arrival just before seven.'

A figure skipped on to the street, walking fast, looking behind her. Glasses, scarf tied up like a fifties movie star. She slipped in the door.

'Anyone following her?'

'That's what DS Ashkani wants to know.' Bridge switched the display to a spreadsheet. 'This is all of the sightings of people going in and out. Your mate Jim Muscat had eleven smoke breaks before seven last night.'

'Must be getting a decent wedge here, given the price of cigarettes.'

'Or he knows someone who works on an oil rig.' Bridge chanced a sneaky look over at Uzma, chatting away, hand covering her mouth. 'This is what's got her knickers in a twist, sir.'

The screen filled with a video of the street behind the hotel: 22.23. Someone standing by the bike sheds next door to the hotel, facing away.

'Why is this relevant?'

'Because . . .' Bridge wound it back and the screen went grey, the time at 22.17. After Katerina left. After someone picked her up. 'This van delivered laundry for the other hotel.' She flipped to another image. 'Before that, the lane was empty.' Then to another one. 'After, our friend's there.' She pointed at the time. 'Either way, it's just after the window of opportunity. And here's the other thing.' She showed him more video, this time showing the man sloping off, face hidden by a hoodie and a baseball cap.

Fenchurch checked the video image again. 'What's he doing?'

'That's what I wonder, sir. It looks like he's having a pee, but there's no puddle.'

'Could be getting rid of something.' Fenchurch walked off. 'Let's have a look.'

———

Muscat was out on the back lane, smoking with a woman laughing at something he said. Muscat caught Fenchurch's eye and she walked off towards the next-door office. 'Catch you later, Mary.' He sucked deep and offered his pack to Fenchurch. 'Smoke, sir?'

'Never got into it, sorry.' Fenchurch leaned against the bike shed. 'Busy?'

'Hardly. Not a lot going on here, is there?' Muscat exhaled slowly. 'You lot shutting the place. No guests for me to guard, eh?' Seemed to think it was the funniest joke ever.

Fenchurch showed him Bridge's laptop. 'Recognise this guy?'

'Oooh.' Muscat squinted at it. 'Can't say I do. Then again, my eyes ain't exactly what they were when I joined the force.' He put his cigarette to his mouth but stopped short. 'Let's see.' He finally took his drag. 'Nah, sorry.'

The Met aren't exactly missing you, are they?

Fenchurch walked over to the spot the man had stood in and crouched down, his knee twanging. Couldn't smell any piss and it hadn't rained overnight.

Wait. What's that?

A copy of the *Metro*, trapped between the wall and a bin. Fenchurch nudged it away with his foot. Underneath was a navy purse, half-open.

So the mystery man threw something away.

Fenchurch snapped on some gloves and went through it. Fifty quid in notes. A load of change fell out, tinkling on the pavement. Inside, house keys zipped away. Gayle Fisher's driving licence.

He got up and put it in an evidence bag, scanning the area for anything else.

Muscat's cigarette smoke was clouding him. Hard to breathe. *Dirty bastard.*

A pink bin bag lay not far from the *Metro*. Fenchurch crouched down and lifted it up.

Underneath, an iPhone. White handset, no case. The screen was a spider's web of cracks, but he could still read the message notifications on the lock screen. A load of them, all from someone called Total Prick, some truncated.

GAYLE, I NEED TIME+SPACE. STEVE X

So Total Prick is her husband. Meaning she's changed the contact, probably after the argument.

AT MY BROTHERS. DON'T CHUCK MY STUFF. BE . . .

Less romantic, less loving. But a possible location.

STOP CALLING, YOU STUPID BITCH

Sent at 20.25. Starting to look like a suspect.

Then three in a minute:

U THERE?

GAYLE? WORRIED! CALL ME!

AT LEAST CALL JOHN AND LET HIM KNOW YOUR OK!

John is his brother . . .
Fenchurch put his Airwave handset to his ear. 'Control, I need an address for a John Fisher.'

Chapter Nine

'Unbelievable.' Fenchurch parked outside a pub and got out on to the street. 'Right round the corner from the bloody station.'

The address was an art deco building wedged between ancient wharves and mills. The pub door opened and two football fans staggered out, red-faced and shouting. One was Spurs, one Arsenal. They took one look at Fenchurch's warrant card and went back inside, best of mates. Funny how their bravery faded so quickly.

Uzma got out of the driver's side and locked the pool car. 'Must be a million John Fishers in London, right?'

'Only one with a brother called Steve married to a Gayle.' Fenchurch set off down the back road.

The building wasn't so nice from the back, the rounded edges all squared off. Six stairwells led up, with a couple of ground-floor flats either side of each one. No security cameras to speak of, though. *Typical.*

Fenchurch looked down the list by the buzzer. Couldn't find number one. 'What's the story with you and DC Bridge?'

'No story.' Uzma was frowning. 'She's a decent copper who thinks she's a great one. Needs reminding, otherwise she'll make a blunder.'

Fenchurch held her gaze until she looked away. 'As long as that's all it is.'

'In here.' Uzma walked over to a door and thumped it with the heel of her palm.

The door opened and a man looked out, his blond hair flying everywhere, covering his mouth in sandy stubble. 'What?'

'John Fisher?' Uzma waited for a nod. 'Police.' She showed her warrant card. 'Your brother in?'

John opened the door wide and went back into the flat. 'Steve!' He stormed through to the kitchen, fists clenched. Guy was like a whippet, barely any body fat. Could see the tendons and muscles shifting round on his neck, like cogs on a bike's gears. He thumped on a door. 'The police are in my flat, Steve!'

'Give us a minute, would you?' Fenchurch gave John a nod, then twisted the handle.

Steve Fisher sat on the bed, bleary-eyed. Didn't have his brother's physique, but had the same blond hair, spiked to a point. He mumbled to himself, but Fenchurch couldn't make out a word.

'DI Simon Fenchurch.' He showed his warrant card.

Steve stared into space for a few seconds, his forehead knitting tighter and tighter. Then he looked up, his focus trained right on Fenchurch. 'It's about Gayle, isn't it?'

Fenchurch took a deep breath. 'I'm afraid we need you to identify a body.'

Pratt walked alongside Steve Fisher, slow like they were in a funeral procession. Then the ID Suite door shut.

'What's your take on him, Sergeant?'

'Pratt?' Uzma was fiddling with her phone, thumbs dancing quick and fast. 'The *om-pom-pom* gets—'

'I meant Steven Fisher.'

Uzma looked up and locked her phone. 'I prefer to let my opinion form over time, Simon. I don't like to prejudice an investigation.'

Through the glass, Steve stood in front of a bed, a sheet pulled over a body.

'Nothing strike you as odd?'

'Should it?'

'I didn't even have to say it was Gayle. And he seemed to relax.'

Through the window, Pratt reached over to lift up the sheet and Steve looked at the body. He nodded then shook his head, but Fenchurch couldn't follow what they were saying.

'Like he was expecting something else.'

'Could just be the natural reaction to having the police turn up.' Uzma pouted, her eyes gleaming under the harsh lighting. 'Or this blazing argument DS Reed's investigating?'

'Maybe. Maybe not.'

Through the glass, Pratt's thumb flashed up.

'So it's her.' Fenchurch let out a breath he didn't know he was holding. 'Take him back to Leman Street. I need a word with Pratt.' He watched her go over to Steve, almost sashaying.

'*Om-pom-pom.*' Pratt waltzed through, about five times the speed of his earlier procession. 'Simon, Simon, Simon. You'll be glad to know that Mr Fisher has given a positive ID for Gayle's body.'

'I saw. I'm not glad there's a dead body through there, but at least we know who it is.'

'Indeedy-doodly.' Pratt grabbed a green Barbour off the rack and slipped his left arm down the sleeve. 'Do you need any more from me?'

'The post-mortem?'

'It's not happening today, kind sir.'

'William . . .'

'Simon. I don't have the staff to do it today.'

'Tomorrow. First thing. No excuses or chess matches.'

'Thank you for your assistance, sir.' Fenchurch leaned back in the chair and watched Steve for any further reaction. Guy looked genuinely devastated. 'I understand how difficult this must be. I can only offer my deepest sympathy and the promise that I'll do whatever I can to bring your wife's killer to justice.'

Even if it's you.

Steve looked at Uzma standing by the window, then nodded at Fenchurch.

'It'd be useful if you could tell us a bit about your wife.'

'Not much to tell.' Steve scratched at his chin, yellow stubble poking through. 'Gayle's an only child. Grew up in South London. She's an English teacher at Shadwell Grammar.'

Fenchurch knew it well. Despite the grand name, it had fallen from its peak in the fifties as the area lost its industry and hope, replaced by drugs and crime.

'We met at uni, Durham, even though we're both London, but it took us going to the north-east to meet.' His laugh died on his lips. 'Then we end up working at the same school.'

'You're a teacher, right?'

Steve nodded. 'Chemistry.'

'Just wondering how two teachers can afford a house like that.'

'It's hardly a palace.' Steve waved through the door. 'John's the monied one. Works in IT at a City bank, but hates it. I followed my passion, he followed the money.'

'That house is worth a packet, though, isn't it?' Fenchurch leaned across the desk, locking eyes with Steve. *God, does he look tired. Guy must've barely slept.* 'Seven hundred grand, I reckon.'

'Gayle's parents weren't rich, but they bought their home in the eighties. They died just after we graduated. Gayle was twenty-one.' Steve stared at the table, started scratching the surface with a nail. 'It completely destroyed her, but I was there for her. She wanted to move into that house, raise a family there.'

'You have kids?'

'Not yet.' Steve shut his eyes. 'Not ever, now.'

Fenchurch left a space, but Steve didn't fill it. 'Nice place, though. Be nicer to see inside it. Shame about your neighbour, of course.'

'Can't have everything.' A smiled flashed on Steve's lips. 'Marjory's been there since the Blitz, I think. She's not too bad, just keep her off the subject of IRA pub bombings or police surveillance.'

'So I gather.' Fenchurch drummed his thumbs on the table. 'Didn't seem to know you, though?'

'That's Alzheimer's for you. Her daughter visits twice a week, but she should be in a home. Joyce won't listen to us. Bethany across the road looks in on her, but she's a bit . . . We try not to have any dealings with her.'

'She saw you arguing.'

Steve went back to scratching the desk. 'See what I mean?'

'Not really. Said it was yesterday afternoon. About five o'clock.' Still nothing. 'You want to tell us what the argument was about?'

'It's none of your business. None of Bethany's either.'

'You say that, Mr Fisher, but then your wife's been murdered and you're staying on your brother's couch.'

Steve dug his palms into his eye sockets.

'Did you kill Gayle?'

'What?' Steve's hands dropped to the table with a smack. 'No!'

'You told her to stop calling you. Called her a "stupid bitch", didn't you?'

'That's bullshit.'

'No, it's not.' Fenchurch took out Gayle's iPhone and kept his eyes on Steve. Sweating, eyes narrowed. 'See, that's the message there.'

Steve kept his focus on it.

'I don't have one myself, but these phones are amazing.' Fenchurch rested it back on the table. 'You know you can share locations with each other? Doesn't even have to be an Apple thing, either. Can do it with— what's it called?'

'WhatsApp.' Uzma grinned wide. 'Bet they regret calling it that now.'

Fenchurch tapped the power button on the side of the phone. 'Anyway, you'd have Gayle's location on your phone, wouldn't you?'

Steve opened his mouth but didn't say anything.

'Before you lie, Mr Fisher, just remember that we will check everything.'

Steve slouched back in his chair, arms folded tight. 'Gayle turned off location sharing.' Couldn't take his eyes off her phone. 'I couldn't see where she was.'

'Probably did that at the same time she renamed your contact Total Prick.'

Steve raised his arms in the air, his fists clenching. 'She was having a laugh. I was angry with *her*.'

'What about?'

Steve let his hands go again, and shut his eyes. His shoulders slouched. 'Usual shit. We're in a pressure-cooker environment. We work together, have the same friends. It gets too much sometimes.'

'So, what, you had an affair?'

Steve rubbed his temples.

'Did you?'

'No. I didn't.'

'But she did?'

And he was gone again, brushing his right arm with his left hand, staring into space.

'Mr Fisher, you keep evading the subject of this argument. Makes me think it was something.'

'It was nothing!'

'Now I *know* it was something.' Fenchurch leaned forward again, resting on his elbows. 'Something big. Something important. Maybe big enough to kill over?'

'I didn't kill her!'

'Really?' Fenchurch gave him space, but he just kept brushing his arms. 'Mr Fisher, please take us through your movements yesterday. Start with lunchtime, I don't need to know about you munching your Corn Flakes.'

'After lunch, I had a double period all afternoon. Lower Sixth.' Steve leaned forward, head in hands. 'Then I went to the pub. Standing arrangement every week. A group of us, nine or ten usually.'

'Was Gayle there?'

'She . . . couldn't make it.'

'Is that unusual?'

'She hadn't warned me she wasn't coming, either.'

'But she had been at school, right?'

'I . . . think so.' Steve sat back and swallowed hard. 'I just had a couple of swift halves, then headed home. Usually watch some telly.'

'But you didn't get a chance to fire up Netflix, did you?'

'No. We . . . argued.'

Fenchurch stared deep into Steve's eyes, but there was no warmth there, just hatred and steel. 'So what happened? You called each other names, then you stormed off?'

'About the size of it.' Steve's sigh was filled with regret. 'I needed space. My brother . . . He broke up with his wife a while ago. His spare room's lying empty, so I thought I'd let Gayle calm down.'

'You want to tell me what this argument was about?'

'I don't. But . . .' Steve shook his head. 'Do you know what it feels like to have everything in your life be a house of cards, eh?'

'I do.' Fenchurch returned the steely glare with interest. 'When it all falls apart, it's very hard to build it up again. When it happened to me, it was over something pretty major.'

'Gayle . . .' Steve rocked back in his seat and stared up at the ceiling. 'She's . . . I can't believe what's happened.'

Fenchurch glanced at Uzma. She didn't seem to have any better ideas. 'Okay, so what did you do at your brother's flat?'

'We talked.'

'And after you were done talking?'

'We went for a walk. Then John took me to the pub and we watched the football. Premier League on a Friday night. Doubt it'll catch on. West Ham versus Man United. He said I needed to take my mind off what happened.'

'And did it?'

'Hardly. It was just people running around.'

'That's West Ham for you.' Fenchurch smiled, but Steve didn't pick it up. 'Do you know when Gayle switched off the location sharing?'

Steve looked at the iPhone. 'You tell me.'

'You know her code.'

'We didn't share them.'

'That the truth?'

'I'm not lying.'

Hard to figure him out. Evasive, but that could be explained by guilt or grief. His wife has just died and his last memory is her shouting at him, then him calling her a bitch in a text.

It all comes down to what the argument was about. Something small and it's unlikely that Steve killed her. But him being so cagey means that the probability of something major is increasing to the point where he's a suspect.

'What about after the pub?'

'Went back to John's. Tried to get some sleep but . . . I was too angry.' Steve rubbed at his red eyes, maybe trying to show how tired he was. *Is it the tiredness of a guilty man, though?*

Steve looked up at him. 'Where was she found?'

'Sure you don't know?'

'What? Just tell me.'

Fenchurch paused. 'The Hotel Bennaceur.'

'On the Minories, right?'

'Right. It's not far from here. Same with your brother's flat.'

'I've told you where I was. I didn't kill Gayle. Didn't know she was there.'

An alibi. Something to probe and tear apart. Until we get into her phone, that's probably about as far as we'll get. Maybe he's innocent, but he's our first suspect. Progress. Ish.

'Okay, Steve, what was the argument about?'

'I . . .' Steve looked at Fenchurch, puzzled. 'Wait, you really don't know?'

'Try me.'

'Gayle was having an affair.' Steve swallowed. 'With a school pupil. It's all over the papers.'

And we bloody missed it.

Chapter Ten

Fenchurch found a copy of yesterday's *Post* in the canteen.
TEACHER-PUPIL SEX SHAME.

And there she was, front and centre — Gayle. Not some model or film star or pop star. A teacher. In Shadwell, of all places.

Yesterday's Post. *The one in my bloody car.*

He sent a text: MEET ME AT JOHN'S. NOW.

Fenchurch tried to wrap his head around it. The something major Steve might've been hiding was now something massive, something colossal. A huge billboard with MOTIVE flashing in bright-red letters.

'So DS Reed missed it?' Uzma was standing in the door, hands on hips.

'Easy, Sergeant. The papers hadn't actually named her yet.' Fenchurch raised his eyebrows. 'Now, I need you to verify that story, okay?'

Uzma leaned back against the wall. 'Fine. You think he killed her?'

'We've got no other suspects.' Fenchurch started walking off. 'I'm going to see what his brother has to say for himself.'

⌣

'Where is he?' John Fisher was pacing around his kitchen, arms flapping, wild like his hair. 'What have you done with him?'

Fenchurch looked out of the window. Still no sign of Reed. 'Your brother's at the station, sir.' He sat on a sofa opposite a monstrous TV, the coffee table filled with game controllers. 'He's giving us a statement.'

'What?' John stopped, arms out, fingers like claws. 'Are you framing him?'

'We're just asking him a few questions.'

'So what do you want from me?'

'We just need to validate a few things about—'

'I need a lawyer. I know my rights.'

'This isn't a formal interview, sir. You're not under caution.'

'What have you done to him?' John lurched towards them. 'You've abducted him! Is he in some government institution somewhere? Are you waterboarding him right now?'

Oh Jesus. Another conspiracy nutjob.

'You might need to stop watching *The X-Files* and *24*, sir.'

'I know what's going on.' John stood up tall, hands in pockets, shaking his head. 'Black sites. Torturing innocent civilians. Disappearing dissidents.'

'Your brother's a dissident?' Fenchurch waited for John to frown. 'I thought he was a chemistry teacher.' He got to his feet. 'If he's starting a revolution, then—'

'You've kidnapped him!'

Fenchurch stepped towards John, leaving a short gap between them, short enough to grab him if need be. 'Sir, if we were up to that sort of stuff, we wouldn't be asking questions in your own kitchen. You'd be in the gulag too.' Didn't have an answer to that. 'Your brother's at Leman Street, confirming his statement with DS Uzma Ashkani. That's all that's going on here.'

John backed away from Fenchurch, but started pacing again. 'What are you fitting him up for?'

'You think we have a file on him?' Fenchurch huffed out a sigh. 'Mr Fisher, we're treating your brother as a suspect in his wife's murder.'

'I knew it was something big.' John's eyes went wide. 'It's definitely Gayle?'

'Steve identified her. We found her body at lunchtime.'

'And you think he did it. Steve? Come on!'

'He had a blazing argument with her about her affair with a school pupil. Next thing, he's staying here and she's dead.'

John collapsed on to the empty sofa. 'You really think he killed her?'

'Do you?'

John's shoulders deflated. 'Steve's my big brother. Always looked out for me. Let me kip at his when I finished uni and had nowhere to go. You think Steve could've killed Gayle? That's my brother, man. My own brother!'

'Mr Fisher, I'm keeping an open mind here. I want to know the truth and I want to be able to prove it. I need you to take us through what happened yesterday. From Steve's arrival onwards.'

John sat back, arms folded. 'I finished work at four, went to Dirty Dick's on Bishopsgate for a couple of pints, then came home. A mate had tickets for the West Ham match.'

'You a fan?'

'I'm Palace, but it's a night out, right? Not been to the London Stadium yet.' John sighed. 'I got back here at six, only Steve's on the doorstep, staring into space, red-eyed like he'd been crying. Asked if he could stay in the spare room. Course he could. So I gave him a cup of tea, but he wasn't interested in it. Took a beer, though, and we had a chat, you know? Like we were back home before our parents . . . you know.' A dark fug settled on John. 'Steve perked up a bit by the second bottle, so I took him out for a walk along the Thames. A lot nicer down that way than it used to be, that's for sure. Went to the pub to watch the match. Had to bail on my mate, but you know, brothers are brothers.'

'Which pub?'

'The Prospect of Whitby in Wapping. Nice boozer, does lovely food.'

'And what was the match?'

John's eyes went wide. 'You think you can catch me out? It was West Ham–Man U.'

'Remember the score?'

'Four-nil to Man U.'

'Did Steve have much to drink?'

'Couple of pints.' John cracked his knuckles, getting a meaty thwack. 'Kept insisting on buying.'

'So, what, one in each half?'

John got to his feet and walked over to the sink. Started spraying water in some Budvar bottles. 'The pub was rammed. Steve missed the opening goal when he was at the bar.'

Fenchurch joined him by the sink. 'What aren't you telling me?'

John stared into the plughole as he tipped out the beer bottles. One of them had the label torn off. 'Steve left the pub at half-time.'

'You're sure?'

'Positive. Ref blew the whistle for half-time and Steve was like "See you, John." Out of there.'

'So, half eight?'

'Think so.' John dumped the bottles in a bucket under the sink. 'I stayed. All this stuff with Gayle, I thought I'd give Steve some time on his own. I got back here about eleven. Steve was in the spare room. Had some Morrissey album on. Can't stand him, but Steve's a huge fan.'

Fenchurch thought it through, trying to piece it together.

Half past eight down in deepest, darkest Wapping. Take maybe half an hour to walk over to the Minories.

Next sighted at eleven.

Plenty of time for Steve to kill Gayle.

Chapter Eleven

Fenchurch walked along the street, scanning around for Reed. No sign of her.

A suspect, finally. But does it feel too convenient? Man murders adulterous wife? Seen it a hundred times. Sometimes it's just as banal as that, no deep conspiracy, just rage in the heat of the moment.

A car rattled along the street and flashed the lights at him. Reed was behind the wheel.

Fenchurch got in the car and tugged at the seatbelt. Bastard thing wasn't shifting. 'It's all over the bloody papers, Kay!'

'I know.' Reed swallowed as she read it. 'I'm sorry. I've messed up. I should've found it earlier.'

'It's not just you . . .' Fenchurch stabbed the belt into the clip. 'I had it in my own bloody motor, Kay. I feel like a prize plonker.'

'Thought you just read the back pages and did the sudoku?' Reed started the car and eased off on the short drive back to Leman Street. 'Sex scandal at Shadwell Grammar didn't attract your attention?'

'Hardly. I see enough bad shit on a daily basis, Kay. I just want to read about someone moaning about West Ham.'

She turned the corner and immediately got stuck in traffic. 'Now I see why you didn't drive to his flat.' She inched forward in the row of cars. 'Still got nothing from their street. Confirmed the argument, but nobody heard what it was about.'

'Figures.'

'Anyway, DS Ashkani passed it over to one of her team.' Reed pushed forward in the queue, not far from the turning to Leman Street. 'I'll get Lisa Bridge looking for CCTV outside the pub.'

'We need to make sure we're giving her some sexier work, Kay.'

'You *like* her, don't you?'

Before he could dive in two-footed, her phone rang. She answered it on speaker. 'Lisa, you're on with DI Fenchurch.'

'Oh.' Sounded like all of Bridge's excitement fizzed away. 'The car that picked up Katerina from outside the hotel? Took me ages because it was a partial but I found another angle. It's registered to a Liam Sharpe.'

Fenchurch heard his own groan echoing. 'Shit.'

Never good when a mate turns up in a case.

———

Reed trundled along Fleet Street, stuck behind another procession of traffic. Felt like the City's buildings were encroaching on the road, squeezing everything like toothpaste. She pulled in on the police parking bay outside the *Post* building and rummaged around for the ON POLICE BUSINESS sign.

Fenchurch's phone blasted out. A shiver shot up his spine and his jaw clamped shut. Then he took a breath and checked the display, wiping the bead of sweat from his brow. Uzma. 'Better take this.' He got out on to the road and answered it, traffic rolling past. 'What's up?' He waited for a gap big enough to cross.

'The manager keeps banging on about when we can reopen.'

Fenchurch darted between a bus and a Volvo. 'The whole place is shut until Mick Clooney or one of his team clears it, okay?'

'Simon, I—'

'Uzma, am I clear?'

'Right, sir. Okay.'

Fenchurch killed the call and set off towards the *Post* building.

'Guv.' Reed grabbed his arm and stopped him. She stood next to him, eyes narrow. 'I saw you flinch when the phone rang.'

He couldn't make eye contact with her. 'It's nothing.'

'It's not nothing. What's up?'

What do I tell her?

Whatever she wants to hear?

The truth?

Sod it.

Fenchurch stopped trying to get past and swallowed hard. 'Every time the phone rings, I think it's about Baby Al. Abi calling me to . . . to say that he's died.'

Reed patted his arm, her forehead knitted tight. 'Jesus.'

'Ten months he's been in that bloody hospital and we get a couple of hours with him every day and . . . and it's just not enough. Nowhere near enough, Kay. It's . . . it's horrible seeing him lying there, just waiting for him to die. *Hoping* he won't.'

'Jesus, guv. Have you talked to Abi about it?'

'I've tried, but . . . it's hard.' Fenchurch stuffed his phone in his pocket. He dropped it, the bastard thing cracking off the pavement. He crouched down to pick it up. Barely a scratch. Stayed down there. 'You know, I wish I was religious. Then I'd have someone to pray to, someone to blame if the worst happened. A philosophy that says I'll get to see my son in the next life.' He stood up, his dodgy knee aching. 'I just want to get to know him in this one. He's not even a year old. What kind of life is that for anyone?'

'I know how hard this is.'

'Do you?'

She looked away. 'My brother died when I was five. He was two.'

'Jesus, Kay. I never knew.'

'I never told anyone. It was—' She covered her mouth and let Fenchurch wrap her in a hug. 'Leukaemia.' Her voice against his

75

shoulder was fighting a losing battle with tears. She broke off from the embrace, rubbing at her cheeks, blinking hard a few times.

Fenchurch stared off down the street, at a crowd of lads larking about. 'Abi said that sometimes she wishes Al hadn't been born. I'm starting to come round to that.'

'Jesus.' Reed lowered her head, her chin trembling. 'You need to help each other. She's not as tough as she acts.'

'Yeah.' But it felt like a no. 'Trouble is, her way of coping is to hope that Al will get better.' Fenchurch bared his teeth. 'I know what hope does.'

'Guv, hoping you'd find Chloe is what got her back.'

'I was stupid to think I'd get lucky again.' Fenchurch stretched out his eyes, trying to shake off the tears. 'Al will get worse. One day he'll stop breathing.'

'We all die someday, guv. The pair of you decided on a fresh start. You've got to give that kid all the love and support he needs. You have to fight for him. For his whole life. That's all you can do.'

Fenchurch looked away from her again. His breath felt like a sledgehammer in the gut. 'You're right.'

'I just wish that being right didn't hurt so much, guv.' Reed pointed at the building. 'Now, are you okay to get on with your job?'

⌣

Fenchurch paced around the meeting room, a glass-and-chrome box in the middle of the office area, open on all sides. Outside, journalists hunkered down for the Saturday-night crunch, all the last-minute revisions to the Sunday edition they'd spent a week preparing.

'Simon!' Liam Sharpe sauntered through the doorway, a grin on his face. Smart haircut and close-shaved face, even wore a business suit. The inevitable destiny of the ex-hipster. 'Sorry, but I was right in the middle of something when you called. How you doing, Kay? Not seen you for a while.'

'Getting by.'

'Getting by, eh?' Liam's grin was still on duty as he kicked the door shut and dropped his phone on the table. 'Simon, you were very brief on the phone. What's up now?'

'Your car was on Vine Street last night, just after ten.' Fenchurch dropped a photo on the table. 'Need to speak to whoever was driving it.'

Liam didn't even look at it, instead seeing great interest in the open-plan office through the glass. 'That'll be me, then.'

Fenchurch put another photo down. 'And you picked up this girl?'

Liam chanced a look. His Adam's apple bobbed up and down. 'She's a woman, Simon.'

Fenchurch leaned back in his chair, eyes closed. 'Are you seeing her?'

Liam glanced at Reed, then got up and walked around the small room. Looked shifty, like he wanted to scratch something he couldn't.

Fenchurch motioned for Reed to leave the room, then waited for the door to click. 'Liam, are you seeing this schoolgirl?'

'It's not—' Liam rested against a chair, stretching out like he was about to run a marathon. 'It's . . .'

'Liam, is Katerina Raptis your girlfriend?'

He jerked upright and started pacing around again. Guy couldn't sit still.

'She's seventeen, Liam! She's at school, you idiot!'

Liam pressed his forehead against the glass, his breath misting, his reflection betraying his self-hatred. Reed was on her phone out there, scowling.

'I need you to be straight with me here. Are you seeing her?'

'Why are you interested in Kat?'

'Kat, is it? Not Katerina? Liam, tell me. Are you seeing her?'

He collapsed into a chair. 'She's older than she seems.'

'She seems like a girl to me.' Fenchurch prodded the photo. 'Looks about twelve.'

'Mentally, I mean. She's wise. Smart. Mature.'

'You're almost thirty. She's just turned seventeen. That's almost double her age.' Fenchurch picked up the photo and tossed it at Liam. 'It's . . . sinister.'

Liam's lip shook. Eyes closed, his forehead knotted. Slow and steady breaths.

'I'm sorry.' Fenchurch reached over for him but he was too far away. 'It's okay for you to move on after what happened to Saskia. God knows I still see her murder when I shut my eyes. But a schoolgirl? Really?'

'It's not what you think.' Liam's face twisted up, tears flowing down his cheeks. His mouth lost all motor control. 'Every time I come in here . . . It's . . . it's where Sas worked. Where we met. So bloody hard. When I met Kat, I thought she was a university graduate.'

'At that hotel?'

'I was meeting a source there.' Liam's face twisted into a snarl. 'What's she got to do with the price of corned beef?'

'A cleaner found a body in that hotel. Katerina saw it and it freaked her out.'

'Shit.' Liam picked up his phone. 'That explains why she's not replied to my texts.'

'So you are seeing her.' Fenchurch shook his head. 'Liam, she left the hotel around the time of the attack. She got in your car. We should be discussing this down the station. But we're not. We're here. I'm giving you a chance to be honest.'

'I drove her home. I swear.'

'Yours or hers?'

'Jesus Christ.' Liam huffed out a breath. 'Hers. She lives with her mum.'

'And you slipped in through her window and had a nice cuddle, yeah?'

And he'd lost him again. Anger flared across his lips.

I trusted him. He helped me out, big style. Now he's shagging a school-girl and holding back information.

'Liam, no!' A tall woman charged into the meeting room, her jaw clenched tight. She got between Fenchurch and his prey. Her bangles shook as she pushed her dark hair behind her ears. 'You can't intimidate a reporter to give up his sources!'

'You might want to get him to stop keeping things from a murder investigation.'

'You need to let your Media Office handle—' She stopped, her face lighting up. 'Did you say *murder*? In the briefing, Superintendent Loftus said it was suicide?'

Reed glared at Fenchurch. 'We're treating it as murder, madam.'

'Interesting.' She picked up the paper and looked at it like she hadn't seen it a hundred times over the last week. 'This is priceless.'

Fenchurch jabbed a finger at her. 'I need you to keep a lid on this, okay?'

'Not going to happen.'

'Who the hell are you, anyway?'

'Cally Morris. I'm the News Editor here.' Cally held up the paper to him, pointing at Gayle's photo. 'Her death killed our front page, you know? We were going to name Gayle tomorrow, lift the lid on the whole sordid affair. We can't, for obvious reasons. But now . . . now, we can focus on her *murder*.' Said like an orgasm. 'Liam, I need three thousand words by midnight.'

'This isn't some tittle-tattle.' Fenchurch blocked Cally's exit. 'Gayle Fisher was murdered. Liam's not typing a word until I say so.'

'Inspector, I get final say on this. We'll publish and be damned.'

'Listen to me. Gayle's killer's still out there. If you publish that story, you're giving them information about an active police investigation.'

Cally stared hard at him. 'If I haven't heard from the Media Office by first thing tomorrow, we'll publish.'

Fenchurch stared hard at her for a few seconds. *Don't have anything else to bargain with for now.* 'Deal.'

Cally set off towards the door. 'Come on, Liam, we need to get back to work.'

Liam's nod came with a sigh.

Cally stopped in the doorway and turned round, focusing on Reed. 'Listen, Ben Maxfield called me. He wanted us to put a stop on the story. Said he's repping Gayle. Apparently, she freaked out when we printed her photo and she went running into Ben's arms. He put her in that hotel room, told her to lie low.' Her eyes narrowed. 'He threatened us with legal action. Named some shyster from Ogden and Makepeace.'

Acid burnt in Fenchurch's gut.

'Oh, I'm sorry.' Cally tilted her head to the side, concern furrowing her brow. 'They're the ones who were involved in what happened with your daughter, aren't they?'

'*Cally.*' Liam stepped in. 'They're just called Makepeace now.'

'Anyway.' Cally smiled. 'I told them in no uncertain terms that we won't be intimidated by vermin like him.'

'That's all very impressive, but we need to find a murderer.' Reed joined Cally by the door. 'We need Liam to share everything. And I mean everything. And now.'

Cally shrugged. 'Fine, but no sources.'

'It's fairly obvious to me that his source is Katerina Raptis, right?'

'She's not my source.' Liam held up his hands. 'Okay?'

'But she is at that school.'

'Yeah, and she told me some rumours. I've been doing pieces on that school for *months*. It's a cesspit. Worse than my one back in Halifax. I've got other sources.'

'Who?'

'A teacher.' Liam's grin slipped away as soon as it appeared. 'Been working on it for a long time. There's a drugs angle, bullying too. Then my source told me that the Head asked Gayle about sleeping with a pupil two weeks ago.'

'Two weeks?'

'Denied it, too. Told him flat out that it didn't happen. Worse, the Head believed her. But I got a video from a source.'

'What sort of—'

'Calm down.' Liam raised a finger. 'We'd never publish anything salacious. It's on a pen drive sitting in Cally's office, along with those photos of what's-her-name at it with a dog.'

'Liam!' Cally shot daggers at him.

Fenchurch got between them. 'You have a video of Gayle Fisher having sex with a student?'

Cally looked at the paper with bitter disappointment. 'You know it's not illegal to possess that video, Simon.'

'Okay.' Fenchurch snatched the paper off Cally. 'One of you two is going to tell me the name of the boy she was sleeping with.'

'We're not allowed to publish anyone's name if they're under eighteen.'

'You can't publish his name, sure.' Fenchurch held up a hand. 'But you can tell us.'

Liam hung his head low.

'Come on. Now.'

'Elliot Lynch. I've got his address on my laptop.'

Chapter Twelve

A long row of two-up, two-downs, overlooked by the railway out to the Essex coast. Looked the same as Fenchurch's old man's flat in Limehouse, just a couple of miles down the road. Party sounds came from a house over the road. Cannabis smell mixed with diesel. Young kids squealing and shouting nearby, out way past their bedtime. Someone kicked a football against a wall somewhere.

'That little shit.' Fenchurch knocked on the door and stepped back. Ant and Dec blared out from the TV, the kind of Saturday-night shit that'd rot your brains worse than white cider. 'He's been banging this schoolgirl and—'

'Banging? Guv, come on.'

'Sorry, Chloe's been watching this show on Netflix . . .' Fenchurch tried the door again.

It flew open. A man stood there, squinting into the evening. Little guy with a checked shirt on, maybe late thirties. Squinting through thick glasses. 'What do you want?' Irish accent, south Dublin maybe.

'Police, sir.' Fenchurch showed his warrant card. 'Looking for Elliot Lynch.'

'Ah, Christ. What's he done now?'

'Derek? What's going on?' A woman appeared, maybe in her forties. Taller than her husband. Grey roots, her face lined hard. London accent, London face. She pushed the door wide and clocked the warrant card. 'Oh, bloody hell.'

'Amanda, I'm dealing with this.' Derek Lynch nudged his wife away. 'Tell us now. What's our boy done?'

'We just need a word with him in relation to an inquiry, sir.'

'Right.' Derek shrugged, then reached for the door. 'Well, our boy's out for the night. Good luck finding him.'

'How about the names of any mates?'

'Amanda, get the list.' Derek waited while his wife brought back a sheet of paper. 'Much easier every time one of you lot comes round to have our answers in advance, you know?' He handed them a photo. 'And this is his ugly mug, yeah?'

Reed took the shot and snapped the list with her phone. 'You've no idea where he is?'

'Do you need a hearing test or something?'

Chapter Thirteen

Fenchurch slammed the door and stabbed the ignition. Started revving the engine, getting a nice roar.

'Guv!' Reed hit the ignition button and killed his fun. 'What the hell?'

Fenchurch reached for the ignition but got a slapped hand instead.

'Guv, it's not the end of the world. We'll find him.'

Fenchurch stared back at the house. The curtains twitched.

'It's not that, is it?'

Fenchurch let out a stinging breath, eyes closed, then clenched his jaw. Ran his hand down his face, rasping across prickly stubble, and he slumped back in the seat. 'My son is dying in hospital, fighting for his life, and they don't give a shit where theirs even is.'

'Jesus. I didn't think.'

Fenchurch brushed his eyelids with his fingers. 'They don't understand, do they? They don't understand how fragile his life is. I deal with all this shit every day and I'm sick of how other people don't care.' He snapped forward in the seat. 'This isn't getting us anywhere.'

Down the road, the curtain twitched again.

'People like that, not giving a shit about what their son's up to now, means that today's cheeky little rascal is tomorrow's gang member. Stabbing people. Dealing drugs. Splashing acid on their face.' Fenchurch took the photo from Reed. A teenage boy, fresh-faced, smirking at the camera, mischief twinkling in his eyes. Elliot Lynch. He took another look at the house, at the parents who didn't care about him.

'We should go in there and batter them with the news about their son's love life, guv.'

'Our priority is finding him. Making their lives a misery isn't going to help anyone.' Fenchurch waved a hand at the swishing curtains. 'Once we get hold of Elliot, we can haul them over the coals. If there's the *slightest* suspicion that he's killed Gayle, then we need to get their reaction on the record. Might've told his dear old mum something. Could've let something slip to his old man while watching the football.'

'Fair enough.' Reed held up her phone, showing the list of friends. 'How about we start with Jarvis Reynolds?'

———

'Couldn't tell you, love.' A heavy man with a red face, greasy hair, beery breath, beer-stained tracksuit. 'Where Jarvis gets to of an evening is a complete mystery to me. I'd ask his mother but she's working.'

'Could he be with Elliott Lynch?'

A shrug. 'I just told you it was a complete mystery. Now.' He scratched his arse and sniffed his fingers. 'My pizza's getting cold and this football's heating up, so if you—'

———

'—don't mind?' A woman in a silk dressing gown, hiding behind the door. 'My Dean's been on a tour of Syria and I'm drying up down there.'

'It's Dean junior we're looking for. Any ideas?'

'Could try his mates, I suppose.'

'You have seen your son today, right?'

'Probably. Those two and Curtis, they're thick as thieves, might want to—'

———

'—try for another one, you know?' Face like a thirteen-year-old beauty pageant girl, body like a fifty-year-old lorry driver. Blonde hair, in a cut that probably cost more than her home. She giggled. 'We've just got six now.' She squeezed her husband's hand, though he didn't register it. 'Owen says he misses when Curtis was a wee one. Course, he's got five sisters, just like I had, but it'd be nice to have a young 'un again, you know? A boy.'

'My boy's ten months.' Fenchurch grimaced, then flashed a smile over it.

'That's my favourite age! They're so cute!'

'We just need to speak to your son.'

'He's a dark horse, is Curtis.' She squeezed her husband's hand again, but his focus was still on the football. 'Isn't he, Owen?'

'The darkest. Like Croatia or Turkey at a World Cup.' Owen sat forward, still holding his wife's hand. 'Oh, go on, son. Go on! Oh.' He fell back in the seat and burped. 'What were we saying, Kelly?'

'Your son, Owen.' She slapped his arm. 'Curtis?'

'Good lad. Smart with the computers.'

'The police are looking for him?'

'Oh, yeah.' Back to the football. 'Come on, ref. That's a stonewall penalty!'

Fenchurch shifted over and blocked his view. 'Mr Ashman, we need a word with your son.'

Owen tried to peer round Fenchurch. 'Why's that?'

'Just need to ask him a few questions as part of our inquiry.'

'You looking into what's going on at the school?'

'What do you mean by that?'

Owen settled back in the chair and reached for his beer. 'You know, the stuff in the paper. Some teacher bonking a student.'

'It's related, sir.'

'Tell you, in my day, the teachers . . . I wouldn't give them a second look. See on our parents' evenings?' Owen's mouth twisted up and he grunted. 'It's like going to a nightclub. Some of them.' He whistled.

'Owen!' Kelly giggled as she batted her husband's arm. 'We wanted to take our kids out of that school, but Curtis is doing A-levels and we've still got three there, three at the primary. We can't afford to pay for their education so we've not got much choice.'

'I don't believe in all that Catholic or C of E bollocks. My kids aren't going to a religious school.' Owen snarled as he took another swig. 'That's *our* school, you know? It's owned by the community, not anyone else. They need to fix it for us.'

Fenchurch leaned back in his chair. *Is this just idle chat or does he have anything useful to say?*

Owen slammed his can down on the table, sending beer spraying up. 'I work mornings, right, so I pick my kids up from school. Have a little chat with the mums and, well, I'm usually the only dad. We're all worried about it, you know? Our kids are at this school that's all over the papers. All that publicity isn't going to do anyone any good, is it?'

'You ever do anything about it?'

'Not me, no.' Another burp. 'Someone spoke to the Headmaster. And he was a prick about it. That guy . . . Real seedy bastard, I swear.'

Nah, he's got nothing.

'We just need to speak to your son.'

'He'll be back eventually.'

'You know where Elliot Lynch might be?'

A frown settled on Owen's forehead, followed by a wry grin. 'Elliot's a right little bugger. What's he done now?'

'Just need a word with him.'

Owen smirked. 'Last weekend, walking the dog with our youngest two, I spotted that boy in the park with a top-class piece of tail. Fit as a butcher's dog.' Another burp. He frowned. 'Recognise the bird from somewhere, though. Gorgeous, she was. Stunning. Like that one off *Tits and Dragons.*'

Kelly giggled. 'Owen, what are you like?'

Fenchurch had more than an idea of who he was talking about. 'You mean *Game of Thrones*?'

'Yeah, you know. I don't watch it for the dragons, if you know what I mean. I just watch it for the tits.' He swallowed a burp for once. 'Think she's the queen. But she was younger. Cracking piece of crumpet.'

'So, where is your son?'

Owen ran a hand across his mouth. 'Don't know about you, but when I was seventeen, on any given Saturday I'd either be out of my skull with my mates at a party somewhere or bollock-deep in this one here.' He gave a loud cackle as he prodded his wife. 'Given how fit the one Elliot's smashing is, I think you should be looking for her, yeah?'

'She's dead, sir.'

'Oh, bloody hell.'

⌣

'They don't give a shit, do they?' Fenchurch slowed as he drove past Shadwell Grammar. No kids lurking in the school grounds. A few punters hanging outside the pub, blackened doors and windows, but definitely still open and serving. Probably never shut. No name on the door, either. The Shadwell United football stadium over the road was still lit up hours after they'd played. 'Not a single shit.' He sped up.

'That prick was right, though, guv.' Reed folded her arms. 'Kid Elliot's age, he'll be at a party or drinking cider in a graveyard or something.'

Fenchurch slowed to inspect a group of kids hanging about down the lane backing on to the stadium. He checked the photo of Elliot again. None looked even remotely like him. 'We're getting nowhere, Kay. Short of knocking on every door between here and the City, we're just drawing a bloody blank.'

Reed took the photo back and tapped it with her fingers. 'I've got an idea.'

Chapter Fourteen

M rs Raptis.' Reed smiled at her from the doorstep. A stench of mushroom pizza and used underpants wafted out from the hall-way. 'We need another word with Katerina, if that's okay?'

Katerina stood next to her mother, using her as a shield. 'Have you caught Mrs Fisher's killer yet?'

'Working on it.' Fenchurch leaned against the door, stopping them from shutting it. 'We need to talk to an Elliot Lynch, any idea where he might be?'

'Well, don't mind me.' Jocasta let go of her daughter and stepped to the side, holding out a hand to Reed. 'It's Jocasta, by the way. Jo for short.'

'A pleasure.' Reed gave a fake smile, then focused on Katerina. 'It's important that we speak to Elliot. So, if—'

'What's he done?' Jocasta was frowning like she was catching up on the latest episode of *EastEnders* or something.

'That's not important.'

'It's got to be, otherwise you wouldn't want to speak to him, would you?'

Reed shifted her gaze to Katerina. 'You do know Elliot Lynch, don't you?' Her steely glare added some hard diamond. 'Because if you don't and you're just messing with us . . .'

'That supposed to frighten me?' Katerina leaned back. Then her head hung low. 'Sorry. I've been bullied a lot at school and Mrs Fisher . . .'

'That woman is a saint.' Jocasta squeezed her daughter's shoulder. 'Helped my baby through it all. Horrible place, that school. We tried another one, but it wasn't as good academically and it's more important that she gets good grades, right?'

'This has reminded me of a lot of things.' Katerina didn't look up. Just grabbed her mother's hand. 'That's why I'm messing with you. It's how I coped with it until Mrs Fisher taught me how to focus on how I feel and figure out what I can do. I'll miss her.'

Jocasta wrapped her arms around her daughter. 'Are you okay, my little pumpkin?'

'Katerina, we really need to find Elliot.'

'I hate that prick.' Katerina pouted, her bottom lip sticking out like she was six again. Not that she looked much older. 'He was one of the worst bullies. But I—'

'Kat, I thought that was all over? Didn't Mrs Fisher—?'

'Mum, shut up!' Katerina pushed her mother away, then leaned forward. 'Look, not that I'm ever invited to these things, but there's a house party this weekend. This prick Jayden, his parents are away. Elliot's got to be there.'

'You got an address?'

Katerina got out her phone. 'I can show you on Google Maps?'

Fenchurch noted the address and handed her a business card. 'Give me a call if you think of any other likely places, okay?'

The address was a big house in that American east-coast style, all weatherboards and verandas. Stuffed down a back lane not far from the school and not the sort of place you associated with Shadwell.

Deep, deep bass came from inside the house, loud enough that Fenchurch felt it in his chest. Teenagers visible in both front windows, laughter and shouting just about audible over the din.

Fenchurch remembered a few parties like this. More than a few. Someone's parents away for the weekend, leaving just one idiot to bring his mates along. And their mates. And theirs. Then it gets out of hand. Once, the police got involved. Fenchurch's dad wasn't impressed, his son at a party where structural damage was done to the house.

Not something I had to contend with — Chloe grew up hundreds of miles away. Did she go to any parties like this? Did she vomit up a gutful of cheap vodka? Did she ever get too pissed to stop some idiot taking a sledgehammer to a wall?

Not that I'd know. Parents are the last to know, unless something bad happened. Just the nagging doubt of her absence, sitting in front of the telly on a Saturday night, watching the clock. Going to bed and she's still not home. Lying there, listening for drunken giggles as the keys drop. Listening to her being sick all over the bathroom floor. Putting her in bed and clearing it up.

His scalp itched.

All that time, all that history . . . Someone else had to deal with what should've been my trials and tribulations. Mine and Abi's.

'Come on.' Fenchurch walked up the path, the bass squeezing his heart.

'This takes me back, guv.' Reed joined him by the door. 'So, we just going to enter?'

'Don't see any reason why not.' Fenchurch opened the door and walked in like he owned the place.

The bass was joined by mid and treble, some knuckle-dragging dance music. *'Por-por. Por-por-por. Selene. Por-por. Por-por-por. Selene. Por-por. Por-por-por. Selene. Porcelain. Goddess.'*

The place stank of cheap perfume, vape misting a long hallway done up like a John Lewis catalogue. At the end, a pile of teenagers lay together, laughing and joking on their phones. In the dark living room, twenty or so kids were dancing, lights flashing.

'*Por-por. Por-por-por. Selene. Por-por.*'

No sign of where the music was coming from.

'*Por-por-por. Selene. Porcelain. Goddess.*'

Fenchurch traced it to a white box under the silver telly. No buttons. He fiddled about but couldn't get it to stop. Nobody even noticed him.

'*Por-por. Por-por-por. Selene. Por-por. Por-por-por. Selene. Por-por. Por-por-por. Selene. Porcelain. Goddess.*'

He pulled the cord out of the back of the machine and the music died.

Loud groans and jeers. 'What!?' A plastic cup of punch hit the wall behind him, spraying pink gunk everywhere.

'Police!' Fenchurch held up his warrant card. 'We're looking for Elliot Lynch!'

Reed flicked on the lights and Fenchurch got a good look at the kids. Some of them were still dancing to the beat in their heads. Nobody matching Elliot's description. 'Anyone seen Elliot Lynch?'

A greasy kid in a tracksuit pointed outside. 'Out there.'

'Come on, Kay.' Fenchurch led Reed back into the hall.

'*Por-por. Por-por-por.*'

'That song's doing my head in.'

'Try hearing it on one-track repeat all day long, guv.'

Fenchurch pushed through four snogging couples in the kitchen, hands in each other's pants, and stepped out into the back garden. A few more couples kissing on the patio furniture, including two boys — so different from Fenchurch's day. Behind, a row of kids sat on the edge of the lawn, one at the side hunched over, vomiting white chunks on to the grass.

A window opened a crack. '*Porcelain. Goddess.*'

Fenchurch checked the kid vomiting. 'Shit, it's Elliot.' He grabbed hold of him and pulled him to his feet.

'You can't do that, man!'

'He's coming with me.' Fenchurch tried to drag Elliot away, but the kid was stumbling. His T-shirt was soaked through with sweat like he'd run two marathons.

'Goddess!' Elliot laughed as he spun round. 'Goddess! Gayle's my goddess, you punk-ass bitch!' He started dancing, fists in the air. 'Por-por! Por-por-por!' He fell to his knees. 'Selene.' Then face down on the grass, right in the pile of sick.

Fenchurch tried to lift him up. No hope, just a dead weight. He rolled Elliot over and peered into his eyes. The pupils wiggled from side to side, rapid, like fish evading the hook. He lifted him up to sitting. 'Elliot, can you—?'

'I love you, man!' His head rolled forward, then back. Eyes wiggling worse now. 'I love everyone!'

'Ecstasy. Shit.' Fenchurch grabbed Elliot and set him on a garden chair, while Reed kept the other kids at a distance. 'Elliot, I need to ask you some questions about Gayle.'

'I love her, man. She's my goddess. Por-por! Por-por-por! Selene!'

Kid's too far gone to take anything in or give anything out except deep, deep love.

'Por-por! Por-por-por!' Sweat trickled down his forehead like a flood after heavy rain, drenching Elliot's face. 'Por-por! Por-por-por!' He started twitching, his pupils a blur. Then he groaned and collapsed back in the chair.

Fenchurch caught a whiff of something sharp. 'What the hell?'

Chapter Fifteen

The paramedics loaded Elliot into the ambulance. Kid was out of it, not even muttering.

A few kids were hanging around, faces etched with panic and fear as the real world interrupted their party. A squad of uniforms marched into the house, heading for a gang of kids still shouting that bloody song in the back garden.

The first paramedic came up to Fenchurch, leaning against his car. Tall and looked like a grizzled copper who'd just decided to focus on helping people rather than convicting them. 'Hey, buddy.' His Canadian drawl sounded really out of place on the streets of London.

'James Mackay, as I live and breathe.' A familiar face from crime scenes over the years, but Fenchurch hadn't seen him in a while.

'One and the same.' Mackay thumbed behind him. 'We've sedated the kid. Going to take a good scrub to get that stink out. You're sure it's ecstasy?'

'I know the signs, James. His eyes were waggling. Then he started sweating and twitching before he had his little accident.'

'Much as I hate to say it, you've probably saved the kid's life.' Mackay glowered at the house. 'Looks like it's Blockchain. That super-strong MDMA.' He snarled. 'Had two corpses from it in the last month. Whoever's dealing that . . . Give me two minutes in a room with them. Least they deserve.' He bared his teeth. 'A shitload of deaths, even more hospitalisations. We're saving people's lives, but they're suffering brain damage or kidney failure. You need to check—'

'—every kid here. I know. I'll get on it.' Fenchurch looked around. 'Nobody is in the same state as Elliot.'

'I'll take that as a good thing.' The ambulance tooted and he looked over. 'We're taking him to the Royal London. I'll keep you posted, all right?'

'Save him.'

'I'll try.' Mackay patted Fenchurch on the shoulder and marched off and hopped in the side. The ambulance hurtled off down the street in a blaze of sirens.

A fresh batch of uniforms showed up, same time as a pair of silver SUVs, angry-faced parents demanding to see their kids.

Fenchurch joined Reed standing by the pool car. She was on the phone so he just stared at the mayhem. Yellow-jacketed officers trying to manage parents through the discovery of their kids' drug taking and heavy drinking.

And Elliot Lynch almost dying in the middle of it.

Going to a house party and almost dying. Kid is way off the lead.

Weird how nobody else seems to be suffering the same effects.

Reed killed her call and flared her nostrils. 'And that song's stuck in my bloody head. It was on all the time in—'

Fenchurch's phone rang. He checked the display — Mulholland. 'Here comes trouble.' He put it to his ear. 'Dawn. You got my voicemail, then?'

'You need to make them shorter.' Mulholland's yawn hissed into the microphone. 'Does it look like we'll get to speak to him tonight?'

'He might die.' Fenchurch got in the car. 'The paramedic thinks it looks like Blockchain.'

'Jesus.' Mulholland paused. 'You think he's a suspect?'

'Could be any number of reasons he'd kill Gayle Fisher, but until we get in a room with him or find something, we're snookered.' Fenchurch checked his watch. Way past time to see Baby Al. 'Do you mind if I go to the hospital?'

'Not now. I've got a better use for you.'

———

Mulholland was waiting outside an interview room in Leman Street, thumbs tapping out a text. She looked up at Fenchurch's thunderous approach and put her phone away. 'How are you doing, Simon?'

'I've had better days, Dawn.' He folded his arms. 'So, what's this better use for me?'

'Brendan Holding.'

'Doesn't ring a bell. Another suspect?'

'Simon, Simon, Simon. You really need to do your homework.' Mulholland stared right into his eyes, then wrapped her scarf tight around her throat. 'He's the Headmaster at Shadwell Grammar.'

'And why are you treating him as a suspect?'

'I like to unnerve intelligence sources, Simon.' She pointed at the interview room door. 'Mr Holding was having a nice evening at the British Film Institute when we got hold of him.' She opened the door and entered.

Fenchurch followed her in.

Brendan Holding was early fifties, but dressed young. Bulging biceps and a checked shirt open to show off chest hair. Sunglasses pushed up over greying hair, shaved close. His face shone, smooth skin like a teenager but without the acne. He smiled at Fenchurch like he recognised him. 'Do I know you?'

Fenchurch sat opposite. 'I've got one of those faces.'

Mulholland gave Fenchurch a weary sigh. Then a beatific smile at Holding. 'Thanks for joining us, sir. We're sorry for your loss.'

'Well.' Holding nodded slowly. 'I'm struggling to process it, but you're right — she'll be a loss. Gayle was a great teacher. One of the most popular I've ever worked with. The kids loved her.'

'I understand how upsetting it can be, sir.' Mulholland adjusted the box of tissues in the middle of the table. Didn't look like Holding was going to use it. 'And the staff?'

'She and her husband were the ones who herded the cats for the Friday-night drinks. Great for team bonding. Always knew there was a crowd heading out. I popped in a couple of times to buy the first round, but I suspect my name was mud.'

'You mean you didn't get on well with her?'

'Not at all. Just that . . .' Holding offered a tight shrug. 'Well, I'm keeping Shadwell Grammar afloat. Treading water, at best. Means I have to make a lot of hard decisions.' He tilted his head. 'Sure someone in your position understands?'

'Feels like drowning.' Mulholland gave a coquettish smile. 'My father went to Shadwell Grammar in the sixties. Hated it, but said it set him up for life.'

Holding took his sunglasses off his head and folded them carefully before setting them down on the desk. 'What does he do?'

'He's retired.'

'You've got a retired father?'

'I'm not that young.' Mulholland blushed. 'NatWest, man and boy. Worked his way from the mailroom to senior management. Put me and my sister through a proper education.'

'You mean private?'

'Of course.'

'Well, a lot of people hated that school. Which is why they're trying to stop all my good work.' Holding locked eyes with Fenchurch. Then started wagging his finger, getting faster as he added in nodding. 'Good God! Simon Fenchurch!'

'That's me, sir. You've probably seen me in the papers.'

'Well, yes . . .' Holding leaned in like they were old mates down the pub. 'How's Abi?'

'You know my wife?'

'Worked together at Lewisham. Great times. We . . . lost touch a few years back. How's she doing?'

'New baby, sir. Sure you know what it's like?'

'I never married.'

'Oh.'

'It's fine. I mean, I like children, but I couldn't eat a whole one.' Holding laughed, making Mulholland grimace. 'When you work with kids all day long, you quickly tire of them. Last thing you want at home, you know?' He left a pause. 'Tell you what, though, I could do with Abi at Southpaw Grammar.' He flicked his head as he grinned. 'Sorry, Shadwell. A little joke there.'

Fenchurch frowned. 'Morrissey album, right?'

'His last good one, if you ask me.'

'Hard to disagree with that.' Fenchurch took a deep breath. 'We need to ask you some questions about certain allegations made against Mrs Fisher.'

'Her affair, right?' Holding picked up his shades and stared into the lenses, like he was using a mirror. 'I heard rumours that a teacher had been sleeping with a pupil. Get them all the time and it just becomes noise. Always complete balderdash. This one, though . . . This one just kept bubbling up. Smoke and fire and all that.'

Fenchurch frowned. 'They mentioned Gayle by name?'

'Not the student, though.' Holding finished preening in the mirror and rested the glasses down again. His head flicked again, like he wasn't in control of the movement. 'I spoke to Gayle. She denied it.' An angry flick this time, definitely deliberate. 'And I believed her, didn't I? Then this little oik from the *Post* turned up, looking for quotes on the story. I thought it was just a smear against me. That bloody paper hates me for turning around an inner-city school. I asked them not to publish.' Another shake. 'But they did, didn't they? Put her photo on the front page. Suggested she'd had sex with a student at another's house.'

'How did Gayle react?'

'How do you think? She panicked. Didn't come in yesterday. Had to arrange a supply teacher.' Holding gritted his teeth like he had to arrange it himself. 'I visited her at home yesterday. Had a cup of tea. She was . . . repentant. Said she'd let me down. Let the school down. That old cliché, but I could tell she meant it. I told her I had no choice but to put her on suspension, pending an investigation.'

'How far have you got with that?'

'I just started it this morning. Most of my week is filled up and I only get round to the meaty stuff on a Saturday.' Holding swallowed hard. 'That said, my little friend from the *Post* did share some information. Turns out it wasn't a one-off. And he had evidence that Gayle and Elliot had . . . Jesus Christ. That they'd had an affair. They'd had sex in a park, for God's sake.'

'Why didn't you go to the police? It's a criminal offence.'

The only answer Holding had was another shake of the head.

'You should've come to us about this, sir. It's a criminal matter. A prison sentence for the offending teacher.'

'I know, I know, it's just . . .'

'Worried about your reputation?'

'Look, of course I would've spoken to the police. I'm sorry. It's just . . . We didn't *know* who it was until—' His shoulders deflated. 'Until I saw that story in the papers.'

'Did you speak to his parents?'

'Not had a chance.'

Fenchurch laughed. 'You should've—'

'Simon.' Mulholland grabbed Fenchurch by the arm and led him outside. 'We'll be back in a second, sir.' She shut the door and glared at Fenchurch. 'You need to calm down.'

'He should've gone to the police.' Fenchurch jabbed a finger at the door. 'Not that the parents would've cared.' He folded his arms. 'You heard him, the *Post* are all over this. They've already got a deep involvement in the case, Liam's mucking us about. We need a media strategy now.'

Mulholland gave a patronising grin, her forehead creasing. 'I'm consulting with Julian on the matter. In the meantime, I really need you to stop leaking, accidentally or otherwise.'

'I'm not leaking to anyone.'

'Not to Liam Sharpe and Cally Morris?' She held a smirk for a few seconds. 'Just make sure they don't get anything else they shouldn't. Am I clear?'

'I don't know who you think you're talking to.' Fenchurch stared at her until she looked away. 'I'm going to catch up with Elliot's parents at the hospital. Then I'm going to spend time with my family. Any objections to that?'

'Fill your boots.' She pushed back into the interview room and shut the door behind her.

———

'Mr Lynch was close to dying.' Dr Lucy Mulkalwar snorted. Sniffed. Tiny and pale-skinned, her black hair cut into a severe bob. Her accent was purest Glasgow. 'He's not out of the woods yet. And it's worse than it looks.'

Elliot lay in the hospital bed, his faced covered with an oxygen mask, an IV drip driven into his wrist. Looked comatose, but his eyes were flicking open. Even caught Fenchurch's eye.

'It looks pretty bad to me.'

Mulkalwar snorted again. 'To be perfectly frank, it's about seventy per cent that he might not survive the night.'

'He took Blockchain, right?'

'Yes. And technically it's serotonin syndrome that's killing him.' Mulkalwar barked out a cough. Then snorted again. 'This is becoming quite common. We see it a lot with patients taking too many of their anti-depressants. Or having an adverse reaction. He had a fit, but we've sedated him. Restlessness. Sweating. Tremors, shivering, muscle twitches, jerking. Mental confusion.'

'Diarrhoea?'

'That's at the less severe end of the spectrum, but yes.'

'Because he—'

'We know. The nurses are nipping my head about the mess.' Mulkalwar gave a sour look. 'It's not just that, it's the risk of infection and so on.'

'Do you know if anyone else at the party took it?'

'Doesn't look like it. According to the attending sergeant, only five of the partygoers were on ecstasy. None of them showed signs of serotonin syndrome.'

'Some better news, I suppose.'

'Here, you!' Derek Lynch was charging down the corridor, anger burning his face red, his stocky frame all bunched up and aggressive. 'What's going on with my boy?'

Mulkalwar stepped behind Fenchurch. 'I am awaiting test results and will—'

'That's bollocks.' Derek tried to get round Fenchurch, but had to settle for prodding a finger in her direction. 'You know what's wrong with him! You know!'

'Sir, I am await—'

'I want the truth, and now!'

'We're awaiting—'

Fenchurch held out a hand. 'Doc, give us a moment?'

Mulkalwar swallowed hard. 'You can't tell him anything!'

'But there's nothing to tell.' Fenchurch frowned at her, adding a wink for good measure. 'Right?'

'Of course.' Mulkalwar left them, her Crocs squelching down the corridor.

'Sir.' Fenchurch gave Derek a reassuring smile. 'The doctor—'

101

'You.' Derek scowled at Fenchurch. 'I know you, by the way. Seen your face in the papers. You seem like a good guy, so I'm asking you to help me out here. What's going on with my boy?'

'The doctor is still assessing your son's condition. You need to let her get on with her job.'

'But she won't tell us anything.'

'I know the feeling. There's no agenda here. She genuinely doesn't know.'

'Is it drugs?'

Fenchurch looked away. 'Probably.'

Derek laughed. 'Boys will be boys, eh?'

'Your son's practically comatose and that's all you can say?'

'Why are you so interested in my boy, anyway?'

'He was sleeping with a teacher.'

Another laugh. 'That's my boy.'

'It's a criminal offence.'

'Aye, for *her*.' Derek bellowed out a laugh. 'He's the victim, right?'

'This isn't funny.'

'Ah, come on. Shagging a teacher. What a boy.'

'You don't care about him, do you?' Fenchurch wanted to pick him up and shove him in the bin upside down. 'He's having sex with a teacher and you just don't give a shit.'

'This is the first I've heard. Honestly.' Derek's head fell forward. 'Elliot . . . He's not a bad lad, just . . . When I was a boy back in Dublin, I was a bit cheeky, you know. Like I say, boys will be boys and all that, but . . . Elliot's out of control. We can't keep him from doing whatever he wants . . . We threatened to go to the police before, but it just bounces off him, you know?'

'You maybe need to follow through on the threat.'

Derek just shrugged.

'Sir, I'll be honest with you. Elliot almost died this evening. I saved his life.' Fenchurch waved down the corridor. 'When I picked him up, he was showing all the signs of serotonin syndrome. Dr Mulkalwar is undertaking tests to confirm that the ecstasy he took was going to kill him.'

'Ecstasy?'

'There's a batch called Blockchain on the streets just now. It's very strong. If you're not aware of what you're taking or you're inexperienced, it can be fatal.'

Derek didn't look too bothered. Like his son's death would solve a problem, more than anything. He walked off, shaking his head like he'd been wronged. Like he'd not raised a boy with no care or attention, let him run wild.

I'd give almost everything to have raised Chloe. Same for the chance to raise Al. And people like him, just barrelling through life like—

Fenchurch's phone rang. Abi. He answered, the spiders crawling up his spine again. 'What's up?'

'Simon, the doctor's taken Al away again! He won't tell me what's going on!'

Fenchurch started running, pushing his dodgy knee.

Not again . . .

Chapter Sixteen

Fenchurch charged down the corridor. His feet felt like lead, when he needed feathers. He pushed through the door. Abi sat on the chair, head low, face screwed up in grief. Chloe hugged her, stroking her arm. The inversion of what it should be. Abi looked up at him. 'They took him!' Her eyes were red-raw.

'Who did?'

'*They* did!'

Not getting anywhere with this . . .

Fenchurch switched his attention to Chloe. 'What happened?'

Chloe frowned, letting Abi pull her closer. 'We were sitting here, playing with Al. It was like he was going to walk, Dad.' She let go of her mother and walked over to the cot, shaking the mobile hanging above it, a pale-blue whale hanging out with its mates — a fish, a crab and an octopus. The cot was empty. 'That doctor came in and grabbed him. Big guy. Grey hair, grey suit.'

'Stephenson?'

'That's him.' Chloe's frown deepened, her breath speeding up. 'He took Al. A nurse spoke to us, said they needed to do tests.'

'Was it like—' Fenchurch's voice caught in his throat, stuck in the quicksand. He coughed and cleared it. 'Was it like when he was born?'

'It was.' Abi was leaning against the side of the cot, breathing hard, tears streaming down her cheeks. 'Just like the last time.'

Fenchurch grabbed her in a hug, rubbing a hand down her back. Trying to reassure her, but his heart pounded in his temple, in his chest, up his arm. 'It's okay.' He tried to keep his voice level, stop any of the fear bleeding through.

'Mum, I'm sure this is normal.' Chloe squeezed Abi's hand, her face showing the same twist of emotions as Fenchurch. 'Right, Dad?'

Fenchurch could only nod. He stared deep into Abi's eyes, smiling like he could suck out all the pain and fear and darkness. 'I'll see what's going on.' One last forced smile and he left them, stepping into the corridor.

Stephenson was standing out there, staring into space, his head rocking slightly, biting his cheek, his face distorted like he'd had a stroke. He jerked back, hands raised. 'Ah, I need to—'

'No.' Fenchurch grabbed his arm tightly. 'Where is he?'

'Let go!' Stephenson stared at Fenchurch's hand until he complied. 'Listen—'

'No, you listen to me. You don't take my son away without explaining to my wife what the hell is going on.'

'Right. I'm sorry.' Stephenson thought it through, his lips quivering. 'I didn't know if it would be a goer, that's all.'

'What would be? You need to start talking.'

'I've been in touch with a colleague, a specialist in congenital heart defects. He's in London for a conference. I spoke to him at lunchtime and briefed him on Baby Al's condition.' A smile crept over his lips, lifting some of the gloom. 'He's agreed to assist.'

Fenchurch felt a surge of joy, spearing his heart.

'Keith Oates, pleasure to meet you.' A short doctor stood behind Stephenson, almost as wide as he was tall, rocking Baby Al in his arms. He held out his right hand, still holding the baby in perfect balance. 'This little guy's a heck of a kicker. Might get him playing for Harlequins.'

'He's going to play for West Ham.'

'A soccer man, eh?' Oates handed Al to Fenchurch, taking care that he held him just right. 'Well, come on.' He led into the room, Stephenson following.

Fenchurch held Al close, smelling his head again, tears stinging his nose. The little bugger was wriggling, but grinning at his old man. *What I wouldn't give to see him turn into an old man.* He gave him one last cuddle, then took him into the room and handed him to Abi.

'Now . . .' Oates was leaning against the cot. Looked like he could sleep in it. 'I've had a good look at Baby Al and, like I just told his daddy here, the boy's a fighter. I'm going to do everything in the power that God has given me to save him.'

Abi hugged Al tight, suspicion crawling over her face. 'What power?'

'As Mr Stephenson has no doubt briefed you, I'm the NHS's primary specialist in congenital heart defects. The last six months, I've been based at the Cleveland Clinic in Ohio. Number one for cardiology in the States, meaning it's the best in the world.'

Stephenson lurked by the door, but couldn't look at any of them. 'Mr Oates has been working on—'

'They get it. I'm the best there is.' Oates held up his hands and gave a humble shrug. 'Atrial septal defects is my specialty. Basically, the "hole in the heart" that young Alan here suffers from.' His eyes were hooded by his thick cranium. 'It's quite common, more than two babies per thousand. You'll know that the standard treatment is to insert a device into the heart to encourage Al's own tissue to grow in the exact way we want.'

Fenchurch focused on Al's chest, hidden under the cream onesie. 'But it's not?'

'The hole is growing.'

Fenchurch locked eyes with Oates. 'How long has he got?'

'We're nowhere near that stage, my friend.' Oates reached over to tickle Al's chin as Abi held him. 'The surgery will close the ASD and prevent it from reappearing. It'll be like Al's never even had it. He'll be happy and healthy. Might even play for West Ham.'

Fenchurch let out a breath. Felt light-headed and giddy.

Abi glared at Stephenson. 'Why hasn't this been tried before?'

'Because you want the body winning the battle on its own.' Oates pinched Al's cheek. 'The vast majority of cases resolve with the regrowth technique. There are risks, of course. But, if you don't want to throw the dice and have the surgery, then Al will be in here for six months, and his heart will just stop beating.'

'I can't deal with that.' Abi's damp eyes pleaded with Fenchurch. 'We need to give him the chance.'

Fenchurch could taste the bitter fear in amongst the sweet hope. 'What happens if the surgery fails?'

'With these hands?' Oates held them up and twisted round to let everyone get a look, his confident grin lurking for a few seconds. 'You need time to think it through?'

Abi kissed Baby Al, her forehead creased, lips pursed. She gave a nod and Fenchurch passed it on to Oates.

———

Fenchurch stopped at the lights at the start of Upper Street. The car was baking hot and he was sweating.

Putting our son's life in the hands of a surgeon we've just met . . . Is that the right thing to do?

Do we have any other choice?

He set off and took the left turning.

What if he's overconfident? What if Stephenson's the better bet? He saw Al in the womb, ran the tests, then led us through the worst of it so far.

But he had the humility to plead with a rock-star surgeon, persuading him to look at Baby Al. That shows it's the right thing to do, doesn't it?

Fenchurch pulled up opposite Abi's car. She was still behind the wheel, staring into space. Chloe got out on to the street and hugged someone.

Fenchurch joined her on the pavement. And let out a groan. 'Dad.'

'All right, son.' Dad was swaying, battling gravity, clinging to Chloe. The whisky fumes wafted from him. 'Just back from the wake. Poor old Doc. Poor old Al.'

'Looks like it was fun.' Fenchurch opened the stairwell door. Abi was still in her car. 'You coming in?'

'Can't stay, son.' Dad squinted at his brand-new phone, then dropped it. He scrambled about, trying to pick it up. Then fell forward, flat on his face. Fenchurch had to help him up. Could taste the whisky coming from his pores. 'Chloe texted me. Can't for the life of me figure out how this blessed thing works.'

'I'll show you, Grandpa.'

'Not just now, Chloe, love.' Dad burped and it turned into a long yawn. 'What was the text about?'

'Hope, Dad. Hope. For Al.'

'I've always had hope for that little sod.' Dad put his phone away. Almost lost his balance again. 'I want to see him lighting up the London Stadium, son. Number 9, Fenchurch on his back. Maybe even England. Who needs Harry Kane when we've got Al Fenchurch?' Dad grabbed Chloe's cheek and squeezed. 'Sure you don't want a trial with West Ham Ladies?'

Chloe nudged his hand away. 'You need a cup of tea.'

'I need my bed.' Dad staggered off down the road, using his hand to feel his way past the buildings. 'See you later.'

Fenchurch followed him. 'Dad, I'll give you a lift.'

'I'll get a cab, son.' Dad waved Fenchurch off. 'You spend time with your family.' And he was gone.

Fenchurch watched him flag down a cab, then walked back to the flat. 'Daft old goat.'

'He's something else, isn't he?' Chloe pushed open the door and entered the building.

'I'll be up in a minute.' Fenchurch opened Abi's passenger door and crouched. 'You okay, love?'

'I'm good, actually.' She leaned back against the headrest, smiling. Then she got out and joined him on the pavement, her car's lights flashing as she locked it. 'One day soon, we'll have both kids under one roof.'

Fenchurch grabbed her hand and followed her inside. 'Thought you had three children?'

'Chloe's growing up, Simon. It's just you and Al.'

Fenchurch laughed all the way up the stairs. Felt good. Felt right. Normal.

Abi was still coasting on the smile. 'Two years ago, I was on my own. It's a big flat just for one person. It'll be nice to have them both here.' She led him inside.

The kettle was boiling in the kitchen. Chloe was at the table, going through her post. Only took her two days to get round to it, a lot less time than her old man. 'Here we go.' She showed a glossy prospectus to Abi. Dundee University.

Fenchurch groaned. 'Dundee, really?'

'Their teacher training course is supposed to be good.'

'Much better than the one I did.' Abi took the booklet and sat next to her daughter. 'And you don't have to do it in the evenings.'

'Those were long, hard months.' Fenchurch sat opposite, his tiredness hitting him. 'But we got through them.'

Chloe looked up from the prospectus. 'No regrets?'

'Not for a second.'

Chloe let her mother kiss her, then walked over to pour out her camomile tea. 'You guys want anything?'

'I'm fine.' Abi was staring at the prospectus again.

Fenchurch smiled at his daughter. 'I'm drowning in tea, love.'

She poured in some cold water then blew on her tea. 'Early start tomorrow. No rest for the wicked.' She trudged off with a wave.

Fenchurch watched her go. The weird reality of their long-missing daughter back under their roof hit him again. Hit him hard.

'Chloe!' Abi got up and darted over to the door. 'You got any ideas what I can make Pete for dinner tomorrow?'

'What?' Chloe frowned. Then her eyes bulged. 'Crap, I forgot.'

'We can reschedule.'

'No, let's do it. He likes Thai and Mexican.'

'Just like your father.' Abi pecked her on the cheek. 'Sweet dreams.'

'You don't have to tuck me in, Mum.'

'Okay. Sorry. Goodnight.' Abi waited until Chloe's bedroom door clicked shut then sat down, scowling. 'Wish I did.'

'I know.' Fenchurch reached across the table and held her hands. 'Oh. I met someone who knows you. Brendan Holding.'

'Christ, that takes me back.' Abi stared up at the ceiling. 'Brendan Holding, eh?' She blew air up her face. 'We worked together at Lewisham before I moved to Highbury.'

'Should I be worried?'

'As if.' Abi's shoulders slouched. 'What's the case?'

'The victim's a teacher at Shadwell Grammar. Gayle Fisher. Know her?'

She pulled her hands away. 'Never heard of her.'

'We've got the pleasure of this Pete's company tomorrow?'

'Don't tell me you forgot too?'

'Love, my son's in hospital and my boss has just been put in the ground. Cut me some slack.'

'Nothing to do with Pete being the same age as you?'

Fenchurch looked away. 'Of course not.'

Of course it is. Guy's twice her age. She should be finding out who she is, not settling for some old bastard like her dad.

Fenchurch picked up the prospectus. 'Dundee?'

'She's right. It's a good course. Not a lot in London for a trainee teacher these days.'

'Her going off again, though. These last few months are time we never thought we'd have.' Fenchurch laughed, then it caught in his throat, back in the quicksand he'd let build up.

'What if this surgery goes wrong, Simon?' She leaned forward, resting her eyes on her palms, elbows cracking off the table. 'We've got our daughter back, but we're going to lose our son.'

'It's not like that. There's no link, Abi. It's just bad luck. That's all.'

'Well, I wish we were luckier.'

Day 2
Sunday, 10th September 2017

Chapter Seventeen

Fenchurch eased the bedroom door shut and padded through to the hall. The morning sunlight blazed in from the living room.

Chloe's door was open, curtains drawn. The posters on the wall were bands whose names Fenchurch couldn't even pronounce, let alone hum a bar of their music. She'd personalised the room. Made it her own. Abi's old typewriters were gone. The bed was made.

No sign of her.

Fear spiked Fenchurch's chest, sunk through the pit of his stomach. No sign of her in the bathroom, no sounds of running water or singing.

He opened the kitchen door.

'—por-por. Selene. Porcelain. Goddess. Por-por. Por-por-por.'

Chloe was slaving over the cooker, hair tied back. The scar on her temple caught the spotlights and almost glowed, making Fenchurch flinch. She noticed him and turned the radio down. 'Hey, Dad. I think this is going to be the best porridge yet.'

Fenchurch kissed her then filled the kettle and stuck it on to boil. 'What's special about this one?'

'Himalayan pink rock salt. Think that'll be better than sea salt.' She spooned up some porridge and held it out for him. 'What do you think?'

Fenchurch tasted it. The salt brought out the sweetness in the oats. 'Lovely.'

'Worried it's not sweet enough now?' She ladled it out into two bowls and set them on the counter. 'Drowning it in maple syrup like you do seems . . .'

'Base?'

'Right.'

Fenchurch sat and drizzled brown liquid on his porridge, leaving just enough for Chloe. 'I'll drop you at work on my way in.'

'Southwark isn't your way in.'

Fenchurch grinned. 'Still going to drop you off.'

———————

'Starving already.' Fenchurch pulled up in the supermarket car park. Over on the Old Kent Road, a cleaning truck trundled down, clearing up Saturday night's vomit and stale beer. Another area of London, nowhere near gentrified, still stuck in the eighties. 'Your grandpa calls porridge "cheat the belly". You feel full, then twenty minutes later you're starving.'

Chloe let her hair down, covering up her scar. 'Sorry, Dad.'

'I'm criticising my metabolism, not your cooking.'

'Well, I must have it too because I'm ravenous.'

Fenchurch laughed. *Not so long ago she was denying anything to do with us, now she's making jokes about having my genes.* Sent shivers down his spine. 'What does Pete like to drink?'

'What?'

'Tonight. I'll get something nice in. Beer, wine, whisky. You name it.'

'Umm.'

'First time we'll meet him. Properly. Been a long time.'

She opened her door and let the noise in.

Fenchurch waved a hand at the supermarket. 'What, you don't know what he drinks or you don't want him to come round?'

'He doesn't drink.' Her tongue rolled over her lips. 'Can't.'

'Doctor can't or alcoholic can't?'

'I don't know.'

'Chloe, are you seeing an alcoholic?'

'Get off your high horse, Dad. I see how much you tuck away.'

'Touché.'

'If anyone's a borderline alcoholic, it's you.'

'They say alcoholism's a disease. It's not. Alcoholics drink to escape their lives. It's not stopping drinking that cures them, it's dealing with their deep psychological issues.'

'What are you drinking for?'

'The shit I see every day. Dealing with that. Compressing my head so that I'm just in the present with you and your mother and I'm not thinking about the crime scene I've been to that afternoon.'

'I didn't think.' She unpinned her name badge and stuck it on. 'Dad, I don't know whether Pete's an alcoholic. Honestly. He never drinks, even on nights out. It's one thing I like about him.'

'Just one?'

'Buy whatever you like and you can sit there getting hammered. Sure Mum won't mind.' Chloe tugged her hair up and scratched at her scar. 'Sorry. Shouldn't have said that. I'm upset about my brother.'

Fenchurch looked away. 'We all are.'

'Yeah, well, I'm struggling. You're attuned to it, obviously.'

'You never get attuned to loss.'

'He's just a baby. How can there be something that wrong with him?'

'When you were that young, I worried about you all the time. I thought you'd just stop breathing, but you were a lot stronger. *Much* stronger.' Fenchurch leaned back in his seat and smiled at her. 'Listen, I might be able to get away at lunchtime. Do you want to meet, just you and me?'

'I'd love it. Mexican?'

'Like there's any other food.'

She laughed, then opened her door fully. Then let out a sigh. 'Dad . . .'

'What?'

'There's . . .' Another sigh.

'Is it about me or your mother?'

'Well, duh.' She shut her eyes. 'We should talk about it at the session tomorrow.'

'What's wrong with now?'

Chloe got out of the car and leaned back in. 'I've been spending a lot of time with Mum. I'm really loving getting to know her, but . . .'

'Is she being too clingy?'

'Dad!' She sighed again. 'Look, we'll talk about it in our session with Paddy tomorrow.'

'Chloe, you can talk to me. About anything, everything. Whatever it is.'

'It's fine, Dad. Tomorrow.' She leaned over to kiss his cheek then set off across the car park, meeting a colleague halfway.

Fenchurch's phone blared out, rattling the holder. A mobile number, unknown caller. He answered it, watching Chloe traipse over to the store. 'Yeah?'

'Hi.' A woman's voice exploded out of the car's speakers, set to Led Zeppelin volume, not phone calls. Sounded young.

'Hi back. Who is this?'

'Katerina.'

Liam's jailbait girlfriend.

Fenchurch sat forward, gripping the steering wheel. 'What's up?'

'I . . . Look, it's nothing.'

'What's happened? Have you got something?'

'No. I just . . . I need to talk to someone. About Mrs Fisher.'

Fenchurch stared at the speakers like he could see into her eyes. 'I keep thinking about seeing her lying there.'

Seeing a body hits people hard, especially if it's someone they know. Nobody thinks about them, the silent victims. Can take days to kick in. And it'll take forever to leave.

'I've been there.' Fenchurch exhaled slowly. 'A few times. It's not easy, believe me.' He caught a last glimpse of Chloe as she entered the supermarket. 'Is there someone you can talk to about it?'

'Mum doesn't understand. And no.' She paused. 'You thought your daughter was dead, didn't you?' She gasped. 'Sorry, I shouldn't have bothered you.'

'It's okay.' Fenchurch's turn to pause. 'Do you need to talk to someone?'

Another long pause, long enough to make him think he'd lost her. 'I've got nobody.'

'Look, come into the station at lunchtime. I'm busy all morning, but I'll fit you in then. How's that sound?'

'Okay.' And she was gone.

Fenchurch started the engine and drove off. *What the hell was that about?*

———

'Moving on, then.' Fenchurch sat in the Incident Room, looking around the morning briefing. 'DS Reed, are we any further forward in proving that Steve Fisher's behind his wife's murder?'

'Ish.' Reed was sat on a desk halfway across the room flanked by a squad of uniformed knuckle draggers, the sort Fenchurch would've been twenty years ago. Trouser suit today, flat leather shoes, so at least she was dressed for work and not a baby shower. 'His alibi's still wide open. Lisa's got the CCTV for the route he allegedly took.'

Bridge sat on her own, laptop clutched tight. 'Not started it yet, sir. It's literally just turned up.'

'Right. Okay.' Fenchurch focused on the rest of the group, trying to spot any other likely sources of hope. Didn't find any. 'I'm attending Gayle Fisher's post-mortem at ten. Dr Pratt will hopefully figure out what killed her.'

'Doubt it.' Clooney covered his smirk with a cough. Laughter bounced around the room.

'Let a guy hope, Mick. You got anything for me?'

'Just a shit-ton of forensics to process.' Clooney tapped at his tablet's screen. 'Hairs, a bit of saliva. Probably all from the victim. Most likely from the cleaners or previous guests.'

'But possibly our killer?'

'You know the rules, Si. You give me a suspect; I'll tell you if they were there.' Clooney hid his face behind his tablet, blocking Fenchurch's view. 'Tammy's still at the crime scene this morning. We'll hopefully finish tonight and get it all off to the lab. Then we're waiting on the lab to get back to us.'

'Can we—'

'Simon, you always ask me to speed up. I don't know why you think your cases are more important than anyone else's.' Clooney lowered his tablet just enough for Fenchurch to see his stupid face. 'If it was the Queen or the Prime Minister going under Pratt's knife, fair enough, you could bump it up. But if this was someone that important, Si, let's be honest, you're not going to be investigating it, are you?'

Fenchurch tried to hide his irritation with a sip of tea. 'Do what you can, Mick.'

'Always do, Si. I've also got that acid attack in Hackney and it just doesn't end.'

'I get it.' Fenchurch switched back to Reed. 'Kay, can you keep tearing apart Steve Fisher's alibi?' He waited for her to write it down, then raised his eyebrows at Uzma. 'DS Ashkani, I need you to track down the two missing guests at the hotel.' He got a nod, then clapped his hands together. 'Okay, let's find the killer.'

The squad dispersed in a puff of noise. Those words always rang hollow, no matter how many times he said them and how hard he meant them.

Mulholland joined him on the bench by the whiteboard. 'A victim and no suspect. The hardest time in any case.'

'Feels like every case, Dawn.'

Mulholland turned to face him, her left eyebrow raised. 'Let me know if you want any coaching on running a more effective briefing.'

'Excuse me?'

'Mick Clooney ran rings around you. And your team look somewhat deflated.'

'You're welcome to run it, what with you being SIO.'

'Simon, as my Deputy, I need you to be able to run a briefing.' She waved an arm round the room. 'And you need to make this team work hard for you.'

Fenchurch finished his tea, though it tasted sour, like the milk had curdled. 'I'll bear that in mind.'

'My offer of coaching stands.' Mulholland sprang to her feet and patted his arm. 'I can get Uzma to deputise if you want?'

Fenchurch put his mug down, though really he should've smashed her face with it. 'I just need that media strategy.'

'It's with Julian for review and sign-off.'

'And we're keeping a blackout until then? It's been over twenty-four hours since Gayle died. Almost that since she was found.'

'It's with Julian.' Mulholland scanned around the room, tugging hard at her scarf. 'What's your take on Elliot Lynch? Is he a valid suspect?'

'Wouldn't put my money on him.' Fenchurch joined her standing. 'When we picked him up last night, he seemed to be in love with Gayle. Didn't know she was dead, either. Usually if someone's killed someone they love, it's long since turned to hate. And the state he was in, he couldn't have lied if he wanted to. We saw the boy's soul.'

'I take your point, however florally put.' Another sharp tug at her scarf. 'Well, the doctor called me. Could barely understand a word she said. I *think* Elliot's ready for interview.'

Chapter Eighteen

Fenchurch pushed through the door into the waiting area and held it for Reed. No sign of Dr Mulkalwar. He walked over to the nurses' station, but spotted her standing near the ward, a pained look on her face. 'Doc, I need a word with Elliot Lynch.'

'DCI Mulholland passed on my message, then.' Mulkalwar led them down a corridor. 'Elliot is in a stable condition but, to be perfectly frank, we need to tread carefully. The ecstasy he took last night was definitely Blockchain. We found some of these in his pocket.' She stopped and held out her hand. A white pill inside a plastic bag.

'This is evidence.' Fenchurch took it off her and inspected it closer. The Bitcoin logo was stamped on the pill, a capital B with two vertical lines. 'How sure are you that he took one?'

'Fairly sure. Elliot was suffering from the early stages of serotonin syndrome, caused by an overdose of MDMA. It was progressing rapidly, so I suspect he'd taken more than one pill.'

'Any more victims overnight?'

'One in Croydon.' Mulkalwar tried to take the drug back, but Fenchurch closed his fingers around the bag. 'Okay. Well.' She stared through the darkened window into the corridor, where an orderly was helping a limping man. 'Anyway. I confirmed with your uniform colleagues — Elliot was the only one at that party who suffered these effects.'

'Small mercies.' Reed scowled at the doctor. 'Can we see him?'

'He isn't taking visitors.' Mulkalwar huffed out a sigh. 'It's easier if I show you.'

'Elliot?' Mulkalwar stood over the bed, pulling back the covers to take a look at Elliot. Kid was staring up at the ceiling. It was like they weren't even there. 'Two police officers are here to speak to you.'

Elliot took one look at them, struggling to keep his face straight.

'They need to ask you some questions.'

Elliot lay back on the bed then burst out laughing like he was at a Billy Connolly gig.

Is this what Mulkalwar meant about his condition?

Fenchurch glanced at Mulkalwar, frowning. She just shrugged. So he crouched next to the bed. 'Why are you laughing?'

Elliot didn't stop, his sides shaking.

'What are you laughing at?'

He gave a shrug, still laughing.

What's up with him?

Fenchurch even touched his own head to make sure his hair was flat or that he wasn't covered in bird crap. Nothing. He grabbed Elliot's arm. That got his attention. 'Listen to me. We found Gayle Fisher's body yesterday.' He waited, but didn't get a reaction. At least the little sod stopped laughing. 'We need to know your whereabouts on Friday night.'

Elliot leaned on his elbow, smirking. Then he started laughing again.

What the hell?

Fenchurch took Mulkalwar to the side. 'Is this related to the serotonin syndrome?'

'To be perfectly frank, I think he's just messing with you.'

'Right.' Fenchurch walked back to Elliot. 'Son, we think that the drugs you took almost killed you. Can you tell me who sold you them?'

Elliot lay back again, laughing hard.

'I'm serious.' Fenchurch reached out and grabbed the kid's arm again. 'Listen to me. What you took almost killed you. Has anyone else got it?'

'Must have.'

Progress. Of a sort.

'Who? Your friends from school?'

'Don't be daft.' Elliot snorted with laughter. 'I mean, seven billion people on the planet. Someone else *must* have some, right? I didn't make the stuff.'

Cheeky bastard.

'Elliot, I need to know where you were on Friday night.'

Elliot gave Fenchurch the up and down then started laughing again, bellowing out.

Fenchurch reached for Elliot again. But Mulkalwar stopped him. 'Time to leave.'

'Why the hell was he laughing?' Fenchurch pulled out and overtook two buses trundling along Commercial Road. 'It's not like my fly was undone, was it?'

'Guv, that kid was off his face.' Reed was in the passenger seat, her face blank. 'Who knows what he's up to?'

'That stuff almost killed him. I don't understand why anyone would take the risk.'

'Part of the thrill.' Reed gave a shrug. 'Looking for escape from their lives. The risk of death ups the thrill.'

'I've seen a lot of heroin overdoses in my time and I could never understand why. Every time you stick some in your arm, it's just rolling a dice.' Fenchurch focused on the bag in Reed's hands. 'These Blockchain pills . . . Jesus. The dice is loaded with them.'

Reed shrugged again. 'Better to die laughing than live in misery.'

Fenchurch's phone rang. The spiders crawled up his spine again. He glanced at the dashboard display. Mulholland. He let out a breath, then nudged answer with his thumb. 'Dawn, did you get my message?'

'It was somewhat garbled, Simon.' Fenchurch glared at the display, catching a smirk from Reed. 'There's a course at Hendon on clear communication. I advise—'

'Elliot definitely took Blockchain. Dr Mulkalwar found some on him.'

Mulholland's pause was long enough for Reed to get four full jerks in of the universal 'wanker' gesture. 'She didn't tell me that part.'

'Elliot could've died last night, Dawn. Those kids at the party would've stuck him in a bed and woken up to a cold body. We need to find the supplier and the dealers.'

Another pause. Fenchurch reached over to stop Reed wanking the air, then turned right off the street between a bookie's and a miserable council block.

'Well done for saving him, Simon. Is that what you're after?'

Fenchurch accelerated towards some new flats overlooking the train line. 'I'm not asking for praise, I just—'

'I don't think this is a valid lead in our case.'

'Don't you think we should stop other kids dying?' Another pause. Felt like victory, but you never knew with Mulholland. 'All I'm asking is that you pick up the phone to the drug squad and let them know.'

'Like I said, I don't think—'

'I've got contacts over there.' Fenchurch took a sharp left. 'You want me to go over your head? Fair enough.'

'Fine.' Mulholland sniffed. 'Did Elliot give you anything at all relating to our case?'

'He's . . .' Fenchurch took a right. Then stopped to let an old lady cross, her shopping basket rolling behind her. 'He didn't play ball.'

'Do I need to send Uzma?'

'That won't help.' Fenchurch was close to revving to hurry the old woman up, but she stopped in the middle of the road and said something to them. 'The kid's just mugging us off. Maybe an anti-police thing.' He waved her over, then set off before the old dear reached the other side. 'We're going to speak to his parents.' He turned on to Elliot's street.

Rammed.

People lined both sides of the road. At least two cameras and a BBC van.

Bloody journalists.

Who told them?

'I need to go.' Fenchurch killed the call and pulled up behind a Sky News van. He got out and barged through the scrum, warrant card out. 'Police! Coming through!'

'Si!' A hand grabbed his arm. Liam, eyes pleading. 'Give us a quote?'

'You can take a running jump.' Fenchurch tried to shake him off, but he was like a cat digging its claws in. Just wouldn't let go. 'You shouldn't be here. Nobody should.'

'Cally wants a quote.'

'Get her to speak to the Media Office.' Fenchurch finally shook him off and pushed past the last few reporters. He trudged up the path and knocked on the door. 'Mr Lynch! Police!'

'I've called the police!' Derek Lynch's voice boomed out of the letter box. 'Can you just piss off?'

'Sir, it's DI Fenchurch.' He crouched down and showed his warrant card through the letter box. 'We need a word.'

'Must've been you lot!' Derek Lynch hovered over his chair, one of those wooden-framed jobs you get from IKEA. He seemed unable to sit but unable to commit to standing. The living room was crammed with furniture, barely any room.

Amanda Lynch's voice droned through from another room, the kind of phone call where the other side was much more interesting. 'Yeah, yeah, ah-ha. Well, I'm not sure about that. I'd need to speak to my husband.'

Fenchurch peered out of the window again. The reporters waved at him, their cheer inaudible through the double glazing. Then he shut the curtains.

Derek was waving his arms around. 'We can't get out of the house!'

Fenchurch leaned against the windowsill. Amanda's voice was louder, but he still couldn't make out much beyond 'yes' and 'no'. 'Our media strategy at present is to maintain a press blackout.' He raised a finger to stop Derek. 'We spoke to Elliot at the hospital. Dr—'

'Yeah, I know. We're picking him up once you've got that rabble off my front lawn, Inspector. Okay?' Derek finally sat on his chair, getting a creak from the wood. 'That stupid little sod . . . Elliot was supposed to have a trial at Millwall this afternoon.'

'He's a footballer?'

'The one thing he's good at. Crafty midfielder, you know? Can hit a pass like you wouldn't believe. But this is last-chance saloon for him. Put it this way, he's not doing well at the school. That new Headmaster's great, but the damage is already done, you know? Hard to turn round an oil tanker.' Derek punched the wooden arm of his chair. 'The football's all he can be arsed with, you know? Spurs and Chelsea watched him when he was fourteen. Came to nothing. Had a trial at West Ham, but of course he's not gone through a boys' club so he didn't learn the West Ham way.' He spat it out. 'Charlton, too, but they didn't like his attitude. We thought it was over, but then Millwall start sniffing about. Now he'll not play in that trial.'

'Sure they'll reschedule.'

'Why, because he OD'ed? Yeah, good one.' Derek rocked himself up to standing, then walked over to the doorway. He squinted at something but Fenchurch couldn't see what. 'It's all gone to his head. Thought he'd made it when West Ham were sniffing around. Best if it all dies away, then Elliot can treat it as a hobby and focus on the school.'

'He needs to focus on proving his innocence first.'

Derek twisted round, scowling at Fenchurch. 'What are you wittering about?'

'He's a suspect in the murder of Gayle Fisher.'

'That's horseshit.' Derek stomped across the wooden boards and stopped inches from Fenchurch's face. 'Horse. Shit.' Then he seemed to remember he was dealing with a police officer. 'He *told me* there's nothing in it. And I believe him.'

'There's evidence. Photos and videos.' Fenchurch left it hanging. Derek took another step forward, baring his teeth, but kept quiet. 'Your son won't give us an alibi for Friday night.'

'My boy did not kill that woman!' Then Derek was off, wheeling around the room, throwing his arms in the air. 'You can't seriously think he did it, can you? Killing a teacher?'

'Sir, it's my job to think everyone did it until they tell me otherwise.' Fenchurch waited for his logic to click round in Derek's skull. 'Where was he on Friday night?'

Derek collapsed into his seat and started kneading the bridge of his nose. 'I've no idea.' He let out a deep sigh. 'Soon as he leaves school on a Friday, we're lucky if we see him before Sunday night.'

'Even when he's got a trial with Millwall?'

'Even then.'

Fenchurch wanted to walk over there, pick him up and throw him on the floor. Tell Derek he should look after his son, be grateful to have any time with him.

'Stop!' Amanda Lynch clomped through from the other room, waving her hands at her husband. 'Derek, Mr Maxfield is going to represent Elliot.' She gave Fenchurch a sour look, eyes narrow. 'He told us not to speak to the police without him or a lawyer present.'

Fenchurch felt his neck tighten, like someone had stuck an Allen key in a bolt and twisted and twisted and . . .

Ben Maxfield. Time to put that little shit in his place.

Chapter Nineteen

Reed pulled up outside Maximum Exposure and killed the engine. 'Right. Here again.'

Fenchurch stared up at the office. Signs of life inside, blue-tinged lights in the meeting rooms and offices, but nobody visible from the street. He opened his door and got out.

'It's really, really good to see you both.' Maxfield stood in the office doorway, smoking, his face stretched tight. Dark rings under his eyes, like he'd been up all night working. Or partying hard. Maybe both. 'I'm so, so busy.'

Fenchurch barged past into the office. 'You're getting on my nerves.'

'Good.' Maxfield blew out a plume of smoke. 'What am I supposed to have done?' He started yawning. Didn't seem like he'd ever stop. 'There's nothing I can help you with, I'm afraid. Gayle's dead, end of.' He reached into his jacket pocket and took out a can of WakeyWakey energy drink. 'The plan was to ride out the publicity, then start doing tabloid confessionals. Raise her profile.' Syrupy-sweet mist hissed as he opened the can. 'Then we could think about *Celeb Big Brother*, then move up to *Strictly* or *I'm A Celebrity*. It's all about how you spin it.'

'She was going to go to prison for having sex with a pupil.'

'Think you'll find she was going to go to the jungle with Ant and Dec.' Maxfield winked as he took a long slug. 'Sorry, I should've offered you some.' Another glug. 'But I can't be arsed. Anyway, you'll know that

I've got the very, very best lawyers on retainer. Gather you're acquainted with Makepeace and company?'

Fenchurch sat forward, his gut fizzing with rage. 'Gayle wouldn't have got away with it.'

'You wouldn't even get into court, Fenchurch.'

'I wouldn't personally, no. I'm murder squad. But someone else would. There's solid evidence.'

'Inspector.' Maxfield covered his yawn with another sip. 'All we did was book a hotel to keep the papers away until it worked to our advantage.'

'And now you're advising a suspect to stay away.'

'I'm not representing Steve Fisher.'

Fenchurch glanced at Reed. 'What?'

'He told me in no uncertain terms where to go.' Maxfield finished his drink and tossed the empty in the bin, a couple of dots spraying on Fenchurch's trousers. 'Could've helped him so, so much but them's the breaks.'

'I meant Elliot Lynch.'

'Oh, him.' Another yawn. 'Right, I really don't give a shit. Now, I need to get out to Stamford Bridge, okay? I'm meeting a client at the Butcher's Hook for a spot of lunch before Chelsea annihilate West Brom.'

'Elliot's a murder suspect. We need to speak to him and you're stopping us. Time to use that retainer.'

Maxfield yawned again, his mouth staying open for a few seconds. Then mischief twinkled in his eyes. 'At this stage, it's just an offer. I've not signed anything with the boy.' The mischief turned into full-blown mayhem. 'Elliot's mother told me about that scrum on their doorstep on Sky News. Must be hell out there.'

'You did that, didn't you?'

'You got evidence I did?' Maxfield got up and collected a navy Barbour from his coat stand. 'Promising young kid, though. Like Gayle, he's really, really good-looking. I've got a Stateside sports agent calling up Major League Soccer clubs, seeing if they can use this current profile to get him a club over in the good ol' US of A. Good money to be made and the standard is so, so low in the States. Even worse than Scottish football.'

'You're sick.' Reed got in his face. 'You've stopped his parents talking to us.'

Maxfield stopped zipping up his coat. 'And?'

'He's a suspect.'

'And?' Maxfield zipped his coat up to his chin. 'Have I done anything wrong here?'

'You're hindering a murder case.'

Maxfield held out his hands, ready to be cuffed. 'Come on, then. Stop me watching my football. I'll come with you, refuse to answer your questions while you could've been doing some good with taxpayers' money, then you let me go.'

Reed looked at Fenchurch, fury burning in her eyes. Fenchurch gave a light shake of his head.

'Thought not.' Maxfield walked over to the door and opened it again. He waved out of the door. 'Now get out of here, you pair of arseholes.'

Reed grabbed him by the jacket and pinned him to the door. 'Say that again.'

'Pair. Of. Arseholes.'

'You want me to rip you a new one, do you?'

'Let go, Sergeant.' Maxfield waited until she complied then laughed in her face. 'Atta girl.'

'Kay, it's bad enough when I go over the score.' Fenchurch pulled up outside Leman Street and killed the engine. 'I need you keeping calm.'

'That guy deserved a whole lot more, guv.' Reed scowled as her seatbelt whizzed up. 'What now?'

Fenchurch checked his mirrors. Clear, for once. 'Right, I'm heading out to Lewisham for the PM. Can you get on top of Lisa?'

Reed opened her door and planted her feet on the ground. 'Thought you didn't approve of sex tapes?'

'Jesus, Kay.' Fenchurch started the car with a rev and flicked on his indicator. 'Don't let that prick get to you, okay?'

'Spoken like you bother doing it yourself.'

'Do as I say, Kay. Do as I say.'

———

'Well, my dear fellow.' Pratt stood over Gayle Fisher's body, humming something from an opera, probing at her innards with some shiny tools. 'I have the great pleasure in confirming that our victim was indeed bound by ties on her wrists, hidden under those pink handcuffs.'

Fenchurch was leaning against the wall, his legs close to falling asleep. 'Two hours for this?'

'Two hours?' Pratt looked up long enough to register a glare. 'I've been in since *four*, dear heart. Your edited highlights take a lot of work behind the scenes.'

Fenchurch shook his legs, trying to wake them. 'What killed her?'

'She died between eleven p.m. and midnight of . . .' Pratt stopped, a frown twisting his brow. 'How do I record it?'

'It's not my place to put words—'

'I'm thinking out loud.' Another glare. 'So far, I've got "A twenty-eight-year-old woman was found dead in a hotel room. No history of depression. No containers of medication or narcotics paraphernalia were found at the scene. Autopsy findings included fully developed rigor mortis and pulmonary oedema with haemorr—"'

'Fluid on the lungs?'

'So you *do* pay attention?' Pratt stood up tall, arms folded, grinning. 'Her lungs filled with fluid and she stopped being able to breathe.'

'What a way to go . . .'

'There are many worse. Besides, I think she probably wasn't aware of what was going on.' Pratt settled back into his crouch. 'The cause of death is clearly drug intoxication resulting in serotonin syndrome. Like I say, she died between eleven and midnight, but the drug was administered earlier. As noted at the scene of the crime, the blood marks on her wrist show a struggle happening circa nine o'clock.'

'You mean someone got into her room and held her down?'

'That much is certain. Now, as to the *manner* of death, my good friend, well, that's something else.'

'If your next word is suicide, I'm handing in my warrant card.'

'Sadly, I won't be sparing the Met from any lawsuits.' Pratt stood up again. 'What I'm trying to figure out is whether it's an accidental death from drug abuse.'

'Don't follow.'

'I mean, she took the drugs and some as-yet-unknown lover tied her down as they were partaking in some edge play. A cheeky bit of chemsex going too far.'

'Taking ecstasy and having sex?'

Pratt gave a nod, then tapped Gayle's cranium. 'The issue with that theory is we have a blow on the head here. It looks very much like someone attacked her and subdued her. Tied her up. And drugged her. Her blood toxicology shows rat poison, caffeine, all the usual crap, but also a huge amount of MDMA. A very high dose.'

Fenchurch took out the Blockchain pill Mulkalwar had given him. 'Like this?'

Pratt was transfixed by it. 'Precisely.'

'So someone stuck a pill down her throat, enough to kill her, then she overdosed, slipped into a coma and died of fluid on the lungs?'

Pratt clicked his fingers and pointed at Fenchurch. 'Correct! Worse ways to go.' He stared into space, then chuckled. 'In a way, whoever did this killed her with kindness.'

'Jesus, William.'

'It fits, though, doesn't it? Tie someone up, pop some of these little babies down her throat.' Pratt held up the pill and clicked his tongue a few times. 'Working it back, my calculations indicate a single twelve-hundred-milligram dose of MDMA.'

'That's a lot.'

'A heck of a lot. The strongest we used to see was the so-called UPS pills at two seventy-eight. Killed a few inexperienced clubbers. Then Burger King came in at the three hundred mark.'

'And Blockchain?'

'Four hundred milligrams per tablet, my friend.' Pratt seemed to shudder. 'Gayle had three. Enough to kill an elephant.'

Jesus. Three super-strong pills. Nobody would take that themselves. Whoever did this knew what they were doing.

And they meant to kill her.

Chapter Twenty

Fenchurch stepped out into the warm air. Smokers huddled outside the Lewisham police support building, soaking up the sun as they shortened their lifespans. Summer still lingered. Just. His old man would no doubt call it an Indian summer, like that meant anything.

He set off towards his car. His phone rang. He picked it up, sweat pricking his spine. Mulholland. 'Dawn.'

'You called me?'

'And I left a voicemail, if you'd care to listen.' Her pause showed she hadn't bothered. 'I'm just out of the PM. Pratt reckons someone had forced three Blockchain pills down her throat.'

'Not suicide?'

She's out of her depth. Clinging to a suicide so she can massage the figures. Doesn't want to face up to the truth.

'No.'

'What about an accident?'

'Dawn, she was tied up. How could it be an accident?'

'What did Pratt say?'

'He said, "They killed her with kindness."'

Mulholland laughed.

'It's not funny.'

'It's *so* Pratt, though.' A long pause. 'Okay, if he's saying that, then she was likely murdered. Whoever killed her didn't bludgeon her, they made her die laughing.'

Fenchurch unlocked his car and got in. Sat there watching the smokers joking like there weren't twenty or so dead bodies in the building behind them, murder victims like Gayle Fisher.

Maybe Pratt's right — whoever did this killed Gayle with love. The least-worst way to kill someone. Maybe. Ply them with enough strong drugs that they don't know where they are or what the hell's happening to them.

But who?

Someone whose love for Gayle had turned to hate, who wanted her to die, but couldn't stomach a knife to the guts or couldn't afford a hitman.

'I'm thinking through the suspects, Dawn. Steve Fisher has a strong motive — cuckolded by a young lover, then shamed in the press. Anyone who knew them would see the photo and know about Gayle's adultery. That's enough to drive most people to action.'

'Enough to kill her, though?'

'Don't know. Tying her up and chucking three Blockchain pills down her throat . . . It's cold-blooded, and Steve must've been angry. A knife frenzy, yes. This? Not so sure.'

'Okay, so means and opportunity?'

'His alibi's still wide open, mainly because we've got such patchy CCTV coverage. Said he was watching the football with his brother, but he left in time to have attacked Gayle and given her the Blockchain. As for means . . . A school teacher getting hold of super-strong ecstasy? Unlikely.'

'But possible.' Mulholland shut a door. The sound changed. *Probably in Docherty's office. Hard to think it's hers now.* 'What about Elliot Lynch as a suspect?'

Fenchurch thought it through, an ache in his gut telling him Elliot might be their prime suspect. 'He had the means. He almost died from taking a Blockchain last night.'

'What about opportunity?'

'Every time we've asked for an alibi, he's . . . refused.'

Squeaking, like she was writing on a whiteboard. 'An open book, then?'

'When we picked him up on Saturday, when he was coming down with serotonin syndrome, it was like he was still in love with Gayle. Kept saying she was his porcelain goddess.'

'That *bloody* song . . . My son can't stop listening to it.'

'Right. Well. In the state Elliot was in, there's no lying. He thought Gayle was still alive. He still loved her.'

'So slightly less likely than Steve.' More squeaking. 'Anyone else?'

'That's where I'm drawing a blank.' Fenchurch turned on the ignition and set off across the car park. 'Have you got hold of the drug squad yet?'

'I reached out, but I'm waiting for a call back.'

Take that as a no, then . . . Like 'reached out' means anything.

'Dawn, this is linked to their Blockchain investigation.'

'Operation Lydian.' The squeaking started again. 'The investigation into Blockchain. Bitcoin is a new currency. The Lydians were the first to mint coins.' She laughed. 'Anyway, what do you propose as next steps?'

Fenchurch gripped the steering wheel tight. 'I want to search both of their homes. We have enough for warrants.'

'Fine in principle, but the press are camped outside Elliot's home. We can't go in there all guns blazing. Am I clear?'

'Clear. I'll start with Steve, then.'

'I need to approve this.'

'No, Dawn, you don't. It'd be better if you backed me, though.'

She huffed. Sounded like she sat down at the desk. 'I've got a meeting with Julian in five minutes. Hold off on raiding anyone's home until you hear back from me.'

Fenchurch twisted his fingers round the wheel like it was her neck.

Another pair of smokers waddled out of the front door.

'Am I clear?'

'Crystal.' Fenchurch hit the end call button.

Way out of her depth. Drowning.

And he was late for Chloe.

———————

Fenchurch walked into the restaurant in Southwark, checking out each table. No sign of Chloe. He walked over to the poncho-wearing, handle-bar-moustached maître d'. 'Got a reservation. Fenchurch.'

'Over here. Oh.' He stopped by a table. Empty. 'Your, ah, lunch partner must've left, sir.'

'Right.' Fenchurch sat at the table and got out his phone. He dialled Chloe's number. Light streamed through the full-height windows. Absolute shithole of an area, but at least there was a decent burrito place.

Straight to voicemail.

Well played, you arsehole. You let her down and didn't even warn her.

Fingers dug into his shoulders from behind. 'You're late.'

'Chloe.' Fenchurch looked up, then let out his breath. 'Sorry I'm so late. Thought you'd left?'

'Had to go to the toilet.' She sat opposite. 'Mum said you're always late, but you only let her know when you won't make it. So I waited.'

'Even so, you don't deserve that.' Fenchurch picked up the menu. Didn't know what to say.

She took it off him. 'I've ordered for both of us. Steak chimichanga for you.'

'I wouldn't have gone for that, but . . . not had one in ages.' The waiter put two lemonades on the table. Fenchurch took a sip. Perfect mix of sour and sweet, with a minty tang. 'How was your morning?'

'Do you want me to list the aisles I stocked up or the customers I served?'

'Just asking if it was good?'

'It's fine. The work's shit, but the people I work with are a good laugh.'

Fenchurch shut his eyes. 'I'd kill for that.'

'Not a good day for you, then?'

'Just . . . tough. This case. I feel guilty even having lunch.'

'You need to eat, Dad.'

'I know, but . . .'

'What is the case?'

'I can't tell you.'

'Really? Because you kept trying to get me to help on that one last year.'

'And I shouldn't have done that, Chloe. I'm sorry.'

'You did what you had to. I wasn't easy to deal with.'

'It's a family trait.' Fenchurch took another sip of lemonade. 'I'm investigating a drugs case. Murder. Super-strong ecstasy.'

'Blockchain?'

'Jesus, Chloe.' Fenchurch's scalp prickled again, like someone was digging needles into his skin. All that time they'd missed, not having a firm enough hand on her, and now she was au fait with the latest killer drug? Shit. 'How do—'

'I read about it on Vice. Killed ten people in the last month.'

'Please tell me you've—'

'Jeez, calm down. I'd *never* take it. Never take any drugs.'

'That's a relief.' Fenchurch sighed. 'The number of drug dealers I've arrested over the years. You can't trust them.'

'But you trusted them enough when you were seventeen?'

'What?'

'Aunt Rosie said you were a party boy.'

'Christ. The mouth on her.' Fenchurch tried to hide his snarl. 'I took one pill, once. Ended up vomiting for hours. One of the worst nights of my life.'

Chloe picked at her straw. 'She's a bit of an arse, isn't she?'

'Rosie's okay. Just . . . I don't know. She had it harder than me. Your grandfather hasn't always been sun and light.'

She pinged the straw. 'That husband of hers . . . He's an idiot, Dad. No two ways about it.'

The waiter reappeared and set down their plates. Fenchurch had a mouthful of hot steak before he'd even asked if they wanted sauces. He shook his head as he took another bite. 'God, I'm starving.'

Chloe was chewing her chicken burrito. 'This is good.'

'Well ordered.' Fenchurch followed a mouthful with some more lemonade. 'How are you finding living back at our place?'

Chloe took her time chewing. 'I don't remember much from before. Bits here and there. The bathroom used to be turquoise, right?'

'Forgot about that.' Fenchurch chuckled. 'I spent a bank holiday weekend getting rid of that colour when you were seven. Hideous. Can still see it.'

'I remember the smell of pee in there.'

'That'll be your grandfather.' Fenchurch laughed. 'Always misses.'

'Gross.' She held her burrito over her mouth. 'How are *you* coping with having me back?'

'I love it.' He held her free hand. 'It's the best thing that's ever happened to us. It's like we never lost you.' He caught a flash of her scar, which sent waves of revulsion up his spine. 'Then I see that.'

'I'm not going to hide it, Dad.' She brushed a finger over it. 'I was so insecure about it at school. Now I want to own it. It's who I am.'

'That's a good way to be.' Fenchurch gave her hand a squeeze, then went back to his food.

'What are you up to after work?'

'Meeting Mum at the hospital.'

'I'm glad you're getting on well with her.'

'It's not easy, but I like her.'

'What's wrong?'

'Nothing with her, it's just . . . all the noise in my head, you know?'

'Oh, I know. Believe me.'

'It's like drums beating.'

'You've got that from me. It's not drums, it's an inner-ear problem. Stress makes it worse. I'm on pills to stop it.'

'You get it a lot?'

'All the bloody time.' Fenchurch finished his food. 'Work is usually my trigger. Sounds like John Bonham pounding away.'

'John who?'

'He was the drummer in Led Zeppelin. Do you have a trigger?'

'Pete.'

'Your boyfriend? Why?'

'I don't know.'

'Is it his age?'

'What?'

'Well, he's a lot older than you.'

'It's not that. Christ.'

'So what is it?'

'I don't know, Dad. It's just . . . Sometimes, I . . . There's a lot happened, you know? I feel turned inside out sometimes.'

'I get that.' He gave her a smile. 'Believe me, I really get that.'

Fenchurch got out of his car and checked his phone messages. Some garbled shit from Dad, hard to make head or tail of. Didn't look urgent.

'Hey!'

Fenchurch swung round, frowning.

Katerina was standing there, biting her lip. 'I asked for you at the desk, but they said you were out.'

Shit, I forgot.

Fenchurch moved towards her, trying to disarm her with a smile. 'You okay?'

She gave a slight shrug. Sucked on her hair like she was seven.

And Liam's seeing her?

'I couldn't sleep last night. Kept seeing Mrs Fisher's dead body. Can't believe she's gone.'

Fenchurch nodded. 'Come on, let's go up to my office. Get you a cup of tea.'

'I don't like tea.'

'Coffee, then?'

Another shrug. She wasn't moving.

'Last night, you said Mrs Fisher was helping you out?' Fenchurch leaned back against his car. 'I take it you were close?'

'She was the best.' Katerina smiled like she'd heard there was a coming rapture and she was on the spaceship with all the true believers. 'I don't know what your school was like, but I'm not that popular there. And when you're not popular, you get picked on.'

'I went to a similar school, just down the road.'

'Didn't know that.'

'Why would you?'

Yet another shrug. 'I've read a lot about you. Your situation. They didn't mention you were an East End boy.'

'With a name like mine?'

'Still. Mrs Fisher knew what the bullying is like. She helped me deal with it. Listened to me. Understood. Tried to stop it, but it's just impossible, you know?'

'And you've got nobody to talk to, right?'

'Right.' She bit her lip again. 'I'd like to talk to you.'

'Look, I understand, but . . . I'm leading a murder inquiry. I can recommend a counsellor. He's good.'

'Did that help you?'

'A lot. Took a while for me to open up. That's the hard part.'

'Was that about your daughter?'

144

'It was with her. You know, I wish I'd spoken to Paddy before. Would've made the whole thing easier.'

'But you're reunited with her, aren't you?'

'She's living with us again. It's hard but good.'

'I'd love to meet her. Chloe.'

Fenchurch swallowed. 'That's not appropriate.'

'Oh, okay.' She tore at her lip again. 'Sorry.'

'Look. I have to keep my private life private. I worry about who knows things about me.'

'Because that's how they kidnapped her?'

'I thought it might've been. It wasn't, but . . .'

Fenchurch's phone blasted out. Reed. 'Sorry, I've got to take this.' He walked off.

'Wait.'

Fenchurch stopped, holding his phone out. 'What?'

'I don't know if this is any use or not. On Friday night, I saw Steve Fisher get out of a cab outside the hotel. Thought you should know.'

Fenchurch stared hard at her. Saw the truth in her eyes.

If Steve Fisher got in a taxi on Friday night . . . He's been lying to us. His alibi is bullshit.

And he had ample opportunity to murder his wife.

Chapter Twenty-One

L et me get this straight. He told us he went back here—' Fenchurch pointed at John Fisher's flat on the laptop screen. '—but he never showed up?'

'He did, but at ten fifty, sir.' Bridge circled the time. 'Just before his brother got back.' She wound the CCTV on to show John Fisher walking down the road, stuffing chips in his mouth. He dropped one and stopped, staring at it like he was going to pick it up and eat it.

Then Bridge switched to another view: outside the Prospect of Whitby pub. Steve Fisher stepped on to the street to hail a black cab. 'That cab's heading towards the City.'

And towards the Bennaceur. Fenchurch mulled it over. *Definite progress and enough to shunt Steve into pole position, but still nothing concrete.* 'What about near the hotel?'

'Just that bloke doing . . . something.' Bridge brought up a still of the mystery man. 'Whatever it is.'

'Could be Steve, guv.' Reed tapped the screen, then frowned at Fenchurch. 'Where did this hunch come from?'

'Katerina Raptis.'

'When did you speak to her?'

'She was outside the station, hanging around like a stray cat.' Fenchurch stared at the screen again. '*Is* it him? I was expecting the cab to drop him off.'

'That's the problem, guv.' Reed shot Bridge a glare. 'Someone in Tower Hamlets Council got wind of the back channel Lisa was using to get street CCTV. Said it should come through from operational command.'

Fenchurch groaned. *Another admin nightmare.* 'What do you need me to do?'

Reed passed him a piece of paper. A name and a number with a Limehouse area code. 'If you wouldn't mind?'

Fenchurch dialled the number and walked off. 'Is that Mohammed Singh?'

'Speaking.' A rasping yawn.

'This is DI Fenchurch of the Met's Major Investigation Team.'

'Oh, okay. How can I—'

'One of my officers needs access to the CCTV cameras on the Minories.'

'Well, *she* shouldn't have been using that login.'

'I can only apologise. Any chance you can issue a new one?'

'Not until tomorrow.'

'This is important. I'm running a murder investigation and that evidence is crucial.'

'I don't have the authority to—'

'What's stopping her using the old login until you sort your side out?'

Singh paused. Fenchurch could make out him licking his lips. '*She* has committed a criminal offence by using someone else's credentials to access the central London CCTV network.'

'Listen, mate, we really need to access those cameras, so if you want me to have a word with your superiors?'

'That's not going to wash, sir.'

'You want to speak to my victim's husband and explain to him why we can't let him out of custody because you won't let us verify his alibi?'

Singh sighed. Then an even longer pause. 'That's it reinstated.' Didn't even hear him typing. 'But I expect DC Bridge to fill out a form tomorrow and we can do this properly.'

'Thanks for your—' Fenchurch had been cut off. *Cheeky bastard.* He walked back to Reed and Bridge. 'Well, I've sorted him out for now. Sounds like the sort of arsehole who doesn't forget stuff, you know? Make sure you apply for a new login first thing tomorrow, Lisa. Okay?'

'I did it two months ago.' Bridge was focused on her laptop. 'I phone him every day and he does nothing.'

'Then find out who his boss is and I'll speak to them.' Fenchurch sat down with another groan. 'Are we back in business?'

'Oooh.' Bridge clicked on a link. 'Yup.' The screen filled with footage of a taxi pulling up just down the street from the Third Planet and the Hotel Bennaceur's separate entrance. 'That's the cab Steve hailed in Wapping.'

The cab drove off the far side of the frame. No sign of Steve.

'Shit.' She smacked her keyboard and scowled at the screen. 'Sorry, sir.'

'That's it? We just see the cab outside the hotel?'

'Afraid so.' Bridge wound back until the cab reappeared, then flicked around a few other viewpoints. 'None of the cameras on that street point at the hotel or the bar.'

Fenchurch stood up tall and stretched out. 'We need to find that taxi driver.'

Bridge tapped at her keyboard. 'I've got his home address?'

'We're not keeping you, are we?'

'You are, as it happens.' Sid Milford shot Fenchurch a glare. Dark-orange skin, but more from being outside all day than lying in a tanning bed. Dressed in salmon Pringle and casual slacks, he stood behind the wooden bar in his living room, stocked with vodka, gin and whisky optics. Classy. Milford sprayed some lemonade into a glass and took a sip. 'Start my shift in twenty minutes.' He waved at the front window, towards a gleaming black cab. 'Got a transfer from Shoreditch to Gatwick. Be a nightmare this time on a Sunday.'

'We'll try not to keep you.' Fenchurch showed a photo of Steve Fisher. 'Recognise this man?'

Milford took the image and stared hard at it. 'Should I?'

'You collected him outside a pub on Friday night.'

'The Prospect of Whitby in Wapping.' Milford tapped the photo off the bar top. 'Lovely little boozer. The scampi's to die for.'

'So you recognise him?'

'Never forget a face.' Milford topped up his lemonade then washed down some ibuprofen from a large tub. 'My wife won't let me touch scampi, says it's baby lobsters and they boil them alive or some shit like that. I don't believe it but there's no telling her. So I sneak in there every so often, try and keep schtum. And that's when I picked up that geezer.'

A woman appeared at the door. Tight leopard-skin dress. Late twenties. Thai or Vietnamese, probably came out of a catalogue. 'Milfy, did you get the rice milk?'

'It's in the cupboard, love.' He waited for her to leave, then leaned on his bar top like he was running a village pub somewhere in rural England. 'Everyone calls me Milfy. Even though it's something to do with porn these days.'

'So where did you take this guy?'

'Now that I can't remember.' Another spray of lemonade. 'Guy looked crazy, though. Wild-eyed and all that. If you told me he shot up a McDonald's, I'd believe you. Full-on Millwall, mate.' He cackled. 'Full-on Millwall.'

'He told us he was dropped off in Shadwell.'

'Lying bastard!'

'Milfy, language!' Milford's wife leaned in the doorway, eating cereal from a navy bowl.

'Sorry, love.' Milford studied the photo again. 'I dropped him off on the Minories.'

'Sure about that?'

'Not far from that hotel, the posh one where some girl got killed.' Milford frowned. 'This is about that, isn't it? Oh, come on, mate! I've gotta get to Gatwick!'

Fenchurch checked with Reed, got a shrug back. 'As soon as you've dropped them off, I need you straight into Leman Street, okay? Ask for DS Uzma Ashkani.'

'I might have another fare.'

'No, you're giving your statement.' Fenchurch took the photo from him. 'It was definitely him?'

'Clear as day, mate.' Milford slurped his lemonade. 'I never forget a face.'

'Don't forget to come in.' Fenchurch nodded at Reed. 'Come on, Kay.' He led her out on to the street. 'Time to bring Steve Fisher in for an interview.'

Reed shut the door. 'You don't want to search his house?'

Fenchurch stopped by the taxi and looked back through the window, where Milford was getting an earful from his wife. 'I doubt it'll play well.'

'Play well? Christ, you're sounding like Loftus.'

'I mean it, Kay. Raiding the house of a grieving widower isn't good form. Let's interview him and if he trips up, we arrest him and we've got every right to search his home.'

———

'Can I get a cup of tea?' Steve Fisher sat in interview room three, nibbling at his nails. 'Please?'

At least he's not asking for a lawyer. Fenchurch sat next to Reed and motioned for her to take the lead.

'You don't want the tea here, sir.' Reed smiled. 'Just need to ask a few questions, if you don't mind?'

Steve looked like he could get up at any minute.

'On Friday, you said you went back to your brother's flat after watching football in the pub.'

'That's right.'

'How did you get back?'

'Think I walked.'

'Think?'

Steve shrugged. 'I walked.'

'You didn't get in a cab?'

'What?'

'This is outside the pub.' Reed held out a still. 'And this is you, isn't it?'

Steve took it off her and stared at it like it was the Bible code. 'It's me, but . . .' He flung it back at her, sending it skittering over the table. 'You've been spying on me?'

'We're validating your alibi.'

Steve screwed up his face. 'You can't think I killed Gayle!'

'Of course we can.' Reed held up the photo again. 'Where did you get the taxi to?'

'John's flat. Like I told you . . .'

'Have you got a receipt?'

'For a taxi?'

'Sir, this is a chance for you to change your story, okay?' Reed tapped the recorder. 'We're on the record here.'

'Like I told you, I went back to John's. And I . . . just sat there and cried.'

Reed put the photo away. 'Did Gayle ever take drugs?'

'Drugs? What are you talking about?'

151

'Ecstasy, in particular.'

Steve shot to his feet, fists clenched.

'You might know it as MDMA.'

'She . . . she's a teacher. She doesn't take *drugs*.'

'Has she ever?'

Steve sank back into his seat. 'Look, the only time I can think of is when we were students at Durham. Had a few nights out in Newcastle.' He swallowed hard, caressing his bobbing Adam's apple. 'We . . . took an E at this club down by the riverside. Neither of us particularly enjoyed it. Still dancing at midday, no idea where we were. You know how it is.'

'I'm a police officer, so I don't.' Reed folded her arms. 'Sorry.'

Fenchurch let out a shallow breath. *Glad he didn't ask me.*

'This was seven, eight years ago. We're teachers now. Can't do that sort of shit any more.' Steve massaged his eyes. 'Gayle . . .'

Reed tapped her foot, waiting for him to stop. 'That was the only time?'

'I can't account for her every waking moment, but it's the only time we took anything together.'

'She never smoked a joint or—'

'Who do you think she was?'

'A human being. People need to relieve stress.'

Steve bit his lip, his gaze shooting between them. 'Look, a few weeks ago Gayle was out with the Friday club from the school. I didn't go, went to the England game with my brother. Got back home about half ten, but no sign of Gayle. I went to bed and woke up about midnight. Still no sign of her. I texted her, but her phone was off. I tried her friends but they weren't picking up. So I started looking for any sign of where she'd gone.' Another deep swallow. 'In one of her bags in her wardrobe, this Louis Vuitton knock-off we got in Tenerife last year . . . I found a load of pills.'

Fenchurch scowled at him. 'What did these pills look like?'

'White, stamped with, I dunno. Like a letter B? But it was like a currency.'

'I know.' Fenchurch felt a spear in his gut.

Blockchain.

Time to accelerate the search.

Fenchurch stood outside the house, dial tone burning his ears. He held the warrant in his hands, could almost feel the favours he'd had to call in from the judge weighing down his shoulders.

The curtains across the road twitched and he waved at Bethany's flat. Almost saw her scowling through the gloom.

He got through to Mulholland's voicemail. 'Dawn, it's Simon. Just to let you know that, based on intelligence received by Steven Fisher, I am authorising a search of his and Gayle's home. We believe she might have had her own supply of drugs. Possibly Blockchain.' He ended the call and pocketed the phone.

Reed walked over to Fenchurch and gave a conspiratorial grin. 'You think Mulholland's going to be happy with us searching?'

'She's not answering her calls, so I'm not waiting for her.' Fenchurch leaned back against the car and checked his watch. 'Besides, if we find it, maybe it gives some credence to the suicide theory she's clinging to. Anyway, there's no press here, so it should be fine.'

A squad car pulled up and a pair of uniforms got out. Male and female.

Fenchurch sidled over, Reed following close behind. 'Okay, I want a nice, orderly search here. Nothing moved that can't be put back where you got it. Am I clear?' He got two nods back. 'We're looking for drugs, especially those marked with a Bitcoin symbol. Any questions?'

The male PC stuck up his hand, a cheeky grin on his face. 'Shouldn't we have a sniffer dog, sir?'

'Happy for you to get down on all fours, Constable.'

'Right, sir. Sorry, sir.'

'They're all busy on Operation Lydian, if you must know. We're getting in now rather than waiting for the sniffer team.' Fenchurch pointed at Reed. 'Follow DS Reed's lead, okay?'

She walked over to the door and tried Steve's keys. Took a few goes before she found the right one and opened the door.

Nice place inside, well decorated. Smelled fresh and clean, like they got new flowers every day.

'DI Fenchurch and I will take upstairs, okay?' Reed pointed at the cheeky sod. 'Stay by the door.' Then she started up the stairs.

'Sorry about Brian, sir, he's just new.'

Fenchurch flashed a grin at the female PC as he followed Reed up. 'I was like that when I started.'

Reed opened the bedroom door. Looked like a spare room, a single bed freshly made up. Wardrobes either side of the window, one twice the size of the other.

'Got to be in here.' Fenchurch went over to the bigger one. Shoes, watches, shirts and jeans. At least three generations of games consoles and tons of games, mostly still packaged. Steve's, pretty obviously.

'Guv.' Reed was kneeling in front of the other wardrobe. 'Got it.' She held a clutch bag in her gloved fingers. Blue with a pearled handle, the LV logo in silver. 'You'd think this was the real deal.'

'Couldn't tell you what a real one was like.' Fenchurch took it off her and looked inside. A baggie lay at the bottom, four little white pills rattling around. He picked it up. 'Looks like Blockchain, all right.'

Thumping came from downstairs. 'Everybody out!'

'What the hell?' Fenchurch tossed the bag to Reed and charged out into the hall. More thudding downstairs. He looked over the banister and groaned.

'Guv.' Jon Nelson stood at the bottom, sucking on his vape stick. 'You got a warrant for this search?'

'Course I do.' Fenchurch stomped down the stairs and passed it to him.

Nelson took a look at it. 'Well, I'm afraid that Superintendent Loftus has given my team priority in enacting it.' He gave a shrug. 'Sorry, but Operation Lydian trumps your case.'

Chapter Twenty-Two

Out on the street, Fenchurch hit redial. Got Mulholland's voice-mail. *Hard to remember a time when she answered my calls.* 'Dawn, it's urgent. Call me now.' He stuffed his phone away, scowling across the road.

Nelson was on his mobile, sucking his vape stick between laughs. He'd lost weight, looked back to his best. *What shagging a young DC at his age does for the waistline . . .* He put his phone away and nodded at Fenchurch, then started chatting to Reed.

Fenchurch walked over. 'Sergeant, you care to tell me what's going on here?'

Nelson waved at Reed. 'Kay?'

'Why are you asking her, Jon?'

'Because she's a Sergeant.' Nelson grinned. 'I'm an Acting DI.'

'I hadn't heard.'

'No, just like you don't get my texts about the broken boiler in your flat.'

'I told you, Jon. Get it fixed and I'll square you up.' Fenchurch scowled. 'How's Operation Lydian, then?'

'Operation Dildo, more like. Total shambles, but what do you expect?' Nelson bared his teeth. 'And it's not all sexy dawn raids, like you'd think. There's this guy, Coldcut, supposed to be behind the Blockchain, but we can't get close. They've got me investigating murders. Four undercover cops.'

'Shit.'

'Yeah, shit. Still, we took down Younis and, well, they think I'm the golden boy. Not often someone brings down a drug lord like that.'

'That's all gone quiet.'

'It's tied together, guv. We're still prosecuting him, but he's linked to Coldcut, we think. Geezer keeps teasing us, but sod it, it's getting to the point where we're just going to do him, you know?'

'I know.' Fenchurch started pacing around. 'How did you find out about this?'

'My new gaffer got a call.'

'Bloody Mulholland. Can't bring herself to answer my calls but she can go behind my back to the drug squad.'

'It was Loftus, actually.' Nelson held out his hands. 'What's your interest?'

'Someone's used Blockchain as a murder weapon. Our victim had three in her bloodstream. And I've seen what one can do.'

'Elliot Lynch, yeah?'

'Right.' Fenchurch handed him the evidence bag containing the Blockchain and the fake Louis Vuitton. 'Found that inside.'

'I can get it processed in an hour, if you want.'

'Please.'

'Heard that your victim was a teacher at Shadwell?'

'English.'

'I went there. My brother, too.' Nelson gave a dark look. 'Bad, bad place.' His expression lightened. 'Anyway, I'll get this lot checked. See you around.' He jogged off towards a female detective and handed the bag to her.

Reed watched him go, shaking her head slowly. 'Does that mean we've lost this case, guv?'

'Far from it.' Fenchurch started off towards their pool car. 'Jon's looking at strategic stuff. Bringing down dealers and suppliers. Whoever's making this shit or bringing it into the country.' He unlocked the car and got in. 'We're the other side of the coin.'

'So, what next?' Reed did up her seatbelt. 'As it stands, Steve found some pills in Gayle's bag a couple of weeks ago. Think she got them from Elliot?'

'Or Steve put them there.' Fenchurch put the key in the ignition. 'Steve's a suspect, but so's Elliot.' He looked around the street. 'If Gayle Fisher was out with someone that night, it was probably Elliot. Either way, we know he had Blockchain. Let's see if he's the source.'

'Out of the way!' Fenchurch pushed through the press scrum, warrant card out, leading Reed and their pair of uniforms through the crowd, then up the garden path.

'Only ever seen this sort of thing on TV.' Reed stopped by the door, eyes wide. She knocked on it and waited. 'Think they'll cause us hassle?'

'Undoubtedly.' Fenchurch spotted Liam near the back, talking with a tall skinhead. 'It's almost like they want us to—'

'What's going on now?' Derek Lynch stood in the doorway, glaring at them. 'You? Not had enough of us, eh? You don't fancy getting that lot to clear off, do you?'

Fenchurch showed his search warrant. 'We need access to your property, Mr Lynch.'

'On what grounds?'

'I'd appreciate it if you could just let us get on with it.'

Derek rummaged in his pocket for his phone. Couldn't stop Reed and the two uniforms barging inside. 'I'm calling Ben Maxfield about this!'

'Very pleased for you, sir.' Fenchurch entered the house. Thumping and clomping came from upstairs already.

Derek hit a button on his phone and put it to his ear.

'Stop!' Elliot was at the top of the stairs, going spare at the cheeky uniform. Fenchurch couldn't believe they'd let him go home so soon, but there he was. 'You've no right to do that!' Cheeky grabbed him in an armbar and led him downstairs.

'What's going on?' Derek got in Cheeky's face, still on the phone, still a foot too short to intimidate a police officer. 'You let go of my boy now!'

'Sir.' Fenchurch dragged Derek away from his son. 'I need you to—'

'He's here now, Ben!' Derek held up the phone. 'He wants to speak to you.'

Fenchurch took the phone and put it on speaker.

'This is a really, really—'

'Mr Maxfield, we have a search warrant. Goodbye.' Fenchurch hung up and gave Derek his phone back.

'How dare you?' Derek stared at his mobile like Fenchurch hadn't just done that. 'You come into my house and start throwing things around. Then you hang up *my* phone!?'

'Sir, I need you to calm down.'

Something cracked against Fenchurch's bad knee. Pain seared up the back, bit at the front and he toppled over.

'You want some, do you?' Elliot stood over him, ready to fight. 'You thick bastard!'

Fenchurch reached up and grabbed his hand, twisted it into a lock and pulled Elliot down. He pushed him over, face down. 'That's not a very smart thing to do, son.'

Face on the wooden floor, Elliot just laughed at him.

Fenchurch helped him to stand. 'What's so funny?'

Just made the laughing worse.

'Elliot, this is a murder case.'

Much worse.

Fenchurch pushed him towards Cheeky. 'Take this little punk down the station.'

'This is horse shit!' Derek had his phone to his ear again. 'Mr Maxfield's got a lawyer on his way!'

'Can you tell him to get that lawyer to meet us at Leman Street?' Fenchurch waved at Cheeky to take Elliot away. 'And tell Mr Maxfield I appreciate his efforts. Usually takes a few hours for them to turn up for an interview.'

'You're a cheeky, cheeky bas—'

'Guv!' Reed was at the top of the stairs, holding an evidence bag in her gloved hands. 'I've found drugs under his bed.'

Fenchurch met her halfway up and grabbed the bag. At least thirty Blockchain pills.

'And a big chunk of coke.' Reed held up another bag. 'At least a hundred grams, I'd say.'

Elliot slumped back against the wall. 'Ah, bollocks.'

Chapter Twenty-Three

'Still no sign of Mulholland?' Fenchurch sighed. The lights were on the blink in the corridor outside the interview rooms. 'Are her and Loftus on a spa break or something?'

'Your guess is as good as mine, guv.' Reed opened the door and peered in at Elliot. He caught sight of them and started laughing again. She shut it and leaned against it. 'Any sign of—'

'Well, well, well.' Anna Xiang stood behind them swinging her briefcase, full of papers for the evil scumbags she defended. Despite the name, she looked about as Chinese as Fenchurch. 'I should've known by the nature of the arrest that I'd be dealing with you, Inspector.'

'You know you're only really supposed to defend innocent people, not drug dealers and brutal rapists.'

'And what makes you—' Xiang huffed out a sigh. 'Never mind. Just so's you know, I shall forego a private session with my client before the interview.'

'Sure about that?'

'He's innocent and has nothing to hide.'

'Meaning that you've already coached him.'

'Never change, Fenchurch.' Xiang entered the room, strutting on her kitten heels. She dumped her briefcase on the table and started chatting to Elliot, just out of earshot.

'Kay, start the tape.' Fenchurch walked off, phone to his ear.

Mulholland bounced his call his time.

Bloody hell.

So he sent her a text: DAWN — IT'S URGENT.

He stormed into the room and stayed standing by the door. 'Mr Lynch, you know that we found a large quantity of drugs in your house. Care to explain that?'

'No comment.'

Here we bloody go. Definitely schooled.

'One hundred and twenty grams of street cocaine. Thirty-four MDMA pills. Now.' Fenchurch walked over and crouched next to Elliot. 'The MDMA — ecstasy, X, E, call it what you want — is stamped with a Bitcoin logo.' He held up an evidence bag containing one of the pills. 'These have been turning up all over London. They're called Blockchain. And they're a killer. Of course, you almost discovered that yourself last night, didn't you? Almost died after you took one.'

'No comment.'

'Elliot, you know what one can do. Someone gave Gayle Fisher three of them.'

'Shit.'

A slip, however minor.

'Three pills is a twelve-hundred-milligram dose. That's making sure. Did you give her it?'

'No comment.'

'Your lawyer's got you on a tight lead, hasn't she?' Fenchurch got up and started pacing the room. 'It beats you laughing at me, I suppose. What's that about?'

Elliot smirked at him. 'No comment.'

'This is a murder case. You're looking at over twenty years inside. And all those drugs we found in your room, that's at least another five, ten. On top.'

'Those drugs were planted in my client's property.'

Fenchurch stopped by Xiang and stared at her. 'I've got the discovery on body-worn video camera.'

'What about footage of your officer planting it?'

'These are your client's drugs.'

'Are they? Because you've not proven that. Where did he get them from?'

'He took one of them himself.'

'One of those very drugs? Same batch? You're positive?'

Fenchurch ignored her and focused on Elliot. 'Someone tied Gayle Fisher down and gave her three of them.'

Elliot locked eyes with Fenchurch. He brushed a tear from his eye.

'You loved her, didn't you? Your porcelain goddess, right?'

He wiped at more tears.

'Did you tie her down, Elliot? Did you give her the drugs?'

He shook his head at Fenchurch.

'Instead of giving me an alibi for Friday, you've laughed at me. You clearly think it's funny, but I don't care why you're doing it. There's just too much connecting you to Gayle, isn't there? Finding these drugs in your room and refusing to give us an alibi. Makes me think—'

'Football!' Elliot hit his fist off the desk. 'I was playing football.'

Xiang let out a sigh.

'I was playing for Shadwell United Under Eighteens.' Elliot folded his arms. 'Quarter to eight kick-off. You can work out the rest, can't you?'

'Inspector, my client has given you an alibi — I suggest you verify it.'

'Bloody Shadwell.' Fenchurch double-parked outside the football stadium and got out. The street was rammed with cars, even parking on the school playing fields over the road. Shouting came from inside the ground. The solid boot of a football. He led Uzma towards the stadium, a proper old-school job. Wood and corrugated iron. Turnstiles designed for men's physiques in the fifties, before the advent of beer bellies and saddlebags. He walked up to the door and knocked. 'Every time this lot play West Ham or Millwall, I swear it's like World War Three.'

'Don't have to tell me.' Uzma pouted as she applied some more lipstick. 'Back in uniform, I had to police an FA Cup third-round match here between Shadwell and West Ham. The Shadwell crew blocked off the DLR station.'

A club official came through the door, blazer and comb-over. 'We're a bit busy just now.'

'Police.' Fenchurch got out his warrant card. Sounded like someone scored. From the groans and swearing, it wasn't Shadwell. 'Thought you were playing yesterday?'

'Reserves today. Portsmouth are tearing us apart.'

'I need to speak to whoever was in charge of Friday night's match.'

'Under Eighteens.' The blazer sniffed, then thumbed behind him. 'Follow me.'

Down in the dark recesses of the stadium, the walls were bare concrete blocks, the floor dirty lino. The place had that stink of mud mixed with the bittersweet tang of Ralgex. The blazer knocked on a door. 'Jack?'

'Referee!' Dirty Cockney accent shouting inside. 'He was a mile offside!'

The blazer opened the door. 'Jack, it's the police for you.'

A tiny little office, football playing on two giant screens on the wall. Chelsea–West Brom in glorious HD on the left. Shadwell Reserves played Portsmouth Reserves on a dodgy CCTV feed on the right, shot from high up in the main stand, half the pitch out of shot, the players like ants.

Jack spun round on his office chair and scowled at them. His hair flopped down. Mid-forties if a day and had the look of a shagger gone to seed, his face bearing the brunt of his youthful exertions. 'What?'

'Police, sir.' Uzma held out her ID. 'Need a word.'

Panic filled Jack's eyes, darting around like he was going to run. Looked fit enough to be a bastard to catch. 'What's this about, darling?'

'Friday night.'

Jack let out a sigh. 'Come on, then. Cheers, Wilbur.' He waved at the blazer, then cleared some of the shit off his desk. No computer, but loads of notepads and DVD cases. Ten bottles of red wine, one uncorked and breathing. His glass was ringed with dark red, wet like he'd just finished a bottle. 'Don't mind if I keep an eye on this, do you? Reserves playing upstairs but I've got a touchline ban.'

Uzma raised her eyebrows. 'What did you do?'

'Told the ref a few home truths.' Another sniff. 'Don't mind if I keep it on, love?'

'Not a problem, sir.'

Jack sat back, eyes locked on the TV. 'Good, good.'

Fenchurch sat in his eyeline, blocking the Chelsea match. 'I know you from somewhere, just can't place it.'

'Jack Walsh.' He held out a hand, adjusting his position so he could see the match again. 'I played for Charlton in the late nineties.'

'That'll be it.' Fenchurch scooted over to block him again. 'Saw you against West Ham a couple of times.'

'Scored a hat-trick against that shower. March 1998. Only hat-trick I ever scored in the top-flight. Fell out with the boss not long after, got loaned out here, they sold me at the end of the season and I've been stuck ever since. Player, coach and now manager.'

'Must be busy.' Uzma pressed her notebook flat on the desk. 'The bloke upstairs said you were in charge of Friday night's match?'

'For my sins.'

'That was Under Eighteens, though, right?'

'Right. The manager here covers a multitude of sins. Only thing I don't manage is the Ladies' team.' Jack waved a hand at the screen. 'I make the bleeding tea in the morning for the lads.'

'We need to ask you about Elliot Lynch.'

'Stupid bastard.' Walsh glowered. 'Got a call from my mate over at Millwall. Elliot didn't turn up for his trial today. Kid's on his last chance of making it as a pro, otherwise he'll end up stuck down here in the non-league. Not enough money to live off, I tell you. Trouble is, he's good enough to make me think of moving him up to the seniors. Tell you, he'd make a difference to the Reserves, if he could stay on the pitch.'

'What do you mean by that?'

'He's a walking red card, that lad.' Walsh followed an attack on the screen then settled back in his seat and wrote something in a notebook. 'I mean, fair enough if you leather someone and break a bone. I can stand by that. But he's doing cheeky little stamps here and there.' Rage flared across his lips. 'Caught him slapping a left-back two weeks ago. *Slapping?* What's that going to achieve? I keep telling him, if you're going to hurt someone, *hurt* them.'

Uzma was keeping her patience, a polite smile on her lips. 'And Elliot played on Friday?'

'He played.' Eyes locked on the screen, the rage building. 'Had to sub him off after thirty minutes. My stupid prick of a goalkeeper got sent off. The way he was playing, Elliot was going to be next so I took him off to bring on my sub goalie. Kid did well, too. Saved a pen in the second half and that was after he took a hefty whack in the cobblers.'

'I take it Elliot stayed around after he was subbed?'

'Do me a favour.' Jack poured out some red wine into his glass and sniffed it. 'Soon as the board went up with his number, he was off down the tunnel. Got changed, then pissed off with his mate, my stupid prick of a goalkeeper.' He sipped the wine and sat back, clutching the glass. 'That's the trouble with Elliot. Thinks he's already made it. Much more interested in drinking and partying than playing football. Pair of them spend their bloody wages on booze, when they should be knuckling down.' A deeper glug of wine. 'Him and Ollie, the bloody pair of them.'

'Did you say "Ollie"?'

'Yeah. Stupid prick went flying at the opposition centre forward, arms out. Poleaxed the poor bastard, like Schumacher in '82 except he didn't put the lad in a coma. Ollie's a big unit.' Another sip of wine, then he reached for the bottle. 'Do you want a glass?'

'We're good, thanks.' Uzma rolled her eyes. 'We could do with speaking to this friend.'

'Oliver Muscat-Smith. Think I've got his—'

'He's on our radar.' Fenchurch played it through. *Elliot's mate is the barman at the hotel. Does that give him an opportunity?* 'Any idea where they went?'

'Oh yeah. The bar in that bloody hotel on the Minor—' Walsh cut off.

'Which one? The Bennaceur?'

'Maybe.' Walsh shrugged. 'You know kids, though. So bloody fickle. Could be anywhere. Hackney, Shoreditch, Brixton, you name it.'

'Why did you cut off?'

'Just didn't want you going to the wrong place, that's all.'

Guy's hiding something. But what?

Doesn't matter. Nail down Elliot's movements as a priority.

Chapter Twenty-Four

The Muscats lived in a square box at the arse end of Shadwell. Not far from the school and the football stadium. A small front garden, well tended, but just not much of it. Even though it was still afternoon, a sodium streetlight flickered outside.

Fenchurch got out of the car first. 'You lead here, okay?'

'I know what I'm doing.' Uzma marched up the path, a spring in her step. She thumped the door and waited for Fenchurch to join her. 'That guy . . .'

'Footballers live in a different world from the rest of us.' Fenchurch peered through the window. A kitchen, the counters covered in plates and bowls. 'I pay a small fortune for the privilege of watching West Ham getting battered every fortnight, but—'

The door opened and Oliver Muscat-Smith blinked out at them. He seemed to relax when he saw who it was, his scowl fading. 'My old man's at work.'

Uzma nudged a foot in the doorway. 'It's you we want to speak to.'

'Come in, then.' Oliver stooped as he led through the door. 'Have a seat.'

Fenchurch sat in a nice comfy chair by the window. A bulky TV in the corner of the living room, hooked up to a stack of games consoles of varying vintages. The fan on one sounded like a jet engine taking off. The place had the look of a bachelor pad — the Smith in Oliver's surname was long gone.

Uzma stayed by the door, gesturing for Oliver to sit on the green sofa, waiting until he complied. 'A little birdie tells me you were a naughty boy on Friday night.'

'What?' Oliver's eyes shot between them. Then he let out a breath. 'You mean getting sent off, don't you?'

'Is there another way you've been naughty?'

'Not like I get much of a chance.' Oliver took another deep breath, slower, puffing up his cheeks. 'That clown Walsh told you, right?'

'Had a thing or two to say, yeah.' Uzma got out her notebook and read down a page. 'Said you got sent off after half an hour.'

'That ref was a useless prick. It was a fifty-fifty. Their striker went down like a sack of spuds. Total joke.'

'Did you have a nice long bath afterwards?'

Oliver put his feet up on the coffee table, knocking a pair of PlayStation controllers on to the floor. 'You fantasising about me or something?'

'Just like to know what happened.' Uzma was blushing. 'That's all.'

'I'd just got in the shower when Elliot comes in. Walsh had subbed him off.' Oliver leaned over and picked up the controllers with his long arms. 'Then we started wanking each other off.' He shook his head. 'Who do you think I am?'

Uzma's blushing got worse, but she was otherwise keeping her cool. 'You didn't hang around to support your teammates?'

'Bugger that. Under Eighteens, man. I'm doing them a favour.' Oliver hugged his legs tight. 'I'm nineteen in February. I should be in the first team. Our first-choice keeper's *forty*. Swear he weighs forty stone, too. Walsh is holding me back, for some reason.'

Try focusing on your attitude first, son . . .

'The guy's a dick. Said I could make it pro, but he's keeping me in the Under Eighteens. Just to mess with me, you know? Swear we're all praying that knobber gets caught fiddling the Under Sixteens.'

Uzma perked up. 'Is that likely?'

'Nah, just a forlorn hope.' Oliver stood up and walked over to the sideboard. Picked up a ship in a bottle. No doubt his old man had spent ages putting it together while his son played on his games consoles. 'Me and Elliot went into town. Had a few beers, then we hit a club in Hackney.'

'Where did you go for these beers?'

'Third Planet.' The bottle thunked to the sideboard. 'Get staff discount.'

'Was Elliot with you all that time?'

'Yeah, he was. We got chatting to these girls at the bar. Lovely tits on one of them.' Oliver leered at Uzma. 'Much bigger than yours. More like that MILF who was chatting me up the other day.'

Uzma rolled her eyes. 'And?'

'Anyway, I like to fly with a wingman, know what I mean? So I kept trying to set Elliot up with this bird's mate, but he was having none of it. Kept going on about his own bit of filth.'

'Oh yeah?'

'Gayle. His bloody teacher.' Oliver curled his lip as he inspected the damage to his father's ship. 'I mean, she's fit and everything, but what's the point in seeing someone ten years older than you?' He set the bottle down and took his place back on the sofa. 'Took me a while, but I got this bird's number, said we'd see her up in Hackney. And that's when I spotted Elliot again.'

'You said he was with you?'

'Not in a biblical sense, sweetheart. Like I said, he wasn't interested in this bird's mate, so he sloped off, left me with them. She was definitely up for it. Gagging for it.'

'You meet her up in Hackney?'

'The bouncer's a regular in the Third Planet, so he let us straight in.' Oliver rubbed his neck. 'He let this bird and her mate in, too. Elliot was still being weird about it. I went back to theirs after. Pair of them were students at Southwark. Wanted a threesome. Not my scene, you know? So I got out of there quick smart. One pair of tits is enough for me, you know?'

Fenchurch leaned forward in his chair and gave Uzma a warning glance. 'Where had Elliot been?'

'No idea.' Oliver picked up a PlayStation controller like he was away to get stuck into FIFA or whatever the latest thing was. 'Anyway, we went to that club and—'

'Let me get this straight.' Fenchurch got up and crossed the small room. 'Elliot wasn't with you all night?'

'Kid's like that. Floats in and out, you know?' Oliver frowned at Fenchurch. 'What's this about, anyway?'

'We just need to know where he was.' Fenchurch shrugged. 'When did you get to the bar?'

'Got an Uber from Shadwell.' Oliver reached for his phone and fiddled about with it. 'Half eight.'

'And when did Elliot go missing?'

'Now you're asking . . .' Oliver frowned. 'Why are you so interested in him?'

'Just help us, son.'

'We left for the club at half ten, so . . . think I found him about half nine? And he'd been away for a good few minutes.'

Right in the middle of the window of opportunity.

———

Fenchurch signed the clipboard and passed it to the uniform still manning the hotel's front entrance. Bloke seemed more interested in the women on the street than his job.

'Eyes on the prize, son.' Fenchurch walked through the front door to the reception. 'Lisa, what you doing here?'

Bridge was sitting at the security desk, scowling at her laptop. 'What do you think?' She slapped the keyboard. 'CCTV. I really need to do something else, sir. This is driving me up the wall.'

'Next case, I swear.'

'Believe it when I see it.' She sat back, arms folded. 'Tammy said she's found another seven cameras here that I don't have footage for.'

Fenchurch scanned around the room. 'You got it yet?'

'I'm waiting on Jim Muscat.'

Fenchurch peered through the door to the bar. Jim Muscat was sitting on a stool, yawning. 'Lisa, he's right there.' He walked over and opened the door. 'Need a word with you, Jim.'

'This is a bloody joke!' Roderick, the manager, stomped towards him, like a small child with low blood sugar. He stopped and kicked a chair, toppling it and sending it skidding across the floor. 'I need to open my hotel!'

Fenchurch got out of Roderick's way. 'Sir, that whole floor is a murder scene.'

'I get that.' Roderick didn't look like he did. 'Believe me, I do. Shut that floor off, by all means, but for the love of goodness, let me open the other three?' He thumbed behind him. 'And the Third Planet . . . You know how much I lost last night? A Saturday! Eh? And the Chelsea game today. It took years to build up that crowd of regulars. Years!'

'I understand your concerns, sir.' Fenchurch spotted Tammy's hair glinting in the reception light. 'Give me a minute.' He left the office and caught up with her. 'Have you finished?'

'The room, yes.' Tammy shook out her platinum hair, still looked bunched up from her crime scene suit. She was an inch or two taller than Fenchurch. 'Nothing that'll solve it for you, but as soon as you get yourselves a suspect, we'll be able to prove they were there. In a week or so.'

'It's just, the manager—'

'I know.' Tammy narrowed her eyes at Roderick, shaking her head in disgust. 'He keeps asking me to open the place. Every hour, on the hour. Had those owners in earlier. The brothers. Swear I think Mick can spot a nightmare crime scene a mile off and passes it on to me. Every bloody time.'

Fenchurch smiled. 'That's his speciality.'

'Yeah, well, doing the graft isn't.' Tammy zipped up her coat. 'Next time, he can deal with those brothers. One of them was sleazing all over me. Dirty, dirty bastards.'

'Anything I can do them for?'

'If looks could rape, you know?' Her smile was half-grimace. 'If he stepped over the line, I'd have taken him down, big time.'

Fenchurch didn't doubt it. 'Well, if you're just about done, I'll let you get off.'

'Cheers.' Tammy walked off, still shaking out her hair.

Fenchurch walked back into the bar. Empty. *What the hell?* He walked back to reception and got Bridge's attention with a wave. 'Where did the manager go?'

'Got a call. Took Muscat with him.' She was still focused on her laptop. 'It's like they're hiding something.'

'I'm getting that a lot on this case.'

'Managed to get hold of this myself.' Bridge swivelled her laptop round. The screen showed grainy footage of a man speaking to a woman in a corridor. Looked like the hotel, but the quality was so bad. She circled the woman. 'We have two missing guests, sir. She is one of them.'

'So who is she?'

'Don't know, but that is the bloke outside.' Bridge pointed at the staff door. 'The guy out in the lane who chucked her bag?'

'Right.' Fenchurch squinted at the image. So hard to make out. Could be Elliot. Could be anyone. 'Have you got any more?'

'That's all Muscat got.'

'One out of seven?'

The staff door cracked open and Muscat wandered through, shoulders slouching. 'Swear that guy will be the death of me.'

Fenchurch walked over to Muscat. 'Jim, I need the other six cameras. Now.'

Muscat's gaze shot over to Bridge. 'I've given her access!'

'No, you haven't.'

'I bloody swear I have!'

'Follow me.' Bridge grabbed his arm and led him back through the staff door to the corridor near the exit. 'Three here.' She pointed at three cameras. 'And another three round that bend.'

'Come on, Jim.' Fenchurch got between Muscat and Bridge, tilting his head to the side. 'We need your help.'

Muscat looked away. 'They're dummy cameras.'

'Make me believe it.'

'What?'

'I think you're lying.' Fenchurch reached up to the first one. 'It's wired in.' He shook his head at Muscat, his bitter disappointment hopefully shining through. 'You're an ex-cop, Jim. Did you hand back your integrity with your warrant card?'

'I . . .' Muscat jerked his head around like he was going to run off. 'Look, they told me to keep quiet.'

'Who? The brothers?'

'Them, they . . . I can't.'

'What are you hiding, Jim?'

Muscat slumped back against the wall. 'Nazar'll kill me.' He brushed sweat from his forehead. 'Okay.' He took a deep breath and swallowed hard. 'Nazar Bennaceur co-owns this place with his brother, right? Trouble is, he's asked me to help him out.'

'With a secret?'

'Sort of.'

'The kind that makes you switch off half your CCTV?'

'That type, yeah.' Muscat wiped at more sweat on his brow. 'If the press get hold of it.'

'Just tell me.'

'Nazar's got a mate who . . . Well, he's set this place up as a . . .' Muscat looked down the corridor, then back towards reception. 'A shagging pad.' He walked over to the bend and waved a shaking finger at a door. 'That one there.' He opened the door. The bed wasn't made, but otherwise it looked like any other room in the hotel. Six used condoms in the bin next to the door, though. 'Nazar's mate meets his mistress in here every afternoon for a bit of how's your father.'

'Someone famous?'

'Ish.'

'Just spit it out.'

'I can't!'

Bridge held up her laptop, showing their missing female guest talking to the mystery man. 'This is Nazar's mate, right?'

'Right, no. I don't know that fella.'

'Who is she?'

Muscat shut his eyes, waving his hands. 'I can't.'

'Come on, Jim?'

'They'll sack me!'

Fenchurch grabbed Muscat's collar and spun him round. 'And I'll lock you up. You'll struggle to get any security work with a criminal record.'

'It's not connected to your case! I swear!'

'Rather find that out myself, if it's all the same.' Fenchurch grabbed the other lapel. 'Jim. Where is the video?'

'It's . . . That video gets wiped every hour.'

'Why don't I believe you?'

Muscat reached into his collar and pulled out a chain, a USB drive dangling from it. 'I keep a copy on this. Every hour. Just in case something happens, you know?'

'What, like a murder in this hotel?' Fenchurch stepped forward, going head-to-head with Muscat. 'Anything on that I should see?'

'It's nothing.'

'Jim . . .'

'Look, I'm in a difficult situation here. I don't want to be stuck in the middle of this.'

Fenchurch snatched the drive off him, snapping the chain, and tossed it to Bridge.

Muscat tried to break free. 'No!'

Fenchurch grabbed his arm in a lock and pushed him face first against the wall. 'Jim, I want to let you go, but I need you to behave, okay?'

He mumbled something. Could barely make out a word.

Fenchurch slackened his grip and Muscat shook himself off. *Good to his word.*

'It's not even encrypted.' Bridge showed the laptop screen. Their missing guest stood in the corridor, her hair fanned out over a long, black expensive-looking coat. Checking her phone and her watch every two seconds. Maybe early twenties but pretty and she looked like she knew it. Then she entered the room they were standing outside.

Bridge tapped the screen. 'Shit, this is from Thursday night.'

Fenchurch let go of Muscat. 'So it's a waste of time.'

'It's the same woman, though.' Bridge held up her laptop again. A man sloped up to the room, checking behind him. Then down the corridor. Then behind him again. He swiped the door and looked straight into the camera.

Jack Walsh.

Fenchurch grabbed hold of Muscat again. 'Is this who you were protecting?'

'I swear it's not!'

'Come on, Jim. You used to be able to stand up in court and tell the truth. Now look at you. Who is he sleeping with?'

'I can't tell you!'

'Right, James Muscat. I'm arresting you for perverting the course of justice. You do not have to say anything, but—'

Bridge's nose was wrinkled up. 'Sir, he's got a video of them inside the room. They're . . . at it.'

'So that's why you kept it, eh?' Fenchurch pushed his face against the wall, hard, making it hurt. 'You're a filthy pervert, Jim.'

'That's all you're getting out of me.'

Chapter Twenty-Five

Y ou're messing us about here, sir.' Fenchurch stood in front of
Walsh's TV screen, blocking the view of the punditry. 'We know
about your little love nest at the hotel.'

He got a sideway glance from Jack. 'Oh yeah?'

'Nice little room. Bin full of used rubbers. You're not denying it,
either.'

'Ain't done nothing wrong, mate.'

'Poor Jim Muscat, having to cover for you.'

'Jim who?'

'The security guard.'

'I've no idea who you're talking about.'

'Well, he had this USB drive. Full of video from outside the room.'
Fenchurch reached into his jacket pocket for a screen grab. 'You look
very shifty there, sunshine.'

'You can piss off, you arsecandle.'

'Charming. Only thing in your favour is this was Thursday night
and you've got a few hundred people who can alibi you for Friday
night.' Fenchurch passed him another shot. 'Trouble is, we really need
to speak to this woman here. That's all I care about.'

'Don't know her.'

'I'll spare your shame, sir.' Fenchurch put the photos away. 'Jim also
has a video of what goes on behind that door.'

Walsh's head slouched forward. 'Oh, Christ.'

'Some stamina you've got. At it for hours. Viagra, is it? And six rubbers? I couldn't even fill that many when I was fourteen.'

'Piss off.'

'We just want to speak to her.'

'Well, you can piss off.'

'My colleague here did a bit of googling on our way back here.' Fenchurch grinned at Uzma. 'Turns out that old Nazar Bennaceur owns a few things, doesn't he? Hotels, shops. And Shadwell United.' He crouched in front of Walsh. 'He's your chairman, isn't he? And a good enough mate to set up this love nest for you at his hotel. Nazar ever get any action behind the green door?'

'Don't be sick.'

'What?'

'Nothing.' Walsh rocked forward, clearing his throat. 'You said this Mustard guy has—'

'Muscat.'

'Whatever. You said he's got a video of me . . . Isn't that illegal?'

'We'll prosecute Jim Muscat for this. Don't you worry about it.'

'Deviant . . .'

Fenchurch tapped the shot of the mystery woman. 'We need to speak to her. It's looking like she might've spoken to the murderer.'

Walsh looked like he was close to cracking. Then steel filled his eyes again. '"Might have" isn't worth me getting my arse handed to me by Nazar.'

Why the hell is he keeping this a secret? It doesn't make any sense. Unless . . .

Fenchurch checked the image again and nodded slowly. 'Is this Nazar's wife?'

Walsh hung his head low. 'His daughter.'

Explains a few things . . .

'And he doesn't know about it, does he?'

A slow shake of the head.

179

Fenchurch got to his feet, hard not to laugh. 'Got to admire getting Nazar to give you a room at his hotel so you could shag his daughter behind his back. Impressive.'

'He'll sack me if he finds out.'

'He's going to have to, sir.' Fenchurch gave him a flat grin. 'I've no choice but to tell him.'

'Whatever you want. Anything. Just keep this away from him.'

'Her name and address. Then I'll see if I can keep a secret.'

'Unbelievable.' Fenchurch pulled past a new development, bus-sized pot plants dotted around the pavement to somehow advertise the flats, then on to an old back lane spitting distance from Borough Market. A row of three-storey brick townhouses, old-style gas lanterns above the door. 'How much do you reckon it's worth?'

Uzma exhaled slowly. 'Over a million.'

'And all paid for by her old man.' Fenchurch got out on to the street and pressed the buzzer. They were blocking the road, but he didn't really care.

'Excuse me?' A woman was behind the car, late teens, early twenties. Expensive dress. Striking cheekbones. Fenchurch didn't even have to check the print — it was Claudia Bennaceur, the woman from the hotel CCTV. 'I need to get past?'

Fenchurch blocked her way. 'Claudia?' He unfolded his warrant card. 'Need a—'

She shot off, back towards the main road.

'Shit.' Fenchurch darted off after her, his knee cracking with every step, an ache drilling into his bones.

Claudia was fast, but heels hampered her long stride. She stopped, spinning round as she kicked off her shoes, then she was away again, dodging round the oversized pot plants. For every agonising step of Fenchurch's, she took two, getting further and further away.

Then she shifted left to avoid a woman pushing a pram and bumped into a man coming out of a shop. The pair of them tumbled over in a heap, a carton of milk splatting and spraying all over the ground. Claudia tried to get up but slipped in the white liquid and fell face first.

Fenchurch grabbed both arms and held her down, wriggling and kicking. She lashed out, kicking Fenchurch in the thigh. Then another caught him in the groin. 'Shit.' Pain burnt at his gut, flared across his stomach. He let go and she was off.

Fenchurch pushed himself up, could only watch as she ran off, leaving milky footprints on the tarmac.

Then Uzma tackled her, pushing her on to a planter and pinning her to the ground. 'Stop!'

Fenchurch staggered over, pain shooting from his balls all the way up to his brain. 'Get her back to the station!'

———

Uzma was driving, rattling along the cobbled back street. Every bump speared Fenchurch's gonads. Felt like they'd swollen up to twice normal size. She'd caught both of them. Even breathing hurt. Made him think about Docherty, the testicular cancer that ate him up, that killed him because he hadn't gone to the doctor about it, just left the lumps growing. Had to start somewhere — a blow to the balls seemed as likely as anything.

Uzma pulled up at the lights. 'What are you running from, eh?'

Claudia sat on the back seat, cuffed to the post. Covered in milk. Her dress, the back seat, even the window. Be smelling the sour odour for months. 'Nothing.' Didn't even look at him.

Fenchurch looked back at her. 'We know about you and Jack.'

That got her attention. She gave him a sharp look.

'A real stallion, isn't he? Proper alpha-male type. You like older men?'

She snarled at Fenchurch. 'You're too old.'

Uzma smirked. 'Nothing wrong with what you were doing at your father's hotel, is there? Consenting adults and all that. I don't get why you'd run from us, Claudia. Your old man doesn't know that his manager is at it with his daughter, does he?'

'What do you want from me?'

'This is you, right?' Fenchurch showed her the still. All crumpled now, but still good enough to see the detail. 'On Friday night. I just want to know who you're speaking to. That's all.'

She looked out of the window, nostrils wide. On the main road now, smoother, fewer painful jolts.

'I know this isn't Jack Walsh because he was at the football. So . . .' Then it clicked into place . . . Fenchurch groaned. 'You're charging him, aren't you?'

'No!'

'You bloody are.' Fenchurch leaned round and got a fresh stab of pain in the balls. 'This isn't *his* love nest, it's *your* knocking shop. Right?'

She shifted her arms, rattling the cuffs.

'Listen to me, Claudia, I know people in Vice. I can have a word with them, yeah? See what they want to charge you with.' He watched her squirm. 'Uzma, head to the Empress Sta—'

'What do you want to know?'

Uzma pulled in at the side of the road.

'This man here.' Fenchurch showed her the photo again. 'You spoke to him on Friday night. Is he a client?'

'No.' She nibbled at a nail, the only one where the natural colour was exposed, instead of the fake powder-blue. Must've been knocked off in the scuffle. 'The client was staying in the hotel. His wife was in the gym and he came to visit me. Don't ask how we got in touch. I spoke to this man when I was leaving.'

'I don't care about that.' Fenchurch tapped the page again. 'Just his name.'

'I don't know it. He just started talking to me. Asking me where the rooms were.'

Fenchurch showed her a photo of Elliot Lynch. 'Was it him?'

Claudia didn't take much of a look at it. 'He was much, much older. Not as old as you, though.'

Fenchurch sat back in his seat. *Thought it was Elliot. After Oliver landed him in it, it made perfect sense. Who else could it be?*

Another throb of pain, not as sore as the realisation.

Steve Fisher.

Fenchurch searched through his Airwave Pronto and found a photo of him buried in the case file. He showed it to Claudia. 'Him?'

'That's him!'

What the hell?

'You're sure?'

'One hundred per cent. I'd recognise that face anywhere.'

Why is he lying to us? And what the hell was he doing at the hotel? Other than killing his wife . . .

Chapter Twenty-Six

Though here.' Martin, the Custody Sergeant, opened the door to the identification suite and led Claudia in. He held the door and grinned at Fenchurch. 'Should be out in a jiffy, mate.'

'Make sure it'll stand up in court, okay?'

'Like a judge's hard-on.' And Martin was gone.

Fenchurch leaned against the cold wall. His balls were aching. *Really should see the doctor about it.*

'Guv?' Reed was in the opposite doorway, frowning at him.

Fenchurch stood up tall and cleared his throat. 'Kay.'

'Got a sec?' Reed motioned towards the room she'd come out of. A woman sat the table. Ginger hair, short. Swaying like she'd been on the sauce and like she was out of touch with the Earth's movement through space. 'Once we got rid of all those drunks and so on, we were left with two people. Two women came in, but only one left again, yeah?'

Fenchurch's turn to wave at the ID Suite. 'We've got the one who left.'

'Oh.' Reed frowned. 'Well, this is the other one.' Her friend kept running a hand across her forehead and blowing air up her face. 'Alison McBrain. Just found her in her room. Two down from Gayle Fisher's. Says she was out all day yesterday, but must've torn through the police tape when she came back . . .'

'She's still off her skull.' Fenchurch was already walking into the room. He gave Alison a warm smile as he sat. 'Thanks for coming forward.'

Reed shut the door and air wafted through the interview room, blowing a strong mint smell and also the sort of alcohol reek you only got from someone's pores. Alison McBrain had obviously been drinking, and hard.

'My name is DI Simon Fenchurch and I'm leading the—'

'Your colleague here says that woman was poisoned with an ecky?' A Glaswegian accent, but more on the lilting side than the stab-you-in-the-face-pal one. 'That right?'

'Where in Glasgow are you from? Partick?'

Her head jerked up, a coy smile on her lips. 'How'd you guess?'

'Based there for a bit.' Fenchurch returned the smile. 'Anyway, we're looking for anyone who saw anything suspicious on Friday night around nine o'clock.'

Alison grunted. 'So why am I in here?'

'Because you were there?'

'You sure about that?'

'We've got you on CCTV in the reception area.' Reed reached into a pocket for a still of Alison lumbering through reception, lugging a hessian shopping bag in each hand, big packets of crisps on the top. 'This is you, isn't it?'

She patted her head. 'Will you look at my hair?'

Fenchurch caught a fresh wave of second-hand booze. No guessing what was in those bags. A pisshead getting out of her skull in a London hotel. Two possible witnesses, neither of them anywhere near credible. 'Did you see anything in your corridor as you came in?'

'Well, aye, now you mention it, there might've been this boy in the corridor, but look, I was at my pal's wedding and . . .' She let out a mournful sigh. 'Had a shite time, you know? Big do at St Paul's, then at a posh hotel round the corner. Bloody hell, it's a bit of a mission on a Friday, isn't it?' Her lips pressed tight. 'Tell you, people say Glasgow's bad but London's a shitehole. Total shitehole.'

'You saw a man in the corridor?'

'Aye, but that wedding was in St Paul's Cathedral, you know? My wee pal Jodie, we grew up together in Partick and it's not the same place as it was, I tell you. It's all flash pubs and that now. No, when we were wee, it was a lovely place. Full of right characters and that, and people looked out for each other, you know? None of these hipsters and trannies and what have you.'

Oh, Christ . . .

'Did you—'

'Anyway, Jodie's husband's ma did some charity stuff way back when, got an MBE or something. Means you can, like, have your wedding at St Paul's? So there's my wee pal Jodie having her big day there. Can you imagine? A wee lassie from Partick in there? Brilliant, eh?'

'Heartwarming.' Fenchurch tried to keep a smile on his face but it was a struggle. 'When you got back to the hotel, you saw a man in the corridor?'

'Aye, I said that.' Alison's expression darkened with a deep sigh. 'Look, I don't know what Jodie was playing at, but she invited my ex to her wedding. That total scumbag, Dan. Thinks he's some big shot now. I don't know what she was thinking. No danger I'd get back together with that fanjo. He's worse than he was at school as well. Made a total prick of himself at the disco, trying to feel me up while he was snogging some other lassie. Can you imagine? So I just left and—'

'You went shopping?' Fenchurch showed her the photos again. 'Crisps and stuff, right?'

'Right. Found a nice wee shop round the corner. Bought three bottles of vodka and enough Diet Coke to get me to Mars and back. Soon as I got in my room I was stuffing crisps down my face, mascara dribbling everywhere, tanning the voddy as quick as I could pour it.

I went out for a bit yesterday, found a nice wee pub that's been there since before the Fire of London. Thanks to Jodie and Dan, I've fallen off the wagon, haven't I? Pair of pricks. I mean, what was she thinking?'

'You fell off the wagon?' Fenchurch showed her the photo again, her lugging her shopping into the hotel. 'You were sober here?'

'Sober as a nun, aye. Didn't even have a glass of fizz at reception.'

'Okay, so let's wind back. The man in the corridor, what do you remember about him?'

'Not as old as you.' Alison glanced at Reed. 'Older than her, for definite.'

Fenchurch got a stack of photos and started placing them in front of her. 'Recognise any of these guys?'

'Oh, he's a honey.' She pointed to a photo of Tom Hardy. The actor. 'Was it him?'

'Eh, no, but . . . Got his number?'

'Anyone else?'

'Oh.' She scanned the photos. 'Oh, aye. That's the boy.' She snatched it off him and stabbed a photo. 'Definitely.'

Steve Fisher. Inside the hotel and he says he didn't know she was there.

———

'You'll be ready to go in about ten minutes, Miss McBrain.' Martin got one of his Custody officers to take Alison into the room next to the ID Suite, his smile lasting until the door shut. 'Busiest Sunday in ages, Si.'

'Is Claudia still in there?'

'No idea what she's doing, Si. Takes less time to watch those *Lord of the Rings* films. Surely nobody can take that long to ID a bloke?'

'The important thing is that she's sure who she saw.'

'Well, I'll let you know when she's done.' Martin disappeared back through the door.

Fenchurch looked around. Uzma was over by the interview room, tapping away at her phone, no doubt updating Mulholland. He joined her, trying to look casual.

Uzma put her phone away. Fenchurch still hadn't seen who she was texting. 'You thought it was Elliot, didn't you?'

'He's got a gaping hole in his alibi. He had the drugs. He was perfect.'

'Have we got enough on Steve?'

Fenchurch huffed out a breath. 'He's got a solid motive. And we've got the drugs. Two people now have placed him inside the hotel at the time of death.'

She frowned at him. 'And that's not enough for you?'

'Nothing's ever enough for him.' DCI Howard Savage was charging down the corridor, hands in pockets, a knowing grin on his face. The strip lights bounced off his bald head. A long splodge of tomato sauce ran down his tweed jacket. Hadn't noticed or didn't care. Either would fit. He held out a hand. 'Simon, good to see you.'

'Wish I could say the same.' Fenchurch shook it then waved at Uzma. 'You know DS Ashkani?'

'We're acquainted, yes.' Savage tucked his hands under his arms. 'Thanks for the call. Surprising to get a vanilla prostitution case from you.'

'It's more a raspberry ripple. Her old man owns that hotel and she's wangled a free room there, which she's using as a bordello. And her father owns Shadwell United, too.'

'Well, now I'm intrigued.'

'Didn't know you were a football man?'

'I'm not. Where there's money, there's usually sleaze, though in this case it appears to be coincidental.'

Uzma's phone rang and she walked off, smiling.

Savage returned the grin, then scowled at Fenchurch. 'Watch her.'

'Oh?'

'Cut from the same cloth as DCI Mulholland. Not to be trusted.'

'I thought you were going to tell me something I didn't know.'

Savage chuckled. 'Well. Anyway. How's . . . everything else?'

'Good, Howard. Good. Chloe's staying with us now.'

'Good heavens.' Savage's eyebrows shot up, creasing his forehead. 'Well, I'm glad to have helped out.'

'You did the admin, that's all.'

'Very true. Very true.'

The ID Suite door opened and Martin led Claudia through. He gave Fenchurch a nod. 'It's Steve.'

Fenchurch let out a sigh of relief, then patted Savage on the arm. 'She's all yours, mate.'

Savage wandered over to Claudia. 'Let's get you over to my office and have a nice little chat, shall we?'

Claudia glared at Fenchurch. 'You said that you'd let me go!'

'I had a better offer. Sorry.' Fenchurch smiled at her, holding it as she was led down the corridor towards the Custody Suite.

Chapter Twenty-Seven

Fenchurch opened the interview room door and had to do a double take.

Dalton Unwin sat with Steve Fisher, chatting away like they were on the train to a football match. Fenchurch had had run-ins with him in the past, the sort of vermin who called themselves criminal defence lawyers and thought they were helping people. Stopping crimes against wronged innocents. More often than not, stopping victims getting justice against the toerags that'd stabbed them. Stopping families getting justice against the animals who'd killed their sons or daughters.

Unwin had been out of the game for a while now, but here he was, his earring stud catching the light, twinkling like a mirror ball. His skin was as dark as his hair, grown out from a skinhead to sponge curls, ultra-short dreads all over his scalp. He wore a dark-grey suit, the same purple handkerchief in his breast pocket as ever.

'Inspector.' He got up and charged over to the door, grinning wide, his hand reaching for Fenchurch. 'How the devil are you?'

'Uzma, get the tape rolling.' Fenchurch beckoned Unwin out into the corridor. 'Heard you got struck off.'

'The term is disbarred.' Unwin's glee slipped from his face. 'And I personally wasn't. My firm was closed down, thanks in no small part to your activities, Inspector. A lot of innocent people will—'

'You're defending people like him now?' Fenchurch nodded at Steve. Sitting in the room, head low. 'Murderers?'

'My speciality is criminal law. As far as I can tell, Mr Fisher is guilty of nothing other than having a murdered wife.'

'If he's so innocent, he should stop lying to us.' Fenchurch joined Uzma in the interview room with Steve. The recorder in the middle of the table was blinking. 'Mr Fisher, we know you killed Gayle, so let's—'

'I didn't.' Steve thumped the table, making the recorder jump. Uzma reached over to check it was still working. 'There's no *way* I could . . .' His voice was thick, like he was close to tears.

'Here's the thing.' Fenchurch leaned across the table, his gaze trained on Unwin. 'We know you've been lying to us, Mr Fisher. Only guilty men lie.'

'I didn't kill her!'

Fenchurch sat back and laughed. Still gave most of his attention to Unwin. 'I'll ask again, where were you between eight o'clock and midnight on Friday?'

'I've told you.'

'Want to try telling the truth this time?'

'I told you the truth last time.'

Fenchurch slapped a CCTV image in front of him. Their mystery man in the lane. 'This is you, isn't it?'

Steve glanced at his lawyer, then gave a shrug. 'You've got nothing on me.'

'A hotel guest confirmed this image is of you.' Fenchurch smiled. 'And another guest saw you outside Gayle's room. They've just sat through our VIPER system. It means Video Identification Parade Electronic Recording. Cute, I know. Witnesses look through a lot of videos, much cheaper and more effective than the old way. Weird thing is, both of them identified you. And you were outside the hotel, throwing Gayle's bag away. And just after nine o'clock, in the corridor outside Gayle's room.'

Steve focused on his lap.

'Just admit that you murdered your wife.'

He looked up at Fenchurch, teeth bared. 'No!'

'We know you had access to the pills used to kill Gayle. You said you found them in that knock-off Louis Vuitton bag, but you and I both know that you planted them there. Maybe you thought we were mugs and we'd think her death was a suicide. Maybe you thought we'd assume that Gayle was out with her young lover. Which is it?'

Steve picked up the CCTV print and started folding it. First in half, then again, and again.

'Word of advice, though. If you want to make it look like a suicide, best not to tie your victim down and give them three times the fatal dose.'

'Inspector.' Unwin unclipped his briefcase and put his yellow legal pad away. 'My client has nothing else to say on the matter.'

'That right?' Fenchurch ignored Unwin, locking his glare on Steve. 'Mr Fisher, if you keep this up, you're going to face trial. The jury will find you guilty and the judge will put you away for over twenty years. You're not an old man, but when you get out in 2038, the world will be a very different place. You won't be able to go back to your old job. It'll be very tough for someone who's been inside. That'll be you, Steve. You.'

Unwin buttoned up his suit, looked ready to get up and leave. 'Inspector, this is wholly inappropriate.'

'I just want to know exactly what your client was up to before and after he murdered his wife.'

Steve started folding the page again, each twist taking much more effort.

'Mr Fisher, you're going to prison for murder. If you didn't do it, now's the time to try and convince me.'

Steve tossed the folded-up paper on the table and watched it uncurl. Then he whispered to his lawyer. But stopped. Muttered, 'Bugger it.' He stretched out his shoulders. 'Right. Okay, so I didn't get that taxi to John's flat. I visited . . . a friend.'

'A friend, eh? Well.'

'He lives just off the Minories.'

'And he exists, right?' Fenchurch stared at Unwin. 'I've been here before with your lawyer and his clients.'

'That's a preposterous accusation.'

Fenchurch switched his glare back to Steve. 'Name.'

Steve looked up, eyes wide. 'I don't know it.'

'Good mate of yours who'll let you into his house and you don't know his full name?'

'I swear I don't.'

Fenchurch wagged a finger in the air. 'Steve, just tell the truth. Please.'

'I can't . . .'

'You're going down for murder, Mr Fisher. I suggest you—'

Steve thumped the table again. 'Okay, he was my dealer.'

What the hell?

'You bought some drugs?' Fenchurch got up and started pacing the room. 'You said the only time you took drugs was once in Newcastle?'

'You really think I'd tell the police about my drug taking? You must think I'm stupid.'

'You must think I am if you expect me to believe this crock of shit. You need to start telling me what you were doing in that hotel, because this story is tripe.'

'I needed to take my mind off what Gayle was putting me through.' Steve rested his head on the table. 'So I visited my guy. I bought some E, a bit of coke and some Special K. Ketamine, in case you don't know.'

'That's quite a haul.'

'I take stuff once or twice a month. Try to keep a lid on it, you know?'

'I want evidence. Names of who else was there. Now.'

Unwin picked up his briefcase and rested it on the floor. Clearly knew he was in for a long one with this. 'As a result of that confession, my client faces up to two years and will lose his job.'

'Even so, I still don't believe him.' Fenchurch crouched next to Steve and waited until he dared look at him. 'I want a name to check this alibi with. And I want the drugs.'

'What's left of them . . .'

'To raid my client's brother's property, you will, of course, require a search warrant.'

'It's a formality, Dalton, you know that.' Fenchurch got up and sat on his chair again. 'But let's start with this dealer's name and address.'

'I can't.'

'We're back to the murder charge, then. And Class As, Steve. No personal-use amount for those.'

'I've just given up my future and you're . . .' Steve leaned back in his chair, staring up, breathing hard. 'You don't *believe* me?'

'You're messing us about. Instead of life for murder, you think you can get off with a drug charge. Couple of years versus twenty-odd.' Fenchurch leaned across the table. 'Names and addresses *now*. And I need them to verify your presence there, otherwise you're spending your next few sleeps on remand in a very vicious prison.'

'It's not . . . I can't.'

Fenchurch stared at him, blood pumping hard in his chest. *Getting nowhere with him.* 'Where did you go after you visited this fictional dealer?'

'I went back to my brother's. Took some of the coke. Then some of the Special K to get me to sleep.'

'You didn't go to the hotel your wife was staying in?'

'No.' Steve unfolded the paper and looked at the CCTV still. 'Yes. Maybe.'

'Were you there or not?'

'Maybe.'

'Steve, I need you to stop messing about, okay? This is serious.'

'I know.'

Unwin leaned over and whispered into his ear. Steve nodded and rested his head on the table again.

'Are you going admit that you were there?'

Steve shook his head slowly, his forehead rubbing against the wood.

'Okay, back to that, is it?' Fenchurch looked over at Uzma and saw his irritation reflected. He gave Steve a few seconds, then started tapping a finger on the table. 'Let's go back to your dealer, then. Probably aren't that many drug dealers left in that neck of the woods. We'll find him.'

Steve looked up at Fenchurch's finger, still tapping away. 'He'll kill me.'

'It's much better if it comes from you, Mr Fisher.'

Steve stayed focused on Fenchurch's tapping finger. Then he looked up and locked eyes with Fenchurch. 'How about I show you the drugs?'

Chapter Twenty-Eight

The pool car reeked of sour milk.

Fenchurch turned on to a side street, his phone ringing through the car's speakers, almost distorting. Bloody voicemail. *Like people have just stopped answering their phones . . .* 'Jon, it's Simon. Give me a bell, okay?' He killed the call and turned the corner, parking behind a squad car.

A uniformed officer got out of the passenger side, wearing mirror shades, and helped Steve out of the back.

Maybe he'll see sense, be a good boy and confess.

Or maybe he's innocent and telling the truth. Just wanted to get out of his head for a bit, trying to cope with his wife being all over the papers for shagging a school kid.

Maybe it was Elliot who killed her.

Or maybe it was someone else entirely.

Fenchurch opened the door and his phone rang, still paired with the stereo. *Another Al call?* Panic crawled up his spine. Not Abi, not even Nelson. Mulholland. The worry took on a different flavour as he answered it. 'Dawn, I'm in the—'

'Simon, when I last saw you, you had no suspects, now I gather you've got two. Why do I have to hear that from a third party?'

'Nice to speak to you too, Dawn.' Fenchurch looked around and finally found someone to place his angry look at. Uzma, getting out of the other side of a pool car. 'I'm in the middle of an operation here.'

'Well, you should be awaiting my instruction before executing any tactical actions.'

'Excuse me?'

'Simon, you're running wild again, aren't you?'

'I've been trying to get hold of—'

'Julian and I have spent the last three hours locked in a deep dive with Operation Lydian over at Scotland Yard, trying to figure out if the supplier of this Blockchain is involved.'

'Dawn, it's possible that a dealer tied Gayle up and—'

'Simon!' Her shout echoed round the car. The uniform wearing shades looked round at Fenchurch. 'As of now, Acting DI Nelson is seconded to our investigation, of which Blockchain remains an active part.'

'As long as he reports to me.'

'He reports to me, Simon.' Her sigh hissed through the speakers. 'Now, I've got to update Julian on the— I was going to say progress, but I'll settle for latest. I need to see you before you leave for the night. In person.' Click and she was gone.

Fenchurch pointed a finger gun at the speaker and shot a finger bullet. He got out on to the street, where Uzma and Nelson were laughing further down the road. He walked over, trying to keep it cool.

'I'll get them to ready Steve.' Uzma left them to it, heading back towards the squad car.

Fenchurch waited until she was out of earshot, even with her super-human hearing. 'You know her, Jon?'

'Went through Hendon together.' Nelson laughed. 'She's okay once you get to know her.'

'Bit too close to Mulholland for my liking.'

'I don't mean to overstep the mark, Simon.' *Not guv any more.* 'But I really think you need to let that go.'

'I'll think on it.' Fenchurch leaned against the pool car and counted along the street until he was at John Fisher's flat. 'Nice to have you back in the land of the living.'

'For now. What's the plan?'

'That idiot's given his drug dealer as an alibi. First, I want to check whether there's any drugs. Then, you'll help me find this dealer.'

'That all?'

'Someone near the Minories.'

'I've got some candidates.' Another laugh from Nelson. 'Trouble is, we can't just burst in there and start asking questions. We need to be smart about it.'

'You're telling me.' Fenchurch caught a thumbs-up from the uniform. 'Come on.' He walked over to Steve, getting close enough to get a waft of Lynx and bike oil, unsure whether it was Steve or one of the uniforms. 'Mr Fisher, you're here to show us your drug stash. That's it. Any shenanigans and, well, it's not going to look good, is it?'

'I know what I'm here for.' Steve let himself be led over. He took the keys from Uzma and unlocked the flat door. 'John?'

Nothing, just his voice echoing round an empty flat.

'Looks like he's gone out.' Steve led inside, through the fug of stale coffee grounds and burnt toast, and took them into the spare room at the back. A massive gaming PC sat there, sucking enough power in seconds to keep Ecuador going for a year. 'It's inside the computer. This thing is super-cooled so the gear won't get hot.' He opened the DVD tray.

Nelson slapped his hand away and snapped on a pair of blue gloves, then reached in. 'What have we got here?' He held up a package containing white powder. 'That'll be the ketamine.' He passed it to Uzma and she put it in an evidence bag. He kept his gaze on it. 'Good stuff, too. Usually tell by the colour what it's been cut with. This is pure.'

'So far so good, then.' Fenchurch took the bag from Uzma. So much pain in one little bag. Then he looked at Steve. 'Next?'

'Right.' Steve reached round the back of the computer for a large silver box, attached to the PC by a couple of long cables.

'Stop!' Nelson took it off him. 'I'm doing it, okay? How do I get it open?'

Steve pointed at a small screwdriver. 'That one.'

Nelson picked it up and started working away at the screws, then carefully lifted the lid. The inside was filled with bags of white powder.

'Shit.'

'What?'

'The E's missing. Shit.' Steve crawled behind the computer, frantically searching. 'Shit.' He crawled out from under the desk and dusted himself off. 'Shit.' He looked up, focusing on Fenchurch like he'd just noticed he was there for the first time. 'Look, those tablets in the Vuitton bag, they weren't my wife's.'

'I knew you'd lied to us.'

'But someone's taken the rest of them!'

'Your brother?'

'John doesn't know about this.'

'So someone's broken in here and only taken some of your drugs?' Fenchurch perched on the edge of the desk and tapped the computer. 'One of these things costs a few grand. Is your brother involved in the drug trade?'

'No!'

'Sure?'

'He's got a job in the City. I told you!'

Fenchurch switched his focus to Nelson. 'This sounds like bollocks to me. What do you think?'

'Bollocks.'

Steve raised his arms in the air and a uniform grabbed them. 'I told you about that E I found in Gayle's bag! It's from the same batch!'

'Which makes me think you planted it in your dead wife's bag. That's low.'

'I didn't kill her!'

199

'The only way you can recover this is if you give us your dealer's name, okay?'

'I can't . . .'

'DI Nelson here works for the drug squad. His team are looking for your man. Not that many left in that area, is there? It's going to be a lot better for you if you just tell us.'

Steve walked over to the window and looked out on to the street. 'His name is Daniel.'

'And does Daniel have a surname?'

Steve leaned back against the glass.

'Okay.' Fenchurch clapped his hands and bounced to his feet. Got a slight twinge in his balls, but didn't let Nelson or Steve see any discomfort. 'We're done here. Let's get—'

'Dodoo.' Dough-doo. Steve sat back, frowning. 'Daniel Dodoo.'

'Jon?'

'Oh, I know him. Had him at Daniel.'

⁓

'Daniel Doo-doo.' Uzma covered her mouth as she drove, struggling to keep her eyes open. 'What sort of name is that?'

'It's pronounced Dough-doo.' Nelson was in the passenger seat, scowling at her. 'It's Ghanaian.' He folded his arms. 'My family's Jamaican, right? When people enslaved us in Ghana, they took our names from us and gave us theirs. Nelson is Scottish or Irish. My ancestors could have a Dodoo or two. I don't know. Daniel does, though, so please give him that respect.'

'I didn't know that.' Uzma wiped a hand across her lips. 'Sorry. But he is a drug dealer, right?'

'We've got a longstanding operation against the organisation he's working for.'

'And he's selling Blockchain?'

'Among other items. It's not simple.'

'But he's sold super-strong E?'

'Yes, but there's a lot more to it.'

'So he's a drug-dealing scumbag. I'm not giving him any respect.' Uzma smiled at him as she pulled up outside the Bennaceur. The place was dead inside, the lights off, silent. *Good.* 'How are we playing this, Simon?'

'We're playing the daft laddie.' Fenchurch felt a stab of pain in his balls. 'As Docherty used to call it.'

Uzma undid her seatbelt. 'Come on, then.'

'Not you, Sergeant.' Nelson opened his door. 'DI Fenchurch and I will deal with this.'

'But, I—'

'No buts. Stay here and keep an eye out, okay?' Nelson got out on to the street and headed down a side lane.

Fenchurch followed him and caught up by a gate. 'See what I'm dealing with?'

Nelson walked up to a house. A rotting red-brick tomb, wedged between new office developments, restaurants, pubs and hotels. House music blasted out of the windows further down the lane. He pressed the buzzer in a weird pattern. Bz-bz, bz-bz-bz, bz-bz, bz-bz-bz.

The door clicked.

'What the hell was that, Jon?'

'Secrets of the trade.' Nelson opened the door and stepped in.

Inside, the hallway was empty. Race-driving noise droned from somewhere in the flat. Seemed to come from the door on the left. Clanking noises came from another room, but Nelson led into a large living room, clean and pristine. A massive TV sat on a wooden unit, that Mario racing game in all its garish cartoon glory. The sound was earsplitting, exploding out of huge floor-standing speakers.

Nelson cleared his throat. 'Evening, Daniel.'

Dodoo sat on one end of a leather sofa, the room's only chair, barely acknowledging them. Tall and black, head shaved. Wearing baggy clothes, his sleeves pulled up to show off tattoos. 'Pull up a pew, Jon.' He waved at the screen. '*Mario Kart 8* is *the bomb*.'

'Heard that.' Nelson sat next to him and picked up a pink controller, tiny in his giant hands. Each nudge of the stick pinged from the speakers. 'Need to ask you a favour.'

'I don't deal drugs.' Dodoo sneaked a glance at him, raised an eyebrow at Fenchurch, then back at the screen as the race countdown started. 'Whatever you want to know, that shit's off the table. Okay?'

'That's cool.' Nelson leaned forward, concentrating on the game. Looked like he was controlling a green dinosaur in a cartoon racing kart with monster-truck tyres. 'You know a Steve Fisher?'

Another nervous glance. 'Never heard of the cat.'

'See, he's given you as an alibi for Friday night.'

'What's he done?'

'Killed his wife.'

'Shit.' Dodoo sat forward, exhaling slowly. 'Well, I ain't even heard of the cat, you know?'

'Sure about that? Said he was here.'

'Did he say why?'

'We're not talking about that, Daniel.'

'Good to hear it.' Dodoo leaned forward. Then tossed his controller on the floor. 'Bastard blue shell, man.' He picked it up and set off again. Looked like he was driving as a fairy-tale princess, emerging from a mushroom cloud attack.

Maybe you needed to be on drugs to play it . . .

Nelson punched the air as he overtook. 'So?'

'So what?' Dodoo leaned left as his character did the same on screen, veering down on Nelson's dragon. 'Cat wasn't even here. Wasn't doing nothing.'

A big white guy dressed in hip-hop gear entered the room, eyeing them up.

Nelson's eyes bulged as he saw him, then went back to the game.

Hip-hop walked over to Dodoo and whispered in his ear.

'You mean Steve the teacher?' Dodoo's forehead knotted in concentration. 'Cos he was here. Cat came round and we played *Mario Kart* for, like, half an hour? Just got it that day, man, and the cat helped me set it up. Not that it was complicated or anything. Cat's good at this game, man. Beat me all ends up.'

Fenchurch couldn't take his eyes off the Ali G clone. 'It was Steve Fisher?'

'Definitely. You can put my name on it.'

'How long was he here?'

'Maybe forty minutes, man?' Dodoo grinned as he overtook Nelson. 'He left at ten past nine at the latest, man.'

Steve, Steve, Steve . . .

Why do you keep doing this to us? And yourself.

Nelson glanced at Dodoo. 'You're sure about that?'

'My Domino's guy turned up at ten past nine.' Dodoo reached for his phone and held it up. 'Steve was gone by then.'

'Thanks for that.' Nelson put his controller down. 'We'll be on our way.'

'Sure you don't want to keep playing?' Dodoo pointed at the screen. 'Domino's man is on his way again, bro.'

'Sod your computer games and pizza.' Fenchurch got in Dodoo's face, so close that he couldn't focus on the kid. 'This Blockchain you're selling is killing people. Stop it.'

'I told you, I ain't discussing drugs.' Dodoo grinned at him. 'You see any round here?'

'Just because I don't see it doesn't mean you're not selling it.'

Dodoo's friend pointed at the door. 'Mate, leave.'

Fenchurch laughed. 'What did you say?'

'*Come on.*' Nelson grabbed Fenchurch by the jacket and pulled him away, tugging until they were out of the flat, only letting go when he slammed the door. 'What the hell are you playing at?'

Fenchurch stomped off down the path. 'Ali G in there thinks he can tell me to leave?'

'Simon, forget it.'

'I'm not forgetting anything. That prick's going down.'

'It doesn't matter. You've got a giant hole in Steve's alibi. Focus on that. He left with enough time to get over to the hotel and kill Gayle. You've got him there. He did it. End of.'

'I suppose.' Fenchurch got in the back of the car, ignoring Uzma. 'Who was that, anyway?'

Nelson got in the passenger seat. 'Thought it was just going to be Dodoo. If I'd known . . .'

'Jon, who was it?'

'Coldcut.'

'I remember the band name.' Uzma smirked. 'That's going back a bit, though, isn't it? *Doctorin' the House?* Yazz? Lisa Stansfield?'

'Whatever.' Nelson looked like he'd seen a ghost. 'I told you about Coldcut. He's the supplier of Blockchain.' He stared back at the flat. 'This is the first time we've got close to him. We don't even know his real name.'

'You mean he wasn't christened Coldcut?' Fenchurch's smile bounced off Nelson's glare. 'You okay?'

'Not really. He's seen my face and now he knows we're sniffing around. This isn't good. Not good at all.'

'You need a minute?'

'We need to take him down.' Nelson buckled up. 'Let's start with Steve Fisher and see where he leads us.'

Chapter Twenty-Nine

Inspector . . .' Unwin leaned forward on his elbows as he gently shook his head. 'I'm bored of your attempts to goad my client.'

'I'm just trying to save everyone a lot of time and hassle.' Fenchurch leaned against his chair back, resting on his hands. 'This sort of case costs millions of pounds if it goes to court. You're telling me you'd rather that money didn't go to something more useful than convicting a guilty man?'

'You can't put a price on making sure innocence is preserved.'

'Let me out.' Steve's breathing was laboured, his mouth hanging open. 'I've given you an alibi. Cast-iron.' He hit the table. 'Cast. Iron.'

'Your alibi's made of talcum powder. Could drive a bus through it.'

Steve looked up at Fenchurch. 'What?'

'Turns out you were at your dealer's house all right, but you left just after nine o'clock.' Fenchurch gave him a few seconds, which he didn't fill. 'Five past at the *very* latest. Gayle was given that Blockchain at quarter past. The drug that killed her, Steve. And you were right next door to that hotel.'

Steve rocked back and forth.

'Are you denying it?'

'I . . .'

Unwin leaned over to whisper in his ear. Steve frowned, then nodded slowly. 'I went for a drink with a mate. Left after ten.'

Fenchurch laughed. 'A mate now?'

'He paid.'

'And does he have a name?'

Steve rested his head on the table.

'Back to that, Steve? Come on. You're mixing with some dodgy, dodgy people here. Drug dealers. Pretty soon, you'll be inside. Coldcut knows people inside, I suspect. Killers. You've rattled their cage — can you trust them not to kill you?'

'Colin's cool.'

Nelson frowned at him. 'Colin?'

'Shit.' Steve started banging his head off the desk. 'Shit.'

'What do you mean by Colin?'

'Nothing.'

'You know Coldcut?'

'That's who I went for a drink with.' Steve shook his head, rubbing his forehead off the wood. 'We went to the Third Planet. The bar next to the Bennaceur. That's why I was there.'

'You were drinking with a drug supplier?'

'I was at school with Colin. Our lives took different paths. I went to Durham; he . . . stayed in Shadwell.'

'Any chance we can confirm this story with him?'

'I've got a mobile number, but I'm not giving you it. Like you said, I'll have a target on my back.'

'Give us his full name, then?'

Steve thunked his forehead off the wood. 'What's the bloody point?' Again. He looked up at Fenchurch. 'Colin David Cutler.'

⌣

Nelson almost fell over as he tried to sit at a computer, the chair spinning underneath him. He shuffled over, his fingers typing faster than the machine wanted, making it spit out error beeps. 'This is the first lead we've had on Coldcut.' More typing. 'If we can get him and Younis in the same year . . .' His typing was furious, like it would crack the keyboard. 'Colin David Cutler. Col D Cut. Coldcut.' He grimaced. 'Quite cute when you think about it.'

'If that's your thing.'

Still typing, Nelson glanced at Fenchurch. 'You're welcome to get back in there with Steve.'

'The moment's passed, Jon.'

'Sweet Jesus!' Nelson punched the air like he'd just overtaken Dodoo on *Mario Kart*. 'We've got ourselves Coldcut.' He showed Fenchurch the screen. 'Born at the Royal London on the twelfth of June 1988. Grew up in Shadwell. Parents divorced at six. Shoplifting charge at fourteen. Stolen car at sixteen. Dealing at nineteen.' He frowned. 'Then nothing until—' He punched the desk. 'Shit.'

'What?' Fenchurch focused on the screen, reading all the detail: 'Colin Cutler died on fifteenth April 2008. Not even twenty. Shot in the face in Woolwich. This is bollocks!' Fenchurch pinged a nail off the screen. 'He was in the room with us!'

'Give me a second.' Nelson started typing again, like that'd do any good. 'Got something.' He let Fenchurch see. 'There's a note from Social Work. Says that after his parents' divorce, he lived with his paternal grandmother, Irene Jean Cutler.' He brought up a PNC. 'God rest her soul. Died in 2010.' Then he grinned wide.

Fenchurch scowled at him. 'Why aren't you pissed off?'

'Because I know that address.' Nelson pressed hard on the screen. 'Tower Hamlets have thirty-odd flats in Shadwell which they know they're renting to dead people. We've told them to keep it like that.'

'You think Coldcut's staying there?'

'One way to find out.'

Nelson parked outside a grim council house a couple of streets over from the school. Bare concrete blocks, flat roof. No greenery for miles around, just urban hell. 'You know you should tell Mulholland, don't you?'

'I know.' Fenchurch grinned. 'You're leading here. I'm just support.'

'Glad that's clear.' Nelson got out of the car and started off towards the big squad surrounding a meat wagon. He stopped at the garden gate. A settee and an old telly sat on a patch of bare mud, still splattered with rain days after the last shower. 'Now, let's bring Coldcut down.' He put his Airwave to his mouth. 'Kay, you in position?'

'Ready, Jon. Just like old times.'

Nelson laughed. 'Just waiting for Serial Alpha to sort themselves out.' He stopped by the squad.

A female DS was briefing them, getting nods and grunts for her trouble.

'Been years since I've seen you like this, Jon.'

'We're going to bring down Coldcut.' A broad grin. 'No bigger rush than that.'

The building looked empty. Whole row did, eight grotty little houses. 'You honestly think he's in there?'

'Fingers and toes crossed.'

The DS nodded at Nelson. 'We're good to go, Jon.'

Nelson's Airwave blasted out. 'Serial Bravo in position.' Reed's voice. 'Waiting for your signal, Jon. Over.'

Nelson checked around behind them. Six uniforms had followed them. He gave them a thumbs-up and got nods in return. Airwave to his mouth. 'We're good to go, Kay.' He waved at the house.

The first officer lugged an Enforcer over to the door. He primed it, then it swung, breaking the door in half. The uniform got out of the way and four of his mates piled in.

Fenchurch followed Nelson in, leaving two uniforms out front. Tiny little box, freezing inside. A battered old table near the front door, still had a rotary telephone on it. Mrs Cutler probably sat there every Sunday, speaking to her friends and family, getting all the gossip.

Four other doors, torchlight flashing in each. Looked like a burglary until an officer stepped out of the first one. 'Bathroom clear.'

'Kitchen clear.'

'Bedroom clear.'

'Got something in the living room.' Three officers piled through towards the voice. 'No, it's just a cat.' The uniform held up a ratty-looking tabby, then set it down outside the window. 'Stinks like a tramp's pants.'

Nelson slumped on to the chair by the phone table, looking destroyed as his golden thread had turned to shit.

'Come on, lads.' Fenchurch went over to the living room. 'Swap rooms, okay? Double-check each other's work. This isn't personal. We're just looking for evidence.'

They clattered about, torches flashing everywhere. Fenchurch clamped a hand on Nelson's shoulder. 'Jon, this isn't the end, okay?'

'I thought it was solid.' Nelson rocked back on the chair. Then the chair collapsed under him and he thudded to the floor. For a second he looked like he was going to murder someone, then he lay down and started laughing. 'And I thought it couldn't get any worse.'

Fenchurch grabbed his wrist and winched him up. 'You okay?'

'Just my pride injured.' Nelson stood up, dusting off his trousers. 'Really thought we—'

'Sir?' A uniform was in the bathroom doorway. 'This bath panel's wonky.'

In the room, another uniform was on his knees, his fingernails digging in behind the edges of a panel. It toppled back and he pulled it out. 'Holy shit.' He reached in and pulled out some pills. 'Blockchain, guv. Tons of it.'

Fenchurch clapped Nelson on the back. 'There's your result, Jon.'

His Airwave chimed. Reed. 'Guv, we've got movement in the garden!'

Fenchurch ran back into the hall, then into the kitchen. Empty, the back door swinging open. *Whichever muppet did this room failed to notice there was someone in here.*

Outside, a figure in a hooded top and dark trousers sprinted away from the house. Reed appeared at the end of the lane and Hoodie jerked back towards Fenchurch. He snapped his baton and lashed out. Missed by fractions of an inch. Hoodie darted across the grass, each stride long, and jumped over the hedge into the next-door garden.

'Get after them!' Fenchurch bombed over. The hedge was too tall. He jogged over to the gate and out into the back lane, then through the gate and into the garden.

Just in time to see Reed catch a whack and tumble over, landing on her back with a sickening thud.

Hoodie ran into Fenchurch, sending him flying. Managed to grab hold of a sleeve as he went down and pulled Hoodie to the deck too. Prick landed face first. Fenchurch squirmed over and yanked his wrist behind his back, putting all of his weight on, pinning him down. Caught a glimpse of dark skin. Hoodie twisted away from him. Then Fenchurch caught an elbow in the jaw. Hoodie shook off Fenchurch's grip and rolled on to his back. Two feet planted in Fenchurch's gut, pushing him back over.

Hoodie was standing over him, breathing hard, features hidden. He reached out a fist, ready to smack Fenchurch.

A uniform piled in from the lane, distracting Hoodie. A ninja kick to the face, full of grace and poise, and the cop tumbled over. Then Hoodie was on him, kicking and punching.

Fenchurch reached for his baton and swung out, catching Hoodie on the arse. He yelped, then was off, vaulting the fence. Fenchurch got up and tried to give chase.

By the time he was at the lane, Hoodie was long gone.

Chapter Thirty

Fenchurch leaned against the wall, wrestling with his knee until it popped. He let out a sharp breath. 'Oh, you bugger.'

Nelson swallowed hard. 'Is that supposed to happen?'

'It helps.' Fenchurch pulled himself up tall and tried to support his weight without the help of a building. His knee still ached, but he set off towards the lane. 'That wasn't Coldcut, Jon.'

Fenchurch had to rest against the gate. *First my balls, now my knee. What next?* 'The guy I chased off was' — he glanced at Nelson — 'African.'

'You can just say he was black, you know.' Nelson flared his nostrils as he started off down the back lane. 'Let me get this straight. We pitched up at Dodoo's flat, asking about Steve Fisher. Coldcut's there and he panics. Gets Dodoo to clear out this place, but didn't expect us to connect the dots so quickly. We've found his supply of Blockchain.' His nodding switched to a grimace. 'Only trouble is, it probably means Coldcut's gone to ground now.' He stuck his Airwave to his head and sped up. 'Sasha, I need you to bring Daniel Dodoo in for questioning.' He paused to open the squeaking gate for Fenchurch. 'Leman Street's fine.' He put his radio away and started off across Coldcut's grandmother's back garden, the weeds at waist height in places. 'I wish we had Coldcut in an interview room.'

'Cheer up, mate.' Fenchurch clapped his back. 'You know Coldcut's name now. This is just the start. You'll find other links. You'll get him.'

'We know who he is now and we've linked him to a stash.' Nelson stomped through the house, his boots cracking off the bare floorboards, then out the front door.

Fenchurch scanned the street, barely covered by street lights, let alone cameras. Didn't want to bring it up. He smiled at Nelson instead. 'Nobody else will die from taking Blockchain.'

'Very true.' Nelson stopped by his pool car. He rubbed his face, rasping the stubble on his chin. 'I'll keep you updated, okay?'

'Cheers, Jon.' Fenchurch walked off towards his own pool car, shoulders slumping.

'Guv.' Reed joined Fenchurch leaning against the car, dabbing at her lip. 'Bastard caught me right in the mouth.'

Fenchurch had a look. 'I get worse cuts shaving.'

'He got away.' Reed gritted her teeth, her gaze sweeping to the neighbouring house.

A silver Audi pulled up next to them.

Reed's eyes rolled. 'See you round, guv.' She wandered off towards Nelson and his squad of uniforms.

Mulholland got out of the car, her face pinched tight. 'Inspector.'

'Dawn.'

'I'm surprised that you're not in the Observation Suite watching DS Ashkani interview our chief suspect.' Mulholland pointed at the houses, torches flashing inside. 'What doesn't surprise me is finding you out here on a complete tangent to our case.'

'It's not a tangent, Dawn.' Fenchurch could barely look at her. 'Steve gave us an alibi, DI Nelson and I chased it down.'

'Chasing isn't your strong point any more.' Mulholland glanced down at his knee, then flashed her eyebrows. 'I take it you didn't find this Coldcut?'

'Not even close.' Fenchurch looked away. 'We've got hundreds of Blockchain pills, but—'

'Meanwhile, Steve Fisher needs to be interviewed. We still haven't charged him.'

'We're working on it.' Fenchurch folded his arms. 'He told us that he was at the hotel when Gayle was tied down and given the drugs. He had a personal supply of Blockchain, more than enough to kill his wife. And his alibi is a drug dealer who said Steve wasn't with him at the time in question.'

'We need *evidence*, Simon.' She waved a hand at the house. 'And upsetting drug suppliers isn't achieving that goal, is it?'

'Dawn.' Fenchurch stood up tall and squared his shoulders. 'Jon Nelson is your officer. I was happy to take responsibility for him, but you insisted.'

Mulholland looked hard at him for a few seconds. 'You've been going against my explicit orders all day. Raiding half of East London, running drug searches. You're not the one who has to field angry calls from newspapers. And from Ben Maxfield and Elliot Lynch's parents!'

No, but I'm the one who has to work for you.

Fenchurch didn't say anything.

'Simon, you're lucky I've not got you on an insubordination charge.'

'Try it, Dawn.' Fenchurch couldn't help but laugh. 'See where it gets you.'

'You're still angry about my dirty little secret, aren't you?' She licked her lip slowly, her thin tongue like a snake's. 'That happened a long time ago. There was nothing that linked him to your daughter's disappearance.'

Fenchurch stared at her for a few seconds then shook his head. 'I'll see you tomorrow.' He marched off towards his car, leaving the case behind for another night. Leaving her to run it. Of all people. He stopped by the car and opened the door, looking back at Mulholland. Let it go. Let her have her minute in the sun. It'll soon be over.

'You okay?' Nelson's car pulled up next to him. He sucked on his vape stick. 'You should've told Mulholland.'

'You're not wrong.' Fenchurch got in his car and wound down the window, face-to-face with Nelson. 'Can you get in a room with Steve Fisher and get him to confess?'

'Si, that's Mulholland's remit.'

'I just want you in there with him. Get him to talk. We've got this place to press him with. At least destroy his alibi.'

'Fine.' Nelson started his car. 'I'll keep you posted.'

Fenchurch watched the motor trundle down the lane. *Just hope he keeps me in the loop.*

———

'You know your daddy, don't you?' Fenchurch held Baby Al high up in the air, got him to giggle. And gurgle. 'Yes, you do!' He pulled him close and hugged him tight. 'Oh, you do.' A lump caught in his throat. His nose prickled. His eyes watered. 'You do.'

'He's been a lot better today.' Abi stood next to Fenchurch, grinning as much as their son. 'Smiling and playing.'

Chloe was on the chair next to the cot, elbows on her knees. Didn't look so sure.

Fenchurch hugged Baby Al again, smiling at Chloe. 'You okay, love?'

She just shrugged.

Fenchurch handed the baby to Abi, then put his arms round Chloe's shoulders. 'You get back to work in time?'

She didn't even look up. 'Course I did.'

'So what's up?'

'Nothing.'

He saw right through her thin smile. 'Come on, what's up?'

Chloe looked up, brushing her hair out of her eyes, then over at her mother.

'There you all are.' Dr Oates marched into the room, his heels clicking on the floor, Stephenson following. 'How are we all today?'

Fenchurch rested against the cot. 'Getting there.'

Abi tickled Baby Al under his chin, got him to laugh. 'He's been happier today.'

'I spent a while with him this morning.' Oates took him off Abi. He focused on the baby, puckering his lips like a fish. 'He's a great kid. Vibrant personality.'

Abi chanced a cheeky smile at her husband. 'He gets that from his father.'

'Sure he does.' Oates gave Al back to her. 'Have you decided on whether you want to give these fine hands a shot?' He fanned out his fingers in the time-honoured 'jazz hands' tradition.

'I thought we'd agreed?' Abi was frowning, first at Fenchurch then at Oates.

'You need to sign paperwork, I'm afraid.' Oates clicked his fingers for Stephenson. 'Luckily I have it right here.'

'Okay.' Abi put Al on Chloe's lap and grabbed the paper from Stephenson. She barely looked at it before signing it, then passed it over.

Fenchurch took the form and started reading the small print. *Nothing particularly untoward in there. But . . . Jesus, it's all the reasons my son can die during surgery.* He put the page on the table next to the cot, unsigned. 'Before I sign that, I need you to take me through the risks.'

Oates couldn't look him in the eyes. 'It's going to be fine.'

Fenchurch snorted. 'It's not your son's life in the balance here. I just want to know what could go wrong.'

'Well.' Oates sighed, then locked eyes with Fenchurch. 'Like any surgery, we may lose the patient. There's also risk of infection and—'

'You may lose him?'

'It's an incredibly small risk, but things may not go how we plan during the operation.'

'And he'll just die?'

'That's right.' Oates reached over and tickled Al's cheek. 'It won't happen, though. Will it, my little soldier? No, it won't.'

'I've a very hard time trusting people.' Fenchurch wanted to grab the baby and run away, far away, somewhere this shit wasn't happening. 'I need more than you saying it's not a problem for me to give my son's life. I need more than jazz hands.'

'The truth is you don't have a choice.' Oates sucked in a deep breath through his nostrils. 'Usually, we have three options. Do this, do that, do nothing. Doing nothing usually means staying where you are. Maybe it's move to another part of London, move out of London or stay in your current home. We don't have that with your son. Doing nothing means he won't get to blow out that first candle.'

Felt like Fenchurch had been kicked in the balls again. Felt like they'd been torn off.

Oates grabbed the form from the table. 'If you sign this, I'll operate on him tomorrow afternoon.'

'That soon?'

'That soon.' Oates nodded as he held out the page. 'We don't have the luxury of time. I'm due back in Cleveland Wednesday.' He grinned. 'Sorry, force of habit. I'm due back *on* Wednesday.'

Fenchurch didn't take the form. Folded his arms instead. 'And there's no chance he'll get better on his own?'

'I've studied thousands and thousands of cases, operated on hundreds myself. If a patient doesn't respond to the closure device, we're fiddling in the margins. And the only way to get them back over the line on to the main page is through this surgery.' Oates picked up the form and waved it in Fenchurch's face. 'Now, you've got the option of having one of the best surgeons in the world operating on your son.'

Fenchurch could barely breathe. His head felt like it was trapped in a car door and someone kept slamming it. 'What does the operation involve?'

'I'll cut some tissue from his right atria.' Oates held up a hand. 'Perfectly safely. It'll regrow.' He smiled. 'In fact, part of the problem is how good Baby Al is at growing tissue on that side of his heart. Then I'll make a series of incisions in his left atria and stitch in this tissue and it'll—' He grinned. 'I'll use layman's terms here. It'll plug the hole and, once he's out the other side, the tissue will knit together and he'll be healthy again.'

'Isn't that what the closure device was supposed to do?'

'His tissue was supposed to grow over it.' Oates sighed. 'It didn't.'

'And how is this any different?'

'Because this will be his own tissue growing over his own tissue, not trying to crawl over a foreign object.' Oates let out another sigh, losing patience. 'Listen, you've got an A-B choice here. Let him die or give him a chance. What is it?'

Fenchurch stared at the form in his hands. 'It's no choice, is it?'

'No. But now you know all those risks? You're giving yourself a whole world of worry.'

Abi was pleading with her eyes.

'Welcome to my world . . .' Fenchurch took the form and signed it.

Feels good to make the decision. Not that choosing between my son's death and giving him a chance at life is a decision. Usually life isn't an option, just someone's death and how I investigate it.

He handed the form back and held it as Oates took it. 'Please, save my son's life.'

Chapter Thirty-One

I just want to focus on what could go *right*, Simon.' Abi was in passenger seat, staring out of the window. Chloe was in the back, holding her mother's hands over the seat rest. 'Why do you always focus on the negatives?'

'It's either my training' — Fenchurch pulled up in front of their house — 'or it's who I am.'

'You weren't always like this.'

'There's your answer, then.' Fenchurch killed the engine and got out.

'Simon?' Katerina was shivering beneath a streetlight.

What the hell is she doing here?

Katerina walked towards him. 'Was that helpful?'

'Was what?'

'The information I gave you on Steve.'

'I appreciate it. I need you to give a formal statement on the matter, so expect some police officers around your—'

'Can't I give it to you?'

'I'm too busy and it's not really my job.'

'Right. Can I come to the station?'

'That works, too.'

Katerina nodded slowly. Then started looking around. She frowned at the car. 'Is that Chloe? Can I speak to her?'

'I told you that's not appropriate.' Fenchurch stepped closer to her. Saw that she was resting against a bicycle. 'How did you know where I lived?'

'The photos in all of the papers . . . I just thought . . .' Her lips pursed together. 'I thought that Chloe might know what I'm going through.'

'She's got her own problems.' Fenchurch gave her a smile. 'Look, I appreciate the lead. It's been useful. Can I give you a lift home?'

'I've got my bike.' She started off, her chain rattling. 'Goodnight.'

Fenchurch watched her go. Couldn't stop himself from shaking his head.

Weird.

And worrying. All the shit Liam plastered over the papers has left me exposed. People know my life like I'm in a book. Know where I live, where I work. Shit, they probably know my favourite burrito places.

Need to get someone to check up on Katerina. Clearly not dealing with the situation at all well.

He looked back at the car. Chloe and Abi were still inside, chatting away. *And I need to keep her away from my daughter.*

He walked over to the flat. Two men walked down from the end of the street. Dad was bellowing with laughter. Same as it ever was.

Pete was following him, dressed for a much more formal occasion — sports jacket, shirt, jeans, shiny shoes. Greying hair, chunky glasses, his chin covered in a wispy beard.

Jesus, he could be me. The silvering hair, the height, the build. Never healthy when your daughter's type is you.

'But I want to leave a nest egg for my grandkids.' Fenchurch's old man was clutching a bottle of Tizer. He looked knackered, liked he'd barely slept. He noticed his son and started limping over. 'Simon!'

Fenchurch let Dad grab him in a hug. 'What are you annoying him about?'

Pete grinned as he offered his hand to Fenchurch. 'Just asking some investment advice.'

'Dad . . .' Fenchurch nudged him towards the door. 'He's not always like this, I promise.'

Pete chuckled. 'He is every time I've met him.'

How many times was that before you met us?

Fenchurch glanced back at the car. Still locked in a deep and meaningful chat.

Dad clapped Fenchurch's arm. 'Simon, he worked for an investment bank! He knows all about investments.'

'I ran the metals desk.' Pete waved him off. 'It's completely different to investing savings.'

'Can't be *that* different.' Dad took a glug of Tizer, gasping as he put the lid back on. 'Bert told me about this thing he's doing where—'

Pete held up his hands. 'Ian, if it sounds too good to be true, it's probably a Ponzi scheme.'

'Bert likes to wear a cravat sometimes, but I wouldn't call him *poncey.*'

'Ponzi, Dad. Like Bernie Madoff?'

'Oh, that Yank who stole all those film stars' money?' Dad grinned. 'Right.' Then he frowned. 'So you think Bert's going to lose his money?'

'It might be legit, but I'd always be suspicious. Get your IFA to look it over.' Pete gave him a wink. 'Anyway, an ex-cop like you shouldn't be trusting people too easily, Ian.'

'Dad's not exactly an idiot.'

'I didn't mean anything by it.' Pete held up his hands again. 'Just ask your IFA.'

'I ain't got one.'

'Well get one. I could recommend a couple?'

'Smashing.'

In the car, Abi and Chloe were arguing about something. He unlocked the front door. 'Right, let's get inside, then.' He let Dad and Pete go first. 'They'll follow us up.'

———

'And then I decided to get out.' Pete sipped his tap water, then rested it back on the table. He was next to Dad, the pair of them crammed in on one side.

Fenchurch looked around the kitchen again. Abi and Chloe were over at the cooker, muttering to each other. Chloe kept scowling at her mother. He put his phone back in his pocket.

'You okay, love?'

'We're fine, Dad.'

'Okay.' Fenchurch felt his phone buzz in his pocket. He got it out and checked the message.

Nelson: NOTHING TO REPORT. I'LL UPDATE YOU IN THE MORNING. OK? OUT.

Fenchurch tapped out a message: NOT GOOD ENOUGH. I WANT HIM SQUASHED, JON. GIVE ME AN UPDATE IN HALF AN HOUR.

The little dots appeared under the message. His phone buzzed again: YOU DON'T GET ANY BETTER, DO YOU? FINE. I'LL CALL WHEN I'VE GOT SOMETHING.

Fenchurch put his phone away and focused on Pete, leaning closer like he was interviewing him. 'Why did you decide to?'

'It was going to kill me if I stayed there. I'd given my life to it and all I had was an AA membership.'

'Oh, I'm an RAC man.' Dad leaned back, picking at his teeth. 'But Bert was saying he gets breakdown cover free with his bank account or something?'

'Alcoholics Anonymous, Dad.' Fenchurch felt a sharp pain. 'Like with Doc.'

'Ah, right.' Dad nodded slowly, still picking at his teeth. 'So your doctor said you had a problem?'

'My liver's not what it once was. Too many client lunches and dinners. These guys were putting in millions every day, but we'd have to entertain them on expenses. Five pints of lager, nothing to eat.' Pete looked like he was reliving the terror, drowning in each remembered pint. 'Bottles of wine with dinner, pubs, clubs. Home at two in the morning and up again at six, trying to get a day's work done before the drinking starts again.'

'Sounds like when I joined the Met.' Dad laughed. 'Only joking.'

Pete stared at his glass of water like it was his tenth lager. 'I wouldn't recommend setting foot within the Square Mile, let alone working there.'

'I've had a few run-ins with the City cops over the years. So's Simon. They run their own police—'

'I've seen them. Uzis on Bishopsgate. Like another country.'

Dad frowned as he took another glug of Tizer. 'Was it cancer?'

'Was what?'

'Why you can't drink?'

'Just common or garden liver damage. That's all. I'm fit as a fiddle otherwise. Run 10k every morning. Do yoga three times a week.'

'You ever try to stop?' Fenchurch leaned back in his chair, getting a creak, and took a sip of his wine. 'Go to your bosses and say, I can do the job but I'm cutting out the booze?'

'When you're at the coal face, it's sink or swim.'

Dad cackled. 'Sounds like your Cornish engine's knackered, mate.'

'It's my liver, not my heart.'

Dad bellowed out laughter, loud enough for Chloe and Abi to look over. 'No, Pete. A Cornish engine's what they used for pumping water out of a mine. If you're sinking at the coal face, you've got a serious problem.'

Pete groaned. 'It was a metaphor.' Then he grinned. 'Felt like I was swimming in Jägermeister sometimes.'

Fenchurch sipped his wine again. 'Are we talking nightclubs or private members' clubs?'

'The latter.'

'I'll assume it's not the Groucho or that artists' one in Soho?'

Pete didn't answer.

'Lap dancing, yeah?'

'Listen, I didn't have a choice!'

Chloe and Abi both had their hands on their hips, synchronised glaring at Fenchurch.

'You've always got a choice, Pete. Go along with it or fight it.'

'It's not that simple.'

'You didn't have to take that money. You didn't have to ruin your body.'

'You're telling me . . . But I'm financially secure. Never have to work again. I can do the degree I want rather than the one I felt compelled to do—'

'And that justifies it?' Fenchurch put his glass down and rested on his forearms. 'This city's going to shit because of bankers and management consultants and property developers squeezing every last penny out of people. Forcing them out of areas they grew up in. Cutting public services just so they can cut their taxes.'

'I worked in metals. I had nothing to do with that.'

'Bet you've got a nice flat, yeah?'

'Kensington. And it's a house.'

'There you go. You know how much that place costs to—'

Abi gripped Fenchurch's bicep. 'Can you give me a hand getting some more wine in?'

'But I'm the only—'

'Need to chill some white for Chloe.' She gave him a frosty glare, her eyebrows raised. 'You know I can't get the chiller to work.'

'Right. Okay.' Fenchurch got up, whispering to Pete on his way up, 'This isn't over, okay?'

'Simon!'

Fenchurch joined Abi in the hallway. 'I've only got—'

'This isn't about the sodding wine.' She batted his chest, then pointed a finger at him. 'You need to start behaving. You're treating him like he's killed someone.'

'This is me going easy.'

'Christ, Simon. He's your daughter's boyfriend. Be civil to him.'

'You've heard his chat. He's an ex-investment banker. Can't drink any more.' Fenchurch leaned against the door. 'Bloody bankers. They're all psychopaths. They don't give a shit about anyone else. I'm trying to stop my daughter getting hooked up with Patrick Bateman and you're—'

'Patrick who?'

'The guy in *American Psycho*.'

'I haven't seen it.'

'It was a better book than a film.' Fenchurch folded his arms. 'For Chloe's sake, I'll treat him like he's not a psychopath, but the second he starts talking about Genesis albums, I'll—'

'What the hell are you talking about?'

'It's in the book. Never mind.' Fenchurch nodded slowly. 'Fine. I'll be civil.'

Abi waved back through. 'Get in there and help me mash the bloody potatoes.'

———

'I know what you're all going through.' Pete reached across the table for Chloe's hand. 'Two years ago. My sister, she had a baby in . . . the same situation as your son.' He wiped away some tears. 'That's the only time I ever had any leeway at work. Didn't have to schmooze, just got on with the job, left at lunchtime, supported Cara through it.' He bared his teeth. 'Joshua died on Easter Sunday 2015, so we've got two anniversaries to mourn every year — the actual date and Easter Sunday. Her husband couldn't even visit the hospital.'

Abi glared at Fenchurch and muttered, 'Not a psychopath.'

Chloe sipped some wine, her glass frosted. 'You poor thing. I didn't know that.'

'You're the ones going through it all now.' Pete pushed his chair back and got to his feet. 'Anyway, I must head off.' He buttoned up his sports jacket. 'I'm working at the university over the summer and it's an early start.'

'I did that when I was a student.' Abi joined him standing. 'Stuffing prospectuses into envelopes for the International Office. Easy money.'

'I'm doing research with a linguistics professor.'

'Oh.'

'It's cool, actually. But taxing.'

Abi nodded. Then thumbed into the hall. 'You can stay if you want.'

'Mum!' Chloe's mouth hung open.

'That's fine.' Pete raised his hands again. Such a bad habit that he must've been deflecting bullets all day, every day in his career. 'I'll politely decline the offer but this has been fantastic. Abi, the chicken was to die for.'

'Just the chicken?'

'And the rest of it.' Pete laughed. 'Simon, I'm sure your wine would've been lovely.'

'It was, thanks.' Fenchurch raised his glass.

'But thanks for having me. I know this isn't easy.'

'You getting a cab?' Dad downed the last of his Tizer. 'I'll join you.'

'I'll get a Travis.' Pete held up his phone, showing the Travis Cars app. 'Hang on, don't you live out east?'

'Limehouse.'

'Well, you were listening when your son got the fact I live in Kensington out of me during his interrogation, weren't you?'

'That wasn't him interrogating you, son. You can still walk.' Dad laughed. 'Anyway, help me catch one of them cab things, would you?'

'I'll help you, Grandpa.' Chloe nudged the table as she got up, then took Pete and Dad into the hall.

Abi collapsed into her chair. 'I'm shattered.' She scanned the mess around them. 'Think that'll keep till the morning?'

'I'll fill the dishwasher.' Fenchurch took his wife's hand and squeezed. 'We should've maybe postponed this, what with—'

'No, you should've been less of an arsehole to Pete.'

'What do you expect?' Fenchurch stared into his glass, just a thin puddle left at the bottom. 'Look, if he's going to take our little girl away from us, I want to know he's right for her, okay?'

She yawned into her fist. 'I'm meeting my supervisor tomorrow morning.'

'I forgot about that.'

'A year's maternity leave almost up and I've not settled our son in here.' She went over and kissed his cheek. 'Thank you for stopping being a twat to Pete.'

'Don't mention it.'

She walked off, yawning. 'Night.'

'Night.' Fenchurch drank the last glug of his glass, savouring the peppery prickle. Caught Abi's yawn.

Shouldn't drink any more and end up like Pete.

One more glass isn't going to take me there, though, is it?

He tipped the rest of the bottle in. Bit more than he'd expected.

The front door shut, a draught of cold air whispering across Fenchurch.

'That stuff any good?' Chloe sat next to him.

'Have some.' Fenchurch tipped half of his glass into hers, didn't spill a drop. *So many years of practice with Nelson.* 'Dad get his cab all right?'

'Pete paid the fare up front.'

'Least Dad's not at risk of paying the fifty-quid vomit fine, unlike last night.' Fenchurch waited for a laugh, but didn't get one. 'Sorry I was being a twat earlier; he didn't deserve it. Pete seems okay. And I'm sorry for upsetting you.'

'It's okay, Dad. Really.' She tried the wine. 'Gah, that's horrible.'

'I used to hate the taste. One of those things you get used to. This is good stuff, too. Twenty quid a bottle.'

'And you say Pete's an idiot with his money . . .' Didn't stop her trying another sip. 'In the hospital earlier, I could see how angry you felt.'

'I hate it when I can't control things, love. At work, I'm working for this woman and . . . it's complicated.'

'What's she done?'

'I told you, it's complicated.'

'You can trust me, Dad.'

'Of everyone, you're the only one that I can.' Fenchurch gave her a warm smile. 'When you went missing, she was on the team. Just a DS. I was a DI, but I wasn't allowed on the case for obvious reasons. And she screwed up. Badly. Made a mess of a lead. The man who kidnapped you. We could've found you a lot sooner if it hadn't been for that.'

She was staring into the glass. 'You had them?'

'Sort of. I don't know.' Fenchurch drank some wine, but it tasted like bleach instead of a rich Bordeaux. 'Maybe it wouldn't have done anything.'

'So you're angry with this poor woman because you've made an assumption?' Chloe nudged her glass away. 'Dad, the people who took me were professional. Organised. Efficient. It was even kind of an accident that you found me. Whatever this is, whatever you're holding over her, you need to move on from it. Okay?'

'Chloe, I—'

'Dad, you see what clinging on has done to Pete, yeah?' She got up and kissed him on the head. 'Just stay sane, okay?'

Fenchurch nodded slowly. Then smiled at her. 'You need a lift tomorrow?'

'Not working. Let me sleep in, okay?'

'No porridge?'

'I'll make some when I get up.' She padded off through the kitchen. 'Night.'

'Night.'

Just stay sane . . . Easier said than done.

Fenchurch got out his phone and checked for updates. A text from Nelson: CALL ME.

So he did.

'Si.' Nelson yawned. 'I'm just heading home now.' Another yawn, halting this time. 'We were in there for a couple of hours, me and Kay. Just like old times, but without you smashing the suspect in the face.'

'Very good. Did you get anything?'

'He knows Coldcut, but that's all he's giving us. Sorry.'

'Right. Well. Thanks for keeping me updated.'

And he was gone. *Charming.*

Fenchurch drained his glass and started on Chloe's.

———

'Simon?'

Fenchurch jolted awake. Heart thudding, head thick. Mouth like an ashtray. Sitting at the kitchen table. Empty bottle of red in front of him. The microwave read 2.48.

'You okay?' Abi nudged the door shut behind her and sat opposite him. 'What the hell are you up to?'

228

'Fell asleep.' Fenchurch went over to the sink, full of dirty dishes he hadn't tidied. Had to angle the glass as he filled it with water. 'I dreamed about Chloe taking a load of this drug I'm investigating.'

'You shouldn't drink so much.'

'You're right.' Fenchurch yawned, then took another gulp of water. Felt pissed. 'Can't sleep?'

'I tried, but I keep thinking of the operation. This time tomorrow, Al will be recovering. But what if he's not?'

Fenchurch put the glass to his cheeks, trying to cool himself down. 'There's nothing else we can do but wait and see.'

'I know. It's just . . .' Her face screwed up, her eyes red. 'I don't want to lose him.'

'Come here.' Fenchurch walked over and held her tight. 'Whatever happens, happens, okay? There's nothing we can do. It's down to Oates and his magic fingers.'

'What if Al dies?'

'Every second of every day since he was born, we've been there for him, fighting for him. All we can do is give him a chance, give him hope that he'll pull through.'

DAY 3
Monday, 11th September 2017

Chapter Thirty-Two

'—another victim in a spate of acid attacks hitting London.'

Fenchurch pulled up outside Leman Street's rear entrance and reached over to kill the radio. First time he'd listened to a music station in years: a terrible mix of vacuous pop and news of the world falling apart. Still, not as bad as the racist idiots on the phone-ins. Maybe.

He got out into the rain, pulling his suit jacket over his head to avoid the worst of it.

'—my authority!' Uzma was by the back door, hands out wide, face twisted up. 'You stupid cow!'

'I'll smash your face in.' Reed stepped forward into Fenchurch's line of sight, fists clenched but still at her side. 'You think you're so much better than me, don't you? Well, I've got news—'

'Oy!' Fenchurch shot up the steps and pulled them apart. A mix of perfume and hissing breath. 'What the *hell* is going on here?'

Reed waved an angry hand. 'She started it.' Couldn't look at Fenchurch.

'Bollocks.' Uzma jabbed an angrier finger, shaking slightly. Eyes pleading with Fenchurch. 'She's out of order, sir.'

Back at the playground . . .

'DS Ashkani, can you please tell everyone that I'm delaying the briefing until my two sergeants can act like adults?'

'This isn't my—'

'Now, please. I'll see you in my office afterwards. Okay?'

With a huff, Uzma swiped through the security door, then glared at Reed as the door shut behind her.

Fenchurch waited until she was inside, teeth clenched. 'Kay, the last thing I expect when I turn up is you tearing lumps out of her.'

'I would've thought it'd be the first thing.' Reed waved at the door. 'She's . . .' The rain was flattening Reed's hair. 'Bloody hell . . .'

Fenchurch stared into her eyes, head tilted to the side. 'What's she done?'

'The same divisive shit as Mulholland.' Reed paced away from him, then stopped and came back, arms folded. 'She said everything has to go through her.'

Fenchurch prodded his own chest. 'It goes through me, Kay.'

'I know that. Didn't help that I couldn't get hold of you.'

Fenchurch got out his phone. The screen was filled with missed calls and texts from her. Not a million miles away from what Gayle Fisher's phone had looked like. 'Sorry, I was driving.'

'And last night?'

'Busy.' The texts were all a variation on Call me, progressing to Have you lost your phone? Fenchurch wiped the rain off the screen and put his mobile away. 'What did you want?'

'Loads of things.' Reed started counting off on her fingers. 'First, we're still getting hassle getting hold of CCTV in the Minories. Lisa lost her account again.'

'I spoke to that guy, Kay. Sure you can run rings around him.'

'Piss off . . .' Reed counted off another finger. 'Last night, I found out that Gayle has a life insurance policy. Steve's going to receive over half a million.'

Fenchurch leaned back against the wet brick. 'Shit.'

'And her will gives him sole ownership of the house. I checked with an estate agent Dave plays squash with. He reckons it's worth eight hundred grand. *Minimum*. No mortgage. She inherited it when it was worth a hundred. Didn't have to pay any inheritance tax.'

Fenchurch totted up in his head. Didn't take long. 'So Steve gets over a million in the event of her death?'

'Except for suicide.'

'Of course.' Fenchurch walked over to the door, wiping rain out of his hair in a spray. 'Let me guess, Uzma's been trying to take credit for the discovery?'

'Taking all the brownie points from Mulholland. I was in till ten last night, guv. On a *Sunday*. I mentioned it to her when we were queuing for coffee next door and she thinks it's hers.'

Fenchurch swiped through the door. 'Get Unwin back in.'

———

Fenchurch nudged his office door open with his wrist. His coffee's cardboard sleeve had slid up the cup and he was holding molten lava.

Uzma was standing there, frowning at him. 'Simon, I need a word.'

'Just a sec.' Fenchurch dumped his coffee on his desk and shook his hand in the air. 'Bloody hell. Why do they have to make it so hot?'

Uzma was frowning at his hand. 'You okay?'

'I'm fine.' Fenchurch stretched it out. Felt like third-degree burns, like those Americans who sued fast-food chains when a Pop-Tart exploded in their faces or whatever. Or he just needed to man up. He snapped the lid off and blew on the coffee. 'DS Ashkani, did you manage to defer the briefing?'

'I did, but I've got something you need to see now.' She held up a sheet of paper. 'One of my officers has managed to get hold of the hotel's security card supplier. This is the access log for Gayle's room.'

'Okay, is there anything interesting on it?'

'Oh yes.' Uzma sucked in a deep breath as she passed him the page. 'The only card used to access the room after Gayle belonged to Jim Muscat.'

Uzma pointed at an interview room. 'He's in there, but—'

'Muscat's still here?' Fenchurch stomped down the corridor towards the interview room. 'He should've been in front of a judge this morning. Why haven't you charged him yet?'

'DCI Mulholland told me not to. Said it's not revenge porn until he publishes it. Also, got to prove that he intended to use it for pornographic reasons.'

'Great.' Fenchurch tried a sip of coffee. Cold. Seemed like all the warmth had gone into superheating the cup. 'Makes sense, I suppose.' He sunk the coffee in one go and dropped the cup in the recycling. 'You okay to lead in here?'

'Sure.' Uzma entered the interview room, head high.

'Sir.' Jim Muscat looked up when Fenchurch entered, sweating like he'd just run from Wales. 'What's going on? When am I getting out of here?'

'Not my remit, sir.' Fenchurch sat down next to Uzma. 'Sergeant?'

'We need to ask about this.' She passed the access log to Muscat's lawyer, who looked a bit too young to be able to represent his client effectively. 'Care to explain how—?'

'This is bollocks!' Muscat snatched the sheet off his lawyer. 'Complete bollocks!' His mouth hung open. 'You think I killed her?'

'It would explain a few things. You've covered up for someone running a brothel in this hotel, now this.'

'I haven't.'

'Just stop. You knew what was going on here. And you're an ex-cop.' Fenchurch shook his head. 'What do they have on you?'

'Nothing.'

'Do you get a free shot or something? Claudia's a nice young woman. You're a single man. That what's going on?'

'I can't lose this job.'

'Security is a growth business in this day and age. There are tons of other ones.'

'It's not that simple . . .' Muscat bit his lip, then snorted. 'The reason Oliver's mother left me is I like a gamble. Horses, football, casino, you name it. Got myself in a bit of debt and Beth left me. Wanted to take Oliver, but he wanted to stay with me. Then, somehow, my sergeant got wind of it, hence me leaving the force. Bet it was that bitch who told him . . .'

'And let me guess, Nazar owns a casino?'

'Sutekh does. Down in Putney. He covered the debt, in exchange for me working the security gig and turning a blind eye to certain activities.'

'Like the brothel?'

'No, like the fact that half the East End drug lords drink in the bar and screw Russian whores in one of the rooms.' Muscat picked at a scab on his lip. 'Anyway, it's all fine. I'm sitting there, pretending to work while all these scumbags are coming and going.' He punched his fist into the table edge. Looked like it hurt but he didn't even flinch. 'I still owe him eighty grand.'

'Jim.' His lawyer elbowed him gently. Then whispered in his ear as he tapped on the page.

'Oh, right.' Muscat leaned back, smiling. 'I wasn't here when that girl was killed.'

Fenchurch shot a glance at Uzma. 'What?'

'I left work at six, then went to the football to watch my boy play.'

'You were at the football?'

'All night.' Muscat's smile widened. 'I'm a season ticket holder at Shadwell, so I didn't have to pay.' Then he glowered at them. 'And, before you ask, I stayed until the bitter end, unlike that little shit, Oliver. Waste of blood and spunk.' His smile returned. 'Beautiful goal in the second half, though.'

Fenchurch couldn't help himself from glaring at Uzma. 'What about after the match?'

'Went to that boozer down the road.' Muscat frowned. 'The one without the name. Can't remember what it's called. We just say "the pub".'

'Did you have your card with you all the time?'

'It's attached to my neck chain. You know, the one you broke yesterday?'

Fenchurch sighed. 'Could anybody else have had your card?'

'Not mine. I mean, someone could've cloned it, right?'

Fenchurch flinched. *Make a copy of the bloody thing. I was too quick to jump to the same conclusion as Uzma.*

'But they'd need that, surely?'

Muscat cleared his throat. 'I didn't have my eyes on it when I was backing up that video . . .'

Chapter Thirty-Three

Y ou didn't even check that he had the card on him.' Fenchurch
stormed down the corridor, pushing between Nelson and Bridge,
then turned the corner. He chanced a glance at Uzma to check she was
still with him. 'You need to tie your shoelaces before you run. Otherwise
you'll knock your own bloody teeth out.'

'What's that supposed to mean?'

Fenchurch stopped outside the interview room. 'You've been grass-
ing on me to Dawn Mulholland, when I need you to focus on your core
activities. Okay?'

Uzma slipped into the Incident Room without a word.

She'll be the death of me. Her or her bloody puppet master . . .

He looked behind him. Nelson and Bridge were locked in deep
conversation.

Take a step back. What does it all mean?

Someone used Muscat's card to get in the room.

But he swore that he had it with him at the football.

So, someone had to clone the card. Time to check.

Bridge walked past on her way back to the Incident Room.

Fenchurch blocked her passage. 'Lisa, have you still got the hotel
CCTV for Friday night?'

'Sure. What time?'

'Around six?'

Bridge walked over to her desk and sat, yawning. 'In or out?'

'Both.'

'Front or back?'

'Start with the front. Looking for Jim Muscat.'

'Okay . . .' Bridge pulled it up. The screen filled with footage of the hotel's front door. Bang on six, Jim Muscat left, like he'd just clocked off in a Victorian factory.

'Is that what you wanted to see?'

'Well, no, but it makes sense.' Fenchurch drew a finger round Muscat. 'Lisa, can you do me a favour?'

'If it involves looking at more bloody CCTV . . .'

'I need you to visit Shadwell United Football Club and check that he was there on Friday night.' Fenchurch retraced the shape around Muscat. 'Oh, and that pub down the road, too. The one without a sign up. He said he was in there after the match.'

'Sir.' She wrote it in her notebook, nodded keenly. 'I'll get right out there. Thanks.' She walked off, striding like she'd just been promoted.

Fenchurch had a look round the Incident Room. Uzma and Nelson were chatting by the whiteboard. *Wonder what that's ab—*

His phone rang. The spiders crawled up his spine. Martin, the Custody Sergeant. Nothing to do with Baby Al. He put the phone to his ear. 'What's up?'

'Got Steve Fisher's lawyer down here for you.'

⌣

Uzma was outside the interview room, looking like she was going to wrap her fingers round someone's throat and just squeeze. Then she clocked Fenchurch and did a double take. 'Sir, his lawyer's just gone in.'

'Could've sworn I told you to delay the briefing, Sergeant, then meet me in my office.'

'I did, sir.' Uzma was looking round Fenchurch at Reed. 'Thought you'd want me in the interview?'

'What gave you that impression?'

Uzma cleared her throat and stared at the corridor floor. 'Sorry.'

'Delay the—' Fenchurch frowned, then started nodding at her. 'Actually, Uzma, can you run the briefing for me?'

'Simon, I'm not sure I'm up to speed with—'

'This is your chance, okay?' Fenchurch leaned back against the interview room door.

Uzma walked off, giving Reed a curt nod as she passed her.

'She looks pissed off.' Reed patted Fenchurch on the arm. 'What happened?'

'Nothing. You okay to run this?'

'Sure thing.' Reed entered the room.

Fenchurch went into the Obs Suite and settled down on the chair. The room reeked of toffee popcorn.

Onscreen, Steve Fisher and his lawyer, Dalton Unwin, were locked in conference, nodding and frowning at each other.

Reed sat opposite, elbows on the table, next to one of Uzma's DCs. Couldn't remember his name. 'You need any more time?'

Unwin sat back, fiddling with his jewelled earring. 'We're good to go, Sergeant.'

Reed gave a polite nod. 'Mr Fisher, did you or your wife have any insurance policies?'

'Car. House.' Steve shrugged. 'Usual stuff. Gayle had one for her phone that I didn't think was good value.'

Reed smiled. 'I meant life insurance.'

'Don't think so.'

'What about when you got married?'

'Not that I can think of.'

Reed nudged a document across the table. 'So this joint-names insurance policy we found isn't yours?'

'I for—' Steve got a nudge from Unwin and shut up.

'Were you about to say that you forgot that you took out an insurance policy?'

'No comment.'

'Okay.' Reed pushed more paper across the table. 'These are copies of your bank statements. You've been paying just short of fifty quid a month for this policy.'

'No comment.'

'Do you pay close attention to your finances, Mr Fisher?'

'Gayle did all that. I fixed up the house, cooked and cleaned. She did the shopping, the garden and all the admin.'

'Sounds fair.' Reed sat back in her seat, taking a few seconds to switch her gaze back to Steve. 'Thing is, I've got a mortgage on my house. Bloody huge one, too. Costs a lot to live in London, doesn't it? Most people in the south-east don't pay down the capital on their mortgages. They just pay the interest, safe in the knowledge that when they sell up, they can pay off the capital, but have a huge amount of profit left over to buy something else when their kids leave home. You and Gayle weren't in either boat, were you?'

Steve just exhaled through his nostrils.

'You owned the house outright. Not far off a million quid.' She nudged the page across the desk. 'Add in the insurance, and you'd be financially secure for life.'

Fenchurch's gut clenched.

Pete and his broken liver, sold in exchange for a life of liberty and freedom. He seemed to think it was worth it. Maybe Steve applied the same calculus to murdering his wife? Cost vs benefit.

'With murders, it's always good to work out who benefits from the death.' Reed prodded the page yet again, ramming home the point. 'That insurance policy and the value of your house . . . Taken together, that seems like a very strong motivation to me.'

The Obs Suite door opened and Mulholland appeared, lips pursed. 'Simon.' She sat next to him but left the door open, the chat in the corridor close to drowning out the monitor. 'I gather DS Ashkani has unearthed some useful evidence against Mr Fisher?'

'DS Reed, Dawn.' Fenchurch turned the volume up a couple of steps but still couldn't quite hear it. 'Not Ashkani.'

'Well, I'll be the judge of that.' Mulholland pointed at the screen. 'I've spoken with Julian and we're going to charge Mr Fisher. Coupled with the items yourself and DS Reed have acquired, Uzma's work gives quite the body of evidence.'

'Still feels very circumstantial, Dawn. And Unwin's got him keeping quiet. Sure you've got enough?'

'Quite sure.' Mulholland left the room, meeting Uzma in the corridor. Looked like they were going to take over.

'Wait!' Fenchurch joined them in the corridor. 'Dawn, you need to let Kay progress the interview.'

'No.' Mulholland patted him on the arm. 'Thanks for all of the work, Simon, but we'll take it from here.' She smiled as Uzma opened the interview room door.

What the hell have I done to deserve this?

Seconds later, Reed stormed out, face like thunder. Straight into the Obs Suite, slamming the door behind her. 'Guv, she—'

'I know, Kay.'

'That's it? You're just letting them win? Guv . . .'

'I'm sorry. There's nothing I can do about it.' Fenchurch switched off the screen. Blank, but it was like Mulholland's face was burnt into it, goading him, teasing him. 'It's all still circumstantial. No matter how good a tale the CPS weave in court, it won't be anywhere near enough to beat Dalton Unwin.'

'Bloody hell, guv.' Reed crunched back in the chair. 'You think Steve will get away with this?'

'Or it's not him.'

'It bloody is.' She huffed out a sigh and stared at him, eyes narrow. Then frowned. 'Hang on.' She got out her Airwave Pronto and tapped at the screen. 'Remember when you had me looking at that press stuff on Saturday? Well, the *Post* ran a story a few months back about Shadwell Grammar, how a teacher was dealing drugs.'

'That school's definitely getting a lot of bad press. Almost like there's something in Holding's theory of a conspiracy against him.'

'He went out of his way to try and make the world a better place, guv. People don't like that.'

'True enough.'

'We found shitloads of pills last night at a house just round the bloody corner from the school.' She switched the monitor on again and pointed at Steve Fisher. 'Those pills belonged to Coldcut. Steve's mate.'

'What's your point, Kay?'

'What if Steve's the dealer? Doesn't matter what happens in the murder trial if we can put him away for that.'

'I see your point.'

'Because it's a really good one.' Reed checked her phone again. Her eyes narrowed as she passed it to him. 'Guv, check the byline.' She tapped on the screen.

Liam Sharpe.

Chapter Thirty-Four

Cally Morris peered round the front door, blinking like she'd just woken up, shrouded by smells of strong coffee and Thai curry. Looked like she'd been on night shift at the paper, working the last details of the breaking case until it was perfect. Her dressing gown hung open, Hello Kitty pyjamas underneath. Liam's cat, Pumpkin, swarmed around her feet, acting like she hadn't been fed in days, but not exactly looking it. 'What do you want?'

'You know who we are.' Reed showed her warrant card anyway. Then frowned as she put it away. 'You sleeping with Liam?'

'I'm his flatmate.'

Liam appeared behind her, stroking her arm. 'I'll deal with it, Cal.'

A mobile rang somewhere in the flat.

Cally hefted up Pumpkin and took her into a room, shutting the door behind her.

'Shacking up with your boss, Liam?'

'We'd been friends for years before she got promoted.' Liam led into the kitchen. 'Can I get you a coffee?'

'Just the truth, Liam.'

'I'm in the middle of something here.' Liam sat at the table and closed a laptop with a click. 'What do you want? Don't you have murderers to catch?'

'You wrote a story about a teacher dealing drugs at Shadwell Grammar.'

Liam got up and walked over to the sink, his cat following him. 'If you're here to get my source, you can go to hell.'

'Very honourable, protecting your sources, Liam. But you're not bringing down a president. You're protecting murderers and drug dealers. Is your schoolgirl girlfriend worth it?'

Liam stared out of the window at the block of flats over the road. 'Don't bring Kat into this.'

Fenchurch joined him by the window. 'She might be seventeen, but Christ, it's—'

'Will you just shut up about it?'

'No! She's a child and you're using her to get some stories. That's low.'

Liam stayed looking out of the window, stroking his cat on the counter. Still couldn't look at Fenchurch.

'Do you actually know who's dealing at the school or are you just attacking Brendan Holding?'

'He's really got to you, hasn't he?' Liam laughed. 'Si, did you know that there was a drug problem at Lewisham when Holding was there? Now there's one at Shadwell. Bullying problem in both places, too. Makes you think, eh?'

'What do you expect, Oxbridge candidates and future police officers? They're both inner-city hellholes, trodden into the dirt until all their hope's gone and all they've got left is drugs and cheap booze. No future. No hope. Just a Blockchain at a rave on a Saturday night.'

'No smoke without fire.'

Fenchurch stared hard at him, then huffed out a sigh. 'Let's play that game, then. Have you got any evidence against Holding?'

Back to looking out of the window. Liam looked round at him, then at Reed. 'Holding knows one of his teachers is dealing. I asked him for a comment, but you know the drill.'

'What evidence have you got?'

'A source is anonymous for a reason.'

'But your source was Katerina, correct?'

Liam just laughed.

'If you had any evidence, you would've published it by now.'

'That's what I'm working on, Si.' Liam walked over and patted his laptop lid. 'Waiting to go to press.'

'Is this dealer Steve Fisher?'

Liam collapsed into a chair. 'So I gather.'

'Help me believe it, Liam.'

'I'm not telling you anything.'

'Liam, I'll take you in for a formal interview.'

'Very pleased for you. I'm not talking. Suggest you speak to Holding about it.'

———

Fenchurch parked at the school and killed the engine. He looked through the gates, couldn't spot any dealing. *But then, it's designed to be secretive, to hide the activity from the law, or anyone who'd take it to the law.*

He spotted Nelson through the rain and gave him a wave.

Nelson got in the back. 'Morning, Kay. Simon.'

'Jon.' Then Reed smirked at Fenchurch. 'Still think you should tell Mulholland.'

'We get ahead of this, Kay, then we take it to her.'

'You know . . .' Nelson took a puff on his vape stick. All Fenchurch could see in the rear view was the mist. 'Sometimes you end up working for someone completely out of their depth. You need to help them, not work against them.'

Fenchurch raised his eyebrows as the mist cleared. 'Are you talking about me?'

'Hardly.' Nelson cleared his throat then took another puff. 'My current gaffer is a bit green. One of those fast-track kids. DCI in less

than ten years. Thinks because he's run a traffic division for six months
that he can run a multi-year drugs investigation.'

'Those guys are good at some things, though.' Reed swivelled
round. 'Politics, statistics, being nice to people.'

'Yet to find a use for any of that shit.' Fenchurch opened his door
and got out. 'Thanks for joining us, Jon.'

'Precious little happening back at base and this sounded sufficiently
sexy.' Nelson pocketed his vape stick as they walked towards the school
and the white noise of the long queue of cars splashing rain as parents
dropped off kids.

The giant Victorian monstrosity loomed into view, the stone blackened as London industrialised then nobody cleaned it after it all left.
Two storeys with a sixties tower at the back adding another two.

*School . . . yet another aspect of Chloe's life I missed. Going from a tot
to an almost-adult in thirteen short years, and I missed all of them. Missed
the three parents' nights when we did have her, too busy with work. Then
we didn't have her and . . . I missed so much. Too much.*

Nelson waved his hand in front of Fenchurch's face. 'You believe
Liam this time?'

Fenchurch blinked away his reverie. 'He's supposed to be a journalist. Trustworthy.'

Reed scowled. 'Jon, he's shagging a schoolgirl.'

Nelson did a double take. 'How young?'

'Old enough, but still too young.' Reed stopped at the gates and
showed her warrant card to the warden. She got a nod then led them
through. 'Oh Jesus.'

A lone figure hid under a rain shelter, tapping at her phone.
Katerina. And by Christ did she look young. Like a very tall child.

Fenchurch walked up to her. 'Need a word with you.'

She looked up from her phone, eyes wide. 'What?'

Fenchurch pointed towards the school building. 'Best do this
inside.'

Someone shouted something over by the front gates.

Katerina went back to her phone. 'I've got school.'

'This is important.'

Then more shouting. A loud roar, like Shadwell United had just scored in the football stadium over the road. A large crowd swarmed around the gates, no sign of any security in the huddle.

'Wait here.' Fenchurch darted over and muscled through the crowd, waving his warrant card. 'Police!'

In the middle, Elliot Lynch was surrounded by journalists and schoolkids. 'I just want to focus on school.' He pushed through towards Fenchurch, eyes wide as he spotted him.

Ben Maxfield had his hand on Elliot's back, pushing him through the throng, giving a cheeky wink to a journalist.

'Stop!' Holding was just ahead of Fenchurch, standing firm in the onslaught. 'This is a school, not a theatre!' He grabbed Elliot's jacket, his fist bunching up the sleeve. 'You need to leave! All of you! Anyone within a hundred metres of the school gates will be having a word with the police!'

The journos cleared off, their chatter dying as they scattered. Maxfield followed, like a shark sniffing blood.

Fenchurch looked around at Katerina. Still there.

'You little witch!' Elliot lunged at Katerina, clawing at her throat. He pushed her into Holding, knocking the Headmaster over.

'Stop!' Fenchurch dragged him off her, locking his arm behind his back.

'She catfished me!' Elliot jabbed a finger in the air behind Fenchurch. 'Pretended to . . .'

'I pretended to be Mrs Fisher.' Katerina's impish grin made her look even younger. 'Shouldn't have been shagging a teacher, should you, you idiot?'

'I'm the victim here!' Elliot bared his teeth at Katerina. 'You—' He lunged for her again.

Fenchurch pulled him back, like a dog on a lead. The kid stamped on his foot and Fenchurch stumbled back, landing with a crack as his arse hit the cobbles. Pain seared all over his buttocks, right up his back. Still had a grip on Elliot. Kid was wriggling. Nelson grabbed Elliot and kept a hold of him while Fenchurch got to his feet.

Holding was dusting himself off, eyes wide.

Nelson pulled Elliot towards Maxfield. 'We're getting him away from the school. Now.'

Maxfield nodded. He looked shocked. Out of his depth. Used to passivity, not slapstick bullshit. 'I'll take him to his grandmother's.'

'Good idea.'

Nelson followed them away from the school.

Fenchurch looked around. No sign of Katerina. 'Kay, can you find her?' Then he smiled at Holding. 'Let's you and me have a nice chat, though, eh?'

'Quite some office.' Fenchurch stood in the corner of Holding's office, overlooking the school grounds on all four sides. He picked up a framed photo of Holding receiving an award, black tie and red face. 'Much better than mine, have to say.'

'It may look special but it's purely functional.' Holding sat behind a huge oak desk covered with paperwork and antique IT equipment. 'Seeing all four corners of my empire is incredibly distracting.' He joined Fenchurch by the window and pointed at the bike sheds. 'I can tell you twenty kids who smoke more than my old man did and he was a forty-a-day kind of guy. Died at forty-two. Heart attack. You try telling this lot that, but they don't think longer than who they're doing Netflix and chill with tonight.'

Fenchurch rested the photo back on the table. 'Netflix and what?'

'It's slang for having sex.' Holding adjusted the frame so it was just right. 'If you don't keep up with the terminology, they run rings around you. Sure Abi can vouch for that.'

Leave her out of this . . .

Fenchurch waved at the playing fields: a few patches of grass, a lot of mud and some football and hockey goals, the crossbars sagging in the middle. 'Did you have this level of control at Lewisham?'

'I wasn't the Head there.' Holding shoved his hands in his pockets and walked back to his desk. 'I went from Senior Teacher to Assistant Head in five years as a result of my achievements. And they listened. Here? Cloth ears, I'm afraid.'

'The drugs problem?'

'It's crippling the community.' Holding sat with a crunch. 'I stamped it out in Lewisham. Community outreach, giving the students a voice, stopping them from feeling so isolated and alone.' He swivelled round, his eyes narrowing as he took in the front gates, and flicked his wrists at the journalists still camped out. 'But you've seen what I'm facing here. The press *hate* me. They want my project to fail. At Lewisham, we were dealing with a single dealer. Here, it's *at least* six. We spend weeks working on taking one down, then they're replaced almost straight away.'

'This is worse?'

'Much.' A smile flashed across Holding's lips. 'You should check with your wife. Abi and I worked very closely together, until she moved schools. It's her baby as much as mine.'

'I'll make sure to get her opinion.' Fenchurch faked confusion, knitting his forehead together. 'Part of the investigation into Gayle Fisher's—'

'A damn tragedy.'

'Indeed. Well. We've heard that Steve Fisher might've been dealing drugs.'

Holding bellowed out a laugh as he slumped back in his chair. His body language didn't add up. 'Well, that's absolute poppycock.'

Fenchurch decided to push his luck. 'We've got evidence.'

Holding thumped his desk. A paperweight thudded to the floor. He didn't bother inspecting the damage. Rage burnt his eyes. 'That bloody story, right?' Another flick of the wrists out of the window. 'This is what I'm talking about. The press are slurring me and my school.'

'I'm sure they're protecting the interests of your students.'

'They're selling papers.' Holding leaned back in his chair and focused on the ceiling. 'Actually, it's all about selling online advertising these days, isn't it? Getting people to click, like rats in a maze.'

'Last night we recovered a quantity of MDMA.' Fenchurch pointed out of the window at Coldcut's gran's flat. 'From a house just down there. They call it Blockchain. What Elliot Lynch almost died from on Saturday night.'

'Well, I will extend any help in your investigation.'

'Good. Do you have any indication that Steve was dealing?'

'None. At all.' Holding puckered his lips. 'Look, if Steve was . . . I had absolutely no knowledge of it.'

'No rumours?'

'This place is full of them, Inspector, but I would've heard if one of my teachers was selling this poison.'

Fenchurch's phone buzzed. A text from Reed: GOT KATERINA. KEEPING HER IN A CLASSROOM.

'What was Elliot talking about?'

'You mean the catfishing?' Holding bit at his cheek. 'We get that a lot. Some of our less academic pupils set up fake accounts, pretend that they're teachers, for instance, or their peers. It goes without saying that we have to be extra-vigilant online. I myself have almost been caught out.'

'He said she was catfishing him. Have you—'

'No.' Holding clenched his jaw and snorted. 'Elliot clearly decided that the only teacher he could confide in was the one he was having liaisons with. Somehow Miss Raptis knew that.'

Fenchurch blew out a sigh. *And she played Elliot. Did she know about the affair? Did she exploit it?*

Chapter Thirty-Five

I'm missing English.' They were talking to Katerina in an empty classroom. 'I need to do well in that or I won't get into university.'

'Which is your first choice?'

'Durham.'

'Where Mrs Fisher went, right?'

Katerina slouched forward, resting her head on a fist. Looked like a child copying her mother's actions. 'Wouldn't know.'

Fenchurch gave her a smile. 'Elliot Lynch said you were catfishing him?'

'Man . . .' Katerina got up, but a glare from Reed made her sit back down again. 'I messed about with him *once . . .*' She shrugged. 'I pretended to be Mrs Fisher on Facebook. She didn't have a profile, so I set one up. Had to make friends with enough people to make it look legit. But I got him. Started messaging him, thinking I was going to get something to embarrass him in English. He sent me a dick pick.'

Reed's eyebrows did a little dance. 'What did you do with it?'

'Let him know it wasn't Mrs Fisher.' Katerina laughed, like she'd never been so impressed with herself. She wiggled her pinky. 'Didn't know it was me.'

'You didn't feel guilty about doing it?'

'No way. He'd been bullying me for years and I found a way to get him. He thinks he's well blaze, but he's just a little prick with a little prick.' Katerina relaxed, crossing her legs in a mirror of Reed's posture.

'I've been in Elliot's class since I was seven. Every day, he's bullied me. Stole my bag. Nicked my dinner money. Stuck chewing gum in my hair. So I started pretending to be different people on Facebook, just to mess with him.'

Reed smiled. 'Why Mrs Fisher?'

'Why not?'

'You know it's a crime, right?'

Katerina jolted upright.

'Relax. It's not our department.' Reed patted her chair and waited for Katerina to sit down. 'You like being other people?'

'I don't like being me.'

'Because of the bullying?' Reed got a nod. 'Must be hard. You ever talk to anyone about it?'

'Mrs Fisher understood. I felt guilty about using her fake account, but . . .'

'I've seen what bullying does to people. Is that why Liam feels so protective of you?'

Katerina's mouth hung open.

'Liam Sharpe.'

'No!'

'You're close.'

Katerina started playing with her hair, twirling a strand through her fingers.

'He's your boyfriend, right?'

Katerina huffed out a sigh. 'Is that what you think?'

'Tell me I'm wrong.'

'It's difficult, because Liam met me when I was fifteen.'

And it just gets better . . .

'Are you an item?'

'Why is that important?'

Fenchurch stared at her, but she didn't say anything. 'Where did he take you on Friday night?'

'Just gave me a lift. I had something for him.'

'A tip?'

'A book. It got me through some tough times. Thought he'd appreciate it.'

Fenchurch didn't know whether to believe her or not. 'Thing is, Liam's publishing serious allegations, the sort that can lead to criminal charges. If what you're telling him is true, I need to see your evidence.'

She tugged at her hair.

'How did you meet him?'

'Like I've told you. Like Liam's told you. I was working at the hotel. He was in the bar, waiting for someone. We got chatting. Soon as I found out he was a journalist, I thought, "Oh, here's a chance to get back at this place." He could get the truth out there about the bullying. Then it became about drugs. I don't take them, but I know who does. Lots of blow, some E. Nothing stronger, but that's enough, right?'

'Any idea who's selling it?'

She looked away. 'No.'

Reed stared hard at her. 'Sure you didn't tell Liam that a teacher was selling drugs?'

Her head tipped forward. 'Maybe.'

'Who was it?'

'Steve Fisher.' She sighed, then locked eyes with Fenchurch. 'I've not seen him do it directly, but . . .' She swallowed hard. 'I've seen him get money off Elliot Lynch.'

'Elliot?' Fenchurch got to his feet. 'Elliot was buying drugs off Steve at the same time he was sleeping with his wife?'

'It's the truth! I saw Elliot give Steve Fisher at least forty quid.'

'This wasn't for a school trip or anything?'

'No. They were in the store room. Must've thought they were being sneaky, but I saw them.'

'Did they see you?'

'Don't think so.'

He stared at Reed. Her hunch was making sense. Holding's drug problem wasn't going away if it was one of his teachers doing it.

Time to get some more evidence.

Elliot's grandmother's street was more Limehouse than Shadwell, and quiet. Two-storey brick houses with front gardens. The gentrification machine had made it halfway up the street — the old boozer was now called the Frozen Moment: a group of bearded hipsters were on the street, taking delivery of a few kegs of beer. Didn't look like they knew what they were doing, just rolling them around the pavement.

Fenchurch got in the passenger side of the car. 'Jon.'

Nelson tightened his grip on the steering wheel. 'Elliot's grandmother lives in that one.' He pointed to a house in the ungentrified end. The brick was so dark a train must've sat outside for a hundred years, blowing soot all over it. 'I had a word with them. Maxfield is a piece of work, isn't he?'

'He still there?'

'Cleared off about ten minutes ago. Like I was going to before I got your call.' Nelson leaned back in his seat. 'You believe Katerina?'

'Don't know. Makes enough sense to investigate.'

'She could be trying to fit him up.' Nelson opened the door and let some cool air in, along with the ozone smell of fresh rain. 'I don't buy Steve Fisher selling drugs in that school. Why risk your career for small money? They didn't need any, either. That house is worth a fortune.'

'All that aside, assuming he was dealing, what if Gayle found out? Maybe even found his drugs?'

'You're stretching here.' Nelson pushed the door fully open. 'It just doesn't feel right. Policeman's hunch.' He got out on to the street.

Fenchurch opened his door and put a foot on the ground. *Maybe he's right. Maybe I am clutching here. Is it just that Mulholland's taking the credit for it? Am I trying to prosecute him through the back door?*

Bike brakes squealed over the road. A bike courier walked up the path and knocked on the door. Then got out a bottle of water and snapped off the cap. The door opened to a crack and Elliot peered out. The courier spoke to him and the door opened fully. The courier splashed the water on Elliot's face and ran off.

Elliot screamed, loud enough to be heard in Glasgow.

Fenchurch charged towards the house. 'It's acid!'

Chapter Thirty-Six

Fenchurch stopped by the door. Elliot lay on his back, screaming. His hands hovered in the air above his face, couldn't bring himself to touch his skin.

Stop the burning as soon as possible.

Nelson shot off towards the attacker. Almost caught him, but he hopped on his bike and started pedalling away. Nelson followed him along the road, his feet slapping off the pavement. Losing the attacker.

'I'm going to help, okay?' Fenchurch bent down and hefted Elliot in a cradle lift, then carried him into the house, the kid screaming. Acid sizzled on the carpet in the hall. The bathroom door was open. Fenchurch lay Elliot on the bathroom floor and tore his T-shirt down the front, tossing it on the floor, away from either of them.

No jewellery. Good.

Elliot's screaming was louder.

Wash the burn.

Fenchurch got the shower on at a slow lick then grabbed hold of Elliot again, still screaming.

'It's burning!'

'I know, I know. I'm going to wash it off, okay?' Fenchurch carried Elliot into the shower. The water splashed his own arms as he directed it on to Elliot's hair, letting it trickle down his face. 'You're going to be okay, son.'

Something hit Fenchurch's back. A woman in her fifties, dolled up like she was out on the pull. She slapped his chest. 'What the hell are you doing?'

'I'm a police officer! Someone threw acid on Elliot!'

She calmed a bit, less likely to smack him again, and focused on her grandson's face.

'What's your name?'

'Marnie. Marnie Nicholas.'

'Marnie, I'm trying to save your grandson's face, okay?' Fenchurch scooshed water on Elliot's face now. The screaming got worse, but the smell got better. 'I need cling film, paracetamol and ibuprofen. And I need you to call 999 for an ambulance, okay?'

'Right.' She took another look at her grandson then set off, purpose in her stride.

'It's okay, Elliot.' Fenchurch held him and got out his phone, hitting dial as he put it to his ear. 'Jon, have you got him?'

'Lost him.'

'Shit. Come back here. I need your help.' Fenchurch killed the call and dropped his phone on the bathroom floor. Water splashed everywhere, like that time when Chloe turned the bath taps on at her grandparents' house and went downstairs.

Marnie was back in the room. 'Here.' She held out the cling film.

'Did you call 999?'

'Ambulance on its way. Fifteen minutes, they said.'

'Good enough.'

Elliot's skin was turning red, but there were no cuts or lacerations.

'Okay, we need to wash the skin for twenty minutes, then put on a layer of cling film, okay? Don't wrap it, put it on in a layer.'

'Why are you telling me?'

'Because I need you to make sure I don't make a mess of it.'

'A layer, right. Not wrapping.' She spilled some pills on the floor. 'Buggeration!' She went down on all fours, waving her arse in the air. Didn't look like she wore any knickers. Then she was back up, hand out.

'Elliot, you need some painkillers, okay?' Fenchurch took four pills from her, two pairs of different sizes, and held them up for Elliot. 'This isn't going to be quick, but it'll help, okay?'

Elliot took them and swallowed them down with water from the shower. His breathing was stuttering.

'You're being brave, kid.' Fenchurch jerked him to his feet. 'You need to stay upright, okay?'

Fenchurch's phone rang. He passed the showerhead to Marnie, who took over the washing, and bent down to pick it up.

Nelson, sounded like he was running. 'I've got him! He's back on that street. Shit! I've lost him again!'

'Keep it on his face, okay? And make sure he stays up.' Fenchurch left the room, then stopped in the doorway. 'Remember, a layer. Don't wrap it!' Then he raced out of the house and got in his pool car. He drove off, wheels spinning down the road, easing off as he hit the long straight.

The attacker was cycling towards him on his bike. Hood up, mask covering his face. He swerved across the road towards the pavement. Fenchurch cut across the street and the bike brakes squealed. The cyclist went flying across the bonnet. Landed on the other side with a sickening crunch.

Fenchurch was out of the car, running towards the attacker. Got a kick in the knee, but he leaned forward, using his momentum to land on the attacker. Squeezed the air of the prick's lungs. He grabbed the attacker's mouth and hauled the mask off. The attacker's teeth clamped shut, trying to bite Fenchurch. Just missed.

Fenchurch cracked the attacker's head off the pavement then reached into the hood to grab hold of micro-dreads, ready to smash his skull again.

Someone pulled him back. 'Guy's not going anywhere.' Nelson, breathing hard.

Fenchurch leaned forward and ripped at the mask.

Daniel Dodoo.

———

Sunlight cracked through the murky grey over Canary Wharf, the huddle of buildings glowing.

'My face.' Dodoo sat in the back of the squad car. 'My face!'

'*Your* face?' Fenchurch grabbed him and took him over to the house. Pushed him into the bathroom. 'Look at *his* face.' Elliot was still in the shower, the paramedics trying to keep him under control. Squealing like a pig. 'You did that.'

Dodoo stared hard at him, then swallowed just as hard.

'Take this bloody thing everywhere, don't you?' Nelson stopped rummaging through Dodoo's bag and held up the Nintendo Switch, the pink-and-blue controllers glowing in the morning light. 'Scratched the screen, though.' He scowled. 'And another bag of Blockchain.'

Dodoo shook his head. Didn't stop, just kept doing it, eyes shut.

'You're going away for a very long time, sunshine.' Fenchurch twisted Dodoo's arm behind his back, slightly more than necessary.

Dodoo just kept shaking his head.

'Come on.' Fenchurch pushed Dodoo back outside, and met the two uniforms from the previous day — Cheeky and his female friend — and gave them Dodoo. 'Take him to Leman Street. Now.'

'Sir.' Cheeky pushed Dodoo in the back seat, then got in the front and the squad car screeched off.

'What a shit-show, guv.' Nelson was wrapping Dodoo's backpack in an oversized evidence bag. 'If we hadn't been here . . .'

'Elliot'd be another statistic with a ruined face. This way, he's got a chance of pulling through.'

The gurney rattled as the paramedics took Elliot over to the ambulance, his screams muffled by cling film. They loaded him in the back, one of the paramedics hopping up to ride alongside.

Marnie grabbed Fenchurch and twisted him round. Stronger than she looked. She waved at the ambulance, its lights flashing. 'I need to be with him!'

Fenchurch led her back towards her house. 'Thanks to your help, you've maybe saved his face.'

'Maybe? *Maybe?!*' She shrugged him off, her face twisted into rage. 'You said it would!'

'I tried. You tried.' Fenchurch pointed at the ambulance, still sitting there. 'Now, the paramedics are trying, then it'll be the doctors' turn.'

Marnie stared at the ground. A little rockery covered in red heathers. 'Is this it?' She pointed at a plastic bottle, mostly empty. Evian, the label burned in half. 'Is this what they . . .'

Fenchurch reached into his pocket for an evidence bag and stored it away. He ran after the ambulance and thumped the back door.

The paramedic scowled then opened up. 'What?'

Fenchurch passed him the bottle. 'This is what they got him with.'

'Thanks.' The door shut and the ambulance shot off, the siren blaring.

Fenchurch watched it go. Trying to control his breathing. A shiver ran up his spine. He couldn't get the smell of burning flesh out of his nose.

A car door shut across the road. Mulholland was walking towards him. Her gaze swept over to the receding ambulance.

'Daniel Dodoo attacked him. Threw acid on his face. The best outcome is he'll be scarred for life. He's lucky we were here.'

Nelson joined them, his jaw clenched. 'Why attack Elliot? I don't get it.'

'Why here?' Fenchurch felt the usual tug at his gut, punching his lungs. 'Dodoo knew he'd be *here*. At his grandmother's. Not at school

263

or his parents' house. Here.' Things started clicking into place. 'At the school, Jon, I told Maxfield to take Elliot away. He said he was going to take him to his grandmother's. You followed him, kept an eye on him, but the next thing we know . . . Dodoo's here, throwing acid on him.'

Nelson took a deep breath and focused on Mulholland. 'Dawn, as far as I can tell, Coldcut is behind it.'

'So it's not connected to the Gayle Fisher murder?'

'I don't know.'

'Then this is your case, Inspector.' Mulholland glared at Nelson, fear in her eyes. 'Interview this Coldcut and get to the bottom of this.'

He nodded. 'I'll add it to the long, long list of questions we've got for him.'

'Less of the sarcasm.' Mulholland scowled at him, then focused on Fenchurch. 'I'll let you both interview him. Just in case this *does* relate to the Gayle Fisher case.' And she was off towards her car.

Nelson huffed out a sigh at Fenchurch. 'You really need to learn to control her.'

———

'You've been a very naughty boy, Daniel.' Fenchurch drummed his thumbs on the interview room table. 'Acid attacks are all the rage these days.'

'Very hip.' Nelson was next to him, rocking back in his chair, legs stretched out. 'Throwing acid on people is like Netflix and Snapchat and Bitcoin these days. It's well blaze, as the kids say.'

Dodoo was keeping his calm. His lawyer had him on a tight lead.

'It's a tough one to prosecute.' Fenchurch got up and walked across the room to stand behind Dodoo. 'Chucking acid on people's faces and running off like a coward. Hoods up, masks on, trying to make it hard for us to track you down.'

Dodoo glanced up, then his owner tugged the lead.

'It's very satisfying when we catch one of you, though. We actually saw you do it.'

'Both of us.' Nelson grinned wide. 'You're going down for it, Daniel.'

Still silence. Not even a glance.

'Don't care what you say now.' Fenchurch walked back round the other side of the table and rested on it. 'Prosecuting someone for an acid attack will be very satisfying. Don't even care if there's anyone else behind this, because we've got you.' He left a gap, but Dodoo kept quiet. 'The best bit is, when this is all over the papers and the internet, the next craven arsehole who gets given a vial of corrosive liquid, they might think twice about chucking it at someone.'

Still quiet.

'Nah, you know what the best bit is?' Nelson chuckled. 'Being able to charge someone with these new acid attack powers. Used to be a few years but, Daniel, you must've heard that they upgraded the sentencing to life.'

'Doesn't look like he did, Jon.' Fenchurch picked up the thread. 'These days, the guidance is to treat you like you've murdered someone. Just because someone's heart is still beating, doesn't mean you've not killed them. Destroyed their future. It's not just the physical harm, it's the mental.'

Dodoo sat back and scratched at his mini-dreads. Still didn't say anything.

'You'll never see this again.' Fenchurch reached down and picked up an evidence bag for Dodoo's Nintendo Switch. 'Not for twenty years. At least. Wonder if they'll still make games for it.'

'Twenty years is a heck of a long time, Daniel.' Nelson shook his head slowly. 'We'll all be living on Mars by then, or the world will be a smoking ruin.'

Dodoo glanced at his lawyer and got a wagged finger.

'Right now, you'll be weighing up your future versus giving up who told you to do this.' Fenchurch sat again and dropped the Switch on the floor. 'I don't care what you've got to say. Any names you give us, doesn't matter. I don't care. I've got you and you're going to prison for twenty-odd years.'

Dodoo looked up, kept up the eye contact. 'Coldcut.'

'I said I don't care.' Fenchurch reached over to the recorder. 'Interview term—'

'I work for Coldcut.'

'We know, you muppet.' Fenchurch held his finger over the button but didn't press it. 'We saw him at your flat last night.'

'He told me to do it.' Dodoo gave a nervous glance at his lawyer, at her angry leer. 'Same as that one in Hackney on Saturday.'

Fenchurch shot his gaze between Nelson and Dodoo. 'What?'

'That kid, some little Pakistani gimp, thought he was a player. Worked for Coldcut then started out on his own. Coldcut wasn't happy.'

'He told you to do that?'

'Course not. I took some initiative. Stole some kerosene from a farmer's tank in Kent. Splashed it on his face. The bouncers held him down so it scarred, you know?'

'Well, it worked, that kid won't be dealing drugs again. His nose is melted off.'

'Like I care. I told Coldcut. Cat was impressed. Solved a problem for him, didn't I?'

'Right. And he was so impressed that he got you to do an encore on Elliot?'

Dodoo sniffed. 'Cat gave me some acid, little bottles. Told me the kid would be at that address. Didn't expect you to be there, though.'

'Why did you do it?'

'No idea.' Dodoo threw his arms up in the air. 'Just do what I'm told.'

'Well, that's not going to save you, sunshine. Nothing is.'

'Wait a sec.' Nelson held up a hand to stop Fenchurch. 'Daniel, if you've got any hope of leniency, you can help us find Coldcut.'

'Piss off.'

Nelson let out a sigh. 'That was you at that drug house last night, wasn't it?'

'What?'

'In Shadwell. You assaulted a couple of officers as you ran off. We're combing the place for forensics. With a murder, we have to prove that you were there when the murder happened. But you being in a drug house is a very different matter, especially when you just admitted to working for Coldcut and splashing acid over some poor schoolboy's face on his orders. That'll be a couple of life sentences for drug supplying on top of the acid attack.'

'I know where he is.' Dodoo's eyes were bulging. 'I can take you there.'

Chapter Thirty-Seven

Another dead woman's home.' Nelson waved at a barren shitheap in Beckton, the wild tree growing in the garden dwarfing the house. So close to City Airport that you could feel your fillings shake when a plane came in to land. 'Dear old Bess Green, no middle name. Died in 2011.'

Three squad cars double-parked on the street, blocking anyone entering the small cul-de-sac. A flash of acid-yellow in the lane running between two derelict blocks of flats.

Fenchurch opened the squad car's back door and craned his neck to focus on the skinny figure inside. 'Why do you think Coldcut's here?'

'Cat's lying low.' Dodoo's gaze darted around behind Fenchurch, like he was expecting to be shot at any moment. Or splashed with acid. 'Keeping away from you pricks. Must know you're on to him now.'

Fenchurch beckoned over a uniformed officer. 'Get him back to Leman Street, okay?'

Dodoo's eyes bulged. 'You don't want me in there with you?'

'Good one.' Fenchurch waved him off then focused on the six officers waiting around. Two of them yawned hard. Someone else's stomach rumbled louder than the BA plane taking off.

Then his Airwave chimed. 'Serial Bravo in place, sir. Over.' He caught a hand waving down the lane.

'No letting them get away this time, okay?'

A long pause. 'Noted. Over.'

'Okay.' Fenchurch took a deep breath. 'We are go!'

The nearest uniform picked up the Enforcer battering ram and sauntered up the back path towards the house. Another yawn, then he hefted it up and forced it against the door. Clunk and it toppled into the dark house.

Three uniforms burst in, leaving two out front.

Fenchurch followed Nelson into a hallway. Full of acrid smoke. Shrill football noises came from another room. A teenage girl lay at the bottom of the stairs, eyes rolling back in her head. Skin covered in black marks. She smiled at them, the sort of slow grin that Baby Al did when he recognised his old man.

Heart pounding, Fenchurch entered the living room, the smoke thicker than in the hall. The bitter taste of toasted marshmallows in his mouth. Four junkies sat around a broken telly, playing a football game on a PlayStation. Four sacks of skin and bone, eyes only capable of focusing on their game. A huge crack ran down the side of the TV screen. One of them looked over, then away again. 'Sod off.'

No bloody sign of Coldcut . . .

Fenchurch stormed back out into the hallway, past the sleeping girl, and looked upstairs. Just got shaking heads. Same in the kitchen. He trudged back outside, sticking his Airwave to his lips, glaring at the squad car. 'Put Dodoo on, right now.'

Muffled sounds, then Dodoo cleared his throat. 'What?'

'Daniel, you said Coldcut was here. He's not.'

'He is! I was there this morning!'

'Son, you're in enough trouble as it is. Leading us literally up the garden path is just going to—'

'Kitchen cabinets.'

'What?'

'Check behind the kitchen cabinets.'

Fenchurch raced back in the house, then through to the dark kitchen.

A bored uniform leaned against the sink, his lips smacking as he chewed gum. He clocked Fenchurch and stood up all, pushing the wad into his cheek. 'No sign of anyone, sir.'

Fenchurch tried the first cabinet door. Locked. He shook the handle but it was solid. Tried another, same result. They were all like that.

The uniform scratched his head. 'What the hell?'

Fenchurch looked at the cabinets again. That beige melamine stuff you used to see everywhere, dark-brown kick plates underneath.

Hang on . . .

He got down on all fours and prodded the nearest kick plate. As solid as the door above. Then he tried the one under the sink. Same. *Hang on.* The far edge wobbled. He shuffled over and pushed it back. The other end swivelled round. Faint light crawled out from behind. He peered in — the bottoms of the cabinets had been crudely sawn off and there was a catch on the back wall, stuck on the bare brick. He grabbed the uniform's baton and flicked it.

The cabinet door clicked and toppled on top of him.

Fenchurch pushed it away and got up to a crouch. The uniform was shining his torch in, pointing at a hole in the back wall. Looked like a tunnel under the house.

The great bloody escape . . .

'You going in there, sir?'

'Not after last—'

'I'm coming out!' Coldcut's face appeared in the hole, his baseball cap covered in dust and soot. 'I'm coming out!' He eased his large frame out of the hole, his shell suit flapping, then bellyflopped on to the kitchen floor. Hands up, he got to his feet. 'I'm coming out peacefully.'

The uniform stepped forward, holding out his cuffs.

Then Coldcut lashed out with a fist. A sickening crack and the uniform slumped back. Followed up with two quick kicks to the gut.

Fenchurch hefted up the baton and started his backswing. But Coldcut was on him, wrapping his arms round his shoulders and pushing him back against the cabinet. Pushed him back over the work-top, jabs raining on Fenchurch's sides, kicks digging into his legs.

Guy's like a wild bull . . .

Someone stormed in, heavy boots thudding on the floor. Coldcut turned round and aimed a punch at someone. Nelson! He ducked it, but caught the low one in the gut. He coughed, doubling over. Then Coldcut hammered his fist into his face and Nelson went down like a sack of spuds.

Fenchurch lashed out and caught Coldcut's left knee. Then kicked out with the right, locking his feet together and twisting. Coldcut fell forward, cracking his head against the sink.

Fenchurch pushed forward, reaching for the spilled cuffs and snapping them round Coldcut's chunky wrists. Even so, he wasn't going anywhere. Out cold.

Fenchurch went over to Nelson and cradled his head. 'You okay?'

Nelson clenched his jaw tight. Blood poured out of his nose, soaked his white shirt. 'Did you get him?'

'Relax, Jon, I got him.'

———

'No comment.' Coldcut pressed a finger on to the bandage on his fore-head. Blood soaked through in patches.

'No comment, eh?' Nelson dabbed at his nose with a hanky. Looked bad but the devil and his horsemen couldn't keep him out of the inter-view. 'This isn't your first time in a police station, is it?'

'What?'

Nelson snorted. 'Your first time in a police station.'

'Struggling to understand you, brother.' Coldcut sounded like he'd been sucking helium. Running a criminal empire with a Mickey Mouse voice was impressive work. He smiled at Nelson. 'It's like someone's broken your nose.'

'Shoplifting. Car theft.' Nelson flicked through a couple of prints. 'And then you died, of course.'

'You think you're smart, don't you?' Coldcut's voice went down in pitch, still sounded like a swarm of bees. 'Who grassed on me? Dodoo?'

'Colin, how do you think we caught you, eh?' Fenchurch splayed his hands on the table. 'Magic? Summoning the devil? Selling our souls at the crossroads?' He grinned. 'You're not as good as you think. Or as dead as we thought. Colin David Cutler. Very cute.'

'Who told you? Was it Steve?'

'Gather you and he go back a ways. Schoolmates, right?'

'Not seen him in years.'

'And you're worried that he's grassed on you?'

'Not seen him in years.'

'He says you went for a drink with him on Friday.'

'Hadn't seen him in years until then.'

Fenchurch nodded slowly. 'Did you have that drink?'

'Bloke was in a state, wasn't he?' Coldcut leaned back until he was almost horizontal. His shell suit rode up to show his hairy belly. 'Found out his missus had been screwing some kid behind his back. Taking him for a pint was the least I could do.'

'And you just happened to be at Mr Dodoo's place of residence when Steve popped in, right?'

Coldcut dabbed at his wound again. 'I was playing *Mario Kart* with Daniel.'

Fenchurch stared at him hard, a few seconds that felt like hours.

Guy doesn't look so bad, but if what Nelson said is true . . . The guy killed two undercover cops investigating him, so he's both smart and dangerous.

'Why did you order Daniel to attack Elliot Lynch?'

'Nobody's died.'

'No, but Elliot's lying in hospital with his face melting. You did that.'

272

'You just said Daniel did.'

'You gave the order. Might as well have tossed it on yourself. Then again, can't see you getting on a bike in your' — Fenchurch looked down at Coldcut's gut — 'condition. You look pregnant.'

'That kid—' Coldcut's voice went up an octave. 'He's an arrogant little shit.'

'So you do know him?'

'I might've played *Mario Kart* with him at Daniel's. Otherwise I've no idea what you're talking about.'

'You got Daniel to scar him for life. What's he done to you?'

'An acid attack on a kid is a nasty business, Inspector.' Coldcut held up his hands. 'But it's nothing to do with me. I hope you throw the book at Daniel.'

———

'You got nowhere with him, Simon.' Mulholland sat behind Docherty's old desk. She tugged her scarf tight around her neck, even though the room was roasting. 'What does someone have to do for you to get a confession out of them?'

Nelson was keeping his counsel, sitting opposite her, biding his time. 'That man is a ghost.'

'Simon, have a seat.'

Fenchurch didn't want to. Didn't want to be in the same room as her. 'His record says he died a few years ago. And yet he's in here—'

'—failing to answer your questions.' She glowered at him. 'Simon, this Coldcut character isn't going to talk to us. He's lived as a ghost for the last few years, why do you think he'll suddenly start talking?'

'Faking your own death might be very illegal. But sod it — he ordered Dodoo to throw acid at Elliot.'

'Simon, I know you want to be the hero cop, but I need you to answer one simple question.' She grinned at him, eyes narrow, like she

273

was a criminal defence lawyer, not his boss. Playing devil's advocate when you were the devil. 'Why?'

'Because—' Fenchurch broke off. He didn't have anything. He looked at Nelson — he didn't either.

'You've no idea, have you? All you've got is that Elliot might've given some money to Steve Fisher.'

'For drugs. We know Steve is a dealer. He went to school with Coldcut. He was at Dodoo's flat.'

'I still don't buy the connection.'

'Is Steve's lawyer still in?'

Mulholland waved her hands in the air. 'You're not getting back in with him until I have a detailed interview strategy from you.'

'I want one last tilt—'

'No!'

Someone knocked on the door. 'You wanted a word, Dawn?' DI Rod Winter stood there, scraping his dirty black hair from his eyes. Clean-shaven for once, looking about ten years younger. Gave Fenchurch and Nelson a nod. 'Si. Jon.'

Fenchurch returned the nod. *What the bloody hell is he doing here?*

'Have a seat, Rod.' Mulholland waved at the seat she'd offered Fenchurch, watching Winter as he slumped in it, arms tight across his chest. 'Gentlemen, Julian and I are uncomfortable with the . . . tone of the investigation so far. What started out as a rudimentary murder now has a sizeable drugs element, not to mention a suspect being the victim of an acid attack. As such, we need to diversify the portfolio and manage accordingly. Starting now, DI Winter will take lead on the acid attack investigation.'

Winter looked over at Fenchurch then back at Mulholland. 'Are you winding me up?'

'Am I in the habit of getting involved in office banter?' Mulholland raised an eyebrow. 'I'm deadly serious, Inspector.'

Fenchurch kicked the door shut. Didn't slam as loudly as he'd have liked. 'Why?'

Mulholland could only focus on Winter. 'Because acid attacks are part of his remit.'

Fenchurch pointed at his own chest. 'It's my case.'

'DI Winter is in charge of the strategic prosecution of acid attacks.'

'Dawn, I keep telling you . . .' Winter shook his head. 'I've got no slack to take on your—'

'Superintendent Loftus has allocated you to this activity, Inspector. Any disagreement, you take it up with him. Am I clear?' Mulholland stared at him until he looked away. 'DI Nelson, your secondment is now officially over. You will run the Coldcut investigation from Operation Lydian.' She shot a withering glare at Fenchurch. 'Which leaves DI Fenchurch. You are to charge Steve Fisher with his wife's murder.'

'Dawn, I disagree with this. We need to—'

'Simon.' She narrowed her eyes at him. 'Let's see if you can focus on one thing at a time without dipping your toes into other people's cases. Mm?'

Fenchurch leaned back against the wall. Couldn't find the energy to argue.

'Now, I need to brief Julian on the latest . . . clusterfuck.' Mulholland got to her feet, wrapping her scarf tightly around her neck as she moved over to the door. 'Feel free to use this office to organise the handover, gentlemen.'

Winter watched the door close, then let out an almighty sigh. 'Well, boys, many thanks for getting me into this.'

'You shouldn't be here, Rod.' Fenchurch walked over and perched on Docherty's old seat. 'This isn't your case.'

'Tell me about it.' Winter took out a tobacco pouch and tipped the contents on to a pair of filter papers. 'Four acid attacks in South London, that one up in Hackney and she's pushing me to take this one, too.'

'We've got someone for the Hackney attack.'

'I gather. Means I've got to put a pair of DCs on interviewing him.' Winter licked the filter and rolled. 'Trouble is, my gaffer's in Majorca for a fortnight and Loftus listens to her over me.' He licked the paper again but slipped, covering his tongue in dry tobacco. He coughed, trying to cover it. 'Anyway, you pair got any ideas how I get back to what I'm supposed to be doing?'

'It's open-and-shut, Rod.' Fenchurch put his feet up on the desk, just like Docherty would've done back in the day. 'Jon and I are witnesses.'

'You saw it? Shitting hell.'

'You just need to run with it.'

'Oh, another one of those cases that's too good to be true? All they do is hoover up resource and I'm scrimping around as it is. Six Acting DCs, can you believe it? *Six*. Big daft lumps from uniform, none of whom I'd take if I had a choice. But I'm desperate.' He spat out tobacco. 'Total farce.'

Fenchurch walked over to the whiteboard and started drawing. 'Here's my thinking so far. We can connect Dodoo to Coldcut, right? Dealer. Supplier.' He joined the boxes. 'Then Dodoo was Steve's dealer, right?'

'Supposedly.' Nelson joined Fenchurch by the board. 'And Steve was at school with Coldcut.' He frowned. 'Add in those rumours that Steve Fisher is dealing drugs on the school playground.'

'Seriously? That teacher who killed his wife?' Winter looked up, his lips still covered in tobacco. 'Talk about open-and-shut, Si. Teacher kills his wife. Bosh.'

'Unproven at the moment.' Nelson uncapped a whiteboard pen, looking like he was back wearing his management consultant hat. 'So.' He wrote Elliot next to Steve. 'Teacher, pupil. Elliot was sleeping with Steve's wife.'

Winter started on another roll-up. 'How does Elliot hook into Dodoo and Coldcut? Why did they splash him?'

Nelson drew lines from Dodoo and Coldcut to Elliot. 'We don't know.'

Fenchurch stabbed his pen on to the boy's name. 'We *think* Elliot bought some drugs from Steve. We were going to speak to Elliot when he was attacked.'

'Could be Blockchain.' Nelson added it with a question mark. 'Elliot almost died from taking it, and Steve's supply is conveniently missing.'

Winter picked some tobacco off his tongue. 'You think Steve used them to kill her?'

'That's Dawn's working hypothesis.' Fenchurch tapped Elliot's name again. 'I haven't excluded him yet.'

'Right, so you don't know.' Winter put his tobacco away and joined them by the board. 'From where I'm standing, it looks like Steve connects Elliot to the other two. Retribution for Elliot bonking Steve's wife?'

Nelson redrew the hard line between Elliot and Steve. 'That's the only thing that makes sense.'

Winter stared at the spidery diagram, then nodded slowly. He tapped on Elliot's name. 'I need to speak to him. Find out if he knows why he was attacked.'

Fenchurch grabbed his jacket off the table. 'I'll join you.'

'You heard Mulholland, Si.' Winter smiled at him. 'You're focusing on Steve Fisher.'

'I heard her. We're handing over, mate. I'll show you Elliot, get him talking, then we're golden.'

Chapter Thirty-Eight

The room was guarded by two male uniforms, big lumps who looked like they could handle themselves. Through the glass, Elliot was lying on his back, wearing a white gown with black polka dots. His face was red, eyes shut and puffed up, skin marked in a few places. White cream covered his jaw, like he'd left some foam on from his morning shave. Cling film held everything in place.

'Jesus.' Fenchurch felt his gut contract. 'Can we speak to him?'

Dr Mulkalwar shook her head hard, teasing one of her hair clips free. 'We need to keep him in a sterile environment for at least two days.' She grinned at Fenchurch. 'Thanks to you, though, we've saved his face. To be perfectly frank, if you hadn't acted so quickly, he'd have lost his skin. It looks bad, but he'll recover in a few days, believe it or not.'

Winter's skin was tinged green like he was going to vomit. 'We've got to the point where an acid attack in London is like dealing with a nosebleed.'

'Inspector, thanks to the work you and other specialist teams are doing across this city, we're getting the message out there. When this sort of attack happens, people like DI Fenchurch now have the knowledge to save the victims. Thanks to you.'

'I guess.' Winter took a gulping breath. 'Just wish it wasn't happening.'

'In six months, it'll be something new.' Fenchurch nodded at the room. 'We really need speak to him.'

'I can't let you in there.'

'Have you got a phone or something?'

'Most people use theirs on the toilet, Inspector. They're like mobile cesspits.'

'There's nothing?'

'Well.' Mulkalwar flounced off with a flap of her white coat.

'No matter how many times I see it, Si . . .' Winter swallowed hard. His phone rang. 'Don't recognise this number. Better not be a bloody accident that wasn't my fault.' He answered it anyway. 'Yeah? Oh. Right.' He fiddled with the phone, sticking it on speaker.

A nurse in a sterilised suit held a mobile out to Elliot. 'Can you hear us?'

Winter gave a thumbs-up. 'Loud and clear.'

Elliot glanced over, but otherwise stayed static.

The nurse returned the thumbs-up. 'He can hear you.'

Winter lowered his phone. 'He's just not bloody speaking. Great.' He held it up again. 'Elliot, my name is DI Rod Winter. You know my colleague. We want to know why you were attacked.'

Elliot jerked forward, his mouth opening wide. He screamed and lay back. Every movement looked like it hurt. Then he looked over. 'I thought you'd caught him?'

'We have, but I want to know who was behind it. Why they did it. What you did that pissed them off.'

Elliot looked away. 'I've no idea.'

'Was it Coldcut?'

Elliot lay flat against the bed, shaking his head. He started shouting. 'No!'

The nurse put the phone down and fussed over Elliot, trying to calm him.

'Well done, Rod.' Fenchurch snatched the mobile off Winter and put it to his mouth. 'Elliot, it's DI Fenchurch. We know who did it. Daniel Dodoo is being charged with the attack.'

Elliot relaxed on the bed, his breathing slowing.

'He'll be away for a long time. Twenty years, minimum. You'll be in your midlife crisis by the time they start talking about letting him out.'

Elliot smirked, then winced with pain.

'I've got a few questions we wanted to ask when we saw you getting attacked.'

'What?'

'Someone said they saw you giving money to Steve Fisher. What—'

'Who?'

'I can't tell you. What was the money for?'

'And *I* can't tell *you* that.'

'We know that Steve's connected to Coldcut. We think he's part of that organisation.'

'I don't know what you're talking about.'

'Listen, we've got Dodoo in custody, but there are a million Dodoos. We've got Coldcut too.'

Elliot breathed out slowly.

'Thing is, if we want to put Coldcut away, we—'

'Steve sold me the E.'

'The Blockchain?'

Elliot nodded. Looked like it was painful. 'The Blockchain.'

'How did that start? You're in a chemistry class, discussing Avogadro's constant or mols per litre or whatever, and he goes, "Here, son, I've got some E"?'

'Hardly.' Elliot rolled his eyes. 'Steve's smart, right? And I don't mean intellectually. He figures people out. Plays poker, I think. He worked out who was smoking dope and who wanted to . . . take it up a notch. One time, we went on a trip to the Science Museum. Steve sat up the back with a few of us and got chatting. Said he could get us good gear. Cheap too. But we had to be quiet about it. Subtle.'

'And you kept your mouth shut?'

'Course. Nobody wanted to waste that opportunity.'

'So you bought some off him?'

'A few pills.'

Winter took the phone back. 'And you're sure that Steve Fisher was dealing?'

Elliot nodded.

'Did Steve ever mention Coldcut?'

'I heard the name. Guy has a rep, you know? But never met him. Never met anyone who knows him.'

'So why did he attack you?'

'Wish I knew, man. Got to be Steve. Me and Gayle . . . Retribution. Payback.' Elliot gritted his teeth. 'He must've known. Must've known how strong that Blockchain was, tried to kill me with it. Wanted me to die, man!'

Fenchurch stared through the security glass, frowning. *The kid looks genuinely upset, like he's figuring it all out now.*

An earsplitting scream burst out of Elliot's mouth, cutting through the glass, distorting on the phone's speaker.

Dr Mulkalwar rushed towards them, arms up. 'Inspectors, I need you to leave.'

Fenchurch took one look at Elliot convulsing on the bed and knew they'd be wasting their time pushing him any more. Elliot needed to focus on getting better. He nodded slowly. 'Okay.' He led Winter away. 'Well?'

'Don't know, Si.' Winter chanced a look back. 'I mean, I could buy it. Then again, I could sell it, know what I mean?'

'Our problem, Rod, is there's precious little evidence. Just rumours. It's like being back on the school playground.'

'Speaking of which, you honestly think a chemistry teacher would sell drugs to kids?'

'I've seen worse. Sure you have too.' Fenchurch waited for a grudging nod. 'And Steve goes way back with Coldcut. He could've seen Shadwell Grammar as a big opportunity, chance to get his poisonous claws into another area. Start at the school. And Steve was his in.'

Winter hit the lift down button and blew air up his face. 'Anyway, you've introduced me. Time for you to clear off, yeah?'

'Suppose so.' Fenchurch hit the up button. 'I've got someone I need to see here.'

'Well, I'll head back to Sutton. Catch you later, yeah?'

———————

'There you are.' Fenchurch slouched into the intensive care room.

'Simon?' Abi sat next to the cot, jigging Baby Al on her lap. 'What are you doing here?'

Fenchurch kissed her on the forehead. 'Interviewing someone downstairs.'

'A murder?'

'Acid attack.'

'Jesus Christ.'

'Feels worse in some ways.' Fenchurch took Baby Al, kissing him on the head. He sucked in his baby smell.

Why did Coldcut target Elliot? Still doesn't make any sense, except as revenge for his friend.

But why risk your empire for that?

Right now, Coldcut is in custody, his world falling around his ears because of this. All for his mate Steve.

'Are you going to make counselling tonight?' Abi's hand stroked down Fenchurch's back. 'It's fine if you can't. Chloe and I can talk.'

'Or we can reschedule.' Chloe appeared, cradling two coffees, their harsh and bitter smell filling the room. Probably tasted of mud. 'Sorry, Dad, I haven't got you one.'

'I won't be here long.' Fenchurch got up. 'If you want to reschedule, does that mean there's something you *need* to tell us? That thing you were going to tell me at the supermarket yesterday?'

Abi scowled at him.

'Dad, it's important to have time with both of you.' Chloe rubbed at her scar. 'There's a lot in my head and I need to get it out, but only in a safe environment.'

'What's not safe about home?'

'I just need to make sure we're not jeopardising anything. Doing it at a session with Paddy . . .' Chloe took a sip of coffee. 'It feels safe, that's all.'

Abi tipped a sachet of sweetener into her coffee. 'Can you make it tonight, Simon?'

'I'll try, but I'm running a murder inquiry.' Fenchurch kissed Baby Al on the forehead. 'We're all here now and we live under the same roof. Surely we—'

'Dad, it's not you. The rug's been taken from under my feet. That's all.' Chloe took a sip of coffee. 'I want to make sure that we're doing the right things and I'm not making problems for myself later. And it's not like even those sessions have been plain sailing.' She shot a glare at her mother. 'Like when you made— When I stormed out that time . . . I'm just saying, it's good to have Paddy there to help.'

'Seems sensible.' Abi's glare told Fenchurch he thought so too. 'Oh.' She reached into her bag for her phone. 'Forgot to say . . . I got a nice text from Pete this morning. Said he had a lovely time last night.'

'Despite my behaviour, eh?' Fenchurch blew a raspberry on Baby Al's belly. Made him laugh. Then he winked at Abi. 'Should I feel threatened that he's texting you?'

'You've nothing to worry about.'

'Right.' Chloe raised her eyebrows.

Fenchurch frowned at her. 'Sorry I was a bit of a dick to him, but he—'

'A bit? You were the whole—' Chloe blushed. 'Thanks for giving him a second chance.'

'I always try to. It's just that sometimes . . .' Fenchurch cuddled Baby Al close. 'Abi, I saw your pal Brendan Holding this morning. Said you and him took down a drug empire.'

'Hardly.'

'I need to call Pete.' Chloe got to her feet and left them to it.

Fenchurch watched her go. 'What's up with her?'

'No idea. She's been like that all day.' Abi stood and tickled their son's chin. 'What was Brendan saying about me?'

'Nothing much. He said you and him had problems with a dealer in Lewisham.'

'Can't remember the guy's name, but he was making our lives a living hell. The school playground was flooded with drugs. Brendan kept at it after I moved schools.'

'Sounds like a *Die Hard* film.'

'More like that Clint Eastwood film, *Gran Torino* or something, where he's a pensioner taking down a local gang. He convicted the guy in the end.'

'Really?'

'You don't believe me?'

'Nah, it's just he didn't mention it. Guys like him like to bring up stuff like that as soon as possible.'

Abi took Al off him. 'He's clean, Simon. Nobody cleaner.'

'This shit follows him, though. Lewisham to Shadwell. Both have severe drug problems.'

'Shit follows you, too, does that mean I should divorce you?' She scowled at him. 'And it's Lewisham and Shadwell. Those are really bad areas. Inner-city. Someone focusing their career on fixing that should be admired.'

'Fair point.' Fenchurch tickled Al's cheeks. 'How long till the operation?'

'Two hours.' Abi looked over at the clock above the door. 'Oates said they need to start prep in an hour.' She hugged her son. 'He's going to be fine, isn't he?'

'I think so. Hope so.' Fenchurch smiled at her, trying to reassure but it just bounced off her glare. 'Are you okay?'

'I was going to take Chloe shopping . . . Take our minds off it.'

'Smart thinking.' Fenchurch kissed Abi then Baby Al. 'A couple of hours not thinking about this shit . . . Priceless.'

Fenchurch walked down the corridor in Leman Street, swinging his Chilango bag. The packet of wine gums he'd bought for Chloe crinkled in his pocket. He unlocked his office door and the sweets tumbled out of his pocket. 'Shitting hell.' He bent down to pick them up.

Bridge came out of Mulholland's office just down the corridor, adjusting her skirt and blouse. 'Sir?'

'Lisa, what are you up to?'

She cleared her throat. 'Thought you'd like to know that Jim Muscat was definitely at that football match.'

'You've got evidence?'

'His season ticket was swiped at the gate and I've got him on the CCTV.' She huffed out a sigh. 'Turns out that pub is called the Rock of Gibraltar. Took a bit of effort to get anything out of the bar staff, but Muscat was in there.'

Fenchurch leaned back against the wall. His alibi stacking up meant someone was mucking about. 'So someone's definitely cloned his card?'

'Right. I spoke to someone from the keycard company and he said it's pretty easy if you know what you're doing. Anyone could do it, given access to the machine. And Jim Muscat doesn't know his arse from his elbow when it comes to tech.'

'That's good news but we need to get to the bottom of how our killer got in the room.'

'You mean how Steve Fisher got that card?'

'That's an assumption. Don't assume things, okay?'

Bridge let out a sigh. 'On it, sir.'

'I'll not keep you, then.' Fenchurch gave her a smile and waited until she was round the corner, then opened Mulholland's office door.

Nelson was behind the desk, typing on a laptop with his right hand, his left rubbing his groin through his trousers. He looked up at Fenchurch, then down at his bag. 'Could've got me one.'

'I did.' Fenchurch tossed him a burrito and he just about caught it. 'Never make the Met Twenty20 team, Jon.'

'One of the lads was on at me to join up.' Nelson tore at his burrito, untwisting the foil like he'd not eaten in days. 'I love cricket but it doesn't love me.' He bit into it and chewed quickly. 'This is like old times.'

'Maybe.' Fenchurch sat in front of Docherty's old desk. 'Hate coming in here, Jon. It's like Docherty's in the corner, watching us.'

'I wouldn't masturbate in here, then.'

Fenchurch raised an eyebrow. 'Or what you were doing with Lisa Bridge?'

'Eh?'

'Don't think I don't know.' Fenchurch winked at him. 'I was thinking more of pissing in Mulholland's drawer.'

Nelson laughed. 'Simon, you need to drop that. The hate's eating you up.'

'It's all I've got left.' Fenchurch opened a drink of lemonade. 'Listen, I was talking to Abi about the drug problem at Lewisham.'

'Which Holding sorted, right?'

'Did he? What I'm wondering is if he's bent?'

Nelson dumped his burrito on the desk. 'Here we go again . . .'

'Hear me out.' Fenchurch took another bite. 'What if he's working with Coldcut. They took a hit in Lewisham, but Holding used it to get a bigger role in Shadwell. Now he's Headmaster, he's hitting that hard.'

Nelson rolled his eyes, chewing.

'Think about it, Jon. Coldcut's got a foothold in East London through that school. I'd never even heard of him until the other day.'

'Last night.'

'Is that all?' Fenchurch huffed out a sigh. 'Well, he's everywhere now.'

Nelson finished chewing. 'Only trouble with your theory is that we got a guy for the Lewisham thing. He's doing two life sentences. We took down his crew and there's no connection to Holding or Coldcut.'

'So I'm barking up the wrong tree?'

'You're barking, that's for sure.' Nelson put his burrito down. 'But' — he opened his laptop and started typing — 'this dealer in Lewisham, Justin Stephens, died last year, stabbed in the showers.' He frowned. 'Well, would you look at that?'

'What?'

'He worked for your old mate, Dimitri Younis.'

'He's neither my mate, or that old.' Fenchurch picked at the steak stuck between his teeth. 'You think Younis knows Coldcut or Holding?'

'Worth a shot.'

Younis . . . Great.

287

Chapter Thirty-Nine

'In here, sirs.' The prison officer led them into the room. Six tables arranged in a two-by-three formation. Just one occupied. 'I'll be outside.'

Younis was slumped in a seat. Little sniffles, mouth hanging open, eyes on the floor. His hair had been shaved to the bone, letting a network of scars get some light. Not that Belmarsh had much natural light. 'Well, well, well.' He held Fenchurch's gaze for a few seconds, then gave him the old up and down. 'Looking good, sweetie.'

Fenchurch walked over to the table and took off his suit jacket. 'You're looking well, Dimitri.' He sat down next to Nelson. 'Prison life clearly suits you.'

'I like it in here, oddly enough.' Younis leaned across the table, resting on his elbows. 'Sure you don't fancy killing someone? I could arrange a bunk-up with little old me.'

'What a lovely offer. I'll pass, though.'

'Oh, you'll keep.' Younis settled on to his elbows. 'Do you mind if I call you Fenchy?' He waited for an answer he wasn't getting, then waved a hand at Nelson but didn't look at him. 'Not sure I like him being here.'

'This isn't on tape, Dimitri. Nothing you say can be used against you.'

'Well, I'm not talking. Even to you, my precious.'

Nelson narrowed his eyes. 'Need to ask you a few questions about your mate Coldcut. He's selling a strain of super-strong ecstasy pills. Calls it Blockchain.' Nelson sat back, arms folded. 'It's very strong. People are dying when they take it. Your people are selling it.'

'Said I'm not talking to you.' Younis chanced a glance at him. 'Case you hadn't noticed, you stupid prick, I'm in prison.' He waved his hands around the room. 'Not that you're in any hurry to get me to trial, eh?'

'I tell you—'

'Justin Stephens.' Fenchurch's glare got Nelson to butt out. For now. 'He worked for you in Lewisham, didn't he? Ran a drug operation at the school. Didn't take to prison quite like you have.'

'No comment.'

'This isn't being recorded. You can just say piss off.'

'Piss off, then. You're wearing a wire, ain't you?'

'That your way of getting me to take my shirt off, Dimitri?' Fenchurch waited for the leer. 'Did you know Justin Stephens or Coldcut?'

'In the biblical sense?'

'In any sense. Did they work for you?'

'Neither.'

'But Justin Stephens knew Colin Cutler?'

'Oooh, get you, Fenchurch. Done your homework.'

Fenchurch winked at him. 'Not just a pretty face, eh?'

'Oh, that's stretching it.' Younis returned it. 'It's your body I'm after, not your face.'

'Speaking of which, one of Cutler's crew sprayed acid on some kid's face.' Fenchurch enjoyed the look of disgust on Younis's face, like he'd eaten from a cesspit. 'Happened this morning. Very nasty.'

'You can't pin any of that on me.'

'You're on trial next month, Dimitri.' Nelson gave a smug grin. 'Be a shame to add another crime to the sheet, wouldn't it?'

'Piss off. I'm in here, not chucking kerosene on people.'

'An acid attack is life these days.' Nelson let it sink in, let Younis add it to the prison algebra in his head. 'If we found out you were involved . . .'

'How the hell can I order someone to throw acid on someone's face from in here, eh?'

Fenchurch started folding up his shirtsleeves, made sure Younis was watching. 'You can stash a mobile anywhere, I imagine.'

'Piss off.'

'If you help us, we can put in a good word with the CPS and make sure you don't face more charges.'

'I'm not involved.' Younis whipped his focus from Fenchurch's bare arms to Nelson. 'I'll help you so long as Laughing Boy here pisses off. Okay?'

Fenchurch nodded at Nelson.

'Your grave . . .' Nelson shook his head as he walked off. The door clunked shut.

'Now it's just you and me, babes. Let's go back to you taking that shirt off for me.'

Fenchurch smiled at him. 'Not yet.'

'Least you could do, mate. I'm sitting in here playing with myself while I wait for his bullshit case to get thrown out of court. Wouldn't mind a bit of how's your father. How is he, by the way?'

Fenchurch steeled himself. 'Not getting enough in the showers here?'

'Sometimes I prefer the cooking to sticking my hotdog in a bun.'

'How about you just tell me whether Coldcut was involved in your Lewisham operation?'

'*I* wasn't involved. That was Justin Stephens. Nothing to do with me.' Younis sat back, hands in his pockets. Seedy bastard probably was playing with himself. 'If I was involved, why did the Met let me build a perfectly legitimate business?' He was definitely playing with himself, the rubbing getting faster. 'Because there's nothing in it.'

'You're telling me you've had nothing in Lewisham?'

'Wouldn't even piss on that place if it was on fire. South of the bleeding river. Not my patch.'

'Very magnanimous of you.'

'I'm going to walk over to that door, babes.' Younis ran a tongue over his lips. 'Slowly, so you can admire the work I've been doing on my butt.'

Just a load of bollocks, then.

Younis wasn't involved in the Lewisham operation. Probably nothing in Holding being bent, either. Nelson's intelligence system is a joke and here I am, pulling together a vendetta against Holding, a man who did some good in the world, probably because he got too close to my wife.

Shit, is that it? Am I worried that Abi was . . . with Holding? She's too smart for a prick like him. No danger.

But . . . she kicked me out for being a selfish prick. And here I am, yet again, being a selfish prick.

Fenchurch cleared his throat as he stood up. 'I'll see you around, Dimitri.'

'Oh, you're just going to leave me with a semi?'

'Good luck in your case, Dimitri. Hope they throw away the key.'

'Offer still stands.' Younis joined him by the door. 'Get yourself locked up and we can make sweet music together.' He reached over to stroke Fenchurch's cheek. 'The pounding of bedsprings, your screaming through a bitten pillow. Sweet, sweet music. You'll love it.'

'That what it's all about for you? Rape?'

'I'm a man who doesn't like asking for things.'

'You ask much of Cutler?'

'I'm in here, sweetie,' Younis whispered. 'How can I?'

'You know exactly what he's up to, don't you?'

Younis stroked his cheek again, his gaze licking Fenchurch's face. 'What is he up to?'

'One of Coldcut's dealers, guy called Steve Fisher. He's a teacher at Shadwell Grammar. We hear that he deals to the pupils.' Fenchurch shifted a little closer to Younis. 'He gets his gear from Coldcut, right?'

'I'm not stupid.' Younis backed off, shoulders slouching. 'You're murder squad and this is all drug squad stuff. Why's Colin on your radar?'

'Steve's wife was murdered using one of those Blockchain pills. Someone held her down, put three down her throat, waited for her to die. Now, we know that Coldcut supplied them. We know that Coldcut works for you. Makes you culpable, Dimitri. Yet another drug death on your hands.'

'This is nothing to do with me.' Younis gave him another stroke on the cheek. 'I'm going to have to leave you with your cock unwanked.'

'And here was me thinking you were all about rape.'

'I've been known to reach around in my time.'

Fenchurch grabbed his hand and held it, twisting the fingers. 'Enough of this shit. Your mate Coldcut arranged an acid attack on someone. I want answers.'

'Why the hell do you think I know anything?'

'Daniel Dodoo doesn't work for you, then?'

'What?' Younis's face fell. 'Is he okay?'

'He's going to prison for life for it. Might get your bunk-up with him.'

'Not my type. He was the attacker?'

'Caught him myself.' Fenchurch tightened his grip until Younis snarled. 'Coldcut got him to splash this kid who'd pissed off his old mate Steve Fisher. You know about it, don't you?'

Younis tried to break free. 'Drop it!' He managed to get his fingers away. 'Never heard of Steve Fisher. Certainly not in my organisation.'

'So you do have one?'

'This isn't on tape. This isn't evidence. You can't use this against me!'

'I was at the hospital. You should've seen the damage the acid did to poor Elliot's face. Couldn't even—'

'Elliot?' Younis stared at Fenchurch, eyes bulging. 'What did you say?'

'Elliot Lynch.'

Younis walked off, shaking his head. 'Jesus.'

'You know him?'

Younis slumped against the wall. 'Rings a bell, that's all.'

'Is he in your organisation?'

'Piss off. He auditioned for my cam site.'

'Bollocks.' Fenchurch tried to work it out. 'Hang on, you've been in here almost a year and he's just turned seventeen. He's too young, even for you and your site.'

'I know precisely how old he is, my sweet.' Younis thumped his fist off the door. 'Let me out!'

'Listen to me.' Fenchurch grabbed Younis by the throat and pinned him to the door. 'How do you really know Elliot?'

'Like I told you, the kid turned up for an audition. Far too young. Told him where to go.'

The door opened behind him and Fenchurch let go. 'You don't want me finding out through some other means. If there's anything between you and Elliot . . .'

Younis rubbed at his throat, still had the filthy pervert's grin on his lips. 'Only thing between us is eight and a half inches of uncut meat.'

———

'You're quiet.' Nelson drove past a row of shops and pulled up at the lights. 'I don't like it when you stop talking.'

Fenchurch ran his fingers down his cheek. Could still feel Younis's hand there. 'I'm thinking, Jon.'

'Even worse.' Nelson grinned at him, then stuck the car back in gear and set off. 'Did you get anything out of that?'

'Waste of time, Jon. He's a bullshit merchant.'

'You were alone a long time.'

'He didn't know Steve's name.' Fenchurch gripped the 'Oh Shit' handle above the door. 'Flinched when I said Elliot's, though. Tried to cover it over with some bollocks about his cam site. Same with Dodoo and Coldcut. What if we've got it the wrong way round? All we've got is Katerina's word that Steve's a dealer. She saw money changing hands. Now, Younis is the daddy of that organisation. He knows Elliot and Dodoo, but he didn't know Steve. What if it was Elliot selling to Steve?'

'But Elliot thought Steve tried to kill him with that Blockchain.'

'We've got so little on that, Jon. Meanwhile, Steve's told us, *on the record*, that he's got a regular dealer. Even gave his alibi as visiting a drug dealer's house to score. He could've said he was visiting his mate Daniel, then he went for a beer with his mate Colin, but he didn't. He *told* us he was buying drugs. Why do that if he's a dealer?'

'Because Steve knows he's going down for murder, so he decides to put a different target on his back. Drugs. It's still a target, still something we can do him for. Just not murder. You know how it works — we're likely to focus on that, get him away for *something*.'

'Maybe.' Fenchurch gripped the handle again as Nelson swerved round another bend. 'That alibi fell apart. Wasn't worth him taking the hit for the drugs. And, if he killed Gayle, why go to Dodoo's first? He had some Blockchain in his own stash. At their house, in her knock-off handbag.' He pinched his nose. 'The way to get away with murder, Jon, is to have as few moving parts as possible. As little a trace as you can get away with. If it was Steve, surely he'd have killed her at home? Why go to all that palaver of tying her up and giving her drugs? Doesn't seem very straightforward.'

'Does it have to?' Nelson stopped at another set of lights, his forehead creased in concentration. 'How about this? Steve finds out that his wife's been sleeping with Elliot. He's angry, wants to harm him, but doesn't know how. He's a lover, not a fighter, all that jazz. But he visits

Dodoo to get some drugs. And he lucks out, because Coldcut's there, his old schoolmate. They go for a pint and talk about it. Coldcut agrees to sort out Elliot.'

'Guys like Coldcut aren't notoriously sentimental, Jon. What does he get from it?'

'Sends a message to the rest of his crew. Don't mess with my guys or their wives.'

'That works.'

'All about how you spin it.'

'Spoken like a management consultant.' Fenchurch got out his Airwave and tapped in a badge number. 'Martin, can you get Steve Fisher's lawyer back in for me?'

Let's see if we can get the truth out of him, finally . . .

Chapter Forty

I told you!' Steve Fisher hammered his fist off the interview room table. 'I was buying drugs!'

Dalton Unwin sat next to him, head in his hands. Not going the way he expected.

'Just happened to be "buying drugs" from the man who splashed acid on Elliot's face? Right?'

Steve swallowed hard. 'What?'

'Don't play coy with me. You got Coldcut to arrange the hit on Elliot. Revenge for—'

'No! I don't know what you're talking about!' Steve swallowed again, his Adam's apple bobbing slowly. 'What happened to Elliot?'

'Daniel Dodoo splashed him with acid. Kid's in intensive care right now, in a sterile room. Chance he might look normal again. More likely that he'll be disfigured for life.'

'Jesus.' Steve had gone white. He blinked hard. 'I didn't know.'

'We've been struggling with why anyone would do that.' Fenchurch left a pause. 'The only link we've got is you, Steve.'

'No!'

'You murdered your wife. That's in the bag. You'll get life. But an acid attack is another life sentence. On top.'

'I didn't do anything!'

'You expect us to believe that? Coldcut got one of his lads to splash acid all over Elliot's face. Your old mate Coldcut. And, you know, the kid who was sleeping with your wife?'

Steve was panting now, his gaze shooting around the room.

'And you know Daniel Dodoo. That's on the record. Same with your history with Colin Cutler.' Fenchurch leaned forward, drilling his gaze into Steve's eyes. 'Daniel did it. Splashed acid over Elliot's face.'

'You're talking shit.'

'We know you're a dealer, Steve. Selling Blockchain, the drug you killed—'

'No!'

'—your wife with. You gave some to Elliot, only he betrayed your trust, didn't he?'

'No!'

'All the time he was selling drugs for you, he was—'

'No!'

'—shagging your wife behind your back.'

'I'm not a dealer!'

'Really? See, we've got evidence that you were. Shitloads of product.'

'That's bullshit.' Another thump of the desk. 'That little shithead was the dealer!'

'Oh, really?'

'*I* bought from *him*.'

Fenchurch stopped. *Does that make sense? Does anything?* He leaned forward. 'How did that work, then? "Here, sir, I've got some super-strong ecstasy, would you like some?" That how it went? Right in the middle of a double period?'

Steve leaned over and whispered in Unwin's ear. Got a shrug in response. 'I used to buy from Coldcut, then things started taking off for him, so he told me to buy from someone else.'

'Daniel Dodoo?'

'No, someone else. A couple of weeks back, my usual guy was out of coke, so he told me to visit Daniel.' Steve sighed. 'Too late to back out when one of your pupils turns up in your dealer's flat.' He shook his head, teeth bared. 'Elliot had a big bag of coke. I wanted some.' He shrugged. 'We came to an arrangement. Neither of us would grass.'

'You expect me to believe that Elliot just happened to turn up?'

Steve pressed his fist into the table. 'Jesus Christ, why don't you believe me?'

'Because you're lying, Steve. You murdered your wife and you got Coldcut to splash Elliot.'

'I didn't kill her!' Steve looked like he was going to thump the desk again. Then he collapsed back, his face twisting up. 'Look, I buy drugs every week, pretty much. Gayle . . . She loved . . . chemsex.'

'Chemsex?' Fenchurch could only laugh. 'Here we go again. Steve, you—'

'It's true! Every Friday, we'd go for a few drinks with the guys from the school, then we'd slip off home. Take an E, put on some music. I'd take a Viagra, then all weekend we'd be mixing E with Special K, maybe some coke.'

'Steve, quit while you're behind.'

'I loved my wife, even after she did what she did.' Steve looked up at Fenchurch. 'I didn't kill her.'

'Steve, you're a drug dealer. Dealers lie.'

'I'm not!'

'We have a witness stating that you took money off him.'

Steve laughed. 'That one time I bought coke off him, he sold me talc or something. He gave me a refund.'

'He just gave you it, yeah?'

'Had to get my usual guy to have a word, but yeah. Elliot must've been worried I'd grass to Colin.'

'And does this "usual guy" have a name?'

'I don't know it. Prefer it that way.'

'Convenient.'

'Yeah.'

'Just tell us where we can find him.'

Steve looked at his lawyer, then shrugged.

'Come on, Steve, have you got a phone number? Email? Anything?'

'No.'

'Cut the bullshit. How can you buy drugs from a guy you're not in touch with?'

Steve nibbled his nails. 'Because he's the barman at The Third Planet.'

'Oliver Muscat-Smith?'

'I don't know his name.' Steve ran a hand through his hair. 'I tried to buy from him on Friday, but he wasn't working. So I went to Daniel's instead.'

'Steve, that bar is in the Bennaceur Hotel.' Fenchurch nodded, speeding up as things started to slot into place. 'Oliver was drinking in there, though, wasn't he? He told you Gayle was there, didn't he? Then you and Coldcut went to kill her. Right?'

'No!'

'You're digging a very deep hole for yourself. You've just reached the bottom and someone's throwing mud on your head.'

———

'Bloody hell.' Nelson pulled on to Aldgate High Street, backed up with traffic swarming round a broken-down bus. 'Be quicker walking.'

Fenchurch held the phone to his ear. 'Yeah, I'm still here.'

'Simon, I'm far too busy for this.' Mulholland sounded annoyed. Loud chatter in the background. 'I need you to take lead from DS Ashkani.'

'I wasn't asking for direction, Dawn, I'm just updating you.'

'Simon, you—'

Fenchurch killed the call. *That could've gone better.* He stuck his phone on silent and pocketed it. 'She's doing my head in, Jon. She's supposed to be SIO but she's just in meetings with Loftus all day long. Sounded like she was at a bloody conference. Wine and bloody nibbles.'

'No doubt you'll point that out to her.' Nelson slipped through a gap in the traffic and pulled on to the Minories. Managed to get a space just down from the hotel. 'Do you believe Steve?'

Fenchurch shrugged. 'He believes his own lies.' He got out of the car and started walking towards the hotel bar.

The place was open again, the lights twinkling in the afternoon murk in the deep shadows of the City's towers. Through the window, Oliver Muscat-Smith was perched on a stool, twatting about on his phone. Looked bored out of his skull. The bar was almost empty, just an old guy at the back watching Sky on the telly and a man in his twenties approaching the bar. Oliver got up and started fiddling with the mountain of whiskies by the till.

'That guy's Steve's dealer? Really?' Fenchurch stopped in the street. 'He's just a gangly idiot. Too young to know anything.'

Oliver looked up at his customer and nodded. Then walked over to pull a pint.

'Someone cloned the room card, Simon.' Nelson sucked on his vape stick. 'His own father's card. He knew his father would be at the football then in the pub. Solid alibi.'

Oliver looked around the bar and nodded again at the punter. Then he slid something across the bar top.

Fenchurch set off again. 'Did you see that?'

'Oh yeah.' Nelson started running, outstripping Fenchurch's pace.

Fenchurch followed him inside, warrant card out. 'Police!'

'What?' Oliver held up his hands.

The punter ran off. Nelson darted after him and tackled him by the door, pushing him on to the floor.

'Oliver, Oliver, Oliver . . .' Fenchurch shook his head at him. 'We saw you. Selling drugs.'

Oliver looked like he was going to make a run for it.

'Looks like a gram of coke.' Nelson stuffed a small packet into an evidence bag. 'Naughty boy, Oliver.' He hauled the buyer to his feet and walked him over to the bar. 'Oliver Muscat-Smith, I'm arresting you for—'

Oliver reached for a bottle of whisky and smashed it on the bar. Toxic fumes belched out along with the liquid. He brandished it, looking like he was going to lash out at them. 'Get away from me!'

Fenchurch held up his hands. 'Oliver, you're making things worse for yourself here.'

Oliver jumped on the bar, agile like a cat. He stabbed the bottle at Fenchurch.

Fenchurch dodged to the right, then grabbed Oliver's knee and pulled him back. Oliver dropped the bottle and it smashed on the flagstones. Then he staggered backwards and fell into the wall of whisky, sending it all falling to the floor. Sounded like someone had pushed over a hundred greenhouses.

Amazingly, Oliver was still on the counter, above the destruction. He looked down at the mess, eyes bulging like his old man's. 'Aw, shit!'

⌣

'I'm not a dealer!' Oliver barely fit on the seat. He was all knees and thighs. 'This is bullshit!'

'We saw you, son.' Nelson held up the evidence bag, the matchbook rattling around inside. 'Give him some coke wrapped in a box of matches, take an extra twenty when he pays for his beer.'

Fenchurch stopped, nodding slowly. 'That's what happened when you got caught with your fingers in the till, wasn't it?'

'What?'

'That was your drug money, not Bennaceur beer money, right?'

Oliver just looked at the floor, no eye contact.

'I'll send this off to the lab when we're out of here.' Nelson dropped the drugs on the table. 'It'll be covered in yours and your punter's prints.'

Oliver's leg started jigging, jerking wild. 'What do you—'

'Oliver.' His lawyer held up a hand. A mess of silver hair and black glasses wearing a navy three-piece suit. 'Please.'

'I've got a trial with Spurs next week!'

'And that's such a shame.' Fenchurch picked up the coke, shaking his head at Oliver. 'You'll be on remand when they're doing those warm-up dances.' He clicked his tongue a few times, trying to be as annoying as possible. 'Though that's the least of your worries, son. You'll be inside for a few years. A promising football career cut short by drug dealing.'

Oliver looked like he wanted to speak, but his lawyer's vice-like grip on his arm stopped him.

'Seen it before, Jon, haven't we? These kids who live the footballer's lifestyle before they've made it. Throwing the cash about, demanding respect. Wanting people to look up to them. "Oh, there's Oliver. He's well blaze."' Fenchurch focused hard on Oliver. 'The problem is, son, your money comes from dealing drugs, not from a football contract.'

'What do I get out of this?' Oliver rocked back in his chair, accidentally kicking Fenchurch on the knee. 'If I was to talk to you, what are we looking at?'

Fenchurch looked at Nelson. 'I'd tell him to piss off, Jon.' He held up the coke. 'This is three years inside, right?'

'Maybe more, depending on the judge.'

'And he's old enough to go to proper prison, too.' Fenchurch put the coke back down again in front of the kid. 'It's your case, though, Jon.'

'Trouble is, I've got no motivation to let you wriggle out of this.' Nelson smiled at Oliver. 'So I'm going to charge you. Shutting down a dealer will look really good in the press.'

'I can give up my supplier. I'll testify in court!'

'You'll appear in court, son, but not as a witness.'

'Come on, mate. I'll do anything, *anything*. Just let me off.'

'That's not going to happen.'

'Anything, I swear.'

'Let's see how serious you are, yeah? Who do you work for?'

'Daniel—'

The lawyer put a hand to his client's arm. 'Oliver!'

'Dodoo.'

'Oliver . . .' His lawyer shook his head. 'You need to listen to my advice!'

'You need to clear off, mate. You're doing me no favours here.'

The lawyer scowled. 'You're refusing my counsel?'

'I'm refusing your bullshit.' Oliver leaned on the table, resting on his elbows, waiting for the lawyer to clear off. Took his time, but Oliver lost none of his resolve.

'We know you sold drugs to Steve Fisher.'

'I get my gear from Daniel Dodoo.' Oliver looked away. 'He works for some guy I don't know.'

'Dimitri Younis?'

'Never heard of him.'

'Coldcut?'

Oliver smirked. 'My old man loves their records.'

'He must be so proud of you. His son, the drug dealer.'

Oliver ran a hand across his face.

'Steve told us you sold him drugs.'

'Shit.' Oliver leaned back and stared up at the ceiling. 'Daniel passed him on to me. Most weeks, he'd come in for a couple of beers and buy some gear. MDMA, ketamine, cocaine. Viagra, when I had it.'

'Did he say what he did with all of that?'

'What do you think?' A smile flashed across Oliver's lips. 'Give it all to a charity for daft kids?'

'I'm warning you, son.'

Oliver's grin died.

'You saw Steve in the bar on Friday night, didn't you? Told him that his wife was staying at the hotel, didn't you?'

'You're talking shit. Maybe I should get that clown of a lawyer back in here.'

'The more you tell us now, the better it'll be for you. Did you sell Steve those Blockchain pills?'

'Elliot.'

Back to lying again. 'Elliot Lynch?'

'I've had enough of it, so I tried passing it all on to him.' Oliver nibbled at his thumbnail. 'Elliot's football career's over. He won't make the grade. So I started shifting stuff to him. But it's hard to break free, you know?'

'Oh, I do.' Nelson grinned. 'That's why people don't get into it, son. They see all this shit in advance. That or they've got a moral compass.'

'Last week, this geezer came to us and told us to start selling this Blockchain stuff. Big guy, built like a brick shithouse.' Oliver punched his thigh. 'Couple of days later, I saw a news story about it, told Elliot we should stop selling it. Elliot wanted to make an impression with this guy, so he took it all off me, said he'd shift it all, show him what he's made of. Shifted it all in a week.' He swallowed hard. 'Then people started dying.'

Fenchurch waited for Oliver to make eye contact with him again. 'People like Gayle Fisher.'

'Right.'

'Did Elliot sell Steve the Blockchain?'

'Look, I've been honest here. What am I getting out of this? You letting me go or what?'

'I'm still waiting to see what else you've got.' Nelson paused. 'Coldcut got Daniel Dodoo to splash acid on Elliot's face this morning. Why?'

'What?' Oliver's eyes bulged. 'I hadn't heard. Been working since ten.'

'They attacked him at his grandmother's. How did they know he'd be there?'

'I've no idea.'

'Did you tell him?'

Oliver waved his hands in the air. 'Why would I?'

'I need to believe you, Oliver. I really want to, but you're making it hard for me.'

'Come on, mate, I'm implicating myself in all sorts of shit. You need to give me a break!'

'You're not giving us everything, Oliver. What else is there?'

'Nothing!'

'Come on, son. I know you're lying.'

'I swear, that's it.'

'Here's the thing. Whoever killed Gayle used your old man's security card. Now, he's got an alibi, watching you getting sent off at the football. But someone cloned his card. You know how to do that, don't you?'

'So does half the bloody hotel!'

'But you knew where your old man would be. You might as well have done it yourself. Steve killed her with your drugs.'

'He didn't.'

'What?'

'Steve didn't do it.' Oliver ran a hand through his hair. 'On Friday night, me and Elliot were drinking in the Third Planet, chatting up these birds, like I told you. Well, I was. I saw Steve over the other side of the bar. With Coldcut.'

'You said you didn't know him.'

'Shit.'

'So you do?'

'That big bloke, yeah. Just told us to call him Coldcut.'

'So why did you lie?'

'That lawyer told me to keep quiet. Deny everything.'

'Coldcut pay for him?'

'Said he was a good guy. Would use him himself.'

'Take us back to the bar, then. Steve and Coldcut.'

'Pair of them ignored us. Steve looked pretty upset. Looked like Coldcut was helping him deal with something. This was about half nine. Ages before we went up to Hackney.'

'Of course, and there's no CCTV in there, is there?'

'No, but I can point out exactly where they sat. They had three pints of Estrella. Spanish lager, nice stuff. Then they caught a cab outside.'

Something at least. Get Bridge on it.

'I still don't buy it, son.' Fenchurch held his gaze. 'Oliver, you know what Blockchain does to people? Gayle Fisher died of fluid on the lungs. Drowned in her own body fluid. Can you imagine what that must be like?'

'She wouldn't have been aware of anything. I read an article on Vice.'

'Almost like you were there, isn't it?'

Shit. He was there.

Elliot.

Elliot went missing during the time they were there. In the hotel.

'You knew Gayle was staying there, didn't you?'

'Kat checked her in. She recognised her, but didn't ask what she was doing there. Discretion, and she didn't look like she wanted any questions.'

'But you told Elliot, right?'

Oliver held his head in his hands. 'He was talking about all that shit in the papers. His Mrs Fisher on the front of the *Post*. I thought he'd want to know she was there. Maybe go to her room and, I don't know, talk?'

'So then you cut a card for Elliot, using your old man's—'

'No!'

'—and let Elliot into her room. You helped him tie her up and force the drugs down her throat.'

'That's not what happened!'

'You just watched?'

'No! I wasn't there!'

'Oliver, you're an accomplice to murder.'

'How do you figure that? You've got nothing on me.'

Chapter Forty-One

Mulholland was in the Obs Suite, drumming her fingers on the table. 'Do you want a round of applause?' She glared at Fenchurch and tightened her scarf. 'DS Ashkani is downstairs, arranging for Mr Fisher's release.'

'What?'

'She confirmed his story with Coldcut. Very helpful. We checked with the bar staff at the hotel and DC Bridge has confirmed it on the CCTV.'

'Dawn, he had all those—'

'Drugs? Steve was in court this morning. Bailed on the drug charges, but we've still got him for murder. Of course, you'd know that if you'd not been involving yourself in DI Nelson's case instead of keeping on top of your own. This is your investigation, Simon. Yours.'

'I'm just out of the bloody interview, Dawn!'

'It feels like you've just chanced upon getting that information. There's no strategy here.'

'He was identified in the corridor outside her room and dumping her bag, Dawn.' Fenchurch fell back against the door. 'You shouldn't let him go.'

'You've still got a suspect. Elliot. He was selling the Blockchain. Killing people. Almost killed himself.'

'I . . .' Fenchurch couldn't speak.

'Simon, Alan Docherty should've put a stop to your behaviour a long time ago.'

'My behaviour?'

'Beating up suspects, blaming everyone for your daughter's abduction.'

'You're actually using that against me?' Fenchurch towered over her. 'That would've all been resolved a long time ago if you—'

'Not this again.' She waved him off. 'Get over it. I've admitted my fault. Yes, I interviewed someone and, maybe, if we'd had the full facts ten years ago, we could've found your daughter earlier. But it's unimportant.'

'*Unimportant?*' Fenchurch wanted to swing for her. Instead, he opened the door, ready to charge out.

'Simon.' Mulholland grabbed his arm. 'As your friend, I'm advising you to focus on the bigger picture. Julian Loftus doesn't care about it.'

'*I* care.'

'And that's the problem, isn't it? I don't want to tell you how to live your life, but maybe it's more important to enjoy your daughter's company than spend every moment of your waking life blaming me? She escaped on *your* watch.'

Fenchurch wanted to lash out and knock her head off. Stamp on it, until it was just bone and grey matter and blood and hate and all the shit she kept in there.

'I thought you'd be spending time with your sick baby son? That's preoccupying you, isn't it? I shouldn't—'

'This is the first I've heard of it.' Loftus stood in the doorway, arms folded. 'Care to enlighten me, Inspector?'

'Sir.' Fenchurch couldn't hold his gaze. 'My son's been in intensive care since he was born.'

'I wasn't talking to you.' Loftus narrowed his eyes at Mulholland. 'Inspector, this disagreement goes back to the end of DCI Docherty's tenure, doesn't it?'

'It . . .' Mulholland couldn't focus on him. 'Yes.'

'Sir. My son's treatment hasn't been working . . .'

'You have my deepest sympathies.' Loftus patted his arm as he brushed past, heading straight for Mulholland. 'Now, you can go and spend time with your family, okay?'

'Sir, I want to—'

'We've got a fresh suspect; we'll work on prosecuting him. I shall see you in the morning.' Loftus gave him a smug grin. 'A word of warning, though. Mr Fisher is being released. I suggest you avoid him on your way out, okay?'

⁓

'Guv!'

Fenchurch stopped halfway down the corridor.

Reed was ploughing along behind him. 'You okay?'

'You tell me.'

'Like that, is it?'

'Just . . .' Fenchurch sighed. 'Mulholland. Loftus.'

'Usual, then?' She grinned at him, but he wasn't having any of it. 'You've been a bit elusive today.'

'I've been busy, Kay.'

'You're supposed to be Deputy SIO on the Gayle Fisher case, aren't you?'

Fenchurch started off again. 'Whatever.'

'Don't you "whatever" me, guv.' Reed grabbed his arm but couldn't stop him. 'You've been doing God knows what all day while I've been managing the case for you. Which means keeping Ashkani at arm's bloody length and updating Mulholland when I can't get hold of you.'

Fenchurch opened the door and set off down the stairs. 'Have you got anything?'

'That's not my point. You've been sleeping on the job.'

'I'm heading to the hospital, Kay.' Fenchurch stopped at the bottom. Couldn't focus on anything. 'Al's operation is this afternoon.'

'Shit, I didn't know.'

'Abi's not telling you everything, then?'

Reed shook her head. 'Is she okay?'

'Hard to tell with her. Chloe's helping. But . . . I don't know. The way my luck's been, I keep expecting a phone call saying . . . Sod it.' He let out a deep breath. 'I'm worried, Kay. Terrified. I spent a few minutes with him earlier, but . . . What if that's the last time I see him?'

'Guv, you're in his corner. Okay? That's important.'

'I just wish I wasn't in this situation.'

'It's tough, guv, but you're tougher.'

'Am I?' Fenchurch opened the door, heading through the Custody Suite towards his car and home. 'Keep losing myself in this case, Kay. I'm all over the place.'

'Mulholland shouldn't be putting you under this pressure.'

'She wants to see me fall.' Fenchurch stopped by the back door, warrant card out, ready to swipe. 'She said you thought to arrest Steve after his court appearance?'

'Right. Well. Anyone would've done that.'

'She didn't. Uzma didn't. You did.'

'And it turns out he's an innocent man.' Fenchurch swiped his card and opened the door.

Steve Fisher was standing in the Custody Suite, inspecting a watch. He smiled at Martin. 'Gayle gave me this for Christmas two years ago.' Then he locked eyes with Fenchurch and started towards him.

Fenchurch walked over, meeting him halfway. 'I—'

'Just get away from me.' Steve pushed past them and walked through the back door.

Fenchurch watched the door swing shut. *I asked for that . . .* He followed him out. 'Hang on.'

Steve was waiting outside, fists clenched. 'I've lost my wife and you've been trying to pin her murder on me. You just wouldn't listen to me, would you? I kept telling you I didn't kill her!'

'Sir, with all due respect, if we listened to everyone who told us they hadn't killed someone, the prisons would be empty.'

'You think you're something, don't you?'

'No, I don't. I'm just a detective trying to do a job. I see vicious murders every day of my life. The worst in society committing the worst crimes. I'm sorry you've lost Gayle. I have some inkling of what you're going through. And I've got the deepest sympathies.'

'You're a prick.' Steve walked off down the back lane, past Fenchurch's car.

'Steve!' Cameras flashed and clicked. 'Steve! Over here!' A huddle of journalists crowded towards him. Steve spun round, panic in his eyes.

Fenchurch unlocked his car. 'Get in.'

Fenchurch pulled up outside John Fisher's flat. No sign of any journalists tonight.

Steve opened the door and put a foot on the tarmac. 'You've treated me like a criminal.'

'You are.' Fenchurch motioned to the house. 'All those drugs we found?'

'Piss off.'

'I'm serious.' Fenchurch grabbed his jacket and stopped him getting out. 'I'm not going to judge anyone for their personal life, but you really need to watch yourself. When you start mixing with people like Coldcut—'

'You don't know my background. You don't know where I've come from.'

'I'm an East End boy myself. I know how tough growing up round here is. You've done well for yourself. Be stupid to throw it all away.'

Steve huffed out a sigh. 'Why did you push so hard?'

'Because I thought you killed her.'

'How could you?' Steve tugged at his jacket, wrenching it from Fenchurch's grip. 'How could you? How could you? How?'

'All that stuff in the papers. You being there. It looked simple.'

'That's what's wrong with the police. You just make assumptions, then you barrel in. Convict the wrong bloody people.'

'Steve, I got you off. I dug and I dug and I dug and we eventually found the truth. Feels like you could've been honest with us earlier.'

Steve slammed the door and walked off to his brother's flat, turning to give Fenchurch an angry look. 'Should never have told you about the drugs.'

⌣

Fenchurch trudged up the stairs, the weight of the case and his life pulling down on his shoulders.

Shouting came from inside the flat.

'You need to tell him!' Chloe's voice.

'It doesn't matter!' Abi.

What the hell?

Fenchurch wrestled with his keys and opened the door.

'Mum . . . Jesus Christ!' Coming from the kitchen.

'You're so pigheaded!'

'Wonder where I get it from?'

Fenchurch raced through to the kitchen. They were close together, teeth bared. 'What's going on? Is Al okay?'

'He's—' Chloe broke off and ran past him. The flat door slammed.

'What the hell?' Fenchurch stopped Abi following. 'Is Al okay?'

'He's still in surgery!' Abi broke free and charged off through the flat.

Fenchurch followed her, the slammed door and their footsteps cannoned round the stairwell. 'What's upset her?'

'You tell me.' Abi raced out of the front door on to the street. A car drove off. 'We've lost her again, Simon.'

Chapter Forty-Two

I t's all ruined.' Abi was clinging on for dear life as Fenchurch hurtled round a corner, his brakes squealing as he took the corner too fast. 'We just got her back and we've lost her again!'

'Will you listen to me?' Fenchurch sped through the corner, narrowly avoiding rear-ending the car. 'We haven't lost her, okay?' He followed the car down Shoreditch High Street. 'She's a grown woman. This is just our first big ding-dong with her outside of Paddy's session. You want to tell me what it's about?'

'Simon, this isn't just a little argument.'

'What is it, then?'

She didn't reply, her eyes scanning the street.

'You remember when she was little? We had so many arguments with her. One time we were at that owl sanctuary, up in Norfolk. We hadn't bought her a plastic football at the petrol station but she just kept banging on about it. Turned into this massive tantrum. She's not like that any more.'

'Because they stole a big chunk of her brain, Simon.'

Fenchurch overtook a bus and had to swerve back in to avoid a taxi. The car pulled into a side street just ahead. 'What were you arguing about?'

'We were . . . Chloe was asking how to break up with Pete.'

Fenchurch looked over, scowling at her. 'Thought she was in love with him?'

'She's still young, doesn't know her own mind half the time.'

'What did you say that got her so angry?'

'I didn't handle it well. I tried to persuade her not to go through with it.'

'And that's what got her so upset?' Fenchurch hurtled down the street. 'Come on, love. I deal with liars all day. What really happened?'

'I swear. It was that. She just . . . exploded. Couldn't handle it. It's the . . . I don't know.'

Fenchurch pulled up at a T-junction. No brake lights in either direction. 'Where the hell is she?' He looked around. Knew the street, the area. It was familiar. He stuck the car in gear and turned left. 'I know where she's gone.'

———

Fenchurch jogged through the park he used to take her to when she was little. Past the basketball court, where some kids were playing, shouting and laughing. Slowing as he neared the benches from behind.

He'd met a witness there a while back and some craven bastard had stabbed his contact, right in front of his eyes.

Chloe was sitting on a bench, her head low.

Fenchurch slowed to a walking pace. 'There you are.'

She looked up at him, eyes burning.

Fenchurch waved Abi off and cut in before Chloe could even start. Nipping the complaint before it started had always worked when she was little. 'I used to bring you here as a kid.' He sat next to her. 'Remember?'

A smile crawled over Chloe's lips. 'You'd always take my last sweetie.'

'Should've taken a lot more than the last one. You'd get into a right grump. Blood-sugar level on the floor.'

'One of the few memories they left me with.'

Fenchurch reached into his pocket for the packet of wine gums. 'Used to meet old grumpy bollocks here.'

'Grandpa?'

'And your grandmother.'

'I . . . I don't remember her.'

'She was nice.' Fenchurch tore at the bag and let her help herself. 'So you're going to dump Pete?'

'Pete?' She held the sweets in her hand, inspecting them like they were poisoned. 'Is that what Mum told you?'

'It's not a lie, Chloe.' Abi was standing in front of them now.

'It's about ten per cent of the truth.' Chloe threw her sweets on the ground. 'Dad, I do want to dump Pete. So I asked Mum for her advice on how to dump a guy who's still grieving.'

'Grieving?'

'He never married, but his partner died of a heart defect. It's one of the things that made him give up that job. And made him stop drinking.'

'So why ask your mother?'

'Because she's been in a similar situation.'

Fenchurch frowned at his wife. Abi looked like she was going to run off. 'What's she talking about?'

Abi shrugged.

'Jesus Christ.' Chloe glared at her. 'Still can't tell him, can you?'

'Chloe, come on.' Abi grabbed her arm. 'You need to back off.'

'Mum!' Chloe shook her off. 'You've been lying to him!'

Abi let go of her daughter and started walking away, head bowed.

Fenchurch sat back on the bench. 'Chloe, what the hell's going on?'

'She never told you, did she?' Chloe picked the bag of sweets off the ground. 'When you were separated, she was seeing this bloke.'

Fenchurch's gaze shot over to Abi. Almost at the car. 'Who?'

'No idea.' Chloe stuffed a sweet in her mouth. 'I'm disgusted, Dad. Seeing some random when she was estranged from you. And you were . . . you were looking for me.'

'Chloe . . .' Fenchurch got up and hugged her. 'It was a hard time for both of us, we . . .'

'You're not angry? You *knew*?'

'I didn't, no.' Fenchurch's gut tied in knots as it hit him. 'But . . .' He let out a slow breath. 'Stay here.'

'Look, I'll stay with you when you split up.'

'Stay here. Okay?'

Fenchurch stopped Abi by the car. 'Love, wait.'

She turned to face him. 'She told you, didn't she?'

Fenchurch felt that gnawing in his gut. Ants crawling across his scalp. 'I'm not judging you. It's understandable.'

Abi nodded, a halting breath bursting out. 'You look like you're going to bludgeon me to death.'

'Part of me feels like it.' Fenchurch closed his eyes as he exhaled. 'The part I don't like, the part I keep hidden. I'm angry, yes, but we were going through hell. Whatever it is, I can understand. Just . . .'

'Brendan Holding.'

'Bloody hell. Really?'

She nudged past, trying to walk off.

'*Wait.*'

'What?' Abi's eyes were filled with tears. 'You want a divorce?'

'Just tell me what happened.'

'Simon, it . . . We were doing that community drugs outreach thing together. Working on it out of hours and . . . one thing led to another.'

Fenchurch nodded slowly, his guts feeling like they were going to spill on to the street. 'Must've been nice.'

'I needed distraction from all that shit. Chloe . . .' She blinked back more tears. 'All the guilt and shame and anger and . . .'

'I know.' Fenchurch held her. 'Abi, I know what it felt like. I'll be honest with you, I never . . . In all that time. Not once.'

'Kay worked for you, Simon.' Abi laughed through the tears. 'I'd know.'

'She's only worked for me for a couple of years. I was in Florida and Glasgow, remember? I wasn't even tempted. I still loved you and . . . I was too focused on finding her to see how much I loved you. The only thing I was married to then was my job and finding Chloe. I barely slept, love. Just worked at catching serial killers. Saint Simon, patron saint of pathetic losers.'

'I thought you'd be angry that I kept this secret. Chloe was asking about Pete and how to dump him without, you know, him killing himself. And it came out. She . . . didn't react well.'

'Reminds me a lot of her at my age.' Fenchurch frowned. 'I mean, me at her age. Bull in a china shop.'

'They can't take that away from her.' Abi kissed him on the lips. 'Simon, if it hadn't been for Brendan, I doubt we'd have got back together. What happened, it reminded me of what I liked about being with you. Made me start thinking about you.'

'Believe me, I understand.' Fenchurch took her hands and squeezed tight. 'I'm fine with it.'

'I'll remind you of that when they're dragging his body out of the Thames.'

'The Thames?' Fenchurch set off back towards the park. 'That's far too obvious. I'd take him up to the Scottish Highlands and—'

'You've thought about this too much.'

'Way too much.' Fenchurch laughed. 'It was the MO of a serial killer in Glasgow. He had this van and he—'

'Okay, I get it.'

'I can't believe this!' Chloe sat on the bench, chewing her way through more wine gums. She jabbed a finger at her mother as she approached. 'She was banging this guy and—'

'That's your mother you're talking about.'

'Okay, she was letting this guy smash her back doors in.' Chloe rolled her eyes. 'Dad, the words aren't important. You should be angry as—'

'I'm fine, Chloe.' Fenchurch pulsed Abi's hand. The gnawing in his gut was still there. 'Really.'

'I don't believe you.' Chloe put more wine gums in her mouth. 'Dad, she had an *affair*.'

Abi's phone rang. She frowned at it, then walked off.

'Chloe, what happened. It's . . .' Fenchurch could only shake his head. 'The pressure, the pain, the *everything*. It was too much. Just because I didn't move on, doesn't mean she had to stay pining for me.'

'I can't believe *you* are being, like, *mature* about it?'

Fenchurch smiled at her. 'I committed to your mother all those years ago. We renewed our vows again last year. If she slept with someone when we were apart, then I forgive her.'

'Jesus.' She handed him the wine gums. 'Just a couple left. Can't believe you let me eat a whole bag of these when I was little.'

'The bags were smaller back then.' Fenchurch squeezed her hand. 'And I might've had a head start.'

'I'm sorry if I freaked you out, Dad.'

'It's okay.' Another squeeze. 'Perfectly natural reaction. Just don't run off again, okay?'

She squeezed his hand back. 'Promise.'

Abi ran over to them. 'Baby Al's okay.'

Fenchurch let out a sigh of relief. 'How's he doing?'

'Oates said he's in recovery, but he's concerned about some minor complications. He wouldn't say over the phone.' Abi brushed fresh tears out of her eyes. 'It's a success, but . . . they're going to monitor the little sod overnight. We can see him tomorrow.' She smiled at Chloe. 'Love, I'm sorry for—'

'Mum, just chill, okay? And stop banging teachers.'

Rage flared in Abi's eyes. 'Chloe, I—' Then she took a breath. 'I shouldn't have told you.'

'No, you were right to. But you should've told Dad ages ago.'

'Chloe, it's fine.' Fenchurch raised his hands. 'Your mother and I are fine. Okay?'

She nodded then rested her elbows on her knees and leaned forward. 'What the hell am I going to do about Pete?'

'Do you love him?'

'Don't know if I even like him, Dad.'

'Meet him for a coffee and tell him it's over.' Fenchurch held her hand. 'He's old enough to get over it.'

'I guess.'

'It's your decision, love.' Abi's eyebrows were standing up. 'You want to have a fashion show for all that swag we bought?'

'Swag, Mum? Jesus.'

Fenchurch's phone rang. Liam Sharpe. He walked away and answered it.

'I . . . I need to speak to you.'

'I'm listening.'

'In person, Si.'

Always some stupid game with him.

Chapter Forty-Three

The bar was rammed, Monday being the new Friday and all that. Giant barn of a place, God knows what it had been before it turned into a pub. Bare stone walls and a really high ceiling — looked like a floor had been taken out, doubling the height. The bar was a stack of wooden crates in front of a row of side-on beer kegs. A din, too, the thumping music lost among chatting and laughter. A waiter walked past with a sizzling plate of satay sticks, the sweet peanut smell lingering, and walked up a set of stairs that led up to a dining area.

Liam Sharpe was up top, sipping at a beer, tapping at his phone. Dressed in a plain white T-shirt with a baseball cap on.

Fenchurch barged past beards, dungarees, bleached denim jackets and clogs, and made his way up. No banister and the steps rocked as he climbed — how it'd got past Health & Safety was anyone's guess. If they even knew about it.

Fenchurch walked over to Liam's table. 'This better be good.'

'Thanks for coming. Have a seat.' Liam was looking around like someone was watching him, ducking his cap over his eyes. 'Quickly!'

Yet more cloak-and-dagger bullshit.

Fenchurch remained standing. 'What's so important it couldn't have been discussed over the phone?'

Liam groaned. 'Always the same with you.' He finished his drink. 'You can order using the app. How good is that?'

'I'm driving.'

'I wasn't offering.' Liam tapped his mobile screen a few times then set it down on the table. 'Sit.'

Fenchurch took the seat opposite. 'What's so important?'

'I had a— Oh.' Liam took his pint off the waiter with a nod. 'Thanks.' He gulped at his beer. 'Oh, that's nice.'

'You want to slow down a bit there.'

'I need as much craft beer as I can get. I'm meeting my girlfriend in half an hour, then we're going to a happy hardcore night in an old warehouse in Dalston. It'll be cans of Red Stripe and WKD.'

'You're taking her to a bloody rave? On a Monday? You'd better make sure she's up for school in the morning.'

'Piss off . . .'

'I'm serious. You're playing with fire. She's far too young. If that comes out . . .'

'Are you threatening me?'

'I'm looking out for you, Liam. She's still at school. She's a *child*. Let her get on with her life and work out who she wants to be.'

'She's got a pretty good idea.' Liam took another gulp, grimacing as he brushed a hand over his lips. 'Right, so Steve Fisher turned up at my flat.'

Shit.

'About an hour ago. Just as I was making myself beautiful. Guy was out of his skull.'

'Drunk?'

'And then some. I know ketamine when I see it.'

'How did he get your address? Even your name?'

Liam took a dainty sip this time. 'My name's all over tomorrow's edition. The story went online at six.' Another gulp, then he picked up his phone and tapped the screen. 'My name's in the phone book. Anyway, Steve was in floods of tears. Wanted me to send him the video of Gayle and Elliot. I thought he'd have seen it, but no.'

'Did you?'

'Who do you think I am?'

'A journalist who's sleeping with a schoolgirl?'

'Har har har.' Liam picked up his glass again and toasted the air. 'You're not interested, are you?'

'I'm trying to help.'

'All this shit about me shagging Katerina.' Liam slammed the glass down. Almost cracked the stem. 'You any idea what she goes through at that school? She's done really well to even get to sixth form. If she gets a decent grade, she can get to a university, escape Shadwell and start to live her life.'

'And you can move in with her, right?'

'You're not listening to me, are you?' Liam took another glass from the waiter, marked with 'The Pterodactyl Head Brewing Co'. 'Cheers.' He sunk the last of his old one and took a sip of the new one. Grimaced but still sunk a second bigger gulp. 'The only person at that school who cared about her was Gayle Fisher. She tried to help with the bullying. Tried to catch them doing it. Tried to make her mother at least *care*. Kat's mother told her that if she just put on some make-up, wore shorter skirts, tighter tops, she'd be more popular. I mean . . .'

'I went to school not far from there. It's tough.'

Liam took a drink. 'And another thing.' Starting to slur his words now. *God knows how many he had before I arrived.* 'Steve said you let him go?'

'Liam, are you just trying to get me to spill some confidential information here?'

'Piss off, of course I'm not. We're off the record here.' Liam burped into his fist. 'Sure I can't get you a beer?'

'Had a skinful last night.'

'Well. Anyway. You let Steve go?'

Fenchurch stared into Liam's glass, focusing on the outline of a human head with a huge fin sticking out the back, just like a pterodactyl. *I'll drip-feed him some shit that'll come out soon anyway, see if he opens up.* 'Dropped him at his brother's myself. He was bailed on the drug offences this morning.'

'And the murder charges?'

'His alibi checked out. It wasn't him.'

'Losing your wife, then you questioning him about every little argument, going through his texts and emails and bank statements.' Liam flashed a grin. 'Makes you wonder who the bad guys are, eh?'

Fenchurch grabbed Liam's glass and held it away from him. 'Did you give him the video?'

'Of course I didn't.' Liam grabbed at the beer like a smackhead reaching for a needle. 'He wasn't making much sense, just wanted to see his wife again. Started threatening me, but I stood my ground. Told him to piss off.' He burped. 'Which he very graciously did.' He sat back and laughed. 'I'm not giving up my source.'

'Doesn't matter. Did Steve say where he was going?'

'Not to me.'

'Thanks, Liam.' Fenchurch got up and passed the beer back. 'I'll see you around.' He traipsed down the stairs and waded through the scrum again, then over to the makeshift bar. A couple of nails hadn't been hammered in properly. Liam's waiter was pouring another beer from a tap at the back. He swung round and nodded at Fenchurch. 'What can I get you?'

'Get my mate another couple.' Fenchurch put a tenner on the bar. 'Oh, and when his girlfriend turns up, she's underage.'

⌣

Fenchurch got out of the car and looked around. No sign of Reed. There was a light on in John Fisher's flat, though. He set off towards it.

'Guv.' Reed was lurking in the shadows down the road. 'Thought Loftus told you to keep clear of Steve?'

Fenchurch just cleared his throat. 'Who told you, anyway?'

'A little birdie.'

'That little birdie hears a lot, Kay.' Fenchurch continued on towards the flat. The air stank of burning wood, like someone had a bonfire going. 'Wondering if that little birdie heard anything about Brendan Holding?'

Reed stopped at the edge of the car park. 'Shit.'

Fenchurch rounded on her. 'You knew, didn't you?'

'Course I bloody knew.' She let out a sigh, hands on hips. 'On a scale of one to kneecapping, how angry are you?'

'I'm . . .' Fenchurch ran a hand down his face. 'It's . . . it's a bit of a shock, you know? All that time, I was like a monk and she . . .'

'Guv, that was one slip.'

'Lasted a while, though, right?'

'She thought it might lead to something. Holding was too focused on his career.' Reed ran a hand through her air. Couldn't make eye contact with him. 'I saw how much you were hurting underneath. I helped Abi see that you weren't being a selfish prick. Helped her remember what she had with you. Someone she loved enough to have a child with.' She looked straight at him. 'And another one now.'

Fenchurch had to look away. 'The op was a success, by the way.'

'Christ, that's a relief.' Reed stroked his arm.

Fenchurch looked at her. The one person who'd been there for him, who still was. The closest thing he had to a friend.

'She thought you'd fly off the handle when you found out.'

'Well, I've changed.'

'You're honestly accepting that she was seeing someone else?'

'I'm not happy, but yeah, I'll accept it. We weren't married. I was a hermit in my little cave, drinking myself stupid every night with Jon bloody Nelson. I'd been a complete arsehole and—'

'You hadn't been—'

'I had. A complete arsehole. Selfish. Thoughtless. Obsessed.'

'Okay, but for obvious reasons.'

'Doesn't matter. I let her down.'

'So long as you're not wondering where you can take him in the Highlands that he'll never be found?'

'There's this little bit just past Kinbrace . . .' Fenchurch grinned at her.

'You're still a complete arsehole, guv.'

'Tell me about it.' Fenchurch walked over to the flat and knocked on the door. 'Anyway, I'm struggling with what the hell Steve's up to.' He knocked again. 'Police!' Then again. 'I dropped him here about an hour and a half ago and I watched him go inside.'

'Next thing you know, he's at Liam's?'

'Right. Off his face on booze and God knows what. I'm thinking he got in, his brother's out, so Steve sits down with a beer, checks the news. Sees another story about his wife and sees Liam's name on it. Tucks into some ketamine he's hidden away elsewhere in the flat. Then he sits there, thinking. And gets a cab up to Liam's flat.'

'How did he get the address?'

'Another hole in Liam's story.'

'You think he's lying?'

'Wouldn't be the first time.' Fenchurch shrugged. 'I just don't know why.'

The door opened and John stood there in a dressing gown, soaking wet. 'What?'

'Steve in?'

'Got back about twenty minutes ago.' John tied his belt tight. 'You can't—'

Fenchurch barged past him.

John clawed at his shoulder as he marched through the kitchen. 'Here, have you got a warrant?'

'You got a reason to not let us in?' Fenchurch brushed him off and knocked on the bedroom door. 'Steve?'

No answer.

'Steve, it's DI Fenchurch. Need to ask you a couple of questions.'

A loud moaning sound came from inside the room.

Fenchurch tried the door. Locked. 'Sorry about this.' He gave it the shoulder and knocked the door clean off its hinges.

Steve sat on the bed, naked, facing his brother's gaming computer, masturbating, tears streaming down his cheeks. The PC's screen played a video, Gayle straddling Elliot, moaning and panting. 'Oh my God!'

Steve glanced round at them, tears in his eyes, waggling around. Then his focus went back to the screen. He kept beating away.

A bag of white pills lay on the edge of the bed nearest Fenchurch, the Bitcoin logo stamped on them. 'Shit!'

Chapter Forty-Four

Fenchurch powered through Aldgate, craning his neck to look in the back. 'How's he doing?'

'I don't know!' John sat next to Steve, wearing a navy tracksuit, his dressing gown wrapped around his brother. 'Stop that!'

Steve's hand went for his penis and John slapped it away.

'I love her!' Steve's words were a blur, all mushed up like baby food. 'If you can still wank over your wife, it must be love. Yeah? Yeah! YEAH!'

Fenchurch pulled off the main road and raced down the street towards the hospital. He pulled up outside A&E and got out, tearing at the back door to help John get out Steve out.

His hands kept going to his genitals.

Fenchurch cuffed him.

'I still love her!' Steve lurched forward, toppling on to the concrete. 'And I'll see her soon!'

A team of nurses rushed out and hoisted him on to a gurney.

Dr Mulkalwar followed them out, her long hair shaken out of their clips. 'You're sure it's another Blockchain case?'

'He'd taken these.' Fenchurch held up the evidence bag. 'I think he was trying to kill himself. Kept going on about seeing her soon. He's probably taken a handful. His eyes are all over the place.'

'Okay.' Mulkalwar stared at the drugs. 'Can you get DI Nelson to fast-track it for me?' She set off. 'I'll work on the assumption that it is.' She jogged off behind the nurses and the gurney.

John looked lost as he followed them in.

Fenchurch sat back against his car, his gut roaring.

Killing yourself like that. Jesus . . .

And he's been telling the truth all along — he didn't kill his wife. He loved her. Still does. Till death do us part.

Why didn't I believe him? It's the same with me and Abi. All the time we were apart and I just wanted to be with her and . . . All the shit we'd been through, everything I did to her, the way I acted, everything I didn't say. I couldn't cope without her.

What Steve must be going through . . .

'Guv, are you okay?' Reed walked towards him, out of breath.

Fenchurch shrugged.

'Think we saved his life?'

'We'll see. Doesn't look like he wants us to, though.'

'This is . . .' Reed shook her head. 'I mean . . . Doing *that* after his wife died.'

'The guy's innocent. Instead of convicting him, we broke him.' Something clawed away at Fenchurch's gut. 'He was trying to kill himself, Kay. Told us his drugs had been taken, but still had them, just hid them. Then took them to top himself. Thought he'd get to see Gayle in the afterlife.'

'There was a case in Scotland a few years back, guv. Almost convicted a guy of killing his ex-wife. Just like this. Turned out someone was framing him, though.'

Fenchurch's head hung low. 'Nobody framed Steve, other than me. His story fell apart. I was convinced he was guilty, that he had killed her. He was just grieving.'

'Come on, guv.' Reed grabbed the drugs off him and put the poison away in her jacket pocket. 'Did Steve say how he got that video?'

'No.' Fenchurch walked off towards his car, parked at a diagonal, the doors hanging open, hazards blazing. 'Liam's the only person we know who had it. He didn't record it, though. We know his source didn't.'

'That Katerina girl?'

'Right. She must've got it for him, but Liam told me she didn't give him the video.'

'Steve must've found him and got it off him. Lisa's on her way over here now. She'll find out how he got it.'

'In the meantime, I want to haul that lying little bastard over the coals.'

———

The bar was even busier, if that was possible. No sign of Liam upstairs or down. Fenchurch charged through the crowd around the bar. 'Bloody hipsters.'

'They're all right, you know.' Reed wrestled through the crowd, following Fenchurch. 'It's supposed to be about being into something. Brewing. Chiptune music. Beekeeping. Collecting fifties paperbacks. Whatever. It shouldn't be about twirly moustaches and Mumford & Sons. It's about being unique.'

'By all looking the bloody same.' Fenchurch pushed into a clearing around the bar.

Liam's barman was carrying two beer glasses, looked like he was about to back into the crowd.

Fenchurch stopped him. 'I was in here with this bloke earlier.' He showed him an old photo of Liam. 'He's got a skinhead now, lost the beard.'

'You sure about that, dude?'

'Wearing a baseball cap. I gave you a tenner to get him a couple of drinks.'

'Oh, I remember now. The underage girlfriend?'

'He still about?'

'No. He snatched that tenner out of my grubby mitts and sailed off into the night.'

'Didn't get a phone call? Anything like that?'

'Come on, dude, it's 2017, nobody *phones* anyone. The guy was messing about on his mobile. Maybe his schoolgirlfriend sent him a WhatsApp?'

'Anybody turn up looking for him?'

'Nope.' He stopped, frowning at Fenchurch. 'Wait. A woman came in. Not a schoolgirl. Late twenties. Tall. Nice enough.'

'Okay. Thanks.' Fenchurch turned to Reed. 'I'm hoping that little shit's gone back to his flat, otherwise we're trawling Dalston looking for a rave.'

Reed started pushing through the crowd. 'Now, *that* takes me back.'

'Still no joy.' Fenchurch put his phone away and knocked on Liam's flat door again. 'Where the bloody hell is he?'

'I can hear something.' Reed pressed her ear against the door and frowned. 'Jesus. Force & Styles. "Heart of Gold". Takes me even further back, guv. Had so many cracking nights in fields near Maidstone or Milton Keynes.'

Fenchurch thumped the door again. 'Pilled off your face, eh?'

'Not *all* the time.'

'With your lapdancing and drug use, it's a miracle you ever got in the force.' Fenchurch thumped the door again. 'He's inside. Why the hell isn't he answering the phone?'

'Think he's avoiding you?'

'Makes me think he gave the video to Steve.' Fenchurch reached out to give one last knock.

The door opened and Liam's housemate Cally stood there, dressed up like she was going out on the town, stinking of perfume. The cat swarmed around her ankles. 'Yeah?'

'Looking for Liam.'

She picked up the cat and got fluff all over her silk blouse. 'He's not here.'

'You haven't heard from him tonight?'

'No.'

Fenchurch checked his phone. Still nothing. 'Shit.' He stepped away from the door, trying hard to control himself. Just furrowed his brow, trying to look serious and in control. 'I need to speak to him. He told me he was meeting his girlfriend then going to some rave.'

'That's right.'

'She here?'

Cally scowled at him. 'What are you talking about?'

'Just wondering if he met Katerina here.'

'That's what he told you? Those exact words?'

Fenchurch's turn to scowl. 'What's going on?'

'He told you he was going with "his girlfriend" called "Katerina"?'

'Not in so many words. Why?'

'Who the hell is Katerina?'

'She was a source. A schoolgirl.'

'*Her?*'

'She's in sixth form. Seventeen.' *Christ, I'm almost defending Liam.*

'He's . . .' Cally huffed out a sigh. The cat scrabbled away from her, then ran off inside the flat, her tail fluffed up. 'Right.' She huffed out a sigh. 'You know how Liam said he was going clubbing with his girlfriend? He was.' She prodded her chest. 'Me.'

'What?'

'I'm his girlfriend. At least, I thought I was.' Cally shut her eyes. 'Few months ago, we went to Marakesh on holiday as mates. We came back, well . . . more than that.'

'I'd say congrats are in order, but I really need to speak to him.'

'Not before I do. I'll kill him. Shagging a schoolgirl behind my back?'

'I'll pretend I didn't hear that. Any idea where this rave is?'

'Just told me Dalston. Supposed to be a surprise.' Cally grimaced. 'Liam got the tickets. Been on all weekend getting the Sunday sorted, then this shit exploded. There's always something, though, so we made Mondays our Friday. There's always something on in London, if you know where to look. Last week, I took Liam to a reggae night in Brixton. He loved it.'

'Okay. Wind back. When did you last hear from him?'

'This afternoon. We arranged to meet in that bar he likes down the road. Supposed to just grab a beer, go for dinner, then off to this rave. So I'm sitting there, all dolled up, waiting for him. And he didn't turn up.'

'How long did you wait?'

'Forty minutes. Didn't answer his bloody phone.'

'Is there anything else that Liam's working on that could get him into trouble?'

'You know what he's like.' She groaned. 'There's always something. I don't know half of what he's got on, but he's never mentioned anything particularly troublesome.'

'No gangs, anything like that?'

'Not after what happened to Saskia.'

Fenchurch nodded in sympathy. 'You knew her?'

'She was a friend, yeah. What happened to her was . . . It hit both of us hard. Kind of brought us together.'

'Have you got that location-sharing thing on your phones?'

'Just a sec.' She went back inside.

'I'm getting a really bad feeling about this, Kay.'

'You think he's involved?'

'Who knows.'

Cally appeared again and held up her phone. 'Says it's switched off.'

Fenchurch parked outside Katerina Raptis's house, a seventies brick-and-wood home not far from the Olympic Park. Tiny, with an even smaller garden. The sort of shoebox they sell to people looking to get on the housing ladder, who then get stuck in debt and misery. He got out on to the street. His phone buzzed in his pocket. A missed call from Uzma. He put the phone away and walked over to the door.

Reed tried the buzzer. 'I'm getting a—'

The door opened in a flurry of hair and fabric. Jocasta Raptis stood there. 'Well, hello, Inspector.' Her eyelashes were fluttering. 'How can—'

Reed took charge. 'Ms Raptis, we're—'

'I told you, call me Jocasta!'

'Is your daughter in?'

'She's not, no.' Jocasta stepped outside, wrapping her shawl over her shoulders. 'Can I help?'

'This is important. When did you last see her?'

'She's not here.' Jocasta covered her face with her hands. 'Has something happened?'

'It's okay.' Fenchurch stepped back, hands up. 'We just need to speak to her. She might be able to help us identify a person of interest on the case.'

'She's not in.'

Getting nowhere with her.

Fenchurch clocked the carpeted stairs behind her. 'Kay, keep her here.' He set off up the stairs.

'You can't do this.'

'He can.'

Fenchurch hauled himself up the last few steps. Four doors, but only one marked 'Kitty Kat's Lair'. He knocked on the door. 'Katerina?'

'You can't just do this!' Jocasta was still downstairs but it sounded like she was right next to him. 'Get out!'

Fenchurch opened the door.

No sign of her. Just band posters. Justin Bieber over by the window, giving way to Rammstein and Marilyn Manson by the bed. *Sweet dreams, indeed.*

Fenchurch felt his shoulders deflate. *Where the hell is she?* He opened her mirrored wardrobes. Just clothes, no teenagers hiding out. On the desk a laptop was sleeping. Fenchurch prodded the keyboard. It unlocked, then flashed back to the login screen.

In that flash, though, Fenchurch caught a still image of Gayle Fisher straddling Elliot Lynch. The same footage Steve was watching.

So Katerina had the video after all. Did she give it to Liam? Or did she record it?

Fenchurch stuffed the laptop in an evidence bag and charged back downstairs.

'You need to get out!' Jocasta slapped at his arms until Reed restrained her. 'What the hell is that?'

Fenchurch showed the laptop. 'I'm taking this into evidence.'

'You can't do that!'

'I can.' Fenchurch grabbed Jocasta's shoulders and held her still. 'Now, I need to speak to your daughter. Where is she?'

'She's at work!'

Chapter Forty-Five

Fenchurch had his phone to his ear, listening to Liam's voicemail as he walked towards the Bennaceur. 'Still nothing, Kay.' His phone rang, right next to his ear. He checked it. Unknown caller. At least it wasn't about Baby Al. 'Hello?'

'Inspector, it's Dr Mulkalwar. Are you okay to talk?'

'Not really.' Fenchurch stared back at Reed. 'What's up?'

'I wanted to let you know that Mr Fisher definitely had at least one Blockchain pill. We're flushing his system just now.'

'Will he live?'

'Unfortunately, we don't know how many he took. It's at least one, possibly as many as three or four.' Mulkalwar paused. 'To be perfectly frank, it's touch and go. More of touch than go.'

Whatever that means.

'Okay, let me know if anything else comes up.' Fenchurch killed the call and put his phone away.

Steve tried to kill himself by taking Blockchain, watching the illicit video of Gayle and Elliot.

He turned up at Liam's flat, demanding to see it. Then Liam goes missing.

Katerina had the video, so she probably gave it to Liam.

So why go missing? And who recorded it?

'Guv?' Reed was holding the hotel door open. 'You okay?'

'I'm fine.' Fenchurch entered the building.

Sutekh Bennaceur was sleeping at the reception desk, snoring and snorting. He woke up and gasped. 'Hey, you!' Then got up, shaking his fists at them. 'Open that goddamn floor!'

'Sir, we're looking for Katerina Raptis.'

'Uh.'

'Take it you're her replacement?'

'I'm here because I don't trust my bloody brother.' Sutekh sat down again, snarling. 'Turning this place into a brothel. Goddamn crook. Him and that goddamn football team. Waste of time and money. Always focused on that. I swear I'll—'

'Is Katerina here?'

'Goddamn—' Sutekh's head nodded forward, snoring.

'Jesus.' Fenchurch went over and shook his shoulder. 'Sir?'

'Goddamn animals!' Sutekh raised both fists. 'Goddamn stinking animals rutting in my hotel! Rutting!'

'Sir, are you—'

'Get that floor open!' Sutekh was on his feet now, glaring at Fenchurch. 'We're losing money every hour!' He collapsed back into his seat. 'Every goddamn hour! The goddamn hotel's open again but nobody's staying! Everyone cancelled! This is like a goddamn ghost town!'

'I'm still thinking about it.' Fenchurch rapped the reception desk. 'Now, do you know where she is?'

'Who?'

'Kat—'

Sutekh was asleep again.

'Come on, Kay. She's obviously not here.'

Sutekh grabbed him. 'She's in the kitchen, getting me a goddamn coffee. Keep falling asleep.'

Katerina plunged the cafetière, humming a tune. 'Porcelain goddess . . .'
That bloody song again . . . The kitchen stank of bitter coffee, strong
enough to keep Sutekh awake for weeks. She turned and jumped.

Fenchurch went over to her. 'You okay?'

'Just didn't see you there.'

'Need a word with you.' Fenchurch pulled up a seat and motioned
for her to sit. She remained standing. 'You seen Liam?'

'I haven't seen him since . . .' Katerina poured out some coffee. 'I
don't know, yesterday? It's been a weird week.'

'Hasn't it just. Thing is, I need to speak to him. Liam has a copy of
the video of Elliot and Gayle Fisher having sex.'

Katerina tipped some milk into the mug. 'What?'

'He got it from you, didn't he?'

Katerina set the coffee down and shook her hand like she'd burnt
her fingers. 'No, he didn't.'

'Sure about that? You're his source, aren't you? I've got your laptop
in evidence.'

Her eyes widened.

'The video of Gayle Fisher on top of Elliot Lynch is on there.'

Katerina collapsed into the chair.

'Were you behind the camera? Did you just copy it?'

'What?'

'This is going to take forever if I need to keep repeating myself.'

'Liam got the video from someone else.'

'Who?'

She shook her head, but couldn't look at him.

'Come on. You know, don't you?' Fenchurch stepped forward. 'We
can do this here or in an interview room. Your choice.'

She didn't say anything.

'Katerina, someone gave that video to Steve Fisher. We found him
in his brother's flat trying to kill himself by taking some Blockchain.'

She stood up, waving her hands. 'I've nothing to do with this, I swear.'

'Did you give him it?'

'No!'

'Did Liam?'

'I don't know. We're not joined at the hip!' She sat down again and swallowed hard. 'Oliver.'

'Oliver Muscat-Smith?'

'He recorded it.' Katerina brushed her hair out of her eyes. 'Liam must've got it from him on Friday night. I saw them talking in the bar here.'

———————

Fenchurch opened the Obs Suite door and popped his head in. Empty. He let Reed go first.

On the screen, Uzma was interviewing Oliver Muscat-Smith, with some young DC sitting in, someone Fenchurch didn't recognise. '—are Elliot's accomplice, correct?'

'I'm nobody's accomplice.'

'You helped Elliot gain access to Gayle Fisher's room, where he murdered her.'

'Bloody hell, Kay. They should show this to prisoners, it's worse than waterboarding.' Fenchurch shifted Mulholland's stuff off the chair on to the table. 'Why is it that when I actually want to speak to that witch, there's no bloody sign of her?'

'I'll pretend I didn't hear that.' Mulholland walked through the door, blowing on a coffee. 'You were sent home.'

'Something came up.'

Reed picked up the laptop. 'I'll get this to Lisa.'

Mulholland waited for the door to click. 'Something came up? Simon, you were explicitly told to leave.'

'Steve Fisher—'

'I heard. Doesn't explain why you're here.'

'Because Liam's gone missing and I need to speak to him.' Fenchurch pointed at Oliver on the screen. 'Our chum there gave the video to him.'

Mulholland sat in the newly liberated chair. 'I hope you've got a reputable source.'

'Katerina Raptis. She saw Oliver here talking to Liam on Friday night. Probably when the handover happened.'

'Is she here?'

Fenchurch sighed. 'She's still at the hotel.'

'I see. Why?'

'She's working.'

'Simon, I know you're going through a very difficult period just now, but this is yet more proof that you're not fit for duty.' Mulholland took a slug of coffee. 'You should've brought her here to give a statement.'

Fenchurch almost bit his tongue. 'My priority is finding Liam. Oliver recorded the video and passed it on to Liam. He might know where he is.' He waved a hand at the screen. 'Give me five minutes with him.'

Mulholland stared at the screen, thinking hard. 'DS Ashkani is leading on this.'

'Looks like she's spinning her wheels. Five minutes, that's all I need.'

⌒

'Sorry for the late substitution.' Fenchurch sat opposite Oliver Muscat-Smith. 'You know Liam Sharpe, right?'

'Who?'

'Cut it out. You know exactly who I'm talking about. Liam Sharpe. Spill.'

Oliver crossed his legs. 'Haven't heard from him in a while.'

'When was the last time?'

Oliver folded his arms now. Any more and he'd collapse in on himself. 'Couldn't say.'

'I gather that Liam—'

'No.'

Fenchurch laughed. 'What do you mean, no?'

'I'm not talking about him.'

'Liam had a video of Elliot and Gayle having sex. You recorded it on your phone, didn't you?'

'Why would you think that?'

'Why deny it, Oliver? Elliot didn't record it.'

'So? Big deal.'

'You filmed it?'

'Elliot asked me to.'

'What?'

Oliver sat forward, clasping his hands on the table. Goalkeeper's hands, huge and strong. 'I knew Elliot from football, we'd played together since we were yea high.' He held his hand pretty low. 'He used to be taller than me, even though he's younger.' He kept his hand there, as if he was amazed that they'd both grown so much. 'Elliot had been flirting with her at school, teasing her a bit. Then one Friday she was in the bar, so I called him up. He came down, started chatting to her. She must've known he was underage, but didn't care. Pretty soon they were out of their skulls, absolutely hammered. Then she told us she had some E.' He scratched at his neck. 'Anyway, we went back to mine. Dad was working. Took the E, put some music on. And he banged her.' His eyes misted over. 'I filmed them at it. You can see *everything*. She's got a great body. So fit. I mean, you could tell that underneath her clothes there was a monster waiting to get out, but seeing her in all her glory . . . Man.'

'Why did you think it was okay to film it?'

'Last summer we were on a club tour of Holland and Belgium. Pair of us would shag anything we could get our hands on. We had a gentleman's agreement. Whoever got lucky would leave the door open for the other one to sneak in and get a video of him banging the bird. He's got more videos of me than I do of him. Kind of like porn, but just for us, you know?'

'That's illegal, you idiot.'

Oliver raised a shoulder. 'Like I care.'

Fenchurch stared at the recorder. *One of those rare occasions when an idiot would spill the beans.* He leaned on the desk, grinning. 'We've got all of your electronic equipment. Phone, computer, tablet, you name it. We'll get the evidence and we'll prosecute you as well.'

'Look, I didn't—'

'You gave the file to Liam Sharpe on Friday, didn't you?'

'What? Of course not. That guy's a hipster prick.'

'What about Katerina Raptis? Did you give her a copy?'

'Maybe.'

'*Oliver.*'

'Yeah, yeah, keep your wig on. I showed her the video and she . . . I don't know. She wouldn't stop talking about it. She was obsessed by it, kept wanting to see it.'

'You give her a copy?'

'Maybe.'

'Can I take that as a yes?'

'Fine.'

'Okay, so who was she obsessed with? Elliot or Gayle?'

'Both. She thought it was beautiful.' Oliver ran a tongue over his lips. 'Doubt she's ever been banged by anyone. Not my type, I'm afraid.' He let out a sigh. 'Did she tell you about that bloke Steve was with?'

'Who?'

'I told you. I saw Steve with his mate when I was chatting up this bird.' Oliver held up his hands. 'I went to the bogs to get a rubber johnny and Steve followed me in. Said hello, then went to the dump station. He wasn't alone. This geezer came in, shut the door. And they weren't taking coke. Believe me, I'd know. Had a big long chat.'

'Who was it?'

'Seen him a few times here. Thinks he's a big shot. Think his name's Ben something?'

Ben bloody Maxfield. What the hell was he doing?

Chapter Forty-Six

'Who said crime doesn't pay?' Reed stopped in the street outside Maxfield's mansion in Hampstead. At least two wings, the whole place wrapped in stucco like it'd been iced for a wedding. Lit up in limes and oranges, the deep thump of house music coming from inside. A party had spilled over the lawn.

Reed stopped by the steel gates. 'Jesus, is that him from *EastEnders*?'

'Wouldn't know.' Fenchurch walked up to the security team, all yellow jackets and clipboards, and held out his warrant card. 'Need a word with Mr Maxfield.'

'Inspector!' Maxfield stepped over a small wall to the side, carrying a half-eaten hotdog bun and a martini. His face was flushed, his hair slicked back. 'You're not here to jump out of my birthday cake, are you?'

'Many happy returns.' Fenchurch caught a waft of cooking meat. 'Need a word.'

'Well, I'm very, very busy.'

'So I see.' Fenchurch looked around. Caught someone from an old TV sitcom. 'Trouble is, I'm not in a good mood and I'd hate to take it out on you.'

'Well, I'd love it. A scuffle with a minor celebrity like you would put me on the front page.'

'A little birdie tells me that you were in the Hotel Bennaceur on Friday night.'

Maxfield snarled at Fenchurch. 'And they say policemen are all thick.'

'You told us that you were on a client's yacht.'

'Ah, now.' Maxfield rested his glass on the wall. 'I checked with my PA and it transpires that I need to update my statement. I'll pop in tomorrow morning, if that's okay? Might be nearer lunchtime.'

'Let's do it now.'

'Inspector, I'd hate to leave my guests waiting.' Maxfield picked up the glass and slurped some martini. 'I can only apologise. I was so, so tired when we spoke. Didn't know what day it was. I've flown over five thousand miles in the last month. It's hard to keep a track of where you are at any moment.'

'Just tell me what you were doing at the hotel.'

'I visited Gayle at the hotel at about eight thirty, and she seemed fine. Shaken up, but fine. Asking about the future, about what I could do for her.'

'Did you meet anyone else there?'

'No.'

'Not, say, Steve Fisher?'

'Well, now you mention it, I had a very, very brief chat with him. It's no crime. I was interested in repping both sides of the couple. So, so many synergies. You can really clean up in the tabloid arena if you control both sides of the story. All sides, if I get a chance.'

'It wasn't an accidental meeting, was it?'

'No, a mutual friend arranged it.' Maxfield flicked away the last dregs of martini on to his lawn. 'Our mutual friend, in fact. Liam Sharpe.'

'Any idea where Liam is?'

'When I say mutual friend, I mean that I've texted and emailed him. Very useful chap to place a story with. But he's not invited, in case you're wondering. Not one of my closest thousand friends, who I really, really must be getting back to.'

Fenchurch blocked his path. 'Did Liam share any videos with you?'

'Ah, the explosive sex tape, eh?' Maxfield took a bite of hotdog. 'I told you before, you cloth-eared gimp, that I would've loved a copy of it. Could've raised Gayle's profile.'

'But you've seen it.'

Maxfield gave a flash of his eyebrows. 'An associate has it.'

Fenchurch grabbed Maxfield's wrist. 'Did you share it with Steve Fisher?'

'No, but I know who did.'

Fenchurch tightened his grip. 'Who?'

'Liam Sharpe.' Maxfield shook off Fenchurch. 'He called me up, said Steve Fisher was at his flat, desperate for the tape. I've got plans for Steve. I want him to get over his wife's death. So I advised yes.'

'Steve tried to kill himself because of that, you idiot.'

Fenchurch got in the car and stared back at Maxfield's house. 'So Liam's in league with him. Turns out you never know someone, right?'

'What does he get out of it?'

'What does anyone get out of anything? Maxfield owes him one. He's got Steve Fisher on his books thanks to Liam. That would've looked good on Friday. Now, it's a poisoned chalice. There'll be a few stories in the paper about us abusing his human rights or something. But that's about it.'

Fenchurch's phone rang. He checked the display, heart thumping. A mobile number. 'Yeah?'

'It's Cally. Have you found him?'

'We're getting closer, but still not got him.'

She paused. 'I've got Liam's laptop here. I could look through his emails?'

'Search for Ben Maxfield.'

Some typing sounds. 'Nothing.'

Maxfield was too smart for that.

'What about Katerina Raptis?'

'That's her surname? I've been looking for her but can't find anything.'

'Try it with a K.'

'Oh? Still nothing.'

'Just try Kat.'

She gasped. 'Tons of emails . . . Most of it's stuff about drugs, some about bullying . . . There's a couple with videos.'

'Can you open one?'

'It's a video of her cat. Same as the other three.' She paused. 'Why did Liam need to lie to me about her?'

'I wish I knew. Can you try Steve Fisher?'

More typing. 'Nothing.' Then more. 'Wait.'

'What is it?'

'A video.' Sex sounds filled the line. 'Got it. Liam sent him it.'

There we go . . . Liam, you stupid bastard. Sending that video to Steve.

'Cally, I know it's upsetting, but I need to find Liam. Can you check his location again?'

She paused. 'Fine.' Then it was like she'd disappeared.

'Hello?'

'I've got something. I think it's off now, but it says his last location, an hour ago, was in the City?'

———

'Here?' Fenchurch stood on Threadneedle Street, just outside the Bank of England. The old NatWest Tower was glowing in the sky above them. He scanned around again. No sign of Liam. No sign of anyone. 'Where is he?'

'You tried calling again?'

Fenchurch got out his mobile and called Liam's number. The calls were stacking up — that was the eighteenth. Same result, voicemail. 'Still off.' He killed it and put the phone away. 'What's going on?'

Reed was looking at her own phone. 'Last time you saw him, he waiting for Cally, but she missed him. Then he's in the City, a few miles south. Where's he going?'

Fenchurch stared at his phone again like it could find him.

'Should we get some units going round Dalston looking for this rave?'

'Needle in a haystack, Kay. Assuming he went on his own.' Fenchurch looked around as a bus swept past. 'Worth getting some of our City mates out?'

'Maybe.' Reed put her phone to her ear. 'Lisa, are you ignoring my texts?' She paused, listening, then waved a hand at Fenchurch. 'It's back on. Lisa, are you tracking it?' Another pause. 'WhatsApp last had it in the City. We're here and—' She started off towards the car. 'Why the hell is he there?'

⌣

Fenchurch pulled up outside the Bennaceur and got out.

'Simon.' Mulholland was pacing around outside, talking to someone on the phone. She waved at them and walked off.

Bridge joined them, carrying her laptop under her arm. 'Guessing this'll be more CCTV work?'

'I promise, Lisa.' Fenchurch followed her and Reed in. 'Next case, you'll get something more interesting.'

'Believe that when I see it.'

At the security desk, Jim Muscat was messing about on his phone.

Fenchurch stopped Reed. 'What the hell is he doing here?'

'Mulholland didn't charge him, guv. Of course, you'd know that if you'd bothered paying attention to your own case.'

'Right.' Fenchurch walked up to the desk. 'Evening, Jim.' He held up a photo of Liam. 'Looking for this man. Seen him?'

Muscat looked at it, then shrugged. Kept his mouth shut.

'You okay?'

'What, you think you can just pitch up here and everything's hunky dory again?' Muscat laughed, but his eyes were full of fury. 'You tried to charge me with revenge porn. Illicit taping! It wasn't even me!'

'You had footage of a couple having sex on a drive round your neck. What else is it?'

'I was covering my arse!' Muscat's nostrils flared. 'It's lucky that Dawn Mulholland got wind of it. Nice to have an old mate help me out.' He shook his head. 'Dropped me back in here in time for my bleeding shift. If the pair of clowns who own this place hear about what's happened, I'll lose my bloody job. I can't afford that.'

'Tell the truth, Jim. You can still hold your head high. Easy to get another job.'

'Getting this one was hard enough.'

Fenchurch held up his phone again. 'Look, has he been here?'

'Not that I've seen.' Muscat yawned. 'I'm off form. Night in the cells isn't conducive to a good sleep.'

Fenchurch smiled at him. 'Sod it. Lisa, can you do your magic?'

'Out of the way.' Bridge barged past Muscat and got at the CCTV console. She sat at the machine and whizzed it back. 'Here we go.'

Liam was outside the hotel, hood up, slipping in the front door.

'This is an hour ago.'

'So he's here?'

'He *was* here, at least.'

'Jim, he walked right past you.'

'I didn't see him. I was with Nazar for a minute. Bleeding nightmare through there. He can't get hold of my boy and his whisky's all smashed.'

'He's in custody.'

'What?'

'Shouldn't have been dealing drugs, Jim.'

'Shit.' Muscat shut his eyes. 'Shit.' He ran off through the front door.

'Perfect. Now, where do we start looking for Liam?'

'I'll look for him leaving, sir.' Bridge punched the CCTV unit. 'The system here is very patchy, as you know.'

'That's all—'

'Simon.' Mulholland was over by the front door. 'I need a word?' She motioned through the staff door.

Fenchurch ignored her. 'Kay, get a team in. We need to go through every room.'

'Assuming Liam's here.'

'Well, if we search everywhere, then we'll know he's not.'

'Guv.' Reed stomped off, Airwave to her ear.

'Come on, then.' Fenchurch followed Mulholland through the staff door.

Sutekh Bennaceur lay on the floor.

Fenchurch raced over to him and reached for a pulse. Still alive.

'Goddamn animals!' His eyes were waggling in his head. 'Goddamn . . .'

Shit — more Blockchain . . .

Chapter Forty-Seven

The foyer was filled with uniform. None of them seemed to know what they were doing. Reed waved her hands around, trying to organise the searches, but nobody was paying attention.

Fenchurch barged through.

The front doors opened. 'Guys, guys, let me through!' A paramedic piled in the front door. James Mackay, pushing a gurney. Cracked it off Cheeky's thigh. Mackay stopped to apologise. 'Sorry, but you were standing in the way.'

'James! Through here!' Fenchurch led them through to the staff room.

Sutekh was still out cold, not that it looked that different to him awake.

Mulholland was kneeling next to him.

Mackay crouched down and pulled his eyelids back. 'Looks like Blockchain.'

Sutekh grabbed his wrist. 'Get off, you goddamn poof! Rutting in my goddamn hotel!'

Fenchurch pulled Sutekh's arms down, pinning him. 'Thought that stuff was supposed to make you happy?'

'Some people need more than others.' Mackay got at his eyes finally. 'Ah, yeah. This is Blockchain. Can you find it?'

Fenchurch let go of Sutekh and looked around. A coffee mug was on its side, but hardly any had spilled on to the counter. Sutekh had drunk it.

Shit.

Katerina made the coffee. Did she drug him?

Fenchurch put the mug into an evidence bag and showed it to Mackay. 'What difference would it make if you drank it?'

'Ecstasy?' Mackay let go and took it. Sutekh flopped on to the floor, snoring. 'You'd come up quicker.'

'Come up?'

'You *know*, Si. Don't joke with me.' Mackay pulled his fingers up from his feet. 'You start with a tingle in your toes and it comes up your body.' He inspected the mug again. 'Your stomach has to dissolve a pill first. If it's all dissolved, it'll hit your bloodstream straight away. Problem with this stuff is it's— Hmm. Super-strong MDMA. The effects are going to hit quicker. Ah, shit.' He tossed the mug back and grabbed his bag. 'Here, Keith? Keith? We need to sedate him, now!'

'I'll get out of your way.' Fenchurch left them with Mulholland and went back to the foyer. 'Getting anywhere?'

'Ground floor done.' Reed let out a sigh. 'Top floor half done. Second is underway. Gayle's floor is still cordoned off.' She frowned. 'Is he okay?'

'Blockchain.' Fenchurch got out of the way of the gurney. Sutekh just lay there, eyes rolling back in his head.

Fenchurch felt that same gnawing at his gut. He stormed over to Bridge at the security desk. 'Lisa, have you got the CCTV from earlier?'

'Here you go.' Bridge hit the space bar and the screen filled with grainy footage. Liam sloped into reception, hood up. Sutekh was sleeping behind the desk. He jerked himself awake, then slipped away again. Liam disappeared over by the lifts, passing beyond the edge of the frame.

'So he's here?'

Bridge squinted at the footage. 'I assume he takes the stairs, but they're not visible on the network either.'

'Great.' Fenchurch sat on the desk with a thump and looked across the foyer, rapidly emptying of uniforms now he was there. That gnawing was back. 'Right, Lisa, you're with me.'

———

Fenchurch charged along the corridor and stopped. 'Shit.' The crime scene tape was torn, the plastic seal flapping in the breeze.

Where the hell is the breeze coming from?

Fenchurch snapped out his baton and looked behind him. Bridge was snapping hers out too. 'Slowly, okay?' He stepped through the tear into the corridor. The door to Gayle's room was hanging open. 'Shit.' He stopped dead.

Liam was strapped to the bed, naked except for his pants. He looked up, his head wobbling. A huge cut in his forehead. Spit dribbled from his mouth, hanging in a chain down to his chin. 'Si? I love you, man. Love you.' His eyes waggled.

'Get those medics back here!'

———

'Come on, guys, out of the way!' Mackay raced over to the bed and dropped his bag at the foot. 'Oh, in the name of the wee man.' He hopped up on the bed and started examining Liam.

'It's . . . Blockchain.' Fenchurch stood back. 'Check his eyes.'

'They look okay to me, Si.' Mackay shone a light into his sockets, then up at the wound on his head. 'I'm more worried about that gash in his head.'

Fenchurch joined him on the bed, following Mackay's inspection. His eyes were straight now.

Maybe he's just pissed? Sinking those glasses of beer at that pub . . .

Why the hell is he in here, all tied up? Some weird sex game?

Liam's eye waggled.

'There!'

'I saw it. More Blockchain.' Mackay went into his bag and pulled out a chunky syringe. He sucked the juice out of a bottle and stabbed the needle into Liam's left arm. 'This diazepam will hopefully bring him down before it hits.'

Liam jolted as Mackay injected the drug. He sucked in a deep breath, then breathed rapidly.

'That'll do for now.' Mackay stuffed his gear back in the bag. 'He's still slap-dab in the middle of the woods, though, not out of them.' He shook his head. 'We're lucky. It's just kicking in now. Unlike your man downstairs.'

'Dr Mulkalwar knows about this.'

'She's good. I'll get her on this.' Mackay beckoned his mate over. They got Liam between them and walked him away.

'Si?' Liam looked round at him from the doorway, eyes rolling. 'Si?'

'It's okay, Liam. You'll be okay.'

'Katerina.'

'What?'

'She attacked me.' Liam tried to rub his forehead but missed the wound. 'She attacked me . . .' Then Mackay led him out.

Fenchurch slumped on to the bed.

Katerina is the killer.

Chapter Forty-Eight

'This is bad.' Fenchurch skipped down the steps. 'Why did she kill Gayle? Why has she attacked Sutekh? And Liam? They're close, so it . . . just doesn't make any sense.'

Reed's look showed she had less of an idea than him.

Fenchurch got out his phone, dialling as he walked. 'Cally? It's DI Fenchurch.'

'Have you found him?' Her voice was trembling.

'He's okay, but we think someone's drugged him.'

'Oh my God!'

'He's in the best hands and we found him quick. He'll pull through.'

'Oh.' Her pause was filled with tears. 'Who did it?'

Fenchurch stared at Reed as they rounded the corner towards the foyer. 'We don't know.'

'Will you hold them down for me while I stand on their throat?'

'I won't get in your way, that's for sure.' Fenchurch grabbed the door handle but didn't open it. 'He's on his way to the Royal London.'

'Okay. Thanks.' And she was gone.

Fenchurch put his phone away then dug the heels of his palms into his eye sockets.

Reed opened the door.

'Where is she?' Jocasta Raptis was fighting against Uzma. 'Where—' Then she saw Fenchurch and raced over to him. 'They're saying my Katerina's—'

'Listen to me.' Fenchurch shared a glare between Jocasta and Uzma. 'Mrs Raptis, your daughter's a murder suspect.'

'Not my Katerina. No.'

'She's been handling sensitive information. She's abducted someone and she's—'

'No!'

'—assaulted another two people, risking their lives.'

'No!'

'We need to find her. Have you any idea where she is?'

'I don't know!' Jocasta looked around, then shut her eyes. 'This is too much.' Her eyes opened again, focused on Fenchurch. Then a light bulb went on. 'She's run off! You sniffing around, it's scared her. You've frightened her! My baby! My poor baby!'

'Could she be with her father?'

'He's dead! My husband and my son died in a car crash. His drinking killed them! Now I've lost *her*!'

'Is there anyone else she—'

'I pushed my husband away. He hated me for being so controlling. I only wanted to love him. That's why I'm so liberal with Katerina. I just want her to stay with me. I can't stand losing her!'

'We need to find her. Is there anyone else she could've gone to?'

'She doesn't have many friends. Just that teacher. That's the only one she talked about.'

'Sergeant.' Fenchurch took Uzma to the side. 'What the hell are you doing bringing her here?'

'Dawn asked me. We thought—'

'Take her to Leman Street and dig into her story. Okay? Find out if she's covering for her daughter. And get a bloody lead!'

'Sir.' Uzma led Jocasta away. 'Come on, let's get you a cup of tea.'

Reed glared at her back. 'What now, guv?'

'I thought she'd be here, Kay. Thought she'd have . . . I don't know, left a trace? Something. But she's left Liam and Sutekh to die, and she's run off.'

'We need to retrace her steps, guv.' Reed walked over to the desk. 'Lisa, have you got anything?'

'Something.' Bridge tapped at her laptop and swivelled the screen round. 'This is what little CCTV we've got of her.' The screen showed Katerina sneaking down a corridor. Bridge thumbed at the screen. 'This is near Gayle's hotel room.'

Fenchurch stared at the image, Katerina looking lost and alone, more victim than criminal. 'This is good.'

Bridge bit her lip. 'Problem is, I can't find her leaving.'

'So she's still in the hotel?'

'Maybe.' Bridge flicked to some other footage. Katerina walked in the front door, smiling at Sutekh behind the desk. Then he started shouting at her, waving his hands in the air. Ran them down her arms and cupped her breasts. She jerked away from him and slouched off to the staff room. Then he fell asleep.

Bridge wound it on and Katerina came out, minus her heavy coat. Another argument with Sutekh and she retreated back through the door. Then Fenchurch and Reed appeared, waking up Sutekh. They went through to the office and Sutekh sat sipping coffee until he had another nap, until Fenchurch and Reed left.

Then nothing, just Sutekh snoozing in an empty foyer until Liam appeared forty minutes later. Katerina followed him upstairs. The video remained static until Jim Muscat limped in, looking shifty as he sat behind the desk like he'd been there all day.

'This is the back door.' The screen showed the Vine Street exit, everyone walking and smoking in superfast speed. Nobody came in or out. 'I'm thinking she's still here, but I don't know where.'

'She's just vanished into thin air. Great.' Fenchurch wanted to collapse. 'Have you got anywhere with her computer?'

Bridge leaned back, arms folded. 'Hasn't DS Ashkani told you?'

Fenchurch sighed. 'Told me what?'

'The photos.' Reed went to a file filled with images of Gayle Fisher.

In school, marking in the staff room. Talking in a class. Jogging in the playing fields. In the street, walking with her headphones on. Walking with Steve. Jogging again. Talking to her batty old neighbour.

In her house, watching a film. Cooking. Ironing.

Upstairs, taking her bra off as she got ready for bed.

Upstairs, having sex with Steve.

Stills from the sex video with Elliot.

Fenchurch pinched his nose. 'She was obsessed with Gayle.'

'I've found poems and stories. Weird shit. They're all about Katerina having sex with Gayle. Dildos, strap-ons, burning each other with candles. Cutting her, drinking her blood. Writing on her skin with a Stanley knife. Then one about killing her. Wrote it just after she got the video.'

Fenchurch got up and started pacing. 'I've had people going round every room in this place. You've covered the doors. Where the hell is she?'

'Wait.' Bridge frowned as she hammered the keyboard. She pulled up some more video. 'Have a look at this.'

The screen showed a corridor, a kitchen porter leaning against a wall, sucking on a vape stick, watching something on his phone.

Bridge tapped the screen. 'Mulholland sent the staff home.'

'Typical.'

Onscreen, the porter nodded as Katerina walked past him.

'Shit.' Fenchurch sat up. 'Where does she go?'

'Just a sec.' Bridge typed into a window and the display switched to a view from further down the corridor.

Katerina walked through a door into a bedroom and shut it behind her.

Fenchurch recognised it — Jack Walsh's shagging pad.

———

Fenchurch and Reed stood either side of the bedroom door. Bridge was further back, baton extended. Ready to rock.

Mulholland put a finger to her mouth then stepped forward and tried the door. Locked. She thumped it. 'Katerina?'

Nothing.

Mulholland beckoned a male uniform over. 'Open that for me.'

He frowned. 'I've not got the key.'

'Can you get one?'

He shook his head. 'This room isn't on the network, it—'

'Use your shoulder, Constable.'

'Right.' The uniform took a step back and a deep breath. Then he shot forward, barrelling into the door.

It didn't budge.

'And again, please.'

'Ma'am.' The uniform was rubbing his shoulder. Grimacing.

'Get out of the way.' Fenchurch nudged him aside and launched himself at the door. It cracked and split down the middle.

The uniform kicked at the handle and the left half of the door flew open.

Mulholland barged past him into the room. Katerina flicked her wrist, splashing something all over Mulholland's face. She screamed. Sounded like the gates of hell had opened.

Just like with Elliot. Acid hitting flesh. Screeching. Squealing.

Katerina ducked under Fenchurch's swing and rushed out into the corridor.

Reed bent down to help Mulholland.

Fenchurch set off.

Katerina ran into the kitchen and slammed the door behind her.

Fenchurch tried the door. Not budging. 'Katerina!' A thump and it jerked open, then slammed again. She was behind it, pushing back. He kicked but the same thing happened. 'Katerina! Let me in!'

'Go away!'

'I'm coming in.' Fenchurch pushed at the door. It flew open and he fell forward, landing face first on the floor. 'Shit.'

'Stay there!' Katerina was over at a cooker, flames licking the base of a pan. She twisted a dial and it turned blue, the gas hissing.

Fenchurch pushed up to standing. 'It's over.'

Katerina held up a bag of Blockchain. 'I'll take these! All of them!'

'If you meant it, you'd already have taken them.'

'You try and stop me!' Katerina held up the frying pan, the copper base glowing red. 'Get back!'

'Come on, Katerina.' Fenchurch stepped closer. 'You don't need to do this.'

'I do!' Katerina held four Blockchain pills in her free hand and put them in her mouth. 'Happy now?'

'Shit.'

Katerina reached for a glass of water on the counter.

Fenchurch lurched towards her.

Katerina swung out with the pan. Time seemed to slow down. Fenchurch jumped towards her, swinging out with his baton. He hit thin air.

Katerina hefted the pan up again and swung for Fenchurch, the air burning as the metal headed towards his face.

Fenchurch lashed out and smacked Katerina in the arm. She tumbled back towards the burner. Stepped on the pan and fell. He moved forward and grabbed her by the throat, then pinned her against the wall. Pots and pans fell around them, clattering off the floor.

Reed was on her Airwave by the door. 'We need urgent medical assistance!'

Fenchurch opened Katerina's mouth and reached down her throat. Got three of the pills out. Then again and he got the last one out. He rocked back, Mulholland's sickening screams biting into his ears. Just like when Elliot was attacked.

Even she doesn't deserve this.

Chapter Forty-Nine

Fenchurch stood in the hospital corridor, watching the paramedics wheel Mulholland away, still screaming. Her face had blackened, her hair burnt away. Way worse than Elliot.

Footsteps clicked behind him and Fenchurch let them past.

Instead, someone grabbed his shoulder. 'You okay, Si?'

Fenchurch shook his head, then turned to face DI Winter. 'Far from okay.'

'Thanks for the call.' Winter collapsed against the window. 'I was going to say it's been a great day. We've done that Dodoo guy for the Hackney attack. Don't know what you did, but he's squealing about a load of other attacks.'

'Don't say squealing.'

'Right. Sorry.' Winter yawned. 'Not that he did any of them, but he knows who did.' Another yawn, then some rapid blinking. 'All the acid attacks I've investigated, Si, you never expect it to be one of our own. Even if it's Dawn bloody Mulholland.'

'Doesn't change anything, Rod. You've got a suspect. Do her.'

'Right.' Winter's shrug showed it was no consolation. 'Anyway, when can I get in with this Katerina?'

'After I've finished with her.'

'Give me a bell, yeah?' Winter set off down the corridor, following the wave of medics, leaving Fenchurch alone with his thoughts.

Mulholland didn't deserve that acid attack. Nobody would. Right in front of my face. A desperate schoolgirl, lashing out because she was caught.

Like I've tumbled out of the window. Up is down, black is white, inside is out.

'Simon?' Liam was sitting on a bed just off the corridor, frowning at him. 'What the hell?'

Fenchurch walked over to the room. 'Jesus, Liam, are you okay?'

'Got the worst hangover ever, but other than that, fine.' Liam pressed at his temples. 'Heard you saved me?'

'I found you, but you and I both know there's no saving you.'

Liam laughed, then went back to pressing his temples, eyes shut. 'What have they given me?'

'Something to counteract the poison Katerina gave you.'

'Shit.'

'Yeah, shit. What the hell were you playing at, Liam? Messing about with a schoolgirl.'

'She was just a source. That's all.'

'Bullshit.'

'That's how it started, anyway.'

'Liam, did you—'

'No.' Liam clawed at the air, cutting Fenchurch off. 'Look, what I've told you is all true. It's just . . .'

'Not all of it?'

'Right. Not all of it.' Liam scratched at his scalp. 'She started out as a source, giving me all this shit about the school. But . . . she started asking me favours. Small stuff, like giving her a lift to work. Then she asked me to put stuff in a story to hurt some kid at school.'

'Who?'

'Doesn't matter. Nobody you've met.'

'Why did you go along with it, Liam?'

'Because she was threatening to go to the police, saying I raped her. When she was fifteen.'

Fenchurch went to shut the door, but Cally was approaching, sucking on a coffee. He left it and turned to Liam. 'You didn't, did you?'

'Of course not!' Liam punched the bed. 'How can you . . .?' He broke off, panting. 'But who are they going to believe? Eh? They'll always go with the girl. I'd be finished. I've worked so hard to get a proper job in journalism and she'd just take it away.'

'And Ben Maxfield? I thought I knew you. What are you doing speaking to vermin like him?'

Liam looked away. 'He said he could help.'

Cally entered the room and smiled at Fenchurch, but it was a glower by the time she spotted Liam. 'You're awake, then.'

'Doesn't feel like it.'

'Liam.' Fenchurch walked over to the door. 'You should've come to me.'

'I didn't feel like I could.'

'About what?' Cally was scowling again. 'What's he talking about?'

'This daft bastard let himself get played by a schoolgirl.'

'Listen. I know you're both pissed off at me, but I'm telling the truth here. She got to me. And you two. You're the only people I've let in since Saskia died. I . . . I wish I'd been honest with you.'

———————

Katerina sat there, head bowed, mouth pinched.

'That's how you're playing it, is it?' Fenchurch sucked air across his teeth. 'Let's start with DCI Dawn Mulholland. You splashed acid over her face. It's not looking good for her. Much stronger stuff than they used on Elliot.'

Katerina ducked her gaze lower.

'How did you get the stuff?'

She shrugged. 'It was for Sutekh. I was going to disfigure him, make it look like one of those acid attacks.'

'You gave him some Blockchain. Put it in his coffee and left him to die.'

'That was just to incapacitate him.' Katerina looked at him, her eyes tiny. 'He's a filthy pervert. Kept touching me in the kitchen. Thinks he can get away with that shit because he's a man.' She smiled to herself. 'Liam's just some idiot who listened to me. People shouldn't do that.'

'You're lucky, though. He'll live. That's probably not what you wanted to happen, is it?'

She shook her head.

'Did you have a plan? Did you think you'd be able to get away with it?'

'Why do I need a plan? I did what I did.'

'You were going to kill yourself, weren't you?'

'Forget it.'

'Katerina, did you murder Gayle Fisher?'

'Do you want me?'

'Excuse me?'

'All the pain you've gone through. You must miss your daughter being young. I could be her.'

'Stop it.'

'I could be her. Take my clothes off for you. Let you put me to bed.'

'We've got your computer.' Fenchurch pushed a printed screenshot across the table. 'Looks like you kept watching that video of Gayle having sex with Elliot. You liked what you saw, didn't you?'

'You want me, don't you?'

'Katerina, I know Gayle was your friend. I know you liked her but—'

'I didn't kill her!'

'We found the stories, the photos, the videos.' Fenchurch shook his head at her. 'You were obsessed with her, weren't you? Like you . . . kept asking to see my daughter. Why did you kill Gayle?'

'No! No! No!'

'Katerina. You bought Blockchain from Oliver Muscat-Smith. You threatened to kill yourself with it two hours ago. If I hadn't got it out of your throat, you would've died.'

She just sat there.

'You tried to kill Liam in the room where you killed Mrs Fisher. Why?'

She tilted her head and bit her lip.

'Liam and Sutekh will pull through, too. They're in hospital now. It's just as well that I found them before it kicked in.'

'You're making a habit of that, aren't you?' Katerina gave an impish smile from under her fringe. 'Elliot. Liam. Sutekh. Me. Such a hero. I want you so bad. Do you want me?'

'You . . . You've scarred DCI Mulholland for life.'

Katerina hid behind her hair again. 'Let me go. I'll be yours, Simon. Your plaything. Your new daughter.'

He saw through the schoolgirl and saw the monster underneath. Christ knows what had caused it, but he could see the evil lurking below the surface. How she could see that killing made sense, that disfiguring someone was better than telling the police about their sexual miscon-duct. Sadism was the first choice.

'Why did you kill Gayle?'

Katerina took some advice from her lawyer, a series of whispers. Then she shrugged. 'Why do you think?' She left a big pause. They'd lost her. Then: 'You've been through my computer.' She shrugged, tears filling her eyes. 'I loved her. I wanted to be with Gayle. I thought I could push her away from her husband. I thought we could be together. Happens all the time, teachers and pupils, think there's a two-year amnesty on it. That's hardly any time.' She rubbed at her eyes. 'Then

Oliver showed me the video of Gayle and Elliot . . . Made me think about her in a different way. I wanted to stop it. Stop her. Stop both of them.'

'So you told Liam about it and he published the story?'

'That's just the start of it.' Katerina pushed her hair back, baring her forehead. 'I wanted to ruin her. She hurt me. Like you can't imagine.'

'Believe me, I can.'

'You can't. What happened to your daughter is because you're a shit father.' Her eyes were all over Fenchurch, looking for a reaction.

He sucked in breath, trying to keep calm, keep quiet. His heart thudded, could taste bitter coffee in his mouth, blood in his throat. 'You were careless. Let some men take her off the street. I wasn't like that.' She craned her neck forward. 'I loved her. I know she loved me. But she rejected me. Went with Elliot. *Elliot.*' She punched the table. 'Elliot.' Another punch. 'Lynch.'

'Did she ever say anything that made you—'

'All the time. Every smile. Every word. I knew. I *knew.*'

'And she just happened to be at the hotel?'

'Meant I had to think fast.' She bunched her hair up again. 'I was working at the hotel on Friday and saw Steve Fisher, guess it'd be about ten past nine. The story had broken Steve in two. Made him angry. Seeing someone feeling the same way I did about her made me feel better. She'd made me feel that way, she'd made her husband feel like that too. So I helped him.' She pushed the desk but it didn't budge. 'I knew which room she was in. I'd copied Jim Muscat's keycard ages ago for when I planned to get Sutekh. Turned out I had a better use for it, so I used it to get into Gayle's room. She was shocked when she opened the door, tried to shut it, but I hit her on the head. Knocked her down. I snapped on the ties, found these handcuffs in her purse — she probably used them with Elliot. She woke up, but I'd secured her. She asked what I was doing. I asked if she loved me, but she . . . she didn't answer. That was it. I gave her three Blockchain pills.'

'You just sat there, watching her die?'

'Right. She was angry with me. I'd never seen that much hate. Then she started smiling. I could see the love in her eyes. She loved me. Deep inside, she wanted me. Wanted me like you do. Right then, I knew I'd been right. I wish I could watch her die in blissful happiness, but I needed to get out of there. I met Liam and he gave me an alibi.' Katerina smiled like a priest hearing God whispering in her ears. 'If I couldn't have her, then nobody could.'

Fenchurch tried to swallow the monster crawling up his throat. 'Where did you get the Blockchain?'

'Oliver. He warned me. Quarter each, max. I thought it was perfect.' She brushed her hair again. 'I knew he was selling stuff over the bar. Kept going on about how good Blockchain was. But I saw a story in the paper about this girl in Hammersmith who died. Then it clicked.' She smiled again. 'Oliver thought he was a big shot. Wanted to be a footballer but that was never going to happen. He was talking about how he's passing his dealing on to Elliot, like he was trying to stop. But he liked the money and the power too much. Loved mixing with people like Coldcut. His supplier. You hear them talk about him, you think he's black, but he's this big white guy. Came into the bar to see Oliver every so often. I started chatting to him one day. He's not too bad.'

'We know who he is. He's murdered people.' Fenchurch smiled at her. 'Then again, so have you.'

'Coldcut came in yesterday, needed to speak with Oliver. He was furious with Elliot. Kept pressuring Oliver, wanted to know where he was. Even asked me. I said I didn't know. It was the truth. Yesterday, I didn't know where Elliot was. But when I got to school this morning, I found out he'd been in hospital. Almost died, but you saved him. What a waste that would've been, dying from drinking his own poison. But I heard Ben Maxfield say he'd take Elliot to his grandmother's. So I texted Coldcut, told him where Elliot was. Next thing I heard, they'd attacked him with acid.'

'His face is scarred all over, thanks to that attack.'

'I wish I'd thought of it.' Katerina shrugged. 'You think I'm ashamed of it? They're all disgusting. They all deserve to be dead. Now they can't harm anyone.'

'So, Oliver gave you the video as well as the drugs, didn't he?'

'He just showed me it.'

'Katerina, I found the video on your laptop. Stop lying to me.'

'I gave it to Steve.'

'What?'

'Tonight. He called me up. Said he wanted to see the video. I met him, gave him a copy.'

'He tried to kill himself.'

'He's the one good guy in this, you know?' Katerina shook her head. 'He just wanted to get back at Gayle.'

'What do you mean by that?'

'When I told him she was there, he wanted to see her.'

'Which entirely contradicts everything you've just told me.'

'I know.' She gasped. 'I can't keep lying.'

Fenchurch didn't know whether to start believing her, but it was worth a shot. 'So what actually happened?'

'Steve said he just wanted to speak to her. I said I couldn't do that. But he said it was okay, he just wanted to speak to her. So I took him up, but she didn't answer the door. So I let him in using that keycard and Steve grabbed her, tried to make her see it was all okay, tried to forgive her.'

'And what happened?'

'Gayle wasn't having any of it. She started laughing at him, saying he was pathetic. So he hit her. Knocked her over. Then he started panicking, so I calmed him down. I told him what I was going to do to Sutekh and he liked it. He just nodded and let me get on with it.'

'Are you telling the truth?'

'Of course I am. But I left him, got Liam to pick me up. Steve stayed there, watching her die. Said he threw away her purse and phone in the lane. Some women saw him, but he didn't think they recognised him.'

'How do you know?'

'He called me up, said he wanted to take the blame for it, but only if I got the video. I said I was framing Elliot, but he didn't think that'd work. You'd be back to him soon enough.'

'So you gave him the video. How was he?'

'Seemed okay, you know? He just wanted to leave.'

'He tried to kill himself. Took a few Blockchain, then . . . planned to watch the video until he died. Just like with Gayle.'

'I wish I'd known. Then I wouldn't be in the shit. I could just let him take the rap.'

'Doesn't work out like that, does it?' Fenchurch got to his feet. 'I'm going to charge you with Gayle's murder and a load of other stuff. You'll be lucky to get out of prison before you're fifty.'

Fenchurch pushed out into the corridor, drained. *The clarity of thought, the evil, the . . .*

'Inspector.' Loftus stood in the door to the Obs Suite. He beckoned Fenchurch in. 'That was quite some performance.'

Fenchurch sat in the chair. 'I think she was relieved to be caught, sir. If she hadn't confessed . . .'

'Regardless, I'm impressed with your work.' Loftus grunted. A nerve twitched in his forehead. 'I've heard from the doctor operating on DI Mulholland. She's going to be off for at least six months. Surgery, recovery, treatment for PTSD. Maybe a year.' He grunted. 'She almost lost her life. But you saved her, Fenchurch. Been saving a lot of people. Like one of those god-awful centre backs who slide in at the last minute because their positioning is so poor. It's all for the cameras.'

'I'm not sure what you're saying, sir.'

'I don't know either.' Loftus chuckled. 'DI Mulholland should be thankful you were there to save her.'

'You said DI?'

'Well, yes. She's only *Acting* DCI. I was going to demote her once I found a suitable replacement. Budgets are what they are and I've had to make do with an acting-up arrangement for this long.' His eyes narrowed. 'I don't like the way she's handled certain matters. Your son's situation is a case in point, among many others.' He reached over and clapped his shoulder. 'Anyway, Fenchurch, I won't ask you if you want the DCI role because I know you don't.'

Fenchurch laughed. 'It'd be nice to be asked.'

'Are you saying you'd take the role if I offered you it?'

Fenchurch's phone rang. 'Sorry, sir, I thought this was off.' He checked the display. Abi. 'I need to take this.' He walked out into the corridor. 'Abi, what's up?'

Silence.

'Abi?'

Monday
2nd October 2017
Three weeks later

Chapter Fifty

Abi got out of the car first, her tears glistening in the morning light, mirroring his own.

He brushed his hand across his eyes, shook the tears off. They clung to the back of his hand, thick and syrupy. As if he hadn't done enough crying.

The stairwell door opened and Chloe came out, eyebrows raised. Looked like she'd been crying too.

Fenchurch swivelled round in his seat as the back door opened.

Abi reached in and kissed Baby Al's forehead. Caught Fenchurch's look and laughed. 'He's home, Simon. Home.'

'I know.' Fenchurch reached over and unbuckled the belt. 'Here.'

Baby Al gurgled as his mother lifted him up. Halfway to being a toddler now, but still so tiny. He arched his back and his top rode up, showing the scar on his chest. The slice that had saved him. His heart growing back. Getting him out of intensive care.

Fenchurch joined his wife and daughter on the pavement, competing with them to stroke his son's face. 'Jesus Christ.' Fresh tears hit his cheeks. 'Jesus Christ.'

Chloe hugged him tight and led him inside. 'Can't let anyone see you crying like that, Dad.'

'Sod it. I'll cry when I want to.'

'Let it out.' Chloe held open the door for them. 'I went over the cot again, tightened everything. Think it's solid.'

'Good girl.' Abi pecked her on the cheek and started up the stairs.

Fenchurch stood at the bottom and watched them climb. His whole family in one place. Their old flat. His son, his daughter, his wife.

They'd soon run out of rooms when Baby Al needed his own. So selling up and moving . . . Like he didn't have enough stress. Positive stress, though. Find a house south of the river, maybe even down in Kent, in the middle of nowhere.

That dreaded bastard called hope dug into his lungs, squeezing his breath, making the butterflies in his stomach flap their wings.

Hope. The thing that's kept me going for so long, that made me find my daughter, that . . .

Jesus Christ. It's so fragile.

All the shit of the last twelve years. It's over.

Time to get on with living.

About the Author

Ed James writes crime-fiction novels. *Kill With Kindness* is the fifth novel in his latest series, set on the gritty streets of East London and featuring DI Simon Fenchurch. His Scott Cullen series features a young Edinburgh detective constable investigating crimes from the bottom rung of the career ladder he's desperate to climb. Set four hundred miles south on the streets of East London, his DI Simon Fenchurch series features a detective with little to lose. Formerly an IT manager, Ed began writing on planes, trains and automobiles to fill his weekly commute to London. He now writes full-time and lives in the Scottish Borders, with his girlfriend and a menagerie of rescued animals.